"An engaging and impressive debut from a new and welcome voice to the literary landscape."

—Yvvette Edwards

author of *The Mother* and *A Cupboard Full of Coats*

"It's great, funny smart but with heart. Love it!"

—Daisy Goodwin,

*New York Times* bestselling author of *Silver River* and

*The Fortune Hunter* and screenwriter of

the ITV television series *Victoria*

This edition first published in Great Britain 2021 by
Jacaranda Books Art Music Ltd
27 Old Gloucester Street,
London WC1N 3AX
www.jacarandabooksartmusic.co.uk

A CIP catalogue record for this book is available from the
British Library

ISBN: 9781913090043
eISBN: 9781913090067

Cover Design: Jeremy Hopes
Typeset by Kamillah Brandes
Cover image: ING Image

Printed and bound by CPI Group (UK) Ltd, Croydon, CR0 4YY

# LIVING
# THE
# DREAM

## Isabelle Dupuy

JACARANDA

*For Felix, Zoe and Lucas*

*It takes a lifetime to learn how to be able to hold your own ground, to go out to the others, to be open to them without losing your ground. And to hold your ground without shutting others out.*

-Martin Buber

*Where you are you can follow*
*The leaves turning to stone,*
*The living branch made patient,*
*The trunk attaining sleep;*
*You can watch from your closed window*
*How true false love has grown.*
Marie Ponsot, Collected Poems

# CHAPTER ONE

## May 2016

Even as I write this, I am well dressed, in a fine white cotton shirt and pale blue cashmere jumper, dark wash mid-rise slim jeans that slide smoothly into tall, flat, brown leather boots. One of my assets is my behind; round, firm and high, I go squeeze it three times a week at Barre Class, around the corner from the tree-lined avenue where our children go to school. I order Ocado groceries, I spend a fortune at Gail's bakery and I select avocadoes by hand, feeling and weighing them carefully before buying them. I drive boys to football games and I keep an extra mouthguard in its plastic casing somewhere in the car, usually in the space between the gear shift and the hand brake. The same DNA that blessed my backside cursed my hair but you wouldn't know this if you met me. I perform well. Better than most of the other Hampstead wives but then again I come from further away. I take nothing for granted.

Yet the ground keeps shaking beneath my feet no matter how small my step.

I have been wired to believe in marriage but not in

feelings. At least not in my own. 'Marry the man who loves you more than you love him,' my mother would say, 'and work hard to keep it that way. Remember love is a fleeting moment in life, like a chilly current that tickles your ankles when you first walk into the water, then is gone and forgotten as you start swimming in the warm, endless sea. What matters are security and stability, power to protect your children and ground them in society.'

I listened to my mother. She was right about the end. Perhaps that's why it didn't occur to me to question the means. I live in London, not Cartagena. 'Society' in this city is a loaded word but I've discovered it doesn't really exist. Not in the Latin American sense, anyway. There is no comfort or shared identity in 'society' here. There is 'networking'. And there's the 'nuclear family'.

We are a nuclear family. I used to think the expression came from the bomb until Tommy came home from school with his physics homework on atoms. I learned that the atomic nucleus is an intense little island of positivity, sur-rounded by free-flying negativity. Just like our family on a rainy Sunday. It's a matter of adaptation.

Thirteen is an awkward number and after that number of years here, I lack a point of reference. Everytime I look in the mirror the same image confronts me, an alien, a multi-breed conceived in violence, lust and sorrow. African, European, a lost Guayabero ancestor, and behind this face, my eyes marking time, more and more time spent in London where nobody will tell you who you are.

One morning, I asked Tom what he saw in the mirror. He had just finished shaving.

'What a silly question,' he said, wiping his chin. 'I see me. Tom. A man. A human being.'

***

I listened for the beep of the car locking, put the keys in my handbag and walked to my friend's house.

Back in 2012, I won a prize for a drab but competent short story about a Caribbean woman growing old in Britain. I received a cheque for £500, my picture went up with a link to *A Rocking Chair* on the magazine's website, and the story was published in the summer issue. Boosted by that small success, I was itching to find a big story, the kind that could carry a whole novel. I was still struggling to find a character with real traction when I met Solange Wolf.

She was one of the 'supermums' at St Francis Prep School for Boys. When she was around the rest of the world: teachers, other parents, even the boys, looked like they moved in slow motion. She'd arrive running in her Louboutin heels—she had an important job in Mayfair and was always late—but she never looked harried, only the opposite. She had an easy charm and a generous smile for everyone around her.

I'd watch her, quietly wondering when she'd trip. Solange was darker skinned than me, from a country poorer and more dysfunctional than my own. She too arrived at Heathrow many years ago with this idea of England. The United Kingdom is special that way. It's not some third world place pretending to be a country. Solange understood this long before I did. She landed so ready to exist, to claim a life here so inconceivable back where she came from, I still can't imagine how she even knew it was possible. Let alone how to achieve it.

Then our sons, Tommy and Baz, became friends and so did we.

One day Solange asked me to write her life story. It was meant for her son, Baz. She was afraid he would never understand where she came from and because of that, would judge her harshly in the future. 'You know what I mean.'

'Yes.' I too had chosen to bear children with a white man, and to raise them in Europe. 'Take Baz to Haiti,' I advised her. 'Show him his roots.'

Tom and I took our eldest to Colombia for this precise reason. It was a difficult trip, both to travel there with young children and to be there. One night we heard gun shots. Tom and I jumped up. Tommy was a baby then, lying fast asleep in the cot at the foot of our bed. The fan was steady on a wicker chair next to the cot, rotating hot air between Tom's side and mine. The half-open window was on the other side of the bed. We moved the cot to the wall underneath the window in case a bullet flew in.

'We spend all year bothering with car seats and safety belts only to...' Tom didn't need to finish his sentence. *Only to spend a lot of money to expose ourselves and our baby here.* He slapped a mosquito against his arm. He was right but what was the alternative? To spend this time in Spain or in France where everything would be nice and carefree and Tommy would only know me as 'London Naomi', a woman forever out of context? I cursed the assholes shooting semi-automatic weapons in the middle of the night.

'No!' Solange's scream brought me back. 'Write my story instead,' she pleaded. 'We all know the past is a different country.'

That was true.

Solange was beautiful and strong in a bulldozer kind of way. Early one Wednesday morning on the way to meet my agent, I saw her standing in the middle of the street in her robe and slippers, negotiating with the rubbish removal men. She couldn't get her head around the recycling rules and was trying to convince them to make an exception for her, to take her un-sorted trash away. I watched fascinated as the two men, Eastern European probably, agreed to hook her bins to the back of the truck. She had retained all the characteristics Tom tried to root out of me the moment I set foot in his country. A deep respect for the hustle. A tendency for loud, sweeping generalisations. A stubborn optimism supported by the delusion that one is made of Teflon.

That's when I knew I'd do it. I told her I'd write her story but only if she allowed me to publish it.

'This should not only be for your son,' I said. 'My children, Tom, his colleagues, the other parents at school—they all need to know about the road you have travelled to be here.'

'Why?' She asked suspiciously.

What I should have answered then was that I needed

them all to know. That her story was important to me, because I couldn't tell my own. Instead, I talked about money. How this book could be a profitable project. Solange liked that. She said yes.

That was four years ago.

We were done. Until she called me at eight this morning.

The manuscript I sweated, a classic rags-to-riches, not-seen-since-Victorian-times, modern fairy tale, and—true—story was incredible. The rise of a poor but spirited girl from the slums of Port-au-Prince with all kinds of odds stacked against her—hurricanes, family, hunger—and yet she prevails, what am I saying, she triumphs. Her story could launch a thousand refugee rafts. If the promised land is a middle-class life in North West London, Solange got there with the added bonus of love. That's how I understood it.

I was wrong.

On this May morning, Solange's husband of fourteen years, Andreas Wolf, showed up on the doorstep of their family home in the prosperous and pleasant neighbourhood of St John's Wood and announced that he had a twenty-eight-year-old Dutch mistress and that she was pregnant with his child.

I rang the doorbell. The Wolfs had a narrow but pretty terraced house with blooming azalea bushes and a large bay window with that special kind of glass that seems to undulate with the light. Someone had taped a blue referendum poster with yellow stars on the inside of the window:

*Vote IN on 23 June*

The last thing Andreas said before disappearing was that he was in love with the mistress and he was leaving my friend. Of course, he also left their boy, Baz who was sleeping peacefully in his room while his father dragged his suitcase down the street. I'm sure Andreas was adamant that the person he was wilfully abandoning was Solange. It just so happened that Baz got left behind as well.

A crazed-looking woman with eyes so big they ate up her entire face; wet, swollen lips; and wild, wild hair opened the door. 'Delete the motherfucker!'

'What?'

'It's all lies.'

'No, it's not. This…' I pointed at the Aston Martin parked down her street, at the manicured magnolias next door, at the clean pavement, at her own pretty house. 'Remember where you came from. This is the truth, with or without him.'

'You're kidding, right?' She waved her hands in front of her face. 'This means nothing. He is what made this place home to me.'

The promised land is Love.

# CHAPTER TWO

## September 2012

*'How does it feel?'*

*'Like home.'*

*'Still?'*

*He kissed her on the neck. She was lying on her back. He was above her, leaning on an elbow to avoid putting all his weight on her. He'd start like that, lightly. Then they'd go for it. He'd put his leg over hers and she'd hold him as well as she could while their sweat formed a little pool in the enclave of her belly button. He'd go stronger, faster but he'd always check her expression, to see if she was happy. And she'd let out a small moan, her face lighting up with each thrust. She loved having him inside of her. And he loved being there. So he wouldn't come. Not the first time. They'd make love two, three times in a night and it was only when the darkness started to fade and they could make out the curtains against the dawn light that he'd let it happen. He'd shudder and cry out her name. And he was done.*

'Hmm.' Tom brushed my heel with his toe. 'Do you really want to go there? Perhaps you should write about less personal things.'

I opened my eyes. We had just made love and somehow through our exertions, we had ended up on each other's side of the bed. I'd been dozing on my back. Tom had picked up my red notebook on my nightstand.

'Oh!' I laughed to hide my panic as I snatched the notebook away and held it against my very pregnant stomach. 'I should be free to write about whatever I feel like; you don't have to read it.' I'd woken up in the middle of the night and spent a couple of hours scribbling, and when I went back to bed I'd left my notebook there without thinking. 'You must trust me. This is just sketching. I'd never write anything to harm or betray you or us.'

'How do you know?'

I hugged him from the back and pressed my big, hard bump against his spine. 'Because you, Tommy, and the baby mean everything to me.' I rested my chin on his shoulder. 'You guys are the reason I left Sportek Marketing.' I threw the notebook on my pile of clothes on the floor to make my point while making a mental note to lock it away in my filing cabinet at the first opportunity.

'You hated your job.' He leaned his head to the side so it would touch mine.

'True... but I didn't go looking for another one. I trusted you.' I reached for the box of Kleenex on the nightstand. Tom pulled a tissue out of the box and handed it to me. I put it in between my legs. I had never been this heavy. This baby was way bigger than Tommy had been. I sat up with difficulty.

'Yes, and I trust you.' Tom stood up and helped me off the bed. He embraced me. We stood naked in each other's arms, inhaling each other, absorbing each other's heat.

There was no part of his body I didn't love. Just thinking about him slowed me down. A few months back, I almost killed Tommy and myself because although my foot was on the pedal and my hands were on the wheel, my mind was still in bed with Tom. I pulled out of a side road and didn't see the car driving full speed across from me. The driver saw me in the nick of time, braked violently and started shouting and only after he called me something very nasty did I connect to the moment. All of that because two hours earlier, Tom had called me his 'joy'.

I padded after Tom to the bathroom in the hall. He turned on the hot water without stepping into the shower. The boiler was old and took some time to heat up.

'Are you going to be all right?'

'You're only away for two days.' I scratched my belly. 'Where are you going again?'

'Stockholm with Virgil. Pitching for a deal.' He was examining me. 'Are you sure you don't feel the baby coming?'

I clicked my tongue. 'Ah, *mi amor*, I still have four weeks, maybe even five. The baby loves being inside of me.'

'Smart baby.' Tom stepped into the shower. 'Look, that's where it's coming from. The shower tray is leaking.' He pointed at a small puddle forming on the outside of the tray, on the tiles.

'I'll call the landlord.' I examined the tiled floor for a

moment. 'Thank you for trusting me. With the writing, I mean.'

'What?' he shouted over the water.

I repeated what I'd said, only louder. I could feel my accent thickening.

Tom switched off the shower and stepped out, dripping wet on the tiles. He took my chin in his fingers and put his lips against mine. We kissed. He whispered to me, 'I'd love that, a famous writer wife.'

We did it right there, against the sink. I was so wet he had to hold me tight to keep himself from slipping out. I never loved him more. I even got that pinch of anxiety all Catholics feel when you realise you have so much to lose. I must produce something successful now, make him proud so he'll never regret choosing me. Even when the children are gone, even when my hair is white and my skin tarnished, I must still shine in his eyes. Yes. Succeed to keep your man.

When it was over, he stood behind me. The mirror contained us both: me, deformed by his child growing inside; and him, with his great, white build like a normalising frame to the small, dark girl with the giant belly. Although I stood alone, in the mirror it looked like I was leaning on him.

'I've been invited to this coffee morning by a mum in Tommy's new school.' I thought for a moment and corrected myself, 'Actually, it was the mum's assistant who called, not the mother herself.'

He took the towel from its peg behind the door. 'That's posh. Are you going?' He began to brush his teeth.

'I won't know anyone there.'

'That's a good reason for you to go. That's how it works here. You pay these horrendous fees so that your child gets to hang out with people like yourself.' He spat out the toothpaste, cupping his hand under the tap.

'The people like me live in Elephant and Castle.'

Tom dried his face with the towel and tapped me on what was left of my waist. 'Don't be silly. You're British now.'

True, I had a brand new burgundy red passport after one three-month tourist visa, one year of six-month temporary resident visas, seven years of Indefinite Leave to Remain visas and a citizenship class where I had to learn about the Welsh parliament and what the 'British' reaction is to a man touching your girlfriend in a pub (no it is not to go find your terrorist friends and plot to blow up the pub). Then came three recommendations by 'real' British people, ten attempts at getting two passport photos where both my irises fit on the same ruler and a swearing-in ceremony where I had to choose between the Queen and God for my allegiance. Of course, none of this made me British. But I discovered the previously unknown joy of breezing through airports. The Colombian passport stoked many reactions from immigration officers but respect was not one of them.

'You're right. I'll go.' I went to switch the shower on and was about to step in when there was a scratching sound at the door.

'Mama? I need to pee.'

Tom covered himself with his towel, opened the door,

rubbed our son's hair, and went to get dressed. I stepped out of the shower, wrapped my towel around my breasts and stood there, waiting. Tommy ran past me to the toilet, dropped his elasticated pyjama pants and pushed his pelvis forward so the stream would hit the bowl without him having to hold his penis. He yawned and his whole little body shivered. 'Mama, I had a bad dream.' A lock of brown hair fell on his forehead as he pulled up his pyjama pants.

'*Pobrecito*! What happened?' There was still a faint hint of the baby in him.

He opened his black eyes wide. He hugged my giant waist. 'You were dressed like an astronaut. And you said you couldn't take off the helmet. Ever.'

'I'm not an astronaut! I'm your mummy, look. They would never want me as an astronaut with my big belly.' I kissed his head. He smelled of sleep. 'Go put your uniform on.'

As I stepped into the shower, I laughed. An astronaut, me? I could barely fit behind the wheel of a car.

\*\*\*

Mrs Von Moncken does not have a house number. She has a house name. How chic but how annoying, I thought, as I drove the length of Redington Road for the third time, looking for 'The Rosary'. I was about to back up and try for a fourth time when I noticed a low brick wall covered with overgrown white roses. I stopped the car. A small bronze plaque was screwed next to the wooden gates, with the name etched into it. I lowered the window and stuck my head out to read the inscription. A tiny camera hung above the entrance. This was it.

I found a resident's parking bay nearby. I wasn't allowed to park in this zone as my old Jetta was registered to an address about two miles and three, maybe four income classes away from here, but I couldn't see another spot. Leaving the car with the blinkers on, I waddled across the street to The Rosary to see if Mrs Von Moncken had any visitor parking vouchers.

Fortunately, the Filipina maid answering the door produced a stack of blue vouchers, peeling one off for me. After scratching off the date and time, I put it on the dashboard so the traffic warden would be able to see it. I pulled down my crisp, new shirt—it had a tendency to creep up on my stretched belly—pushed my hair back so that my diamond studs were *en evidencia* and took a last close look in the rear-view mirror to make sure.

Mama and Abuela Edith ran a plant nursery. We lived in a colonial house in old Cartagena that belonged to my mother's father before the quarter became fashionable. It was dark, with floorboards painted brown with anti-termite solution and windows protected with wooden shutters instead of glass, but the front gallery was shaded and pleasant, with a purple bougainvillea that curled up the left post all the way to the corrugated zinc roof. Our home was on the edge of the university neighbourhood, the kind of street where the dustmen started to give up, where the whiff of urine tickled your nose depending on the direction of the breeze. An uncomfortable place to be.

I wiped my sweaty palms on my pregnancy slacks as I took a careful step into the Von Moncken house. I found myself standing in a space the size of our living room that had apparently no other purpose than to be an entrance hall. There was a round, beautifully polished oak table with a bouquet of white roses in the middle and a number of heavy, expensive art books piled on one side. I cocked my head to look at the spines, *Lucian Freud, Picasso, Francis Bacon.* The maid asked me to follow her down a wood-panelled hall towards the sound of female voices and the clinking of porcelain cups.

Fifteen or so women turned around as the maid ushered me into the dining room. This was no kill time at Starbucks with a Ziploc full of Cheerios and screaming toddlers, no. This was the fucking lottery. Stylish, confident women, still tanned from their summer holidays, stood around a giant table laid out so perfectly, I wanted to take a picture for my mother. Polished French silverware, linen napkins, Japanese teapots, baskets of fresh croissants and pains au chocolat, cut peaches and fresh strawberries in Wedgwood containers.

'Naomi, so nice to meet you.' A beautiful blonde woman stepped forward and kissed me on both cheeks. 'I am Ines Von Moncken, the mother of Marcus. Welcome, welcome. Here, we prepared a name badge for you.' How did she know my name?

'Thank you so much for having me.' My eyes fell on Ines's shoes. Yves Saint Laurent sandals. She must have worn them all summer for the leather to look so dark and supple.

I stopped before large French doors. The sun broke through the clouds, it was one of those warm but unpredictable early autumn days, and I stepped out onto an immaculate lawn with a trampoline in a corner and space, space everywhere. I imagined my boy, Tommy, bouncing out there, falling on top of the Von Moncken boy, rolling together against the mesh walls like puppies. I heard footsteps behind me and I turned around. A young woman in a black and white uniform, different from the one who had given me the parking vouchers, was carrying cups of coffee on a tray. '*Gracia*…Thank you." I smiled as I carefully reached for a cup and saucer.

She looked at me. '*De donde vienes?*'

Ah, a fellow Latina immigrant. 'Colombia.'

'Ah.' She told me in Spanish that she arrived in London from Venezuela only three months ago. That her name was Daniela, and she was of European descent, which is why she qualified for an Italian passport, something most of her friends back in Caracas would kill for because the situation, ay, the situation there was so bad, her boyfriend who had left her the month before asked her to marry him when he heard of her European Union passport. That this was not the kind of job she'd had in mind but don't get her wrong, she was grateful to Mrs Von Moncken because her English was very bad and the rents in London very high.

I nodded in sympathy and tried to walk past her back into the house.

'*Perdón señora, pero…*' Daniela and her tray blocked my way.

I looked at her. She didn't move but started shifting her weight from one foot to the other, and finally asked me if please we needed construction work or even a handyman because her husband (so she married him), he had not found work yet. He was not expensive and I could pay him cash.

'No, I'm sorry we don't need a handyman.' I answered in English with a look beyond her to the doors. It was true: We were living in a rental house.

'Ah, maybe you need a gardener?'

I shook my head.

'Garage work? Mechanic for your car?'

'*Lo siento, pero no necesitamos ayuda.*' Dark clouds squeezed the sunlight out. It was going to rain and that would ruin my carefully straightened hair. I walked around her to get back inside.

Daniela exasperated, shouted behind me in Spanish: 'Come on, sister! Not all of us have been as lucky as you.'

I stopped. Why was I was the only person here who'd managed in a couple of words to breed such familiarity? Yes, I heard the strategic voice in my head telling me to let it slide, it doesn't matter, protect Tommy's and your place in this world. Forget the one this woman is trying to pull you back into, the one she'll never escape from even if she's here. It's not worth it Naomi, I even heard Tom's voice in my head:

*Don't be silly, you're British now...*But the Spanish rolled out of my mouth: 'When a *mulatta* like me,' I rolled back my sleeves so she could better see my skin, 'makes it, it's always luck, isn't it?'

Daniela's blue eyes widened.

'Because if it's luck, it's undeserved.'

She said nothing.

'And if it's undeserved, I owe.'

The chime of a silver fork hitting crystal interrupted me. Daniela took her cue and ran to the kitchen. Me, I couldn't move. I put my hand on my big belly and tried to calm down. *Uno, dos, tres, quatro* I had to calm down.

'Ladies!' I heard Ines through the doors. A heavy drop fell on my head, plop right in the middle of my scalp. I went back in. Our hostess was standing at the head of the table. 'Now that we're all here, I'd like us to introduce ourselves. This is a fresh start, not just for our sons starting their first year at St Francis, but for us as well. We are going to be together as parents for a long time and I thought this little coffee would be a nice, informal way for us to get to know each other, ahead of play dates and birthday parties.'

I had yet to exchange a word with a fellow guest. That was not good. I was failing Tommy, Tom, our family. Ines on the other hand had the entire party wrapped around her cool manicured finger. There was magic about that woman.

There was sweat all over me. My little interchange with the Venezuelan didn't help. There was a console with photographs in silver frames displayed on a chiselled marble top.

From afar they looked like they'd been cut out from Tatler or Vanity Fair but no, I recognized Ines. They were just a very handsome and glamorous looking family. There was Ines and her husband and their four children on top of a mountain in their ski suits, their teeth as white as the snow they are standing on. Here they are at the beach, looking healthy and happy and somehow not tanned, with Ines resplendent in a bikini and wide-brimmed hat, and her husband looking rich and powerful in spite of skinny legs, a soft belly and swimming shorts with flamingos printed on them. It was in his face, in the way his eyes met the lens, so sexy. *Look at what a winner I am*, they were saying. I loved it. Up until then, family for me had something inevitable about it. It wasn't something you could tailor, or invent. It was flawed, it was boring, it was there. It wasn't supposed to perform, to be aesthetically pleasing, to be a project.

'Naomi? How is Tommy settling in at St Francis so far?' Ines saw me examining her family photographs and came to stand next to me.

'Very well.' I looked at her. She was exquisite. 'I can't believe you have four children.' I wanted her life, her looks, her family. I could just imagine their summers. A *finca* outside Sevilla (I loved Sevilla), fragrant with lemon orchards and olive trees on a rolling hill where all her (benevolent) relatives came together and all the kids, cousins, siblings, and family friends could spend their hot, sunny days lounging by the (of course) pool, and their evenings around a giant country table with an endless supply of sherry and *jamon*.

'Oh, they keep us busy.' Ines smiled. Someone called her name from the other side of the room, and she excused herself.

I braced myself and I approached the mother closest to me. 'Hello, I'm new at St Francis. My name is Naomi Perez Barnes, I'm the mother of Tommy.'

The name tag on the side of her silk shirt read *Melanie, mum of Damien*. She was short and, like most women here, blonde and looked affluent: just the watch on her wrist must have been worth tens of thousands. She pressed her lips together in a closed smile. 'How do you do?'

She didn't extend her hand so I, thinking she wanted to be greeted with a kiss on the cheek, moved in to touch her face with my lips but when she understood what I was doing, she jumped back and quickly put her hand forward. I was forced to shift my weight back to my left foot. I tried to shake her hand while doing so but that proved too much; my foot twisted and I had to lean on the table to prevent my fall. My big tummy hit a cup, spilling tea on the white linen placemat. 'Oh, I'm so sorry!'

Melanie abandoned me to my fate. In one swift turn she not only avoided the tea and kept her white trousers intact, but also established enough distance from me, the fool, so that no association could possibly be made between the spillage and her. Without thinking, I patted the tea with all the napkins I could find until I realised that these napkins were also made of white linen and that I was ruining Ines's entire set. I watched helplessly as the stain spread with an evil speed across the various cloths.

Daniela saw this happen from her position next to the kitchen door. She didn't move, stood instead with her arms crossed on her chest, smirking at my demise. I felt like shouting across the table to her, *this is the reason countries like Venezuela will never get ahead*!

Now what? She obviously was not going to help. But the table couldn't be left like this, it looked awful and the linens should be washed at once to prevent the stains from settling into the cloth. I moved the dishes and the cups to the side and gathered the wet linen in my arms, drenching my shirt in the process. It didn't matter, I'd never be invited anywhere again and more importantly, I'd messed it up for poor Tommy. I had reached the kitchen door when Ines came to me insisting on taking the linens. Before I could protest, another lady, her name badge reading Antheia, also offered help but now, of course, Daniela the Venezuelan maid appeared out of the blue, an image of concern and care as she took the load from Ines's arms. As she walked by me she pursed her lips and a low wet whistle came out of her mouth. *You may fool these European ladies but you're not fooling me.*

I ignored her and shook my wet shirt away from my body. 'I'm so sorry...'

'What are you talking about?' Ines would hear none of it. 'I'm happy you made it here at all. When I was eight months pregnant, all I could do was roll around like a barrel. We can't wait to meet your son.' She walked me back to the middle of the room and just like that, everything was fine. Hurray for twenty-first-century London. I smiled as the mums congregated around us. There was nothing to fool anyone about. Oh, I knew what Daniela was referring to. Back in our countries there was no such thing as a girl with a blank slate. You could be an heiress or a bourgeois of (pure) European descent, a *mestiza* or a *mulatta* on the make, a black girl from town, an Indian from the mountains, a street urchin, a girl with no name and no protection. But London is an open city, not a factory for inferiority complexes.

'Naomi! What a lovely name. When are you due? How long have you lived in London?' She had a nametag on her blouse: *Lily, mum of Justin*. She looked scruffier than the other women in the room: her sandy hair was thin and lacklustre, her face pale, her clothes non-descript and grey. Her voice was sharp, cutting even, but it sounded sincere.

'Pleasure to meet you, Lily, I've been here a while, nine years now,' my words tumbled out. 'My husband is English.'

'Oh golly, I'm in the process of divorcing one of those.' Her face fell. 'I'm sorry, I shouldn't be saying this to you. We're a small country but we have a good amount of diversity. In characters too, I mean.'

'Yes... How is Justin settling in?' I asked back on form.

'Oh, he's fine. His dad went to St Francis so he's been hearing about it his whole life. Apparently, the toilet facilities are much improved since Charles's day.'

There was an awkward pause.

'And your son,' she squinted at my nametag, 'Tommy?'

'He seems to like it. The school is new to us too. We're

discovering it all together.'

'But you said your husband is English?'

'*Djes* but he's from the Midlands, that's where he went to school.'

'Ah, and where did he go to uni?'

'Right here, to University College, you know behind Heals' on Tottenham Court Road.'

'That's so funny, that's where I went to medical school. On Huntley street, really right behind Heals'! I used to go there to buy scented candles, it was the only thing I could afford. I loved it.' She frowned. 'It's also where I met Charles. You see, whereas your husband and I are perfectly happy with our credentials, Charles couldn't stand the fact that he didn't get into Oxbridge. It was the beginning of his end. He'd gone to Eton and came out of there with a lethal dose of achievement anxiety mixed with emotional shrinkage that got us to where we are today.'

She lost me there.

Lily sighed. 'And where do you come from, Naomi?'

'Colombia.'

'And what do you do?'

'I used to work in sports rights. I'm home now, focusing on the family.' I patted my pregnant belly, finding myself opening up to her. 'I write. At night, mainly. Sometimes during the day. There's a lot I'd like to say but I'm not sure anyone here will be interested.'

'Oh, you'd be surprised. The English love exotic stories, especially those set in the sun.'

'I don't write "exotic" stories.'

'Did I use the wrong word? I'm sorry. What I mean is, this island is so grey. People jump at anything to take them out of this drabness. Don't you think?'

'No, I don't,' my eyes rested on her charcoal shapeless trousers, 'Escapism is more complicated than that.'

'Oh.' She leaned in to me. 'Is this how women are in your country? Or are you particularly bold?'

I shook my head, no. I was not bold. I'd been working until recently in sports marketing, a male dominated industry. My edge, the angle upon which I built my career, was the fact that I was a woman—a pretty, careful Latina who knew how to put men in the centre. It paid off, first in Colombia, then in New York and in London. You can pretend not to care about your honour, your dignity, about nothing except the bottom line but it's not true. It's never true. Now I was haunted by a need for revenge. My dreams regularly took me back to a shameful moment in my career. In one I take a laptop and I hit a senior Vice President on the head with it. The corner of the laptop slices his thin temple and the blood next to his eye drips down onto his starched, white, collar. 'What is it you were saying again?' I ask him.

In real life, this married father of three and head of my team had cornered me alone in a conference room when I was pregnant with Tommy and told me he would 'make my pregnancy hell' unless I handed over to him my most lucrative client. I was already scared enough, it was going to be my first baby and I was alone in my husband's country. I signed over the client without saying a word and I held it in until I reached the ladies where I cried. In another dream I shove an old man out of a moving limousine in New York. I don't even wait for the driver to stop for a red light. I just open the door as the car drives up West street and kick his fat ass with my heels until he tumbles out.

In real life, this colleague had offered me a ride uptown in his limo after a business dinner and he kept putting his hand on my thigh. After taking it away a couple of times, I shifted away from him on the back seat until I was wedged against the door. Finally I lied and told the driver I had arrived home. I then walked the two miles to my flat.

'Well, for a long time I thought I was bold but all I was doing was repeating like a middle-class parrot whatever outrage of the day was chosen by Radio 4's *Today* programme,' Lily told me. 'I don't think the younger people are like that but we, this generation,' she looked around the room and shook her head, 'while I repeated platitudes, patients walked into my surgery, broken, sickened, weakened by the injustices that surround us and all I noticed was that their back hurt, that they had migraines. It took the breakdown of my marriage...' She laughed nervously. 'It is a cliché, isn't it? The wronged wife becomes a feminist, haha. But I started to recognise them, some of the wives. So tired, and too embarrassed to ask for anything. It's 2012 but they still accept it. That their right to exist rests on their capacity to care for their husbands and their children.' She was on a roll. 'There is something wrong about the marriage contract. And it goes back to our biology.'

I looked around us on this Monday morning. Wives and mothers looking healthy, confident, some were laughing out loud. They were happy in their state, just like me. I thought of my own divorced mother's tears. No, I'd take my married life one thousand times over one like Lily's or my mother's back then. Lily's political awakening was a poor consolation for what she'd lost. But I couldn't say that to her. Instead I asked, 'What do you think a woman should do?'

'Put yourself and your business first, I'd say. The men resent you for it, although that's exactly what they've always done.'

'But how can you love someone and put yourself and your business first?' I didn't get it. After Tom's promotion, which meant more money but also more travel, we had decided together that I would quit my job and focus on the family. 'It's hard for him to be away for three, four days a week. He's missing out on his son's childhood. He was so sad when he got the clip of Tommy riding a bike for the first time. He was sitting alone at some gate in Frankfurt airport, refusing to go to the lounge although his flight home had been delayed, so he could get on the plane as soon as he could. No, in my household the family is our business and we're all working for it.'

Lily squinted at me as if I was speaking in Spanish (which I wasn't).

Melanie of the white trousers joined us. 'Darling!' She hugged her fellow Englishwoman. 'I have three tickets to go see Hedda Gabler at the Old Vic next Thursday. Ines said she'd come. Are you free?'

'So sweet of you, Melanie, I'll see if my nanny can stay late.' Lily put her hand on my arm and looked at Melanie. 'Naomi, would you like to come? I'm sure we can find an extra ticket.'

'It must be sold out.' Melanie's voice had a metallic edge to it, as if she were speaking inside an empty cauldron. 'How about if I send you the link? You can see?' She pressed her lips at me again.

'Melanie!' A tall red-haired woman with a high-pitched voice joined us. 'Isn't your eldest at St Paul's now? Was it really as hard as they say to get in? What kind of tutor did you use?'

'Oh, I don't know, Pam. She just wanted to go there.'

'Antheia—your eldest—where did he end up? I remember you had some problems…' Pam turned her slightly hysterical face to the nice woman who had helped me out with the linens.

'He went to his second choice school.' Antheia raised her hands in a way I hoped was ironic but couldn't be sure.

'Oh!' Pam put her hand over her mouth.

'Can we not talk about schools? I find the topic dreadfully boring.' Melanie yawned.

Tom had long ago explained to me that secondary school is what defines you in this country. It's where you make friends, where you find your place in society. I asked him then what was his place and he told me he didn't have one. He had to make himself one because he didn't attend a famous

41

school.

I knew what he meant. My mother was from an old and cold Cartagena family that disowned her after she married my father. By the time she divorced and her own father relented, the money was gone. Although she could barely afford it, it was inconceivable for her that my brother and I would not go to the same schools she, her siblings, her parents had gone to: Santa Rosa de Lima for girls and Collegio Don Bosco for boys. As a rule, the richer the kid, the worse the student. We were straight A students, my brother and I. Nico got a detention once because he was chatting in math class with a rich kid. The teacher called him up in front of the class. He was ten.

'Señor Perez,' the teacher announced to the entire class, 'do you want to know why I'm punishing you and not your friend, Señor Fanna?' His voice reverberated against the walls. 'Because no matter what he does here, in ten years' time, Señor Fanna will be driving around town in his air-conditioned Mercedes but you, depending on what you do here, you could be sitting on the walls next to the dock, dangling your unemployed feet in the air.'

'What matters is that they are happy at school, no?' Ines was holding a large bowl of fresh strawberries that she offered around.

'You are such a good mother; your kids would be happy anywhere.' Melanie took a strawberry and, holding it by its green stem, bit into it. Not a drop of pink juice fell on her white trousers or her silk shirt. I looked at the juicy, ripe, fragrant strawberries and then at my tea-stained shirt. I passed.

'Things are changing. University is what matters. Just like in America.' Lily scanned the room for support. Her eyes stopped on me. 'Naomi! You're from Cuba right?'

'Colombia. I'm from Colombia.'

'Even better. Tell them, Naomi, where did you go to university?' Without waiting for my reply, she looked at the others. 'And I bet you she went to a secondary school nobody in this room has ever heard about.'

I could have touched the silence in the room, it was so thick. They were all looking at me. Even Daniela stopped clearing the table, waiting for my answer.

'I attended the University of Miami. It was closer to Cartagena than most other places in America.' A sour taste developed in my mouth. I wanted to go home and brush my teeth.

'Oh, that must have been fun!' There was a general sigh of relief.

What the fuck was wrong with me? I had never lied about my life before. I graduated from secondary school and walked down the road together with the poorer students (the rich ones went north to Bogotá, Mexico City, or for the truly privileged, the United States) to the University of Cartagena, a place where dreams do not come true. After two years of squalor, strikes, Marxism, and living with my mother, I dropped out. I got a job in the capital selling media rights with a vague plan of returning to university in a more reputable place one day.

Enough. I picked up my handbag and thanked Ines for her hospitality.

'Must you leave so soon?' She took my hand.

'Oh, I forgot my cleaning lady was coming and I didn't leave her instructions, so…'

I walked straight ahead of me without turning back. As I opened the front door to leave, I noticed one last picture in the hall. It was framed in heavy silver and it was of Ines kneeling and kissing Pope Benedict XVI's hand. I ran out into the rain and shut the door behind me and I couldn't care less if my hair was getting wet. I stood there with my eyes closed, waiting for my heart to slow down.

'Hello, is the coffee morning already over?' A lively black woman with a mass of frizzy hair and a French accent stood in front of me.

I recognised her from the school gates. *Supermum*. Today she was wearing jeans, a light Burberry raincoat and silver Converse trainers. 'No, no, I just have to leave early. I'm sorry, who are you?'

'My name is Solange. I'm Baz's mum. I don't know any of the mothers and I want to avoid what happened at Baz's nursery when everybody thought my nanny was the mum and I was the nanny.'

'You must definitely go in, then.'

'Are you feeling all right?'

'I'm just a bit tired.' I touched my belly. 'I'm fine really.'

She frowned. 'You're sweating. Come back in with me,

I'll get you a glass of water.'

'No!' I yelped. 'I really have to go.'

'Then give me your phone number. Maybe we can arrange a play date for,' she looked at my nametag, 'Tommy and Baz?' She pulled out her phone. 'Do you know what you're having?'

'Another boy. Our second.' I smiled. She was the first person to ask me that question.

'Oh, that is wonderful! Baz is so far an only child. But who knows?'

I looked at her. 'Let's meet on Friday evening. I'll pick up the boys from school and you can join us when you're done with work.'

'Are your details on the class list? I leave work on Fridays around five and I'll come straight to you.' She smiled. 'Do I still need to go in there?'

'It's not so bad. As long as you know who you are.'

With that, Solange disappeared inside Ines's mansion and I walked across the street to my car.

# CHAPTER THREE

Thus began one of the most important relationships of my life. Solange gave shape to my thoughts, credence to my reality. She had no hope of blending in and she didn't give a damn. She had found a way of being married to a Dutchman and living, working, and raising her son in England, while remaining defiantly Haitian throughout. That Friday when she asked me to write down her story, she became my hero. In my work, but also in my head.

I stood at the school gates at three-thirty, waiting for the boys to come out. I smiled and greeted the various mothers I had met at Ines's, replete with their cashmere scarves, dogs, and shiny SUVs. The children were released to us on the playground, giddy with freedom and hunger, and the dogs barked with excitement, the boys sharing their snacks with them while the mothers held the leashes and the sports or violin bags, heading for their cars or their nearby homes. Tommy ran to me, his St Francis school satchel swinging in his hand. 'Is it true Baz is coming to our house today?' He was breathless with anticipation. It was his first play date. His eyes searched my face.

'Where's your blazer?' He was wearing the white polo shirt and grey trousers but the most expensive item on the uniform list, the seventy-five pound woollen blazer with the school's insignia sown in golden threads over the chest pocket was missing.

Tommy touched himself, 'I left it in inside, in my locker. I'll get it tomorrow!'

'It's Friday. Why don't you ask Mister Jones to let you back in?'

'I promise you Mama, it's safe in my locker. I'll get it on Monday in time for assembly!' He scanned the playground. 'Baz will get worried, he said he was coming home with us.' He looked up into my face.

I took a moment to let him see I was serious about the blazer. 'Ok. Go get him.'

'Yes!' He squeezed his little fist and ran off to find his new friend. A buoyant light-skinned boy with a wide smile and a headful of rising hair came running behind Tommy. I listened to their chatter in the back of the car. Spaceships, their teacher's face when she got angry—'she looks like porridge'—and a horror story about a boy who supposedly used sandpaper to wipe his bum. In the background the radio was playing, Pitbull. It was a grey afternoon. The traffic was dense. We were singing. We drove down Finchley Road all the way to West End Lane and to our place on a steep, narrow street lined on both sides with two-story houses linking West End Lane and Kingsway. Towards the top of the hill was our house, white with an unremarkable hedge and a tiled entrance on the street level. We had a small garden at the back that was separated from the neighbours by a chicken wire fence on one side and a wooden one on the other. On the see-through side to the left, the neighbouring house was split into apartments. It belonged to an elderly couple who rented the top two floors to students while they lived on the ground floor. The husband, Ian, was polite but remote. He was a retired chartered surveyor. His wife, Harriet, was much friendlier. She'd come to the fence when the weather was good with her cup of tea, sigh at our disastrous garden—theirs was immaculate—and call out to me, 'Naomi! Are you there? Would you like a cuppa?'

Most of the time I was home, steeped in arcane details about Peruvian history. I was toying with writing the story of British woman with Asian roots (she must look like an Inca) who'd just converted to Catholicism and joins a hiking group in the Andes. They cross a mountain pass with a reflective lake on top and a ring of clouds below and she loses sight of her group and ends up on a path that takes her straight into the sixteenth century. Every time Harriet came to distract me, I'd start by ignoring her, staying quiet to see if she'd conclude I was not there and go away. And then I'd relent, telling myself I had time for a break, and not only was it rude to ignore Harriet, but she was good research for me, writing as I was about someone who grew up here. And then I'd repeat to myself I had time before the school run. As soon as she heard me open the back door, she'd rush to her kitchen to make me a cup of tea. She had taken it upon herself to enlighten me as to the ways of the English. 'You are married to one, after all,' she'd say, reminding me of the importance of avoiding making too many faux pas. 'It could lead to unpleasantness in your relationship.'

My lessons would usually start with 'In this country,' sometimes followed by thinly veiled complaints, 'we tend to our gardens; we don't allow children to scream and shout,' but—and this is the reason I liked her—Harriet had decided some time ago that her purpose on this earth was to learn how to love. She worked hard at it and this made her interesting. She had found a way to be happy for over thirty years with the same man. A man who didn't seem worthwhile to me. He had a subscription to the *Daily Mail.* They ate dinner at six on the dot seven days a week, with the BBC news in the background as ambient noise. They went together to mass twice a month but Harriet would stay on her own to serve tea and biscuits to the congregation on special occasions. They had a grown daughter, Lizzie, who came to visit on Sundays. She usually arrived furious with one thing or another about her life and would curse and scream at her parents for not having done enough for her. Harriet was hurt by this, but she didn't get angry. She tried to love her differently, she read books and articles to find a way to make their relationship meaningful for Lizzie. She prayed for her to meet a good man. The only happiness in life, she would say, is to love and to be loved in return.

I opened the kitchen doors but before I let the boys out, I

checked to see if Harriet was in her garden. It was a nice September afternoon and I didn't want the boys to kick a ball into her while she was tending her geraniums. But she wasn't there and her back door was shut. In spite of our talks, our garden remained a dusty mess of cracked paving, weeds and a small patch of yellow grass. I had no time for plants. Tommy and Baz ran outside after me and started playing football. I left them there and went back inside.

Solange arrived soon after, wearing her afternoon pick-up gear. The designer suit, the battered Hermes bag, the immaculate beautifully shaped pumps—even the air she brought in, of French perfume mixed with the subtle sweat that comes from sitting in badly air-conditioned, overcrowded meeting rooms—it was a different woman from the casual mother on her way to a coffee morning I had met a few days earlier.

'Mummy!' Baz ran in to hug her as soon as he saw her through the kitchen glass door. I remembered her saying she'd been confused for his nanny but he was so obviously her son. Except for their complexion, they looked alike: their eyes, both brown and almond shaped, their wide mouths, their smile. It was also obvious how she adored him. She dropped her bag on the floor and opened her arms to catch him. Tommy came in too and went to the cupboard and asked me if they could have some crisps. I gave him a bag of Walkers and ruffled his straight hair.

My mostly white mama, Marina, had been a rebel and a hippie in her youth and married my black father to the horror of her family. They said my parents would have 'unreliable' children, as in 'Fernando Perez has unreliable lineage'. This is because my paternal grandfather, Anton Perez, ignored his parents' advice to seek a Caucasian wife in order to 'improve the race': the Perez family was already so mixed, my great-aunt once drew a family tree based on hair quality. Anton famously married a young black maid because, they said, he was lazy and complacent and knew she would allow him freedoms no white woman would tolerate with the extra bonus that Edith could make ceviche and fry plantains like no other. My father was born dark brown with a fuzz of cottony hair and the seeds of an inferiority complex that would blossom and grow until it destroyed his family.

Of course things were changing, even in Colombia. Whereas no one today would find it surprising or special that a black person had a degree, was a doctor or an engineer; the last frontier of a race complex is more aesthetic than intellectual. What struck me about Solange was not that she was obviously a successful professional, it was the confidence in her good looks that allowed her to wear her wild hair naturally and to avoid make-up. Maybe growing up black in Haiti is better. 'What do you do?'

'I work for a property developer. I take care of everything to do with public relations, communities, the city, you know,' she waved her hand in a way that reminded me of home, 'all the people who try to prevent my bosses from turning this city into a giant luxury condo site.' She shrugged. 'What I'd really like to do is cook. I'd love to have my own business. Do you know there isn't a single Haitian takeout counter, let alone restaurant, in all of London?'

'No. I don't even know what Haitian food is like.'

'Well, it's very good, of course.' She laughed. 'Although it's a home-based cuisine. It's not an eating-out culture, but that's changing. So classic Haitian dishes like *diri ak djon djon* and *griot de porc* take a long time to prepare, but I've been experimenting.' She took a glass from the drying rack and turned on the tap. 'May I?'

'Of course! I'm sorry, I haven't offered you anything to drink. What would you like?' I opened the fridge and took out a cold bottle of white wine.

'Water is fine for now.' Solange filled up her glass and drank it in one go. 'Ah.' She looked around at our kitchen, taking in the embarrassing water stain on the ceiling from the leaking shower upstairs. 'How long have you lived in London?'

'About nine years now. You?' I opened a pack of dried almonds and poured them into a wooden bowl.

'We moved here shortly after Baz was born. I didn't want him to grow up there.'

I filled my own glass with water from the tap and waited for her to continue.

She said nothing.

'There?' I said softly to encourage her.

'In Andreas's country.' She didn't say what country that was. 'I wanted a neutral place. A culture that was neither his nor mine.'

'Okay.' The thought had never occurred to me. 'What

made you choose here?'

Solange took an almond and bit it in half. 'This is the most open city in Europe. Here Baz won't stick out like a hair in the soup. Here he'll have the best chance to be treated fairly. To compete on an equal footing with everybody else.'

'May I ask where your husband comes from?'

'The Netherlands.' Solange cocked her head towards the boys in the garden and put her finger on her lips.

I had never been to the Netherlands. 'But your husband, Andreas? I guess he agrees with you.'

'Yes. It cost us, though. Can I?' She wanted to open the bottle of wine.

I passed her the corkscrew from the drawer and a wine glass.

'I forced him to see his country in a way he probably didn't want to,' She filled the glass and handed it to me. 'You're pregnant, duh!' She hit her forehead with the palm of her hand and took the wine for herself. 'He compares it to the scene in *The Matrix* when Morpheus offers Neo the choice between the red pill and the blue pill. I keep reminding him that I never even had a choice. It was the red pill for me from the start.'

'Maybe you should remind him instead that Neo wins at the end.'

She gave me a significant look. 'Where do you come from, Naomi?'

'From the Caribbean coast of Colombia, a suburb of Cartagena.' I took a bag of carrots out of the fridge.

'You grew up there?'

I filled up a pan with water and switched on the stove. '*Djes.*'

'They make good wives there.' Her eyes settled on my belly.

I was looking for something to reply with but she shook her head, don't bother, 'I was kidding.' She frowned, 'I love Andreas but history gets in the way. We've been trying to have another baby...'

The water was boiling. I threw in a pinch of salt and transferred a bag of pasta into the pan. 'Whose history?'

She shrugged. 'Ours, the world's... it's hard to say where to draw the line.' She slowly emptied her glass. 'So far nothing. Maybe... you can pray for us too?'

I stirred the pasta more vigorously than necessary. What did it matter that I stopped believing these things the minute I left my mother and Colombia? Solange obviously still needed it. I went outside and called the boys: 'Dinner in five!' To my surprise I found Tommy and Baz, gaping and guilty, standing on our side of the fence and Harriet, her face puce with anger, holding their ball above her head. Waving the spoon, I ordered them to come inside immediately.

Tommy and Baz walked in. They'd been kicking the ball against the fence the whole time they were outside until they drove the poor woman crazy.

'Shame on you boys!' she shouted to their departing backs.

I ran out to her. 'Harriet, I'm so sorry, I had the door

closed and I have a visitor and I didn't see what they were doing.'

'They've been kicking and rattling that fence. Look at what happened to my geraniums.' She had planted flowers along her edge of the fence. The boys had managed to jog the fence onto some of the stems. The flowers were ruined.

'Oh no! They've been very bad. I'll take you to Homebase tomorrow and I'll replace all the plants you've lost.'

'You must teach them to respect boundaries.'

I stepped over the half-bent fence and surveyed the damage. 'Oh, Harriet. I'm so sorry. Would you like to join us for a drink?'

'No, it's almost our dinner time. Ian must eat at six otherwise he can't take his medication. Thank you, though.' Her shoulders fell.

I went back over the fence. The kitchen door had been left wide open. Solange was standing there. I went back inside and shut the door. 'She's upset but she's a really sweet lady.'

'I didn't mean to annoy you when I asked you to pray for us. We are doing an IVF course, the third one. It's just that in this life you need luck too.'

'The prayers I know are about standing still. Enduring. Never about change, or...' I waved at her flat stomach, 'new.'

I gestured to the boys standing next to the kitchen door to hold on.

'Baz! Tommy! What were you thinking?' Solange called my son as if he were her own.

The boys skulked over to her with their heads low.

'What's wrong with you? Why did you do that?'

'It wasn't my idea,' Tommy said to me.

'I don't care whose idea it was,' Solange brought his attention back to her. 'Go out there to apologise.'

Baz looked through the glass door, 'She's not there anymore.'

'I have a better idea.' My classes in Englishness were paying off. 'Why don't you write her a nice letter in which you apologise for your behaviour?'

Solange nodded. 'Yes, I like that.'

I handed them a blank piece of paper and two pens. 'Her name is Harriet Williams. Start with "Dear Mrs Williams".'

Solange had poured the pasta into two bowls. 'Does Tommy want butter?'

The front door opened. Tom was early. 'Hello? I'm home!'

'Tom, *mi amor*, we're in the kitchen.' I immediately started clearing up some of the mess. That word, 'luck', started flashing in my head. 'This is Solange. She's a mum from Tommy's class.'

'From the coffee morning?' Tom looked at me to make sure, 'Naomi mentioned she met a charming mother.' He kissed Solange on the cheek. 'As charming as my wife.' he put his arm around my waist.

'Daddy!' Tommy left the table when he heard Tom's voice and high-fived his father. He was proud to show off his daddy to his new friend. Tom loved for the family to celebrate his return home from work or travels, especially on Friday evenings. He leaned down to shake Baz's hand. 'What's your name?'

'Bathz.' His mouth was half full of pasta.

'Bat?' Tom looked at Solange.

'Baz. It's a mix of the Dutch name Bass and the name of a Haitian singer called Taz,' Solange explained.

'Ah, one of those. Well, *Baz*, it's a pleasure to have you here.' He raised an eyebrow at Solange and her naming ideas but left it at that. He loosened his tie, 'What a day.'

I poured him a glass of wine. 'Ta,' he raised his glass to Solange and me. 'Here's to a really crappy week.'

'Thank God it's Friday!' I said.

He took a bite out of Tommy's plate. 'Mmm, you forget how good plain pasta with butter is.'

I invited him to sit down next to me, 'what happened?'

'You know the Swiss company that was going to buy Ava Labs? Now they only want to buy sixty per cent of it.'

This was the deal he was counting on for his bonus. 'Ay.' I put my hand over his and then I turned it over and kissed it on the small burn scar in the middle of his palm, 'are you going to look for another buyer?'

'My boss wants this deal to happen. He's already counted it for our group revenues for the year. I've been going around town looking for an investor who'd like to take a minority stake in a highly innovative biotech company.' He pressed his eyes with his fingers.

'And?'

'So far,' Tom took out his phone to make sure, 'nothing.'

'Can we go watch the telly in your room?' Tommy and

Baz asked me.

Solange removed their empty plates. 'Baz, pick up your things, we're leaving in three minutes.'

'No! Mummy, please can't Baz stay longer?' Tommy tugged at my arm.

I looked imploringly at Tom.

'Solange, why don't you call your husband and you all join us for dinner here?' Tom ruffled Baz's curly hair. 'The boys can watch a movie in our bedroom.'

'Yes!' I joined Tom. 'We'd love to meet him and as you can see, we have plenty of food.' I opened the fridge door to show her.

Solange hesitated. 'Baz, will you behave?'

'Yes! I love you mummy!'

The boys ran upstairs before we could change our minds. They were excited to have a few more hours together.

Tom took the bottle of champagne from the back of the fridge. 'This is a special occasion. Naomi rarely invites people over.'

Solange went outside to call Andreas, leaving us alone in the kitchen.

'What are you going to cook?' He was looking at my pregnant belly.

I came close to him and encouraged him to touch me. 'Chicken and leeks and potatoes and a salad. I have two avocadoes that are about to go bad. What do you think?'

'Mmm…' He lifted my shirt and put his ear to my stomach. There was a sharp tug inside. 'Did you feel that?'

I looked down at his beautiful, happy face; my huge, golden, immaculate bulge; the black and white checked tiles on the floor; the counter covered in plastic bags. Food, glasses, life, luck. How long could it last? I started coughing violently.

'Andreas is coming!' Solange announced, shutting the garden door behind her. 'He's bringing another bottle of champagne.' She looked at me. 'Are you okay?'

'Here's some water.' Tom filled a glass from the tap and gave it to me.

I drank the water and tapped my chest, '*Mi amor*, can you take care of the boys? Baz can borrow a pair of PJs and maybe you can put a movie on for them in our room?' Once Tom was gone, I sat down. 'I really hope that your dream of a new baby comes true.'

'Thank you.' She put her hand on my arm. 'I bet you grew up in a culture of *madichon* too. You don't worry. It doesn't reach England. It's like *piment zoizeau*, you know—those chilies that will burn you alive but look as thin skinned as blisters. They can't grow here either.' She rolled up her sleeves. 'No one can steal your good fortune. Now, can I help you with dinner?

That word *madichon*, was the Haitian version of the Spanish *maldición*, malediction in English? I went to look for a copy of a magazine in the pile of mail and other papers on the coffee table in the living room. 'Here. It's a story I wrote a few months ago. I'd like to hear what you think. As a Caribbean woman.'

Solange took the magazine and looked at the cover

before flipping the pages to find the story. 'Naomi! You're a writer! And you won a prize too!' she held up the cover as if to show me. 'Hello? What's the story about?'

'It's about an ageing woman who always thought she'd retire back to her home country but in the end never leaves London and dies here.'

Solange sat down to read it. I peeled an onion to pass the time. I was curious, no nervous, to hear what she'd think. I already cared about her opinion.

After what felt like a long time she stood up and put the magazine down. 'It's good. I felt on the inside of the story. You've taken on one of our basic fears—that we never find our way home. And you've translated into something everybody can understand.'

I stuffed the onion into the cavity of the chicken.

'Do you want me to finish that?' She had already taken out some half dried thyme leaves in the fridge. 'I see what you mean. About *madichon*. It's just our way of expressing anxiety.' She chopped a lemon in two and squeezed and pressed each half over the entire bird so that not only the juice but pieces of yellow flesh smeared into the chicken. 'I have a story I'd like to tell.'

While Solange explained to me what she wanted to do, Tom came back downstairs with both thumbs on the keypad of his phone. He picked up his glass of champagne. 'Well, here's to another no.'

'To your company?'

Solange looked at me, then at Tom. 'Who do you work

for?'

'Swain and Nicholls—S&N—it's a small advisory firm.'

'And you need an investor for one of your clients?'

'If you know anyone...' Tom peered into the oven. 'I'm starving.'

'I may know an investor for you.'

'Ah?' Tom stopped in surprise just as the doorbell rang. 'Hold that thought.'

He ran to open the door. Solange just stood there, she seemed frozen. Even I found myself paying attention to the sound of Tom opening the front door, to the new footsteps coming in.

Andreas, an enormous hulk of a man appeared with a magnum of Bollinger. 'Thank you for having us,' he said with a heavy Dutch accent. 'Where is Baz?'

Solange seemed tiny next to him. 'He's upstairs, watching a movie with Tommy.'

'Ah. Which film?'

I didn't know, so I turned to Tom.

'Um, *Spider-Man*.' Tom took Andreas's coat and poured him a glass of champagne. '*Two*.'

'Ah.' Andreas accepted the drink. 'Thank you.' He focused on my pregnant belly. 'Can I see him?'

'Who?' The way he looked at me, I thought he meant the unborn child.

'Baz, of course.'

'Of course.'

Tom, also appearing diminutive next to Baz's father, led

Andreas upstairs.

'Do you really know someone for Tom's deal?' I took four plates out.

'Maybe. It's a hedge fund guy. He's bought some of our debt and I had to go see him to reassure him about our relationship with the council. He is very rich.' Solange peeled the skin off the avocadoes and with her thumb scooped out the green and yellow flesh and threw it in the salad bowl.

'Oh?' I checked the chicken in the oven. 'What's his name?'

'Reginald Danton. Newspring Capital? They have two whole floors in one of those renovated buildings on St James's Square.' As she rinsed her thumbs in the sink and threw the avocado peels in the bin, I realised this whole evening, Solange had somehow prepared most of the food. 'Should I make the dressing?'

'No. You've done enough. Let me do that.' I took a bowl from the cupboard and added olive oil, rice vinegar, a quarter of a lemon, and some salt. I beat it with a fork and put a drop to taste on the back of my hand.

'Naomi, would you write my story?'

I choked on the acid of my vinaigrette. '*Qué*?'

'I'm serious. You can translate it into something a British boy can understand.' She looked me in the eye.

The taste of fear, dirt muddy with beer came into my mouth. I cleared my throat. 'I haven't really accomplished anything yet.' I should have added that she should look for someone more seasoned, a journalist, a memoirist. But I just held my breath. I was thrilled that she'd asked.

'No, I want you to do it.'

'They're thick as thieves, those boys.' The two men came down the stairs. 'Andreas! Can I offer you another drink?'

'Can I have one too?' Solange handed Tom her empty glass and winked at me.

For an impromptu dinner party it was truly excellent. We had no dining room in that first house and we all sat in the kitchen to the flickering light of candles stuck in old wine bottles. While we were chatting, we had prepared a good meal between the salad and the roast chicken and the leeks.

'So how did Andreas convince you to marry him?' Tom liked Solange, I could tell by the way he looked at her.

'Maybe I convinced him.' Her laughter, now that I heard it again, was deep and rich, intact in a way her speech no longer was. There was an old woman who used to sweep the stairs of the law faculty at the university in Cartagena who'd wear a white scarf tied behind her ears like a slave. With every shake of her broom, she'd mutter, 'Life is beautiful but livin' ain't pretty.' And then she'd laugh. She laughed like Solange. 'First you two. How did you meet?'

'We were queuing for coffee in New York. The place was so popular, the lines stretched outside on the pavement. There weren't that many good coffee bars back then.' I smiled at Tom.

It had been all the way downtown, when there was still a big hole where the twin towers had once stood. A coffee shop off Bowery around Spring Street. I was taking a break after an early morning meeting in the area, checking my voicemails before heading back to Midtown. Tom was standing several people behind me but I must have felt his gaze because I turned around and there he was staring at my behind. It was summer. I frowned at him. Instead of retreating, as most men would, and pretend he'd never looked at me, this one stood his ground. His chin pointing at me, he dared me to challenge his right to look at me. That made me curious. Timorous, sensitive types didn't attract me. I liked power. After I paid for my latte, I went to stand at the counter and stayed there even after I got my cup. Soon enough, he was standing next to me, waiting for his cappuccino. There was a boyish eagerness in his blue eyes, a spark, a desire to be seen, recognised. And so I did. I acknowledged him, not Tom, the junior associate/slave at the investment bank who lived with three other graduates in a cramped flat on the other side of the water in Jersey City, no, I nodded at the Tom of the future, the Tom he wanted to tell me about.

'Oh, do I have plans.' He'd taken my hands into his with the best smile I had ever seen. 'So we left the coffee shop and met that evening at a tapas bar and we haven't stopped talking since.' I stopped. There's an old saying in Colombia about dissipating your business through too much talk. I had said enough. I focused on cutting a piece of leek with my fork and putting it in my mouth.

'She was working for this old American pig of a sports agent and I knew right away when I saw her.' Tom beamed at me. 'She looked fragile but beautiful.'

I tried to be modest. I pretended I didn't hear.

'So you… rescued her.' Solange's eyes narrowed.

I spoke up. 'Yes, he did. I think all young women need rescuing, don't you?'

Solange thought about this. 'No. Nobody loves their rescuers anyway. The most ambitious one ended up nailed on a cross.' She turned to her husband. He put his hand over hers on the table and covered it so completely that her forearm looked like it had no end.

'The face of modern London! I'm the only native on this table. What brought you two to the UK?' Tom poured them the last of the second bottle of champagne.

'London is better for our careers than Amsterdam,' Andreas said automatically, like a well-rehearsed line.

'Or Port-au-Prince,' Solange added on cue.

'Come on, Haiti I don't know, but Amsterdam is a lovely, prosperous city,' Tom insisted.

'If!' Solange almost screamed.

I frowned.

'After two years in Amsterdam, I was ready to cho—'

'How did you choose St Francis School?' I interrupted Solange. She was too excited; she was on the verge of saying something she would regret.

'I… I first heard about St Francis from a colleague at work.'

At least she caught on quickly.

Andreas visibly relaxed. 'This is delicious.' He smiled for the first time. That's when I realised how tense the man had been and that this was not the first time the conversation had taken such a turn. He nodded at me, gratefully.

'Wait, you haven't explained what brought you here from Holland. I have to say, I have spent time in Holland and Belgium as a student and I loved it.'

I tried to kick Tom under the table but he was too far away and I was too big to slide down on my chair to reach him.

'It's a nice enough place to visit,' Solange said in a tempered voice. She was back in control. 'I met Andreas as a student in Chicago. I thought I understood *l'étranger*, as they say in Haiti, because I lived in America. But I moved to Holland with the wrong expectations.'

'My wife suffered from racial discrimination in Amsterdam.' Andreas folded his napkin and threw it on the table. 'That is why we don't live there anymore.'

Silence descended.

'It's admirable how you've left your country for your wife.' What the hell do you say?

He didn't respond. His lips became very thin until they were like a dark line across his jaw.

'Tea or coffee anyone? We have decaf, don't we Naomi?' Tom came to the rescue.

'Eh? Oh, yes, and herbal tea. I think we have a nice lemon and ginger.' I escaped to the cupboard above the sink to sift through the boxes.

'Do you have any whisky?' Andreas asked.

Without saying a word, Tom went to the living room

where we had an old-fashioned liquor cabinet we had bought at the market in Church Street. He came back with a bottle of single malt.

'Thanks.' Andreas downed his glass with ease. He was a good-looking man in a Teutonic type of way. Blond, square-jawed, blue-eyed, and big boned. Just like my Tom, Andreas worked in investment banking. Unlike my Tom, Andreas was withdrawn. I could see why he chose Solange. By himself he found life hard, heavy perhaps; Solange provided the igniting spark, the boost when, as the old lady used to say, livin' ain't pretty.

'Do you like living in London?'

'It's an amazing city.' He didn't smile.

Solange pushed her chair back, the scrape on the tiles setting us all on edge. She stood and put her arms around Andreas's head and kissed his hair. He shut his eyes and leant his head into her.

Intense couple. I started gathering the plates.

We went upstairs to see the boys. The movie was long finished and an electric blue light emanated from the screen. The boys were sound asleep on our bed. Tommy had even wriggled under the duvet. I left him there and switched off the TV. Andreas lifted Baz up as if he were a duffel bag and carried him out, while Solange searched for her handbag.

'You mentioned earlier something about an investor?' Tom asked as he helped her with her jacket.

'Yes, I was telling Naomi. Maybe you already know him, Newspring Capital? Reginald Danton?'

'The £3 billion hedge fund? This is way too small for—'

'He's interested in biotech. He told me last week.' There was a glint of pride in Solange's eye.

'You know Reggie Danton?' Tom was impressed. 'It's impossible to meet the man. My boss has been trying for two years. How did you do that?'

'He wanted to see me. I liked him. He was open and calm. Best listener I've seen in a long time.' Solange looked at me. I nodded back. She cleared her throat. 'Tom, maybe I can arrange an intro for you?'

Our deal was done.

Tom's face lit up. 'That would be brilliant!'

'Solange!' Andreas called from the driver's seat.

'Okay, I have to go. Thank you so much.' Solange ran to her husband, holding her thumb and little finger up to say she'd call the next day. They waved at us from the car.

Tom and I stood in front of the house and watched them drive away. From the little I had heard tonight, Solange was 'it'. I had found my protagonist. Or rather my protagonist had found me. Luck. It was all luck and how long would it hold? Already she had me on that one.

'What the hell is a lovely, warm woman like Solange doing with a man like that?' said Tom. 'No wonder she can't get pregnant. His sperm must be as reticent as his character.'

'They love each other.'

We went back inside and closed the door.

'I wonder if she can pull it off... Can you imagine? Reginald Danton.' He shook his head. 'He was just another fund manager until the financial crisis of 2008. He got it right somehow. He knew not only that the subprime market was going to blow and take the banks with it, but he was able to time it too.' Tom carried the salad bowl from the table to the kitchen counter. 'Now, he's a regular top ten in *The Sunday Times* rich list.' He slapped his hand against the counter. 'Damn! Wouldn't you love that?'

'*Mi amor*, can you empty that, please?' I was rinsing the plates and I indicated the salad bowl with my chin.

Tom took the bowl to the bin, put his foot on the pedal to open the lid, and banged the bowl upside down against the metal edge of the bin. 'Where do they live, Solange and Andreas?'

'I think in St John's Wood.' I placed the last dish in the dishwasher.

'Do they? That's quite expensive.'

'I'm pretty sure. In the car Baz was telling Tommy how he knew his home address by heart. Something Carlton Hill NW8. That's St John's Wood.'

'Huh. I guess it goes faster with two salaries. All I got out of him was that he worked in derivatives at Citibank. In a house or in a flat?' He remembered the dirty salad bowl in his hand and handed it to me.

'*Mi amor*, can you take the rubbish out, please?' I found a place for the bowl and placed a tablet in the dishwasher dispenser. I shut the door and switched it on. 'Yes it does.' It was my turn to slap my hand against the counter. 'I'll go back to sports marketing after the baby is born.'

'Ah, darling, that's not what I meant.' He pulled me up and hugged me. 'You think I don't know everything you do? We talked about this. It's our choice, this is how we want to live.' He indicated the mess surrounding us. I tried to disentangle myself, but he held on to me. 'And you're going to write a great book.'

I looked at him. 'Yes, I am.' I hesitated. No, there wasn't enough yet to talk about. 'It's starting to peel.' My eyes moved with my words up to the ceiling. It had a beige ring around it, like someone took a cup of coffee and threw the liquid upwards.

He shrugged. 'Don't worry. We will buy our house this year.'

'We'll buy a house when we can afford to buy a house.' Without thinking, I went on, 'I saw a flat…' I saw his face and stopped. I was about to say that I'd seen a listing, three bedrooms on a third floor on Priory Road, on the other better side of West End Lane that looked reasonable.

'What?' Tom refused to consider apartments, no matter how big.

'Nothing.'

He sighed, gazing at the leftover chicken and leeks and the champagne glasses that had to be washed by hand. 'Darling, would you mind taking care of this? I've had a really terrible week and I'm falling asleep.'

'It's okay, my love. Go to bed.' I tried to lift the rubbish bag but the strain was too much for me. 'Please can you take this one out for me on your way?'

He didn't hear me.

'Tom?'

'Oh sorry, of course.'

Half an hour later, I turned off the tap and finished wiping the countertop. My feet were killing me. It was all that extra weight. I sat down and checked my phone. Nearly one in the morning. I made a mental note to call the landlord in the morning—again—about the damp on the ceiling.

# CHAPTER FOUR

## May 2016

'Solange? *Mierda! Cristo Todopoderoso!*' I crossed myself two times.

'You're right. Exorcise yourself. Don't let your family be infected by mine.'

'Shut up and let me in.' Fumes from my own divorce seeped out of some septic tank in my brain. I call it 'my' divorce but it was my parents'. I was eleven.

Like Baz.

She turned her back on me and walked towards the living room. I shut the door behind me and followed her. She was wearing a T-shirt with Japanese prints on it and a weird pair of electric blue shorts that seemed to be made of plastic. I found her sitting on the sofa like a teenager with her feet up and her T-shirt stretched to the point of deformation across her folded knees. Her head was hanging in the gaping hole that had become the T-shirt's neck and all I could see was a tangled mass of black, kinky hair.

I settled in the armchair opposite the sofa. Behind her was their bookshelf. Her college books were still on the shelves, their once colourful spines fading into yellow so that their American flashiness finally fit with the monochrome Haitian, Dutch, and German titles. She raised her head. I put my hand to my mouth. She looked like she had died. Her eyes were yellow, her lips dry and cracked—a zombie. They did come from Haiti after all. I dropped my eyes to my feet. I found my loafers pretentious.

Antheia had warned me this morning at the school gates but I was too obtuse, too self-centred to understand. 'I was in an Uber early this morning on my way to my chiropractor and we drove past Solange's house,' she'd told me. 'I saw her and Andreas on the steps outside and I asked the driver to slow down. I lowered my window to wave at them and that's when I saw Andreas leave with a suitcase.'

'Maybe he was going on a business trip.'

'Naomi, Solange was standing on the pavement, barefoot, wearing some bizarre blue shorts, and she looked so shattered. I've seen that look before. I think… Anyway, I wanted to tell you. I know you two are good friends.'

I took a deep breath and looked up at Solange. 'Have you eaten anything?'

'I heard his keys in the door,' Solange started in a low voice. 'He was due back from a transatlantic trip. I was up, waiting for him. He was standing with his suitcase on the landing. I was happy to see him. Yes, I was.' She raised her head, as if to convince me. 'I believed, Naomi. In spite of everything, I believed in love, in marriage, in family. I believed in him.'

I nodded.

'But he made no move to kiss me or to come inside. And then I saw his look. The "I'm just a boy in the shell of a forty-five-year-old man, so don't hold me responsible" look. Nothing good could come out of that look. I leaned against the doorframe and waited. I thought he'd been fired. Girl, I have to give it to him. For all our fifteen years together, I did not see this one coming.'

*I've been seeing this Dutch girl and she's five months pregnant.*

Boom.

The morning was still beautiful, the sky as blue as it was when I woke up. I could see Antheia driving by in her mini-cab, the round Transport for London sticker on its rear window. I could see Solange standing there, a crashing sound in the distance.

And now here she was. I was experiencing one of the great mysteries of life. How was it possible that a simple piece of information, *I've been seeing this Dutch girl and she's five months pregnant,* could trigger this kind of physical pain? Women in my country run through the street or stand in front of their house to scream. They scream because they want God to hear their pain and they scream for the relief of screaming. But here? How does one suffer in North-West London? What a silly question, one just does.

The silence was broken by the clang of the metal flap of the mail slot in the front door. Three boring-looking white envelopes, bills probably, fell on the floor. Outside, a postman pushed his mail cart past the azalea bushes. I looked at her unchanged home where our children had played together so often, where we had once spent so many evenings working together on our book and where Solange was now falling apart. So this is hell.

'I still love him. Everything in my body is yearning for him. And he's no longer mine. He doesn't care.'

'My aunt's husband left her after twenty years of marriage without warning.' Yes I was trying to pull away. 'He too had found some young creature on the make. She hung a framed photograph of him on her living room wall and moved a footstool underneath the picture, put a candle on it and a plastic rose in an empty mayonnaise jar. She told everyone who came by that her husband had died and gone to hell and he became known from that day on as 'El Defuncto'. It almost killed a friend of my aunt who saw him walking down the cereal aisle in the supermarket. She thought it was a ghost, some kind of Colombian Lazarus.'

Solange wasn't listening.

'I'm going to buy you something to eat.' I ran out of the house, terrified. I had felt a connection with Andreas. Unlike Tom, who found him a bore, I knew there were layers to that man. Pain, yes, but he had depth and he loved Solange possibly more than Tom could ever love me because she didn't make it easy. She wasn't a 'good' wife but she was authentic and flawed and un-European and he left his country for her. Nausea made me stop on the pavement. I was on St John's

Wood High Street. I watched the traffic. The man selling tomatoes and plums and flowers outside Panzer's Deli was the same as the day before. The Romanian ladies were still painting fingers and toes through the window of the nail salon across the street. Even the front page of the paper,—I stopped before the stand in front of the Post Office—, was the same. There was no rushing headline about a surge in betrayals, in desertions, in heartbreak.

And yet. Tom too travelled a lot, was travelling right now, as a matter of fact. Then my mind, running wild, went there: *I could have a rerun of Solange's scene at my doorstep in twenty-four hours' time.*

What holds a man down? An old man used to sell a potion at the market in Cartagena called *Sientate*. Only a few drops in a man's morning coffee was enough to make him sit down at home and lose the urge to wander. Abuela Edith and I used to laugh at the women who were silly enough to stop at the old charlatan's stall and listen to his nonsense. Now I knew how these women felt. How do you keep your husband, indeed, when you feel covered in cobwebs? After fifteen years of marriage?

I threw up in the gutter at the corner of the road.

# CHAPTER FIVE

## October 2012

People see corruption differently depending on its scale. If you're a foreigner in Latin America and you witness a local slipping a bill to a policeman who then waves him away, you'll say, 'Ah, what a shame that people here have become so corrupt. How lucky that in our green and pleasant land we don't even think of doing things like that.' Everybody in Colombia still believes in the original sin. In England, people are born clean and corruption is an external force that attacks their good character, the way a virus can infect a healthy body. To make sense of it, the English pick apart the childhood and every aspect of their criminals' lives to demonstrate how different, even alien, they are from the rest of the good citizens. Where I grew up, the only difference between a man in handcuffs and one strolling down the street is that one had the bad luck and/or stupidity to get caught.

We had both learned, Tom in Leicestershire and me in Cartagena, that something had defeated our parents and that that something was money. And we wanted a perfect life because in this century we are led to believe we can have one.

That can mean different things for different people and for us, that meant money.

After that first dinner party, Solange delivered on her promise and secured Tom a meeting with Reginald Danton. He came home that evening pumped up, as they say. The only time I'd seen him happier was the day Tommy was born. Danton was incredible, he said. Stepping into his office was like being admitted into a higher sphere of existence. 'It was like being high on cocaine without taking it.'

I had never tried cocaine so I asked him to explain what he meant. 'I felt more intelligent, more creative, more energetic, just sitting there.' He said he dreaded the moment when he'd have to leave. 'Those lucky bastards' enjoyed floor-to-ceiling glass walls overlooking the park, a seventeenth-century reclaimed library from a Venetian palazzo, mid-century classic and cool furniture like Hans Wegner Papa Bear chairs, lighting to ease your eyesight and warm your heart. There were pods in the hallway along the glass wall where you could lie on an ergonomic long chair, plug the supplied headphones into the wall and choose between a selection of classical works, audiobooks or the latest in meditation techniques. If you wanted more out of your 'pod' time, there was a 'therapy room' in the office where you could book massages, neo-linguistic programming or yoga sessions.

'But what is the man like?' My breath was becoming short; I was five days away from my due date. Tom wasn't the only one to open a new vista in his life.

Solange and I had started working on our book. It began:
*Port-au-Prince, 1980*

*We were really poor. We had nothing. So my mother sacrificed herself. She became our slave. The only aim of her existence was to provide for us. This made her hard. She was not loving. She was irritable and would get angry for nothing and beat me with whatever object she could find.*

Tom had opened a bottle and was offering me a glass of wine. 'No?'

'It's not me, it's the baby,' I smiled.

'Okay, where was I? Danton! Yes,' He barely heard me, he was so excited, 'home counties ex-rugby player from one of those boarding schools with black capes and bad heating. He even has the ginger hair. But from the moment we shook hands and sat down to talk, I knew I was in front of someone extraordinary. He doesn't need to project anything. I've never seen that in this industry, a man so unconcerned with his reflection. You know, even if they pretend they don't care, dress casually, try to look like hipsters or victims of arrested development, they're still selling something and you know because they check their image in your eyes. But Reginald Danton, he's rich enough to just focus on you, what you're saying, how you're saying it.'

He kissed my hand. He kissed my pregnant belly. He hugged me and caressed the top of my forehead. This Danton was something. Tom was just like the day we first met, irresistible. His face was luminous, his blue eyes dancing. I watched his big farmer's hands, smoother than any of his ancestors', move as he spoke and maybe it was the late pregnancy hormones, but I felt an overwhelming need to feel those hands on me. We made love for the last time before Sam was born. I was exhausted afterwards but Tom got out of bed and worked until four in the morning on more details about the AVA deal. He came back for a nap, got up again at six and sent the new deal information to Newspring by seven before the markets opened, as promised.

The next day, Newspring offered to plug the hole in the company's financing. Tom had to give in on the valuation, but AVA Labs was so desperate by then that they didn't mind. Tom's boss, a New York transplant named Virgil Brown, was so impressed he invited us both to dinner at his house with his wife, Jenni. As I sat, or rather sprawled on their sofa, an open bottle of Gaviscon in my hand, they congratulated us on our growing family and Virgil told Tom in unambiguous terms that his future at the firm was bright.

'By the way,' he said, putting down his glass of cognac, 'and I'm not saying this because I'm trying to keep you at S&N, but it seems like you've made a strong impression on Reginald Danton. I wouldn't be surprised if he offered you a job. He's always looking for hungry, smart men.' Virgil turned to me. 'Naomi, you listen too, this is about your family's future.' He thought for a moment. 'How do I say this without sounding disingenuous… Okay, Danton can offer to pay Tom two, maybe three times what I can give him. But Danton expects his people to deliver double-digit returns. Year on year. He can't justify his crazy fees if he can't keep what they call the 'alpha' up. That's a lot of pressure. And those who crack, who miss their target, who have bad luck... I don't know. I have yet to meet an ex-Newspring employee in my dealings around this city.' He smiled. 'Or in Palm Beach, Ibiza or wherever the alumni of the other hedge funds hang out.'

'Maybe no one ever leaves Newspring.' I smiled at Tom.

'He only has fifteen, maybe twenty people, no more.' Tom cleared his throat. 'I got a tour of the office.'

Virgil picked up his cognac and leaned back on his arm-chair as if Tom's words allowed him to rest his case.

'Maybe it's the same original team?' I ventured.

'Well we do know an ex-Newspring employee, Nat. He's my second-degree cousin on my father's side. A sad story, really.' Jenni watched me pour the Gaviscon down my throat. 'Anyway, how are you feeling? It's hard to keep anything in the stomach at your stage.'

'Oh, I'm fine. What happened to your cousin?'

'He had a crisis of meaning. That's how he called it. He basically burned out and had a nervous breakdown.'

'He went crazy. Lost his wife. She took the two children, they were what? Ten, twelve? when this happened.' Virgil sighed.

'Marjorie could have waited. Nat may have recovered. I don't think she loved him, not really.' Jenni turned to me, 'He became a preacher. He now lives on an Indian reserve in New Mexico.'

'Native American.' Virgil corrected his wife.

'Sorry, yes Native American,' she shrugged.

I looked at Tom. He shook his head at me. Don't worry, he was saying. I thought of his big strong hands. He was different from these people. Tom was built to work, hard. Both his grandfathers had been miners. His father eventually re-trained as a mechanic but he too started deep in a shaft. Tom was immune to middle-class guilt because he was not middle-class. We weren't secure enough to indulge in existential doubts. We first had to buy a house. I leaned into the cushions. It was a relief to be so pregnant. It gave me an excuse to disconnect from their conversation. I examined the minimalist fireplace in front of me and the colourless painting above. In my head, Solange's voice was full of colours.

*Maman left the house at dawn and only came back when it was dark, crushed with tiredness. She looked like a ghost, drained of strength. She still put her apron on to prepare our one meal of the day. Some days she would show us the little cash she had earned at the factory. It was her way of telling us that we would eat: rice and beans.*

\*\*\*

Sam was born two days later and my mother flew in from Cartagena. She was delighted with her second grandson.

'You have done so well, *mi hija*. He is as beautiful as Tommy.' She insisted I hold the baby in a certain way so

82

she could take pictures of him from all angles to send to the family.

My arms were getting sore. 'Enough already,' I protested but she ignored me, unpacking instead a new baby hair-brush she had apparently bought for the occasion. 'No!' I was furious. I held Sam away from her. There was a curl on top of his head and I knew she wanted to smooth it out. 'Enough, Mama.' I glared at her. Marina glared back at me but she did put her brush and her camera away.

Sam was a beautiful baby, with a perfectly shaped head and big black eyes that took some time to focus on me. Once they did, they didn't let me go. His eyes followed every twitch and smile, every movement of my arms, my fingers. I was his world. He couldn't be mine. It wasn't just that I had his older brother Tommy. I was first and foremost Tom's wife. Sam was a couple of weeks old when Tommy fell on his way home from school with Marina. His forehead hit the hard edge of a low border wall. Blood gushed out of his open wound and fell into his eyes, temporarily blinding him.

I took an Uber with Sam in a baby sling and went to join them at the A&E. The gauze Marina held against the cut was already soaked through; I didn't know a head could bleed so much. I didn't want Tom to see his son like this. We sat together all four of us and I kissed Tommy's tears. I only called Tom once our boy had been cleaned up and the doctor had had a chance to examine him. When he walked in, Tommy stopped crying and tried to sit up.

'What happened?'

'The cut is blunt and deep. He needs more than the simple stitches I do. He'll have to see a plastic surgeon.' The doctor answered automatically.

'What the hell? And what is Sam doing here? Do you know how dirty these emergency rooms are?" Tom moved past me to reach Tommy, taking his hand. 'It's going to be ok now.'

There was nothing for me to do but to go join my mother in the waiting room. 'In the meantime, keep an eye on him.' The doctor walked Tom and Tommy out a few minutes later. He gave me a brochure about the signs of concussion.

Tom carried Tommy to the cab. I could see the expansion of the muscles of his back through his suit jacket. Tommy had his arms around his father's neck. I was relieved when Sam started crying.

That night I stayed with the baby in our bed while Tom spent the night in the armchair in Tommy's room. At some point when Sam was sleeping, I tiptoed next door to check on Tommy. He was agitated but sleeping like someone with a high fever—one of the symptoms of severe concussion. Tom was kneeling by his bedside with a wet towel and a mug of cool water. He showed me the thermometer.

'I've been checking him every hour and he doesn't have a fever. He's just unsettled and a bit sweaty from the accident.'

'Why don't you go to bed, I'll stay with him.'

'No, it's okay. I want to stay here with him.'

After a moment, I went back to bed, vaguely irritated but unable to figure out why.

In the morning, I left Sam with Marina and was about to leave with Tommy to go back to the hospital when Tom caught up with us at the door. 'Were you going to leave without me?'

We went together.

And I came back with a freshly bandaged Tommy by myself.

'It looks like it's all under control so I'm going to the office,' were Tom's parting words as soon as the plastic surgeon cut the last piece of thread.

I slammed the front door behind us.

'Naomi! Come watch this!' Marina called as soon as she heard the door. I left Tommy to hang his coat and I went upstairs to our bedroom, where I found my mother on the rocking chair, burping Sam against a small towel on her shoulder while watching a rerun of a popular soap called *Sin Tetas No Hay Paraíso* (Without Tits, No Paradise). 'Have you ever seen this?'

I sat on the bed and took in the pretty but overly made-up star on the screen. 'No. This is one of those narco soaps, isn't it?' I touched Sam's cheek. 'He's asleep.' The bottle was almost empty.

'My little *gordo* still hasn't burped.' Marina patted his back. 'Ah, the things people do for money. This show's old. All she does is get cheap implants to catch the *capó*. Today she'd fill up her tits with powder. Did you know that the big drug dealer they arrested with that actor in Mexico was actually a clone of the real guy? He's still free, probably drinking whisky with the president as we speak.'

'Mama, clones don't exist.'

'Ay', she made a face, 'they did in Iraq, remember Saddam Hussein? Plastic surgery is very good now.' Sam let out a small hiccup. 'Good boy. Now, you sleep.' She gave me the baby. I laid him on his side in the Moses basket next to our bed and covered him with a blanket. He soon turned on his stomach, his little arms bent, his two hands flat on the sheet on each side of his head.

She watched me settle him. '*Mi hija.* Talking about breasts. Now that you've given Tom two children, it's time you invested in yourself.' She assessed my chest. 'You know this is what happens, they shrink and they sag after two pregnancies, and your breastfeeding doesn't help. You have to think about your marriage. Men, even if they pretend they don't, care about these things—'

'Mama, please.' I indicated Tommy, who'd walked in. For the first time I was happy his Spanish was so bad.

'No, no, I know a very good plastic surgeon in Cartagena. I'd tell you his name but you wouldn't know him. He's just bought two king palms from us worth $20,000 but I gave him a discount and he's so pleased, he said you can come anytime, he'll put you ahead on his list.' She tried to pull my T-shirt across my chest.

'Aagh! We are not like that, Mama.' I left her with the children in the room and went downstairs. It was raining. A brown puddle was growing outside the garden door. My phone rang. It was Tom. 'Oh.'

'Why do you answer the phone like that?'

'Like what?'

'Like you resent me or something.'

'I'm depressed.'

'Forget about it. We're moving! You won't believe what just happened.'

Danton had offered Tom a job to run an investment portfolio. Tom asked to see his holdings. Danton showed him a blank piece of paper. 'You're building it.'

Tom ran home, his face as white as the sheet of paper Danton had shown him. He took my hands in his. 'Do you think I can do it?' The salary was good, slightly higher than what he was getting now, but the bonuses could be brilliant. 'We are talking five per cent of the profits on my fund. He wants me to invest £400 million in biotech and pharma. I must get a minimum ten per cent return, so worst-case scenario, that's £40 million. Four per cent of that is £2 million.' He stopped. I asked him to tell me again to make sure that I had heard the numbers, that we were awake, and that this was real. Tom exploded first: 'Oh my God!'

We jumped into each other's arms and kept on jumping all the way to the kitchen. Tom switched on the speaker and put on Blur's 'Song 2', the one that goes 'Woo-hoo!' He leapt on top of the dining table and turned up the volume, pulling me up to be with him. I kicked off the placemats. He seized the salt shaker as a microphone and handed me the pepper one. We shook our hair in sync to the music. I swung to his invisible guitar.

'Woo-hoo!'

I glued my hips to his. He grabbed me by the buttocks and pulled me tight. I let my head fall back as he shouted, 'When I feel heavy metal / And I'm pins and I'm needles!'

'Woohoo!' I swung my arms around his neck.

The kitchen door opened.

'*Estáis loco?*' Marina barged in, 'You're going to wake up Sam and give Tommy a headache.'

I stepped down and pulled on Tom to do the same. I switched off the music. We stood in silence for a moment, listening to see if either of the children were crying but no, the house was quiet.

'Mama, Tom got offered a fantastic job today,' I explained.

Marina frowned. 'What's wrong with the job he has now?'

'Nothing! But that's not the point.' I went to hug her.

My mother stood stiff. 'What kind of job is it?'

'Very similar to what I do now,' Tom stepped in. 'You know, finance, money management.'

'So why is it so much better?' She was in one of her moods.

'Because the guy who runs the new place is a genius and Tom could make a lot more money.' I switched to Spanish. I pointed at the damp on our ceiling. 'You want us to be able to afford our own house, don't you?'

She too pointed at the ceiling. 'This? Because of this you're in a hurry?' She stood the way she used to when she was trying to impose her will on me, hands on hips, feet apart.

'At my age, you come to learn that some things are too good to be true: *Lo mejor es el enemigo del bien.*'

'Mama, you don't even know what the new job is.'

Tom wasn't bothered; his Spanish only went so far. He had already checked out and was looking at something on his phone. I wasn't pleased with Mama for spoiling our mood, why couldn't she just be happy for us? But what upset me most was that I couldn't dismiss her. As usual she had found her way under my skin. *Minimum return of ten per cent.* What if Tom only makes eight or seven per cent? Virgil Brown's words popped into my head.

Later that evening, I sat on our bed, breastfeeding Sam. *Newsnight* was on but I had turned the volume down. Tom sat next to me on top of the covers with his laptop open.

'What are you thinking?'

He had said very little since Marina came to the kitchen a couple of hours before. Maybe he, too, was worried about this minimum return condition. My breast was empty and Sam was gurgling happily. I gently pulled the nipple away and Tom picked up the baby. I put the muslin cloth on his shoulder. He lay down on the pillow with Sam on top of him and I covered them both with the duvet. My mother didn't understand our world. Still.

'Tom, are you worried about this minimum return? What happens if you don't make ten per cent?'

'No.' His eyes were closed. 'I'll make the minimum.'

'But what if you don't?' I put the cup back on top of my nipple and clipped my bra back on.

'Danton's invited us to a luncheon he and his wife are hosting next weekend. I think we should go.' He started patting around the bed with his hand, taking care not to disturb Sam.

I handed him the remote control. 'So you've decided, then?'

'I want to see the interior of the lion's cave before I sign.' He raised the volume.

Tommy came in and I invited him into the bed too. He snuggled in-between us. The baby snored on Tom's chest with satisfaction, making Tommy giggle. Maybe I was addicted to worry. I was becoming one of those women. I took a deep breath and let my head fall back. Big things happened today. Happy things. I touched Tom's foot with mine. Jeremy Paxman was interviewing Michael Gove. The words 'immigration' and 'referendum' kept coming up.

'Bollocks.' Tom sat up. 'This referendum is the latest trick of the upper classes to keep their power. They've lost their City jobs to better qualified French and Italians. They've lost the law firms to the Americans. And the Eastern Europeans are visible enough for them to pretend that the EU should scare the rest of the population. Bollocks all of it."

I folded my pillow in two, 'Good night *mi amor.*'

Tom didn't answer. He switched off the TV, carefully placed Sam back in the Moses basket, and carried Tommy, who by now was breathing loudly, back to his bed. I was already half asleep when I felt his arm around my hip. He liked sleeping with his face against my back.

# CHAPTER SIX

*Sometimes we were not lucky. We guessed it easily when my mother came home and would not look at us. We knew there would be nothing to eat that day. I still had to study and do my homework, a difficult task. Hunger gave me stomach cramps and kept me from concentrating. I'd go to bed, sucking my thumb, drooling to the smell of the dinners being cooked by our neighbours. During the night, I'd wake up to see the shadow of my mother, lit by a trembling candle, sewing discarded pieces of cloth that she had brought back from the factory to make pillow cases. At dawn, she'd go sell them at the Marche de la Place for a little money so she could buy us food before going to the factory. Maybe she was too proud to display her misery to the world. She asked help from no one.*

'Solange, this is crazy!' I stopped typing. 'How did you ever,' I indicated her beautiful clothes, her manicured hands, 'get to this? St John's Wood, the prep school, your... your job?'

Solange smiled. 'God rewarded me for having chosen the tough and narrow path of hope. I learned that the struggle against life forces us to lose ourselves absolutely and then to find ourselves completely. It is the true baptism and no one can avoid it.'

'You mean the struggle to live, the fight for life?'

'If you're poor enough, you're fighting against life.'

For the first time, I felt I didn't know Solange at all. This worried me. I didn't want to even consider the idea that our backgrounds may not have that much in common after all. It would take away the whole idea of 'our voice', of our book as the story of a new kind of immigrant, my kind of immigrant, what I wanted these British to know about me.

'Wait,' I said, beginning to type once more. '"Struggle", that's the word. "The tough and narrow path of hope."' I cast my doubts aside. After all, having a Spanish speaker write down in English the story of a Creole speaker was bound to lead to some problems of semantics. 'Let's continue.'

*The night my mother died, her last breath was full of worry for us, for what our fate would be. I dare to believe that she is now finally at peace. She earned her peace. We took her body and buried it in the cold mountain, where she was accepted and loved by her peasant family. I realised that my mother had to die to enjoy the peace rich people think is their birth right.*

Which brings us to Danton's lunch.

\*\*\*

I dressed as nicely as I could for a woman still swollen from giving birth and we drove out to Reginald Danton's country house in Wiltshire. When I found out the lunch was out of town, I proposed we book a hotel or a bed and breakfast nearby. After all, my mother was still around; it was a chance for us to have a weekend out. We hadn't been alone as a couple for ages. But Tom had to be at work on Sunday. 'I'm going to the US on a roadshow next week and we need to have everything ready. I'm sure I told you.'

'No, I didn't know.' I turned my head to hide my disappointment. I forced myself to look out the car window. The sky was low and wide in this part of the country. It was almost noon but we were already deep enough into winter that this didn't mean anything. The light was dim, colourless, a variation of stone grey that would soon enough drift into black. He hadn't told me he was working this weekend and travelling all week. We drove past Stonehenge. 'I could never live out here,' I said. 'It's too close to a nature I have no connection to.'

'I think you'll change your mind when you see Danton's house.'

'Why, have you already seen it?'

'No, but based on his office—'

Then it dawned on me.

'Tom, we don't have a present!' Unless we kidnapped a sheep and tied it on top of the Jetta, there was nothing in sight that we could package as a gift.

'The man's a billionaire. There is nothing we could give him that he doesn't have already. I wouldn't worry about it.'

After a few wrong turns, Google Maps eventually led

us to a narrow road hedged in by rectangular, human-height blocks of shrubs. The corners were short and blind. Our car beams got lost inside the tightly wound birch and hawthorn walls. After what felt like a long time, the road ended. We arrived in front of Victorian-style tall grilles, the kind you see in haunted house movies. And, as in those films, there was nothing to be seen beyond the gates, just tall grass and a foggy mist. There was an old stone wall on both sides of the entrance, just high enough to prevent sheep from escaping or coming in. There was no sign, no house number, no name. Google Maps was convinced we had arrived at our destination. I started looking through my phone for the invitation when Tom saw it. 'Wait, this is it.'

We must have hit a sensor hidden somewhere. Out of nowhere there was a pole, like a tall torchlight that rose from the ground until it reached the level of Tom's car window. There was a speaker built in at the top and a keypad right underneath. Tom rolled down the window and pressed a button. 'Tom and Naomi Barnes,' he announced. A professionally cheery voice with a Polish accent welcomed us to Barringdon Park.

'It's really quiet. Do you think we got the date wrong?' I looked around us to see if there were any other cars.

Tom hesitated too, but the gates opened. 'They're letting us in,' he said, stepping on the accelerator.

We drove up the gravel path. At first there was nothing, just vague fields with hazard lights on the ground to indicate the road. There was a soft rise and as the road opened we arrived into a magically lit garden with a perfect green lawn and a lake in the distance and, in the midst of it all, the most majestic native oak tree I had ever seen. Its' proportions were perfect, the trunk like a pillar, with thick branches straight as beams stretching out from all around. The leaves at this time of the year sparse and golden, still provided a thin parasol for the squirrel looking at us from it's position on the trunk, not too low, not too high—the kind of tree you'd like to sit against in the summer when the leaves are green and thick with a book. Actually, that's the cover of *Alice in Wonderland* talking, it's got nothing to do with me, with the kind of places I would read a book in when I was a young girl. But England as a movie set has been projecting false memories into the minds of those of us who grew up in the periphery ever since Walter Raleigh set sail. I was excited. Here I was, little Naomi Perez, about to enter a real-life manor house, to be welcomed by no less than the lord of the manor, Reginald Danton himself, Englishman extraordinaire.

At first I didn't see the house. The path followed a loop so that guests could be dropped off and the cars be driven on out. There was a black Porsche ahead of us. A valet held open the door, waiting for the guests to step out to drive the car to the parking provisions elsewhere. We stopped. Unlike the couple ahead of us, there was no glamour in getting out of a Volkswagen and so we quickly left the car and handed the key to the valet just as he was about to drive the Porsche away.

Barringdon Hall was what is called a Georgian gentry house. It had gone through many restorations and extensions as it moved from being a self-sufficient country estate complete with a mill and working barns to a Victorian grand mansion with extensive servants' quarters. The great rectangular façade of Oolite stone was creamy in texture and cold to the touch. Subtle lighting softened the building, giving it a golden glow against the brown green of the autumn surrounding it. The double doors were open and there was a traffic of people coming in and out and a frenzy of shimmering dresses and sharp suits and red carpet jewellery and gorgeous shoes and we could hear sounds, music drifting out of the house. I tried to imagine what this place would be like the following evening, after the party, when everyone had gone home and those great double doors were shut.

'Naomi! What are you doing just standing there, come on!' My husband was standing next to the door. He looked like them with his fine navy suit from a Jermyn Street type of place, dark suede shoes and no tie. No he looked better than most of them. Tom had his hair and the twinkle. He opened his arms to me.

My heart filled with trepidation.

We walked in together.

I saw what Tom meant about not wanting to leave Newspring's offices. This place, perhaps like the office, stunk of past and present privilege but unlike the National Trust places we'd driven Tommy to, there was no creaky nostalgia for grander times, the signs of decades of decrepitude, from frayed Bessarabian rugs to moth punctured drapes. The future was bright here. I squeezed Tom's hand.

I stepped onto an uneven flagged floor that apparently dated back to the 12<sup>th</sup> century. Low ceiling beams gave a first impression of entering inside a cottage but the mere bareness of the space— there wasn't even a hook to hang a coat on—the ancient speckled mirror hanging on a wall reflecting the only piece of furniture in the room, a massive round table, Ines style but bigger, contradicted the first impression of humility. An expansive bouquet of flowers stood in the middle of the table, made of a wood that looked warm and reddish and familiar. Mahogany. An immaculate young woman wearing a headset and a white suit was standing next to the table with an iPad and checked our name off a list. A waitress took our coats away and offered us a glass of champagne. We were escorted from the hobbit-hole-like entrance hall into a modern take on what must have always been the *wow* space of this house. A grand staircase made of marble started with wide short steps and swirled its way up. The floor and the lower part of the walls gleamed white with the same shiny marble until they gave way to tall stained glass windows that went up the full length of the staircase. It was amazingly bright and the far-away ceiling, a dome painted with a scene of doves flying against a blue sky, brought joy to the hall. Holding my glass, I made a full turn on my heels to take it all in. I stopped before a somber painting in a heavy gilded frame of a deeply serious old man with silver wisps of hair sitting on a chair, surrounded with blood red shawls and heavy dark drapes and a barren winter tree in the background. There was a small wooden sign, dated 1788, nailed into the bottom of the frame.

"John Ash M.D. FRS
Founder of the Hospital"

With the relevant dates and then engraved in tiny print at the bottom,

"painted by Joshua Reynolds"

'Is that a famous painter?' I whispered to Tom.

He shook his head, 'dunno.' A waitress appeared with a tray bearing little slices of pink roast beef topped with horse-radish held together with a toothpick. I tried one.

'I do hope you like it. It's a house specialty.'

I turned around. The voice was friendly, the accent crisply posh. 'Naomi Barnes? I'm Reginald Danton. Thank you so much for making the trip. It can't have been easy to leave a newborn behind.' It was in the eyes. For the rest he looked the way Tom described, ex-rugby player indeed, average height, thickly built with a head of red hair and a slight hunch.

Sometimes, not often, you come across people with eyes like Reginald Danton. There was a young man in my first year economics class in Cartagena. Also, a woman who used to come buy plants at my mother's nursery. I remembered them because their look puzzled me; I didn't understand why some people appeared to see faster, deeper than others. And then I read somewhere that our brains are made of neurons that transmit and receive information like walkie-talkie radios and that we somehow generate the electricity needed to do this, and I realised that some people have so much power, sheer processing power, that the overflow emanates from their eyes.

'Oh, my mother is here and I was able to express enough milk to last till Sunday. It's this new pump I got online, it works so much better than—'

'This is quite the country house, Reginald.' Tom interrupted me, placing his hand on my arm. 'Beautiful Reynolds you have here. Impressive.'

'Tom welcome!' Danton took his hand into both of his. 'So thrilled you both could make it.'

Ha. To my credit, Tom had met the man before whereas I fell like a baby with a tit for Danton's charm: He listened to me babbling about breast pumps as if I were telling him about the Dalai Lama.

'It belonged to a hospital in Birmingham and they were selling it in order to buy the latest cancer treatment technology.'

I tried to redeem myself. '*Dyies.*' My best Eliza Doolittle imitation. 'Eh, have you been in this house for long?'

He looked right through me. 'Yes, but you should have seen it when we bought it from my cousin. The plumbing hadn't been touched since 1940. Lucy and her interior designer, Veere have done an amazing job restoring this old pile. But you haven't met Lucy yet. Come say hello. You know, we too have a baby. Our fourth.'

He walked ahead of us and Tom pulled me close. 'Thanks

for noticing that painting. I would never have known.'

I nodded, careful to stay close to him. I noticed a small screen built into a wall. It was a light switch.

A man about Tom's age with an educated face and a balding head came to us. Danton introduced him. 'Tom, Naomi, meet Adam Porter, one of our portfolio managers.'

'Pleasure.' Adam shook our hands without looking at us. He wanted to speak to his boss in private, that much was clear.

While they were having a closed discussion, Tom and I stood there alone. We were now in a room that looked, I imagined, like what a grand reception room in the 18th century would. It was as if all the sofas and tables and drapes and fireplaces had been frozen for two hundred and fifty years and then brought back intact, polished and dusted. The walls were stuccoed with palm trees and the ceiling was divided into panels with intricate designs on the edges. The panel above the marble fireplace had sculptures of mythological figures, I recognized Cupid and his arrow. It was so lavish, so perfectly 'classical' in taste and tone, I felt for a second, in spite of the thoroughly modern jazz music emanating from a hidden sound system, that we'd tripped on a crack in time, and stumbled into an exclusive gathering of the rich, but circa 1788. I gasped. I was the only black person in the room. And the 18th century was no time to be a black woman.

'Naomi!'

'Ah!' I looked at Tom. There was a waitress holding a magnum of champagne next to him and she was trying to refill my glass. I stretched my arm out to her. 'My God.'

'What is it? You've gone all sweaty. Is it the—' he pointed at my breasts.

'No, no...' I wanted to check my armpits but I couldn't do it discreetly. I took a sip. 'I'm just happy I, my ancestors, we don't come from where these people got their riches from.'

'The Spanish were no better.'

I said nothing. He was right but we were not in a palace in Spain. It's easier to relax when the history surrounding you is not your own. 'Do you recognise anyone here?'

'No.'

The guests knew each other, there was a continuous hum of conversations going on and people moved fluidly from one group to another. We got a few nods and half-smiles here and there but nobody approached us until Danton returned, putting his hand on Tom's back.

'Tom, we need you at Newspring. We just got a commitment from the largest insurance company in Belgium. Five hundred million euros. We don't have enough hands for this deck. You need to get on board.' He took me by the arm as if I were the most important woman in the world. 'Naomi darling, I want you to meet Lucy because I know you won't believe me if I say to you that we are a family firm. I want Tom to come home every night and be a father... and a husband!'

As if Reginald Danton cared about my marriage. I laughed, the sound coarser than intended.

'It's not funny. This country needs stable, reliable families.' He gave me a stern look.

I froze, self-conscious now of my status as guest and foreigner. I had been offered a peek, no, a welcome into the real live version of a legendary but up till now hidden England. This man, these people were serious and I was proving unworthy of their hospitality. Again, I tried to redeem myself. We were now in a kind of anteroom with wood panelling and a fishbone parquet. I looked up into the faces of the dead staring down from their gilded frames above the panels. 'Who are they?'

Reginald Danton's eyes followed mine to the two great portraits hanging adjacent on the wall. 'Which one? That one to the left is my great-grandfather on mummy's side. He was our ambassador in Rome.' He stopped and looked around to make sure nobody else was listening. I stayed very still to make sure I'd hear what he had to say. 'I'll tell you a secret. My father's lineage started with photographs. While mummy's forefathers were posing for portraits, daddy's people were working in shipyards. My grandfather left for Hong Kong as a banking clerk but he sent his son back here to school. Daddy became a Tory MP. Whenever someone asked him about himself, he'd tell them to go look in *Who's Who*.' He laughed.

'Who's what?' I asked.

Reginald raised an eyebrow but pointed at the other painting. It was an interesting portrait of a nineteenth-century woman with an expressive face and messy black hair, but an impeccable Victorian lace necklace. 'I got this one at a Bonhams' country house auction, a repository of abandoned ancestors if there ever was one.' He looked lovingly at the woman. 'Nobody knows who she is, but I'm sure she was an artist or sculptor—look at her hands! Maybe Camille Claudel herself. Looks good here, no?'

'She is a relative too, dyes?'

For a second, a short second he lost it. He flashed me a look of pure spite. I blinked and when I looked at his face again, he was back to his charming affable self. 'No. I'd like to think it's a portrait of Paul Claudel's sister, Rodin's great lover.'

Who the hell was Paul Claudel? I couldn't afford to put my foot in my mouth again so I just said, 'Ah, ah.'

A beautiful woman with a face shaped like the moon, long black hair and skin as smooth and even as a new jar of face cream came up to us. She was wearing one of those unforgiving Hervé Léger dresses made up completely of wide bands of elastic, one I was six kilos and three months of Barre classes away from. She headed straight for Danton. 'Reginald, lunch is ready. Nigel will end up overcooking the filets if we make him wait any longer.'

'Lucy darling, come say hello to Tom and Naomi Barnes. Tom is considering my offer to join Newspring.' Danton put his arm around his wife's tiny waist.

She turned her head in our direction. 'Of course, Tom will join Newspring. It's the best hedge fund in London.' She winked at me as if we were old friends making fun of our husbands. She disengaged from Danton and took me by the arm. 'If we don't lead the way, no one will make it to the table and that would be such a shame, don't you think?'

As I walked with her, I felt so self-conscious about my post-pregnancy body that I couldn't help explaining that I'd just given birth three weeks ago and was still breastfeeding but that as soon as I weaned the baby, I'd be back at the gym, pronto.

Lucy encouraged me to talk with occasional 'oh's' and 'of course's' but I soon realised that her attention was firmly on making her guests find their places at the table. I was in the middle of telling her about St Francis and what a brilliant school it was when she pointed at a place somewhere to the far left of a twenty-seater table fit for Buckingham Palace. 'Your name, I think, is down there.'

I bit my lip and went to find my seat. Where was Tom? His name was nowhere near mine. They had seated him closer to the centre of power, towards the middle of the table. Reminding myself this was all about business, I sat down. A waiter poured red wine in my glass while another filled another glass with water. My napkin stood folded stiff on top of a silver plate. Two small bread plates were to my left and right. One was mine and the other my neighbour's but I couldn't remember which one was which. Reginald and Lucy stood up. I listened vaguely as I focused on which plate the people sitting across from me were using for their bread. Then I saw them all raise their wine glasses. Reginald was proposing a toast. I picked up my glass to his firm, to ourselves 'his friends', to the country. And then it was Lucy's turn. She turned to her husband with a loving expression and after a few words about what a wonderful man he was, she turned to us and said how important it was for her to introduce their baby to us, their 'extended' family. She looked to the door towards the kitchen.

I turned to see what she was waiting for. A middle-aged woman in a nurse's uniform approached, carrying a small baby, a newborn, just like our little Sam. She went straight to Lucy, who took the newborn in her arms and announced to the room, 'This is Anya, our new daughter.'

I texted Tom five seats away, 'Is that her baby?' I looked again at her teenage waist.

Tom shrugged. 'No idea' he texted back.

The man next to me, an older American with long white hair and a velvet jacket noticed my confusion and leaned over. 'They paid a surrogate, using Lucy's egg and Reginald's sperm.'

'Oh my God. Did she have a problem?'

'Of course! Do you have any idea how much money and time goes into a body like that in your forties?' He looked at me as if indeed I had no idea.

Insulted, I turned away from him, a defensive hand on my flabby tummy. Who wants to live like that? I was grateful that I had a husband who was down to earth like me and could see beyond a bit of pregnancy padding.

In the meantime, Lucy and Reginald were going around the table, showing Anya's little face to the guests. When it was my turn to admire the baby, I waved my pinkie at the little girl whose eyes were closed. She was beautiful and tiny and I felt an unexpected tug in my nipples as I experienced a deep longing for my own baby. Please, don't let the milk come now, I pleaded, as the longing turned into an itch. I shook my shirt away from my chest. Danton shook hands, told jokes and never once looked at either his wife or the newborn. Lucy was a picture of fulfilled motherhood in a perfect body. She smiled as she held up the baby for me to see. I was about to say something when I realised she had no idea who I was despite our conversation barely half an hour before. Her eyes brimmed with kindness but she didn't see me. I closed my mouth.

'Did you see the diamond ring on her finger?' I overheard one woman say in an excited voice to another. 'What do you think? Harry Winston? Or Chopard?'

Reginald and Lucy completed their circuit of the table and gave everyone a chance to gush and coo for their meal, sorry, at the sleeping baby. Then the nanny reappeared out of nowhere and whisked the child away.

It occurred to me that the Dantons lived in a parallel dimension where things that are real for us, like pregnancy, are fake for them, and things that are fake for us, like giant diamond rings, are real. Maybe joining Newspring Capital wasn't such a good idea after all. I tried to make eye contact with Tom, but he was completely absorbed in a conversation with Adam Porter. I turned back to the American. His name was George Parkman. He worked in public relations and Danton was his client but he was also an old friend. They'd been at Wharton together. To keep the conversation going,

I asked him if he had a family. He told me that he had two sons and a daughter and the only other thing he said about them was where they went to school. After he asked me what my connection was to the hosts, he told me it was not done to spend more time chatting to the person to your left than the person to your right. With that, he turned his back to me. When the lunch was over, George pushed back his chair noisily. He was heavier than I'd expected. He wasn't wearing shoes but purple slippers embroidered with a coat of arms.

Tom came to find me. 'Danton asked if we could stay a little longer. It's a beautiful afternoon. He'd like us to go for a walk with him and Lucy.'

From a dismal wintry morning the day had switched course and it had become sunny with no wind. The wet grass on the rolling hills outside looked shiny and new. I followed them to the mudroom. There were framed pictures of the Danton children's prep school classes over the years. Apart from the uniform, they looked exactly the same as the one I just bought from Gillman and Soame of Tommy and his class. I swelled with pride. One wall was lined with tall and short Hunter boots. Three or four bouquets of flowers, still wrapped in paper, lay on top of a wooden counter attached to a porcelain sink.

'Naomi, darling, what size do you wear?' Danton motioned to Tom to help him look through the sizes.

'Um, six.'

Lucy took off her heels and, her stockings intact, slipped her feet into the wellies. I sat on a chair to unbuckle the strap of my shoes. I put my foot down on the flagged stone and was surprised to find it heated. Tom helped me find a pair that would fit, we put on our coats and went outside. The guests were still inside the house, chatting obliviously.

We followed a gravel path through manicured beds framed by boxes and yew until we reached a stream lined with bulrushes. It was muddy on the banks and I was glad for the wellies. Three hundred metres further we crossed a small wooden bridge and climbed over a sheep barrier, before proceeding up the hill. At the top awaited a perfect vista: a visual straight line stretching down the slope, framed by trees of exactly the same height, ending with the classical façade of the manor. It was obvious that Danton loved looking at his house like this. He explained the history of the landscaping. It started with someone with a cowboy name, Capability something or other, who'd invented the idea of these wide, unobstructed views. Evidently, you needed large amounts of land just to create such surroundings for your house and the great shame of many an estate was that the vistas were ruined by new constructions.

Lucy leaned forward. 'We had to have it swept for bugs two months ago because we hosted a follow-up meeting on some discussions Reggie had in Davos and half of the people wouldn't come if we didn't do it. Oh, what a job that was. Ten bedrooms to be checked. Isn't that so, Reggie?'

'Are your older children here?' I wanted to make a personal connection with Lucy. I wanted her to like me: Tom would value that, if I had a somewhat intimate relationship with the wife of Reggie Danton.

'One is. The other is in California. Reggie,' she turned to her husband, 'does Mahmut know he's driving me to Heathrow tomorrow?'

Reggie went on talking about the trees as if he hadn't heard her. Tom, who had heard her, became embarrassed and coughed. Reggie then took notice of Lucy. 'Oh? Yes, darling, I'm sure that can be arranged.' He started walking down the hill. 'Now, Tom, I want to know what you think about biotech…'

'Where are you going tomorrow?' I saw my chance.

She accelerated her pace to catch up with the men. I ran after her. 'Are you going to America?'

She didn't look at me. 'Yes.' And then as if she remembered something, she turned to me. 'To Los Angeleez,' she said it like the English, 'on BA. It's much more eco-friendly to do it like that, especially when you're travelling on your own. Don't you think?' Before I could say anything, she left me behind and touched her husband's arm. 'Reggie, you know I have no return ticket?'

'Yes, yes, we're coming back together from New York.' He went back to Tom. 'Do you know New York well? I'm thinking about buying an office block in Midtown, Sixties and Lexington.'

'Oh, would that be your office in New York?' I had caught up with the three of them.

'No.'

'We already have our office on Park Avenue,' Reginald

explained to me kindly, while shooting Lucy a look for her curt answer.

'It took two years and a lot of headaches to redecorate.' Again she avoided looking at me, focusing instead at the guests now visible inside the house.

'Ah?' I didn't know what to say.

'Does Tom like music?' Lucy asked me.

'Yes, of course.'

'What kind of music? We sometimes have concerts here.' And just like that, her demeanour changed. She opened her arms on the expansive lawn we were standing on. 'Young people love it. Last summer we had... Reggie? Which band was it?'

But Reggie was almost back at the house, deep in conversation with Tom.

She sighed. 'I'm terrible at band names.'

'Tom likes all kinds of music but I'm still partial to Latin music,' I offered, encouraged. 'I do like Blur.'

Lucy gave me a half smile and rushed off.

I followed the three of them into the mudroom to take off our wet boots while a butler waited to wipe them and re-line them neatly against the wall.

The whole two-and-a-half-hour journey home, I barely said a word. I replayed the day in my head, trying to understand why I wasn't more excited or even happy. We were not in the 18th century. But it would take me years to understand the rules of the game Tom was about to sign us into. I couldn't imagine that I was not allowed to be the subject of any sentence. That I would never be considered as equal. All I had that evening were impressions. Tom was so excited about his new job, he didn't notice my anxiety. He talked and talked all the way home to West Hampstead.

'What do you think?' he finally asked.

We were in bed. My breasts were aching by the time we got back. I had just brought Sam and the feeding cushion from the other room. It was wonderful to feel his warm body in my arms again. It took some effort to convince him to latch on and only once he was feeding did I turn to Tom. 'This wasn't a party. This was a business meeting masquerading as *Downton Abbey*.'

'So?' He looked at me incredulously. 'Is that all you have to say?'

'No.' I sighed. 'I guess it was more exciting for you than for me. Which makes sense. You're right, Danton is special. It's just that...'

'What?'

'I felt everyone there was cold, including Lucy. They were polite, sometimes charming but it all felt calculated. I don't think they'd ever give a damn about us. We're not their people, you and I.'

'Do you care? It's just a job.' He sat up and kissed little Sam's head. 'A job that will get us out of this dump and into our own home; a job that will take us places, ensure our children's future, give us what those posh fuckers always had, gravity!'

I raised my eyebrow at my normally even-tempered,

politically correct husband. 'Well, well.' I smiled. 'So you didn't buy into all of that...' I waved my hands.

'I'm not blind.' He looked at my breasts.

I laid Sam in his Moses basket next to the bed.

Tom pulled me on top of him.

And our fate was sealed.

# CHAPTER SEVEN

## May 2016

*"I spent the best part of my sixteenth year refusing to adapt to our new circumstances and insisted on keeping the same friends I'd had when Papa was around and paid for our membership at the Club. I no longer had tennis lessons and I could only go there when a friend invited me. I put all my wits and energy in maintaining these connections so I could be seen at the Club as much as before. I kept a tally in my diary of how many Fridays and Saturdays I spent there per month. I'd sit with Alexia and Annabel, joking and flirting with the boys around the swimming pool. We'd all be in shorts and T-shirts and I'd be hyper aware of how they had the latest Swatch watches and of the sign next to the pool area saying that the pool was for the exclusive use of members and I'd pretend not to care while controlling myself not to feel hungry. You could only order on account and I obviously did not have one. I'd drink my water and nonchalantly take a chip or two from my friends' plates and chew them slowly."*

I put my pen down and closed my red notebook. It was my fourth red notebook. The first three were locked in my filing cabinet but this one was the first to contain not just thoughts and fragments of my imagination. In this red note-book I was trying to write my own biography. I had seen Solange literally grow taller, brighter, happier over the past four years as she opened up her past, went down that tunnel and took control of her story. I was making my own small attempt to do the same. I sat at the Cumberland Tennis Club, waiting for Tommy and Sam to finish their lessons, a glass of water in front of me knowing full well I could order any-thing I damned well liked now. I pressed my eyes; I didn't want to cry. What drove Andreas away? I lifted my head, sick of my own thoughts. Other mothers were chatting with one another, some reading the paper, others doing homework with a young one.

'Naomi, how are you? I had lunch with Antheia and she told me about Solange.' A middle-aged blonde in slacks and a loose cashmere sweater pulled up a chair and joined me at my table.

'What did she say?' I examined Melanie to see how con-cerned she really was.

'That Andreas has left her and Baz and run off with a twenty-eight-year-old pregnant woman.' She did look upset. 'What a wanker. And Baz held such promise, too.'

I checked my phone. Two missed calls from Antheia and one from Tom. 'Yes. I was with her this morning. It's very hard. Solange still loves—'

But Melanie was fired up. 'And wasn't she trying so hard to have another baby? I remember picking up Damien from her house a while ago and I was surprised to see her at home and she told me she'd left her job to focus on her IVF treatments. How old must Solange be, our age, no? Mid-forties? And the year when Baz has his eleven-plus exams too. This is when he chooses to do this? Men. Unbelievable.' She shook her head. 'Well, I guess that's what happens when you marry a man who's better looking than you.'

I opened my mouth to say something about that comment and a great weariness came over me. I closed it again.

'Then again, who the fuck knows? Did I tell you Jon has a mistress? Some Eastern European twenty-something he met at the gym. I told him not to fool himself: There is nothing in his fifty-year-old body or receding hairline she's attracted to except whatever pretence of wealth he's been throwing around. I keep threatening to send her our bank statements.'

So it happens to blonde wives with expensive watches too, I almost said. I looked at Melanie. Age and circumstance had brought her down to earth and made her more sociable but... She still had the same rigid expression, maybe now it was just because of the Botox. The past years had not been kind to her: her hair, her lips, even her neck, all seemed to have thinned out since we'd first met. What happened? When we met four years ago, she was still an attractive if snobbish woman. 'Do you remember when we met at Ines's coffee morning? The boys were just starting St Francis. It wasn't that long ago but...'

Melanie looked at the kids playing on the courts outside. 'We were still living the dream. That made all the difference.' There were tiny creases surrounding her lips. 'Didn't you think you had cracked it? I was so sure I had. I had it all and I assumed it'd be forever: husband, children, money, career, body, feet with no bunions. No one told me there was a sell-by date on my life.'

I thought of the other women I had met at Ines's house back then. Pam had started a YouTube channel where she filmed herself working out in her living room in sports designer gear while talking about how to get children into posh private schools. Antheia decided that as soon as her children went to university, she'd move back to Greece. With this in mind she started a small business, importing olive oil and other Greek products to London. She was happy. Lily discovered the art of swiping and never looked back. Ines continued with her charmed existence. 'The other mums seem to be doing pretty well.'

'You're saying that because you're doing so well.'

'Am I?'

'You see, you're so secure you don't even know it. You have nothing to sweat about. Try having no income for over a year, two children in private school and you'll start feeling again. Add to that the ego problems that come with having an unemployed husband... I always thought that having a family was a sideshow, that it would never be an end in itself. That I could continue with my ambitions, my self-realisation. Now I cross my fingers every September that we'll survive another school year.'

We watched the end of the lesson in silence. I decided to go back to Solange's to see if she and Baz had eaten something before going home.

\*\*\*

Solange was wearing the same plastic shorts and strange t-shirt she had on when Andreas left, one day ago. She smelled as if she had just sprayed fresh perfume over her unwashed body. Her laptop was open on the kitchen counter and she was on a live Skype call with her friend in Haiti.

'Sorry, Naomi just walked in.' Solange motioned to me to come say hi to the screen.

'Hi!' I smiled.

A woman with ageless skin and a face full of moral certitudes stared back at me. 'Tell her to divorce Andreas.'

Solange stepped in. 'Cynthia, you never got divorced yourself—'

'And I regret it! Listen,' she opened her hands, 'if he's in love with a twenty-eight-year-old, you get out now while he still feels some guilt. Once that new baby comes,' she smacked her lips, 'you know the Haitian saying: A man only cares for the children of the woman he is fucking... at the time! And he is not fucking you! When I finally decided to cut loose from Jerome after mistress number twenty-five—'

Solange turned to me. 'I can't listen to this.'

'What?' Cynthia shouted from over seven thousand kilometres away. 'You don't believe me? What do you think killed him? How else would a fifty-five-year-old man get the most toxic cocktail of VDs known to humanity? At his funeral last year, I stood with our sons like a good wife next to his coffin and I had never seen a longer line of *poupounettes* in black. One of them even tried to throw herself into the coffin! I said, "Shut the fucking box, let her go down with him since she loves him so mu—'

Haitians shouted more than Colombians, I realised. I stepped back so they could switch back to Creole and I saw another woman come on the video call.

'Bonsoir, Solange.'

'Martine, *chérie*, this is my dear friend, Naomi.' Solange turned to me. 'Naomi, this is my other roommate in Haiti from long ago, Martine.'

I returned to the computer screen and smiled. 'Hello.'

Martine looked sadly at both of us. 'Solange, just walk away. Keep your dignity. Take nothing from that man.'

'*Sa wap di la?*' Cynthia sucked the air between her teeth in a way that reminded me of home. 'She has a kid to raise! Solange, don't listen to this nonsense. You take everything you can.'

'Solange works. She doesn't need that white man's money. I remember when Tatie Ghislaine's husband betrayed her. Tatie packed her clothes and her toothbrush, nothing more! And she walked away. Poor Tatie, she didn't have an education, she sat behind the till at Ti Jean's shop and he never paid her, always said *demain, demain*, which in a way is worse than having no job at all, but she never asked for anything. She had her pride. She went to sit on a rocking chair on the porch of Tatie Lilianne's house.'

'And then what happened?' Cynthia stood there with her hands on her hips.

'Well, uh, actually she, eh, died on that rocking chair last month…' She stopped, confused.

'Oh, I didn't know.' Cynthia's demeanour changed. 'I'm so sorry.' Cynthia picked up a small cup of coffee. It was hot over there you could see it on their shiny faces, in the flashes of blinding light that escaped from the closed shutters behind them.

Solange looked frozen. And ill.

I recognised this kind of Caribbean talk. In Spanish, it's called, *sobremesa*. It's the sun that does it, I think. 'Mesdames, I am so sorry to have to cut this call,' I said in my best French. 'Solange and I have to prepare dinner for the *enfants*.' And before anyone could add any more tales of loserdom, I shut the laptop.

Solange was lost in thought.

'Don't let them in too deep. It's like in Cartagena. Talk is cheap and when there's no money and no prospect of making any, you talk a lot.'

She gave me a blank look. 'I have to make dinner.' She didn't move.

'I'll take care of it. You relax.'

The laptop started ringing. Another Skype call. Solange shook her head. 'Forget it. The news is going around Haiti.' She sighed. 'Can you imagine if this were 1994 instead of 2016? Then you had to pay for these calls and so I'd be sitting here, my heart beating because I knew I'd have ten, fifteen minutes max to talk back home about the end of my life.'

I went into the kitchen.

The laptop rang again. This time Solange answered. I peeked around the doorway:

Another Haitian woman inhabited the screen. She looked completely bewildered.

'Yes, Andreas has a Dutch mistress and yes, she's five months pregnant. He dropped it on me like a bomb,' Solange told her with a straight face.

'A bomb? Where? In London? *Mes amis*! Here they kidnap, there they bomb—'

'*Like* a bomb, Nadine. No, what I'm saying is my husband has made a girl pregnant and is in love with her.'

'So there is no bomb?'

'No.'

'Ah, I get it. *Like* a bomb. Shit. I can't believe a Dutchman would do that. I thought only Haitian men pulled that kind of crap. You spoiled him, Solange. You turned him into—' She was interrupted by the noise of an engine sputtering. 'Hold on, Solange, the generator is skipping again. Jelius!' The image flickered and went dark. Only the voice remained. 'Where's the jerry can with the diesel? Jumps start it ag—' She was cut off.

'Solange, come give me a hand. I found lentils in the cupboard and some sausages in the freezer.' I handed a saucepan to her.

The kids came running into the kitchen, hungry. Tommy made a face when he saw the lentils but Baz said nothing. He sat down and quietly ate about half his plate. Tommy ate the sausage but was still playing with the lentils when Baz got up and went to Solange and wrapped his arms around her waist. He was the same height as Tommy but that day he seemed older. The way he looked at his mother, his silence that came from within.

Baz had never been a *parlanchin*, a chatterbox. He had always been a quiet, thoughtful child. But this was different. Baz was looking at his mother for an explanation, for reassurance. She was all he had, that was obvious from the way he held her but he also knew that she was wounded, fragile, and so he daren't ask. Solange had explained Andreas had left her, rather than him, yet still he held on to his mother, this boy, as if to compensate for the husband's abandonment. Did it matter to him that his father was 'only' leaving his mother? As far as he could see his home had turned precarious, his family broken, his situation insecure. He was bound to ask himself why, why weren't they good enough as a unit? And he didn't even know about his dad's new, upcoming family.

'It's going to be okay, Baz. Look, I'm fine. Naomi and Tommy have come to visit. *Allez, allez*, go play with your friend while he's still here.' Solange gently removed his arms from her waist.

To my surprise, he did as he was told. He looked back one last time then ran up the stairs calling for Tommy to join him at the PlayStation. 'How do you do that?'

'What?'

'I don't think Tommy, let alone Sam would be appeased

so… quickly if this was happening at our house.'

'Oh, they would be. For the love of you.'

How could I say that love was an increasingly abstract concept in my home? Everything else was so perfect, who could imagine that there were entire evenings, nights behind those stone steps, behind those double doors with the brass handles, when nobody said a word to each other? Solange may be right, but that would only be because they saw so little of Tom that they wouldn't notice the day when he stopped coming home at all.

'I am a fool and Andreas is a criminal.'

'You're not a fool. These things happen.' I sounded so North-West London at that moment.

Solange looked at me as if I were crazy. 'These things don't happen to sane, healthy people. A fourteen-year-old marriage with a child, a home, a wife, a husband is not supposed to end. Give me an earthquake, give me a revolution, have thunder strike Andreas in the brain and leave me a widow. I am equipped to deal with catastrophe; I will deal with disease, gunfire, financial ruin. I will not blanch in the face of any of those calamities but to fracture my heart? That is a fundamental, elemental crime that destroys the very structure of my strength. Why did he throw us all in this trajectory of destruction?'

'You sound like a Colombian politician. You think he knows? All he has done is to follow the trajectory of his penis.' I gave up on the NW London thing and replaced it with the angry Latin woman thing. Neither was sincere. The truth was that their love, Solange and Andreas's love, was real but unhappy. They loved each other badly. Because of various factors, his more depressive character, his culture, the fact he was a big, white man, it was he who felt he could leave. But I was afraid she'd poke my eye out with the bread knife if I told her that.

'Exactly. I am a fool.'

'How could you have known?'

'Because I was told, when I was nine years old. I came home from my Catholic school one day and I told my mother the story of Adam and Eve. She laughed and said, "Let me tell you the story of your people, of the black people of Haiti." This is what she said:

"'In the beginning, the invisible light created man and woman as one. But when the Great Almighty decided to grant them His own Intelligence, only the woman was alert enough to receive it. The man, distracted, did not notice. The woman became aware of her new power and her ambition and pride grew. She became greedy and sought out the sacred lizard, the wisest of all creatures. The lizard shaped like a spine with emerald scales and ruby eyes, told her the secret of eternal life. She did not share this knowledge with the man. The Great Almighty then became angry with them both, her for being greedy and him for being so clueless, and he slashed them in two. Man and woman have lived in different bodies ever since, and their minds remain closed to each other. The woman, however, kept a touch of His intelligence. This is known as Intuition.'"

I said nothing. Solange was right, and everything her mother had told her was true. We all walk into our private hells with our eyes wide open, pretending we do not know what we know.

# CHAPTER EIGHT

## January 2013

And then my mother left. And I stopped driving to school. In an effort to shift the baby weight, we walked every morning with the stroller across Finchley Road into Hampstead. Sam would watch me while I talked with Tommy. He didn't need to see anything else, not the silly plastic toys hanging off the frame of his buggy, not the clouds above. Just me. I leaned into the stroller and kissed him.

I hadn't been able to enjoy Tommy like that when he was a baby. As soon as I could walk straight again, basically a week after he was born, I fled back to my job. I was still mortally afraid of losing my independence, my place in the world. I didn't see how I could keep my worth as a human being without earning a pay cheque. I loved Tommy, but he was dangerous.

On the day Tom signed with Newspring, he went to a furniture store and bought a giant dining set. A rectangular walnut table almost three metres long and the twelve plush velvet-backed chairs that went with it.

'What a folly! Where are we going to fit this?' I looked

at our cramped kitchen.

'In the house we're going to buy. I want a big family, Naomi. And now we'll be able to afford it. You will sit here, at the head.'

I kissed Tommy goodbye and he ran into the school playground. Sam had fallen asleep in the buggy. The sun was out. I was comfortable with my coat open and so I pulled back the plastic cover so Sam could have some fresh air too. I walked to a new organic coffee shop where they served porridge with blueberries and chia seeds and sat down with my notes from my last meeting with Solange.

*I suffered. My mother had no food to give us and I swallowed her suffering instead. In my child's mind, our suffering was eternal, endless, God had not decided we had suffered enough. I would watch my mother cry. Cry and work because she worked all the time.*

*At nights especially I'd stay awake, trying to understand why we were so poor. I dreamt of the day I could work and Maman could rest. She woke with the rooster's crow and went to mass at the neighbourhood church. I didn't want her to be alone, so I would go with her. I was still sleepy and resented my brother and sister for staying in bed. Yet that early morning mass is where I built the strength and courage for the struggle. I kneeled so close to Maman that our arms touched. I fell down to the floor with her before the feet of the child Jesus of Prague and I prayed for fortitude, with my forehead on the cold stone for relief, or if that wasn't possible, for death.*

*I became a warrior.*

'Soy milk latte?' The waitress placed the cup on my table. Sam stirred in his sleep.

'They also had them in blue and grey.' Two women in running lycra left the café, their trainers squeaky against the tiled floor.

I left a £10 note on the table. I wanted to get home before Sam got too hungry. I understood why Solange had asked me to pray for her. God had once heeded her call.

\*\*\*

Tom was not there when Sam took his first steps that autumn. I sent him a video on WhatsApp. By then he was gone most weekdays. He came back on Fridays, sometimes Saturday mornings if he was flying from America, but no matter where he came from, he returned to us an exhausted man. He forced himself to sound interested in Tommy's school life, he tickled Sam's cheek and put him on his lap, he kissed me and did his best to listen, but he invariably fell asleep after a couple of minutes. During his travels he stayed in five-star hotels. Our home on the other hand neither looked nor behaved like a Four Seasons. He told me to hire help: 'We can afford it now.'

'But we don't need it.' I was home and besides our house was too small.

December arrived in London with its long nights and boiler problems but whereas in the old firm, bonus time was late January, at Newspring Reggie Danton made sure 'announcements' at least were made before Christmas. And Tom's was a chunk of change as they say, the size of all his former bonuses from S&N combined.

As 2014 rolled round, we started looking for a 'real' house. Tom started to be invited to social events. He wanted to buy art. I hired a full-time housekeeper called Meribel, a lady who had left her own children in the Philippines to come iron our sheets and babysit our children at night. Tom and I would attend gallery openings and private shows where the artist would swoon over my looks or my words and the gallery owners would offer to lend me art to 'test' on our walls. 'We have no walls,' I said on one such occasion, 'only leaking ceilings.' Tom then took me by the elbow and explained to me slowly that this was why we were buying a house.

'I thought we were buying a house to live in it.'

'Ha ha. Yes, to live in it surrounded by objects of beauty.' He pointed at a large rectangular painting of a tunnel. I heard the dealer explain the magical subtlety of the artist's use of light, 'like a millennial Vermeer.' The banks executing Newspring's transactions seemed to have entire departments dedicated to entertaining us, the families of the hedge fund managers. We arrived at a Silverstone trophy event only to discover that we had to listen to an entire sales pitch from the people who invited us before we were allowed to relax in the hospitality box and see the actual race.

'It's better when you become more important,' Danton later said to Tom, 'because they become afraid of annoying you. Not that it matters.' He explained he didn't want his people partying on some vendor's tab. 'It's a form of bribery and we have a reputation to uphold.'

We bought a house.

A beautiful family home in Hampstead.

Tom showed me the mortgage. I gasped.

'It's because I wanted to have enough money to refurbish the house.'

'But the place is okay the way it is. They said they redid the kitchen twelve or thirteen years ago.'

'This is not my dream house.'

I nodded, ok.

By the time we moved into the Hampstead house, we were different people. I stopped walking the way I used to. The ground had shifted. I now took smaller, more hesitant steps. I reported to Tom what the boys and I had accomplished at the end of each day, on the phone most often and sometimes in person. We were trying for a third child and so we made love regularly and diligently, with our goal in mind. Life had become a series of tasks and tests and I had the vague feeling I was failing them all. In the meantime, between the house, the new Range Rover, the well-spoken boys, and my tight 'good wife' butt, Tom did appear to be living the dream. This was important because, together with my growing conviction that I deserved nothing, Tom was receiving more and more affirmation from the world that he was an important man and he deserved everything.

My book with Solange became my only hope. Succeed

to keep your man. Once that book was finished, everything would change. I'd have something to say about myself, who I was, what I had accomplished. I wished the book were already published and that I was receiving just enough attention to make Tom respect and desire me for me. At the opening of legendary Chinese artist Ai Weiwei's show at the Royal Academy sponsored—partly—by the Dantons, I wore a flaming red dress with red heels to match. I was still in the courtyard, looking at his monumental Tree sculpture, thinking about the audacity needed to even conceive of such a thing when I overheard Lucy talking with one of her syco-phantic friends, her chin in my direction: 'You can take the girl out of Latin America but you can't take the Latin—'

She stopped when she realised I could hear her.

*That's right,* I stuck my chin back out at her, thinking of Ai Weiwei. *What's wrong with non-European worlds?* I made a mental note to never buy the grey and black clothes Lucy and her friends favoured. Let them blend in with the ashen skies: This was my time and I wanted to shine. After a couple of glasses of champagne and no petit-fours I realized there was nobody there who wanted to shine with me so I told Tom I had to go. He was busy talking shop with his French colleague Antoine.

'But the exhibit?'

'I've been around twice now. It's very good.'

'I haven't been through yet,' Tom realised out loud.

'I know.' I pursed my lips.

'Naomi, wait please, Nathalie is on her way and she'll be

very upset with me if I tell her that she missed you.' Antoine smiled.

I smiled back and kissed them both, Tom on the lips and Antoine on the cheek. I left.

I arrived at Solange and Andreas' house with my laptop, my red dress and my red shoes. 'Let's do it!'

Solange smiled at my determination. 'Tonight we have an important chapter to write. It's going to be called *The Hurricane*.'

Every word I typed, I typed with a vengeance.

*In those days, my family was homeless. The darkness of night was our accomplice. We would drag our suitcases and sleep on the porches of strangers' houses, those that were welcoming thanks to locked doors and switched-off lights. In the morning, we'd walk the streets asking everyone if they had a room for rent and if they'd agree to be paid at the end of the month. We were tired, we were hungry and I could read the despair on my mother's face every time we were turned down.*

*The afternoon of hurricane Allen the sky turned from blue to white to grey, the temperature dropped from scorching to pleasant, the dogs started to howl and the mosquitoes disappeared. My mother dressed us as nicely as she could. She had washed and combed our hair; she combed my brother's hard curls down with pomade and had pulled my hair back so tightly it made my eyebrows arch. She took us to see my grandmother. The latter had a shop near the harbour. We went there on foot. We passed a pig squealing on top of a pile of trash mixed with rubble.*

*Once we arrived, my mother decided not to go in. She asked us to go beg my grandmother to give us shelter against the coming hurricane. If that was not possible, to give us some money. My mother, who smelled of the earth and whose feet were dirty after walking all the way to the harbour in flip-flops, stood alone with my baby sister behind one of the big iron doors. 'Go, she'll know her own blood.'*

*Holding each other by the hands, the two of us ventured in. Inside, it was dark and big and cool and there were tall rolls of fabric against the walls that looked like they could fall and crush us. My grandmother was sitting on a high stool behind a raised counter. She had beautiful hair, smooth and glossy, and she was wearing those fifties-style pointy rimmed glasses although this was 1980 I sneezed. My so-called grandmother saw us then. My mother was right; she knew exactly who we were.*

*'Am I responsible for these children's existence?' she shouted as if she were on trial. 'Did I ask for this? Who said I had to pay for my son's dirty adventures?'*

*We ran out. I never saw that woman again. In the meantime, the rain had started. Water was rising on the streets. Thunder and lightning sparked like fireworks in the sky. My mother carried my baby sister in her arms while my brother and I hung on to her clothes. She found a tree in between two tall houses as the wind grew stronger. There were things flying now, pieces of tin, branches, tarpaulins. My mother told us to hang on to her legs and, still clasping my sister against her chest, wrapped her other arm around the tree. Time moved slowly that night.*

*At one point, it actually stopped.*

I crossed my arms on my chest and leaned back on my chair. 'What does it feel like?'

'To be in a hurricane?' Solange had been peeling carrots while she spoke. She was now chopping their ends off. She offered me one.

'*Gracias.*' I bit the carrot. 'No... you tell that well. What is it like to be *here*, living here the way you do,' I looked at the cutting board, the Japanese knife, 'when you come from that?'

'I didn't realise until Baz received a book of Hans Christian Andersen's tales on his birthday last year. It was a beautiful book, hardback, an Everyman Classic and, as usual, I had never heard of him. We read *The Little Mermaid* and it was Baz who noticed that my face was wet. I didn't know. My childhood, my Haiti, was my fishtail. I had to get rid of it for Andreas to see me, to love me. And once I did, it all fell into place: my work, St Francis school, our life. What does it feel like to be here when you come from the bottom? When you have risen to this surface alone, when you have left so many behind? It hurts. It hurts enough that the rest becomes easy. Just like the little mermaid with her 'floating walk', because the pain is always there.' She wedged the knife across a large carrot and leaned on it until the carrot split in two with a cracking sound. 'That's when I decided to tell my story. I had been trying to forget it before but that only made the pain worse. I didn't understand that to live fully in the present, you need to make peace with your past.'

I listened to Solange and told myself that in spite of growing up in insane poverty, she was luckier than I because she had that option of making peace with her past, with her family, with her country.

'There is no day that goes by where I don't think back to that night. When I realised that we were still alive, that it was over, that the sun had returned. I breathed with relief and I saw that the fog of my breath was different. It was hotter, stronger. No longer the sigh of a little girl. The breath of a warrior.'

I shut my laptop, and hurried home. Solange didn't need a silly dress to shine.

# CHAPTER NINE

After two years at Newspring, we decided to knock down the existing kitchen with its old wooden worktops and white Electrolux refrigerator and install one of those sleek German ones made of marble and Corian, with cupboards so smooth, it felt blasphemous to press a human finger on them. We now owned a stainless steel Sub-Zero refrigerator big enough to double up as a family morgue once we died. While I argued and bargained with designers and builders, Tom lived in a whirlwind. He was running all around the world researching companies in the biotech/pharmaceutical space, meeting big pharma executives, entrepreneurs, research analysts, and venture capitalists putting seed money in the sector. Although he had Adam working with him, he could never cover everything Danton wanted him to. He was always one step behind. Danton was some kind of a human dynamo who never slept. He'd email Tom at two, three in the morning and expect an answer within minutes. He had ideas all the time and wouldn't allow any of them to be dismissed without proper due diligence. At some point he decided there may be a connection between plastic surgery, the pharmas and biotechs, and the beauty-enhancing medics and model agencies.

'Model agencies?' I was terrified.

To be fair, Tom tried to discourage him. Danton laughed, 'Don't be such a Debbie Downer. You never told me you were a Calvinist! For God's sake, just go take a look. It could be fun.' And so Tom started hanging out in the West End and Soho, looking at these 'sexy' industries. He soon discovered that they had all adopted a business model called 'Bling the Billionaire Blind'.

'I find myself struggling through a barrage of starlets, models, cocktails, and VIP gigs just to reach the balance sheets of these companies,' he told me.

'Why don't you just tell him what you're good at? He wants to make money? He should let you deal with what you know best: pharmaceutical and biotech start-ups.'

'I did.'

'And?'

'I'm flying to New York tomorrow to meet the owner of yet another model agency.'

With that, he was gone.

I shivered on the edge of the football field, waiting for Tommy to finish his training. He was running hard, defence, his left leg covered in mud. It was one of those English days when the weather gives you nothing to build on. When you're on your own, seeking your inner generator because the sun is absent and the wind blows whatever energy you started off with away. Where was Tommy? I looked more closely. Ah yes, there he was, tackling another boy. No, I didn't know those socks. They all looked the same. Of course they didn't... and then I saw my son. His yellow football boots, his sturdy legs, his round buttocks. He was beautiful and separate from me and he too would think less of me one day. He would think of me as disposable unless I managed to show my worth.

'Mama, did you bring water?' He was standing in front of me, his hand touched my arm, casually, without him even being aware of it.

'No, I'm sorry. Let's go home; you can drink water there. I have the car.' I was doing it to myself. Why hadn't I brought him a water bottle like the other parents standing around me? By being unreliable and thoughtless, I was training him to not count on me. To not need me. To forget about me.

I swallowed. Watch out, Naomi. You must try harder.

With Meribel at home taking care of the boys, when Tom was in London, we were out every night. At first we'd laugh on the way back home at some rich people control freak craziness such as this oligarch who agreed to take his son on a holiday cruise, 'like normal people' only to reveal that out of the blue, the owner of the cruise line decided to 'keep them company' and boarded the ship with them to 'hang out' and ensure they were never treated like normal people.

But one day I stopped laughing. The rules were becoming clear. I was made to understand, somehow, that my presence at these dinner parties, supper clubs, opening events, was more than optional. Everything was completely contingent on Tom.

After a particularly exhausting night I declared to Tom in the back of a black cab on our way home, 'I'm not going out anymore. It's too tiring.'

He was typing an email, his face the picture of concentration illuminated in a halo of blue light from his phone.

I gazed out the window. I missed us, our family. Earlier that evening I had been busy getting dressed when Sam came asking for his bedtime story. I started to apologise, 'Mama has to go out in fifteen minutes. Tomorrow, I promise.' He didn't protest, just walked away. I remembered I had also said no the night before. In fact, I hadn't read to him all week. I ran after him.

'Wait!'

I ended up having to go out with my hair in a scrunchie and no make-up. Tom should appreciate the fact that I made the effort to go out with him at all, I said to myself, to expose myself to this world that had nothing to offer me. When I caught Tom's eyes lingering on a perfect-looking young woman—I searched in vain for any flaws—I attributed the ensuing soreness in my stomach to my own Colombian baggage, i.e. the never published, yet known by all—at least all the women I grew up with—'Latin Guide to Staying Married'. It is the inspiration behind wives who throw stones at mistresses, who tail philandering husbands and engage in car chases, who scheme, who plot, who use Botox and inflate breasts and for the real hard-core, who die. One poor wife I knew ended crashing into a lake as she sped behind her husband and his girlfriend. The wife drowned and the husband was so distressed he immediately married the girlfriend.

The taxi stopped; we had arrived home. Tom paid the driver without looking at the man once, his eyes glued to his phone screen. I used my key to open the front door. Tom walked in behind me. He went straight to his study and closed the door.

Meribel called out a good night from the kitchen. I thanked her for staying up and started up the stairs to our bedroom. My feet were heavy. I sat on the bed and started to take off my shoes, then my stockings. I took off my skirt, my top, my bra. I went to the bathroom. I released my hair, which didn't fall down but stayed up, stiff and kinky with humidity on my head.

I hid in bed. I pulled up the duvet until there was nothing left of me on the outside, just a lump underneath the otherwise impeccably made bed, with hospital corners and crisp white linen sheets. This was not our destiny. I had to stop what was happening to us—I had to enlighten Tom. He was too close, sitting in that Newspring office all day and out with the same kind of people all night. He couldn't see what it was doing to him, to us. Shit. I kicked the sheets off of me and then I pulled them back again. I turned. I couldn't close my eyes.

Tom came into the room. I thought of pretending I was asleep but I couldn't do it. My body was too tense, my eyes followed his every move. How he sat on the bed and took off his shoes and his socks. How he stood up and unbuttoned his shirt and left it on the chair and, bare chested went into the bathroom and closed the door.

I listened. He flushed the toilet. He knew I was not sleeping. He wouldn't have flushed if he thought I was asleep. He knew I was awake and watching him and he undressed and went into the bathroom as if I didn't exist. The door opened. I lay very still with my eyes closed. He came to bed. I felt the air that sneaked in under the duvet with him. He lay on his side with his back to me. His wider frame lifted the sheets away from me and I became cold. I didn't dare cuddle up to him. I just lay there uncomfortable and unable to sleep. 'Tom? Tom can you hear me?' I whispered.

He stirred but didn't answer.

'Tom! I'm scared.' I spoke loudly this time.

'Wha?'

I touched him on the shoulder.

He turned to me. He put a hand on my forehead and closed his eyes, 'darling go to sleep.'

'I can't. I'm all worked up. Can't you see? We don't connect the way we used to. I'm scared Tom. I'm so scared. You, our family, I… I can't…'

'Naomi I'm really tired and I need my sleep.' He didn't open his eyes.

'But this is important…'

'Sometimes I feel like you envy me, my job, my career and that you want to sabotage me.'

I reached out to touch him and he turned his back to me. I retreated. I moved all the way to the edge of the bed. I didn't bother him anymore.

Soon he started snoring.

I didn't give up. The hurt only made me try harder. I told him I loved him although I didn't expect him to answer the same to me. I brought the children to him, I organised outings to the zoo, lunches with happy families, I talked until my mouth went dry. I repeated back to him his own words from when we got home from that fateful lunch at Barringdon Hall: *It's just a job. We are not their people, you and I.*

'Exactly.' Tom finally acknowledged with frustration, 'so why do you feel so threatened by my work?'

A few days later, I went to the Newspring offices at St James to pick up our car. Tom had taken it early that morning but I had to take Tommy to play football in Wembley that afternoon. I was waiting for Tom in reception. The lift opened and I stood up. Lucy Danton stepped out. She had it right, as usual, in her beautifully tailored woollen dress, sheer black tights and ankle boots. She moved as if she owned the place, barely casting a glance at the reception staff and she would have certainly ignored me if I hadn't been standing in her way. She hesitated for a short second, and then came to me with open arms. 'Naomi, darling, I'm so happy to see you. Where have you been? I was so disappointed when Tom came alone to our Brexit dinner.'

'Oh, didn't Tom tell you? Little Samcito was sick—'

'Is he all right?'

'Oh yes, completely recovered. Thank you.' I smiled.

The lift doors opened again and it was Tom. He was

dangling the car keys in his hand. He had left his tie and jacket upstairs in his office. 'Lucy!' He called. They kissed each other on the cheek.

'Here,' he handed me the keys.

Instead of pointing out how after making me wait twenty minutes he couldn't be bothered to even greet me, I asked him if he'd like fresh seabass for dinner.

'Sure. I'll try to get out of here before eight but I can't promise anything.' Tom squeezed my arm and ran back to the lift. Lucy and I watched the doors close on him.

'I gave up on Reggie for weekday dinners years ago.' Lucy offered. She waved at me as she walked out of the building.

I stood alone with the keys in one hand and my handbag in the other.

'Can I help you with anything else?'

The receptionist's voice sounded full of scorn. I walked out with my head low.

\*\*\*

*We would end up inside the cage of a bland-looking truck, crawling up the narrow, broken mountain roads with no parapets and I was afraid, sitting on a crowded bench on the inside of the cage with grey bags of charcoal at our feet, that the truck would slip and tumble down the mountain. But my fear was mixed with joy. When the truck stopped, we would run out and jump in the rivers, climb the grenadine trees, pick mangoes or my favourite: a lychee-like fruit that grew in clusters called keneps. I loved hearing the skin crack with my front teeth and then sucking the sweet, peach-coloured flesh off the pit that left a numbing sensation on the tongue and lips. We would marvel at shiny super-smooth pebbles, sometimes black, sometimes white, polished to perfection by the passing rivers.*

'Me too. I liked collecting shiny black and white pebbles. I'd line the rim of the shower basin with the—' A sudden violent burst of coughing interrupted me. My eyes flooded with tears, and I was retching. I couldn't stop. My stomach started to cramp but all I could do was cough and cough.

Solange got up and hit my back a few times. When that didn't work, she held a glass of water to my lips, but I coughed into the glass and almost choked. Then she thought of hugging me. She held me tight like a baby. Only then did it stop.

'You're not well. You should go see a doctor.'

'I'll be all right.' I coughed one last time.

'And you've lost weight. There are dark circles under your eyes. Talk to me, Naomi. What's wrong?'

A flurry of images came into my mind. My father, Abuela Edith and the bra she bought me so my breasts wouldn't sag like hers, the smooth leather seats in Alvaro Sackler's car, my head, my hair rubbing against the mud. I spat in the sink. We were supposed to be working.

'I don't have much time today. Let's finish.' I wiped my mouth with the back of my hand.

Solange hesitated. And then she, as usual, picked up

where she left off.

*Our time of peace was the summer. I couldn't wait for school to end. We would leave for Bainet in the south of the island. Maman would examine the trucks going there and pick one with no or very few religious slogans painted on their sides. 'The trucks plastered with Jesus and the Holy Spirit have reckless drivers,' she'd explain. 'They think God is a free insurance policy...'*

\*\*\*

Two years, eight months and three days had passed since our lunch with the Dantons. We had just been to a Brexit debate at one of the gentlemen's clubs on St James's Square. It was a sober crowd and an alien one I realised when I saw my brown hand with my red fingernails alone together with Tom's the only ones to go up for the Remain team at the end of the hour. The rest of the audience voted for the Leave side in a wave of pale hands sticking out of dark sleeves. We left St James's Square shortly before eight, and walked to meet Tom's colleague, Antoine Hadjaj, and his wife, Nathalie, for dinner on the other side of Berkeley Square, in a glitzy fish restaurant on Mount Street. The date had been fixed six weeks before, in accordance with the new social rules we were now living by. I was looking forward to the evening—we always spotted a celebrity when we went to that restaurant, last time we saw Hugh Laurie—and we had a lot in common with Antoine and Nathalie. Their children were the same age as ours and

Nathalie, like myself, was balancing working from home as a children's book illustrator with running the house and family, to allow Antoine the freedom and focus he needed for his work at Newspring.

We arrived first. I sat on the banquette so I could see the room and Tom took the chair across from me. He had picked up an *Evening Standard* on the way and flipped through the pages. The referendum was nine months away and, in spite of the debate we had just attended ('Full of fossils,' declared Tom), we felt certain that the Remain vote would win. The London paper was supporting that view.

Antoine walked into the restaurant. I stood up as soon as I saw him and waved. For a second I thought he was alone, Nathalie must be coming separately, until I saw he was holding hands with an unknown young woman. I turned to Tom but he was busy texting on his phone. I looked back to make sure it was the right Antoine Hadjaj and at that moment he waved back and started for our table. And that woman was not his wife. Maybe it was his little sister, Nathalie's cousin, a niece travelling through town.

'Tom, Naomi, hello, *oh là là*, it's been so long!' That last comment was for me. Obviously, he saw Tom at work every day. He kissed me on both cheeks. He looked the same as the last time I saw him, maybe two months earlier: he still had his good head of black hair; his small dark eyes still had their sparkle.

Tom put the phone down and shook hands warmly with the Frenchman. The woman stood patiently beside him, waiting to be introduced.

'Tom, Naomi, I want you to meet Vanessa.' He cleared his throat.

She flashed a brilliant smile to my husband and completely ignored me.

Tom greeted her as if he'd known her for years. Antoine sat on a chair next to Tom and Vanessa on the banquette next to me. I was doing all I could to keep my mouth shut. This new woman was like a younger, fresher version of Nathalie. She had the same kind of body, lanky but with big bones; a long face with full lips; and thick, dark hair as if she too had Iranian blood. The wine and bread arrived and a conversation started. Tom asked Vanessa where she was from.

'Florida. That's where we met, Antoine and I.' She said his name surprisingly well.

Antoine, Nathalie, and their children had gone to Miami on holiday earlier this year. Yes, I remembered now, it was over Easter break. Nathalie had invited us along but we had already booked to go skiing in Val d'Isère. So Antoine had been with his family when he came across this Vanessa. 'How did you meet?'

Antoine blushed. Vanessa giggled, and although she was responding to my question, she turned her head so she only addressed Tom and Antoine. 'I was working at a cycling shop that rents bicycles when this handsome man walks in with three adorable children. And then he asked me if I could help teach his youngest to ride. And we realised we couldn't keep our eyes off each other.' She gave the hedge fund manager a misty look.

In the 'Latin Guide' a woman like this is called... well, let's say a 'predator' in English. She had wrested this man away from his wife of twenty years, away from his three children, she had destroyed a family, and here she was sipping expensive wine, enjoying every minute of it. 'You fucking bitch!'

Antoine lowered his eyes into his glass but the girl just gaped at me.

'Naomi, a word please.' Tom tilted his head towards the exit.

'Hold on.' I waved my hand. What did he expect? That I'd pretend nothing had happened? Worse, that this man's behaviour was normal? Acceptable? That because he was rich he should get away with anything he felt like? What about his wife? His kids? 'Where's Nathalie? How is she?'

Vanessa stood up and threw her napkin on the table.

'Wait,' Antoine asked her and turned to me. 'The marriage hadn't been working for years. Vanessa had nothing to do with our break-up.' He wanted to make sure Tom and I heard him, so said it a second time: 'Vanessa had nothing to do with our break-up.'

Tom nodded in support of his fellow male and colleague and I leaned back, silenced. I didn't know enough. I liked Nathalie but we were just acquaintances. We had never spoken about personal things like our relationships. Antoine had moved on to the banquette to hug and reassure his *dulcinea*.

Tom leaned in to me. 'How could you? What he does in his personal life is his business. Now you've just ensured that we can never have a social meeting again. I'll just have to see them on my own.'

'But—'

'Get a grip.' He touched the roots of his greying temples which immediately made me think of my own.

Antoine reluctantly let go of Vanessa and moved back to his chair across from the banquette. Vanessa picked up her glass, took one look at Tom and offered a silent toast to Antoine with a face that said 'you see? They all envy you.'

That night I isolated myself again at the edge of the bed and obsessed about the smell of my armpits, my hair, my fingers. Tom had crashed on his side of the bed and was sleeping like a log with his back to me. In the morning he got up and went straight to the bathroom to take his shower. He did not say a word to me.

I lay there, invisible, insignificant. The sheets, the blinds, the oak parquet, the old hotel slippers from the InterContinental that I was staring at with my head hanging off the bed, everything had gone still, stuck in dusty, indifferent rays of sun.

I rolled back onto the bed and closed my eyes. Everything hurt: my head, my eyes, my heart. I got up. I went to join him in the bathroom.

Tom stood in the middle in front of the double sinks, blocking the way to the drawer where I kept the paracetamol. I stood there squinting at him, the whole bathroom shaking thump, thump together with my head.

'Oh hello, why are you up so early?' He wiped the left-over shaving cream from his face.

'I need some paracetamol.' I pulled my T-shirt down to cover my exposed underwear. 'Did you sleep well?'

He moved aside so I could open the drawer. 'Very well. You?'

'No, I slept badly.'

He untied the towel at his waist and dried his face with it. He was completely naked now. But it had nothing to do with me. His body was his.

'You hurt me last night.' I popped two pills from the packaging.

'Naomi, not now.' He examined himself in the mirror.

I searched his face. 'Why can't you reassure me? I feel awful. It didn't use to be like this.'

'Aw, you poor thing.' He took me by the arms but instead of drawing me to his chest, he gently but firmly moved me out of his way then left the bathroom. 'Adam's very busy so I'm taking over some of his portfolio. I'm afraid it means I'm going to be away a lot more over the coming months.'

'What?' I started to panic. Get a grip, I told myself. I pressed my lips together.

'You're busy anyway. You have a book to write.'

This was becoming a stock phrase with him. 'Where are you going?' I watched him get ready, while gluing my back to the bathroom door frame.

'Warsaw. To check out a biotech venture. Adam called

it pharma but it's a small, technological start-up and they claim they've figured out the ultimate sleeping pill. Can you imagine? It could be the most exciting deal around. The Polish Minister of Health is personally coming to pick me up from the airport.' While he talked, he inserted his cufflinks into the cuffs of his shirt, folding them back and pulling down the sleeves afterwards until they looked just right. 'I'll call you and the kids later,' he shouted as he ran down the stairs.

I followed him as far as the staircase and sat barefoot on the top step. The front door opened and shut with a 'clang'. He was gone.

The day tugged at me. It was raining outside. The kids had to go to school. Solange and I were nearing the end of the book. I had to go over our last notes. I didn't move.

'Mama? I can't find my tie. Mama? Where are you?' Tommy had just passed the open door to my bedroom. He addressed my back as I still sat on top of the stairs: 'What are you doing there?'

'Nothing,' I sighed. 'Nothing at all.' I gestured for him, 'Come give me a kiss.'

'Mama,' he started slowly, 'Every time I ask Sebastian for a playdate, he can't come. He has to study for the exams.' He hesitated, 'Am I going to take the entrance exams too?

Fuck. I had to take care of Tommy's applications to secondary school. I pretended I didn't hear him. 'Go downstairs baby, I'm coming in a second.'

I pulled Sam out of bed and, with him in my arms, joined Tommy in the kitchen and started making breakfast. I put a slice of bread in the toaster and took the jam and butter out of the fridge. Sam started to cry. The toast came up and I buttered it and gave it to him.

'How about me?' Tommy stood there with his big eyes. I realized I should have put two slices in the toaster, I have two children. My head started to hurt again.

'What about you? It's not all about you.' I took a slice of bread and put it in the toaster. And then I felt exhausted and I sat down. Tommy was still standing there with his big eyes except that now they were filled with tears while Sam ate his toast, and I held my head with my hands. Why make Tommy feel bad? Because it was safer than going after Tom the husband. I smelled the toast and I went to the toaster. The toast was black. Meribel arrived in her robe. 'I'm sorry Gordo'—I rarely called Tommy *gordo* anymore—'this is not how I want to be.' I asked Meribel to toast two slices for him and to put anything he wants on them, even Nutella.

I left them and went upstairs to get ready. I spread moisturiser on my face. The cream wouldn't penetrate my skin. I took a tissue and wiped it all off. I reached for the bottle of Chanel perfume. I'd been wearing number 19 since I got my first pay check, twenty-three years ago. I wore it the way I learned from my mother, spraying it against the inside of my wrists and then rubbing the wrists underneath my ears, on my neck. I always wore the same fragrance, whether I was going to the supermarket or to a gala evening. Tom used to love it, not only the smell but the predictability of it. He'd say it was part of what made me, me. Even the boys I felt knew me better because of my consistent scent. I picked up the glass bottle. I lifted the square flat top. I'd like to say the bottle slipped from my hand, that I still had some creamy residue on my palm. The bottle went crashing against the tiled wall. The shards of clear glass lay all over the floor, mixed up with the sharp, pungent Number 19 aroma. The whole bathroom stunk of me and I could barely breathe. I stepped out and I felt the piece of glass sink into my bare foot. It was a straight and deep pain, an honest pain and I breathed out as I let my weight come down fully on the wounded foot. I took another step forward. I noticed the gorgeous trail of blood first on the porcelain tiles and then on the oak floor of the bedroom. I stopped in front of my closets. I opened my lingerie drawer and as I put one leg through the hole in my knickers, blood stained the fabric. That was ok. Don't all women put blood on their underwear sometimes?

The beginning of Hate is Love denied.

# CHAPTER TEN

## May 2016

On the first Saturday after Andreas left, the mothers from school decided to go support Antheia who had started selling her olive oil at a local farmers' market. It was a beautiful Saturday morning. The neighbourhood showed up in their Lululemon tights and their Daunt Books cloth bags and the tradesfolk—who knew their business -, booked a Joni Mitchell-millenium version guitar player, complete with long, tangled hair, dirty jeans and an amplifier so the market not only looked and smelled organically earthy but sounded like that too. Solange came and we all hung around Antheia's white and green stand, chatting, drinking flat whites and trying to attract shoppers to Antheia's Cyclades Olive Oil. Although some shoppers shrieked in horror at the prices, most accepted this 'market' for what it was. Asides from buying two bottles to support my friend, I also bought cupcakes for the boys, a fresh baguette, two boxes of strawberries and a piece of Comté cheese for us. I was holding too many bags to reach my keys so I rang the doorbell when I got back home.

Meribel opened the door. 'Mister Barnes, he say not come downstairs, he busy working.' She was holding little Sam by the hand.

'Mummy!' He tried to jump into my arms. I handed the bags to Meribel and bent down to pick him up.

I went to the kitchen anyway. Tom was sitting in the lounge chair against the glass wall in the kitchen. Pink pages of the weekend paper were spread on the floor around him. He was wearing his glasses and there was a mug with cold coffee and a plateful of crumbs on the breakfast table. Although he hadn't played in at least eight years, he still loved wearing his King's Old Boys FC shirt on Saturdays. He was on a call. 'You can't be serious. New side-effects? Because a woman went sleep-driving two days after taking Zuidex and crashed her car?'

Sam ran to his father. 'Daddy! Mama is home! She got cake!'

'What?' Tom spoke into the receiver, 'Hold on, do not hang up!' He pressed the mute button and examined us, first Sam, then myself. 'What is it?'

'I brought us really nice bread and cheese from the market,' I said, helping Meribel unpack the bags.

Tom frowned and went back to his call. 'Well, if you're so sure it's not the pill, test the hell out of that woman. Forty million! We've put forty million dollars in your idea...' Sam offered him a bite of the chocolate cupcake that was already all over his face. Tom put the phone against his chest. 'Naomi!' he shouted. 'Take the fu—' He stopped himself. '—children away from here, will you?'

Sam gaped, scared by his father's anger, and started wailing. The cake fell from his hand onto his father's lap.

I left them all to it and went upstairs and sat on the sofa in the living room. Andreas had taken Baz out to dinner the night before and had the nerve to bring him back home in the company of his baby mama. Solange threw a hairbrush at his head. Melanie encouraged her to drink red wine at ten-thirty in the morning with the excuse that it was rich in resveratrol: 'Very good for your serotonin levels. Ideal against bitterness.'

Ours was an elegant sitting room with a glass coffee table and a hand woven rug that that the designer assured us would be a good investment. You could see its' geometric patterns through the coffee table, in between the large art books about black and white photography. There was one enormous painting on the wall. It was of the inside of the dashboard of a truck. There were maps, chocolate wrappers, an evil eye hanging on a chain off the rear-view mirror as well as other knick-knacks hanging there and in the mirror, you could see a reflection of the truck driver's face. He looked like Saddam Hussein.

A woman had died taking the sleeping pill created with Newspring's investment.

'Insomnia is a $2 billion market. You think the big guys in Switzerland or in France want to see us wipe them out? It took them years to corner the sleeping drug business with their shitty pills. And we show up with a product ten times better than theirs for the same price. If word about this woman gets out…' Tom was walking up the stairs. He hung up when he saw me. 'What were you thinking leaving Sam there with me on a call?' His sweat pants had chocolate frosting on them.

'You keep saying it's not Saddam Hussein but I think it is.'

'Well, it isn't. I told you to stop saying that. It's a Turkish painting and a valuable one to boot.'

He had gained weight since he started with Newspring in spite of various diets. He was eating out too often. Not that his looks mattered anymore. He was trading in a different currency.

'Did someone die because of your company?'

'Nobody died because of "my" company. Don't be ridiculous.' He glanced at his phone. 'There's Arsenal v Spurs in ten minutes.'

'So she's not dead?'

'That's not the point. People die every day and it's got nothing to do with us.' His jaw clenched. 'Do you understand? Nothing to do with us.'

'I… I'm going to run some errands.'

'Good. If you have a chance, can you put petrol in the car? And you know we have dinner tonight with David and Barbara. It should be fun; we're going to a new wine club in Pall Mall.'

'David and Barbara?'

'David Miller? He's our head of research. His wife's name is Barbara. She's a headhunter. They're both American.

No?' He shrugged and walked away.

Tom was right, I had no idea who he was talking about. When I left the house, Tom was sitting in the middle of the sofa in the TV room with his arms outstretched, Tommy on his left and Sam to his right, an open box of pizza on the coffee table. The sound of the football commentators with the noise of the stadium filtered through to the hallway, thanks to the surround sound system we had installed.

I sat in the Range Rover in silence, clenched the wheel and couldn't turn on the engine. At the market earlier, Ines had said something. She was trying to help Solange but the words stuck with me. *What the money does to him.* I inhaled the smell of the still fragrant leather surrounding me. How about what the money does to me?

We had gone as a family to buy this very car two years ago. At first when I saw the prices, I panicked. I told Tom we could still go to Car Giant, it was just over the motorway. Tom kissed me on the head. 'My wife and children will not drive in a second-hand car. It's always bothered me, this idea of sitting where other people have sat and... farted before.' He looked around and rubbed his hands. This dealership found him in his element, already he loved spending money and the salespeople smelled it. Even Tommy felt the excitement and started running around. I had Sam in the stroller and I called for Tommy to stop, but the staff smiled and told me not to worry, that they loved children and the lady from reception brought him cookies. They allowed him to sit behind the wheel of a model with a price tag of £85,000 and touch everything—he was even allowed to turn on the engine, pushing his tiny fingertip into the ignition button as if it was one of his matching game toys. As for Sam, he complained so much, I let him out of the pushchair and the salesman put him behind the wheel of another £80,000 car and Sam sprayed his saliva all over the dashboard as he made engine sounds. In the meantime, our salesman made us cappuccinos. Tom asked technical questions about the safety and manageability of the 'Autobiography' versus the 'Vogue'. He indicated the boys and me: 'My life is going to be driving in that car every day. I need to be sure.' The salesman didn't miss a beat and, with as straight a face as Tom, told us that in his thirteen years at the dealership, he had rarely seen such a caring and responsible couple.

Tom put his arm around my shoulders.

And I let my head rest against his.

I got out of the car and slipped back into the house, carefully so they wouldn't notice me (not that they would, they were too busy with the game). I took my laptop in its black sleeve and left on foot, making my way down to the high street and the Waterstones book store. Taking a table in the coffee shop upstairs, I clicked on a section of our book, *Living the Dream*.

The plot was linear and ascending, with a few twists and turns, but those were just kinks in an overall arrow pointing up until it reached what I now knew was not the end. Solange was right, this book lied maybe not in its contents but in its conclusion. You don't arrive anywhere. I was finally losing the optimism that had propelled me forward all these years. I fought and fought with Tom to no avail. He just didn't care enough. No. I couldn't believe that. It was a spell, an English spell that had been cast upon him by that warlock Danton, but I would learn how to break it. For this I had to be taller, brighter, happier. I had to venture into my own tunnel. I shut the laptop and took the red notebook out of my handbag.

"Towards the end, we had a beach house. Rented, not owned, but that only came out later. It was on Isla Grande, one of the closest of the Rosario Islands to the city. We would go there on Saturdays, sometimes Fridays if my father was done early. It was a cabin really, with no air-conditioning, and we had to burn spirals at night against the mosquitoes. There was a concrete platform next to the cabin with a thatched roof where Abuelo Anton and Abuela Edith could sit on plastic chairs and look out at the mangroves and the sea. The beach was narrow with fine white sand mixed up with rotting almonds, sticks, and pebbles. About two metres in from the surf, tough root-like vines spread horizontally, like a tree trying to crawl, perhaps because of the wind.

I remember my father from the back, with his black cushiony hair and elegant neck, standing ahead of me in his maroon shorts, an old Guyabera shirt that he kept for the beach, brown socks and wingtip shoes. He would stare out at the Caribbean sea with his hands on his hips, reminding me of the woman emerging from the waves in the cola commercial, except in reverse. I watched his back broaden with each breath, thinking he'd walk into the sea until the water covered him up completely and he'd be gone. I probably never had that thought at the time, only later, once he had disappeared from our lives.

Then again, I have many false memories about Fernando Perez. He didn't want to be known, not by me, not by Mama, not by his parents. Our conversations tended to be formal and impersonal but he looked at me as someone he loved. Sometimes after school, he'd take me into one of his afternoon meetings with his accountant, or one of the transport guys, or the cooperative rep. I'd sit on a wooden chair with a wicker seat, the local type with rough woven strands of palm that left deep marks on the back of my thighs. I spent the time trying to hypnotize myself by staring unblinking at the turning blades of the ceiling fan above my head. I enjoyed it. It was a treat to be with him, even if it meant enduring a long, boring meeting. Every so often he'd look at me and smile. At first I thought his pride was in showing me how important he was, how successful. Then I understood it was me he was proud of, me, his daughter.

It started off as one of those typical stories of a wealthy man leaving behind one family because he can afford to start another one. He had run off with his secretary, a woman ten years younger than my mother. Then it turned out he wasn't wealthy at all. We had to leave our modern suburban house and move in with my mother's parents. Then it transpired that a judge had issued a warrant for his arrest. Marina was either crying or screaming all the time. We couldn't be in the same room with her; our mere presence made her crazy. Of course, we were kept in the dark. In those days, people thought that if you didn't tell the children about the crisis erupting around them that they wouldn't notice.

My maternal grandparents entertained the most terrible ideas about what Fernando had done. In their mind, my father had finally revealed his true morality and character. They were too jubilant in their rage to mind Nico's and my feelings, and anyway they assumed, my grandmother in particular, that we'd agree with them.

'This is what a man with such origins was bound to do. Can you imagine? The son of a maid and a dilettante anarchist. No traditions, no values, no morals: just desire unleashed like a hurricane on our poor daughter. For all we know, he's not in Brazil or Miami like they say, he's right here in the jungle with FARC or worse, with the—' My grandmother stopped. I turned to see what made her quiet. My mother. Marina looked like she wanted to shoot her. That day we moved out of that house.

I tried to guess the end of my grandmother's sentence. Did she mean the government special forces? Another outlaw guerrilla group? Or the drug dealers?

Marina always denied the possibility that my father could have been involved with a drug cartel or with gangsters. He did get into trouble with the law but that had to do with an insurance claim. His father, Abuelo Anton, died a few months after Fernando disappeared and Abuela Edith moved in with us. She too vehemently shut down any suggestion that her son would be involved with banditos.

I stopped talking about it but something in me resisted their version of the story. There was something comforting in the idea that my papa had to disappear from our lives. It wasn't a choice: It was the noble, brave thing to do, a last act of protection. There was a dream I used to have: Papa with his brown socks and black city shoes, runs down a mountain slope, waving goodbye to me with a finger on his lips. As I hide behind a tree, he calls out to the sicarios, 'Here! This way!' and then these creatures that look like men with holsters but bark like dogs run after him like a pack of hounds. And we are left safe behind the Yopo tree.

With every year, my private little tale of Fernando lost some of its power. The love, the sacrifice, the imagined protection—all of these faded before the reality that was thrown in our faces every day. Papa and money were gone. By the time I became a hormonal sixteen-year-old, I was angry. The hole his absence created had not closed. If anything, it got bigger."

I stopped. I paid for the tea I had not drank and started to walk back to the house. As I passed the Italian chocolate and ice cream shop, I spotted parents I knew inside, having a coffee while their children had an ice cream. We waved at each other. I remembered when I used to feel the way they looked. Maybe it was all in my head. Maybe there was no hole, just my paranoid brain, unable to accept a normal family life.

I reached the front door with a spring in my step. I rang the doorbell although I had my keys. I wanted to be welcomed by my family.

Tommy opened the door. 'Are you going out tonight again?'

'Come here, baby.' I wrapped my arms around him and hugged him as hard as I could.

Tom came up from the kitchen holding Sam in his arms. 'There you are! We were wondering when you'd be home. Meribel's making pasta for their dinner. Do you need time to get dressed? We have to be there for eight.'

'Mama, are you going to read me a story?' Sam went from his father's arms into mine.

'Yes. Let's go take your shower first.'

'Naomi, it's already seven-fifteen,' Tom warned me.

'It'll be fine.' I went upstairs and helped Sam wash his hair. Then I dressed all in black, black trousers, black turtleneck, black pumps. I was putting on my make-up when Sam reminded me of my promise to read to him. We'd been reading Antoine de Saint-Exupéry's *The Little Prince* for the past month at the rate of a couple of pages here and there. I had forgotten where we had stopped, so I picked up the book and opened it randomly. 'Ah, this is where the pilot and the Little Prince are looking for water in the desert.'

*"What makes the desert beautiful," said the little prince, "is that somewhere it hides a well…"*

'Mama?' Sam peeked down at me from his bunk bed.

I stopped reading. 'Yes?'

Tommy's head peeked into the room. He came in without a word and climbed onto the armchair with me. I made space for him and he rested his head on the inside of my shoulder. I continued reading.

*I was astonished by a sudden understanding of that mysterious radiation of the sands. When I was a little boy I lived in an old house, and legend told us that a treasure was buried there. To be sure, no one had ever known how to find it; perhaps no one had ever even looked for it. But it cast an enchantment over that house. My home was hiding a secret in the depths of its heart…*

'Does everything have something hiding inside?' Tommy lifted his head.

'I don't know about everything but everybody, yes.'

'Wait, Mama, do you have something hiding in you?' His face was so close, I could feel the heat of his breath.

'Don't we all? You have plenty of things hidden in you, like your heart, your lungs, your brain, your self.'

'Your poo-poos before they come out!' Sam cracked from his top bunk.

'Okay, that's it for tonight.' I shut the book but this time, I marked the page. 'Kiss, Mama has to go out with Daddy now.'

'Mama do you know everything that's hiding in you?' Tommy reluctantly got up from the armchair with me. Sam stopped laughing and was looking at me upside-down. They were both waiting for my answer. I thought for a moment.

'Naomi, let's go!' Tom called from downstairs.

'No, but...' I looked at both my boys and they were listening and I knew this was a moment, a precious chance for me to say something meaningful, to show my boys an alternative way to see me, maybe all women. 'Nobody knows what's inside just like that. You have to work at it, test yourself, overcome big, unwanted problems—'

'Naomi!'

I shook my head. 'For example, I never knew I had anger in me against daddy until recently.' I shouted back, 'Wait!'

'I don't like it either when he shouts like that,' Tommy said.

'Poor daddy, it's because mama's always late.' Sam shot me a mischievous look.

Tom would be furious. But I had to finish explaining to the boys, they had to understand this. It was important.

'We carry all sorts of things inside. The easiest ones to find are the feelings like anger and jealousy and shame. The best parts we have to search and discover and bring out like in a treasure—'

A loud, sustained car honk interrupted me. I looked out the window and sure enough, I saw the headlights of the Porsche as Tom revved it in front of the house. 'I have to go now. Sleep well, *mi queridos*. Your mama loves you very much.' I kissed them both and ran downstairs. 'Meribel, make sure they go to bed!' I shouted in Spanish to the housekeeper and shut the door behind me.

Tom took his frustration out on the streets, speeding like a capo on the run down Haverstock Hill and around Regents Park, with me fuming in silence beside him. If he was hoping to get a reaction out of me with his stupid driving, he could think again.

The club's entrance was discreet. There was only the number on the door. We walked in and the concierge at the desk somehow knew who we were, he even asked Tom if he needed a blazer.

'It's Saturday night,' Tom straightened his plain shirt, 'why would I need a blazer?'

'Club rules.' The concierge opened a closet and showed us a selection of tweed, woollen and linen blazers. Tom grumbled but he picked a blue woollen one and put it on, 'does anyone really care?'

'Please if you will follow me.' He pretended not to hear Tom's question and walked ahead of us.

'Not a word about Zuidex, okay?' Tom whispered to me. 'Remember, these people are not friends.'

'But the children—' I said out loud.

'Naomi, get with the programme!'

'*Vale*, okay.' The good wife. My heels made a dry tapping noise on the parquet floor. We entered a solemn space, with a dome decorated with frescoes and dark wood panelling on the walls. Although there must have been thirty or more people in the room, it still felt solemn, even quiet. The concierge explained that the club owners had re-converted an old chapel into what they called a 'shrine to wine'. They prided themselves on the quality and depth of their wine collection.

'Makes sense,' Tom thought out loud, 'David loves to brag about his private cellar.' The entire wall behind the bar was occupied by high-tech refrigerated units with glass doors and interior lighting so the members could contemplate the wine collection while the bartender prepared their drink. A man stood up and waved at us from a sitting area with Chesterfield sofas and deep upholstered seats. Our host. I made myself smile.

'Tom! Naomi! So good to see you.' David, older, balder, and shorter than Tom but with a bouncy energy, walked up to us with open arms and a wide grin, as if he owned the club. His welcome was so warm, I almost forgot he was not a friend. He led us to a small table away from the main bar, where his wife Barbara was sitting. She stood up to greet us. Barbara was plump and her hair was grey, but she held herself straight and there was a solid peacefulness about her.

'I hope you enjoy wine. They have the best sommelier in London. Name it, they'll have it and by the glass, too.' David motioned to a waiter.

'That's brilliant. Look, Naomi, they have the Côte-Rôtie.' Tom put down the list. 'That's my little test of how good a list is,' he grinned at them. 'I love Côte-Rôtie, even the earthy smell.' He looked across the room. 'Splendid club you have here,'

'Yes,' I agreed, 'so many different wines. How do you know which ones to order?'

'Oh, well, you need to be interested in the industry. For example, I'd like to order the Chevalier-Montrachet tonight because I know they hold a good year and it's the right time to open a bottle.' David waved the waiter over.

Tom was taking it all in. There was something proud, satisfied about his expression that I had never noticed before.

'Look,' he said in a dramatic whisper if only to confirm my thoughts, 'isn't that Mathew Collins? Wasn't he was in the office the other day?' David raised an eyebrow as he followed Tom's eyes. 'Who would have thought, eh, David? That we'd see the day when an arrogant bastard like Collins would come to Reginald for,' he made air quotes, 'advice?' They all three started laughing softly, then to my horror, this Collins fellow saw us and, a stupid grin on his face, he left his wife alone and started towards our table. Barbara was the first to crack into an open laugh and the men followed. They didn't care that Collins could hear them. Tom downed his glass and wiped his eyes with the corner of his napkin. The waiter brought a dish of olives and David asked for oysters, 'Fines de Claires only, I hate the fatty ones.'

I shifted in my seat and looked away.

Yes, when there is no love there is social climbing... and champagne. I ordered a second glass after chugging my first. Collins was nervous and talking non-stop and I took the opportunity to look closely at David and Barbara. Ah, I recognised them; they sent us long, detailed Christmas cards every year. That was one of the reasons their card always stood out from the dozens we now received every December:

It wasn't just the children in the picture, they were in it too, Ines-style, white teeth in the sun. The other reason was the printed letter folded inside the card relaying in mouth-watering detail all the successes and achievements of their offspring. I remember asking Tom what was the purpose of these letters. It wasn't like we knew the Miller children. What emotion were they trying to generate in us lesser mortals with their laundry list of elite schools, sporting prowess, cello and violin competitions and drama awards? This year's letter stretched to cover both sides of the paper (at least they were environmentally minded).

'I don't know,' Tom said, handing the letter back to me. 'It's an American thing. The English would never boast like this. We're too afraid of envy.'

That was back in his first year at Newspring.

Collins finally left and David proposed a toast. 'To friendship!'

We all raised our glasses and looked each other in the eye. Since we were celebrating things we did not have, like friendship, I proposed a toast to love and family. David and Barbara cheerfully agreed. Tom looked at me and there was joy and even love in his face. but it was like a happy mist that took in everything around us, the club, the Millers, even poor Collins, it was not intimate to us. I almost put my hand on his face to see if it would just go through, as if he were a hologram of himself, a ghost made of air. I picked up an olive. Don't you feel the void? I wanted to shake him, my lover, my lovely Tom. The olive tasted salty and bitter.

'David by the way, have you heard about our sleeping pill project? It's going to blow you away.' Tom was glowing. 'Once we get it out, it's game over for everybody else. And we are all going to be sleeping much better!' He looked at me pointedly before picking up his glass and leaning back on the sofa.

'Hmm. I heard about some troubles with the test trials. And you know, the government in Poland is changing.' David stuck his nose in his glass and inhaled deeply.

Barbara raised an eyebrow.

'No, it's okay,' Tom rushed to reassure. 'Yes, we have one trial that is problematic but it's not at all clear that it's related to Zuidex. This woman drove her car into a pole and died. It was days after she took our pill. But because she was part of the trial, we're checking everything, autopsy, her blood, yadi yada. We want to be completely waterproof on this one.' Tom swallowed a gulp of wine. 'Ah, this Chevalier-Montrachet is phenomenal.'

When I first met Tom Barnes, he did not use words like 'yadi yada' or 'phenomenal.'

'I'm glad to see you still feel so confident.'

'The Minister of Health invested his own private funds in Zuidex.'

David frowned. Nobody spoke for a moment.

'On a different topic, we hope you guys are recruiting your friends, the parents at school, everyone you know to vote in this referendum. We need all the help we can get.' Barbara smiled at me.

'Of course! It's going to be close and it would be such a

disaster if we voted out,' I exclaimed.

'Really?' David looked questioningly at Tom. 'We are actively campaigning *for* Brexit.'

'Who? You mean Newspring? I didn't know.' I too turned to Tom.

Tom swallowed what was left in his glass. 'How are you, Barbara? How are the kids?'

'Oh, but the EU is a sinking ship!' Barbara wouldn't be so easily distracted. She inched closer to her husband.

'I went through a great deal of effort to become a British citizen and a big part of what motivated me was that this country was part of the EU,' I said. Tom reached out for my hand. He squeezed it. It took me a moment to squeeze his back.

David's friendliness had vanished. Without it, he looked like a fish: grey and cold. 'I'm sure you and Tom will change your mind.'

'Can you vote?' I held his gaze.

David coughed. Barbara turned to her husband but didn't say a word. Aha. These gringos never bothered to get British nationality. They had no power, so they were trying to vote by proxy through us.

'The EU is what gave me hope about my future. As the son of coal miners from Leicestershire.' Tom held on to my hand. He smiled at me, 'we wouldn't be here, none of us, if it were not for the EU and the doors it opened for us in London.'

I kissed his hand.

A phone started to ring. It was Tom's. He looked at his screen. His face fell. He started typing hard and fast and then, without a word to anyone, he got up and ran out of the building.

They must have found a link between the dead woman and the pill.

David watched Tom leave. He turned to me, 'Barbara just came back from Boston this morning.'

'Djes?' I blinked a couple of times.

'Yes, our oldest two children are at university there,' Barbara added.

'In Boston?' I wondered who the dead woman was, if she had children.

'We did a wonderful tour of Bordeaux last spring. It was Roger's eighteenth birthday and we wanted to welcome him into adulthood in a more European way,' David cleared his throat, 'before he joined the immature social life of a Harvard freshman.'

Tom walked back in. The blood had drained from his face and his hair was dark with sweat. Even his lips had lost their colour. I waved at him and patted the seat next to me. 'Congratulations!' I tried to buy him time to recover from whatever news he'd received. 'David and Barbara have two kids at Harvard.'

He didn't seem to hear me at first. He just sat there for a moment, staring in space.

'Our eldest is sitting the eleven-plus in a few months' time. We are so nervous.' Tom said in a flat voice, his nervousness most obviously not linked to Tommy. 'It takes more than money to get into the good schools, apparently.'

'Yes.' David's eyes narrowed. 'It takes more than money to achieve most things.'

Barbara turned to me. 'Where are you hoping to send your son to school next year?'

'I...'

'Naomi's put Tommy's name down for all the best day schools in London, isn't that so, darling?'

I blinked. We had yet to talk about Tommy's secondary school options; there was a parents' meeting at school coming up and I hoped we could get an idea then.

The waiter arrived with our food. He put a plate of glistening scallops with white froth on top in front of me. I pushed it away. I had a lump in my throat.

'Do you have any tips, ideas for us?' Tom put his hand on my arm as he addressed Barbara and then looked at me in a way that said, 'Listen carefully.'

David laughed. 'Well, to be honest, Tom, it's a little late in the game for that. He's ten? We started preparing our kids for these exams from the day they turned four.'

'Oh, David, why would you think their boy isn't prepared?' Barbara smiled at me, 'Naomi is a wonderful mother, I'm sure.'

I pressed my lips together.

'Naomi is doing the best she can,' Tom put his hand over mine, 'but she didn't grow up in this system so...'

I couldn't believe it. 'As if you did, Ibstock boy!' I wanted to shout. It was too unfair. With his blue eyes, expensive clothes and developing mid-Atlantic accent, he could fool them in ways I never could. I downed my glass of champagne, wincing as if it were Alka Seltzer, and waved at the waiter to bring me another.

Tom went on, 'on careful thought, I think Naomi and I will vote for Brexit after all on the 23rd,' he said to David and Barbara.

'What?' I spilled my refilled glass over my turtleneck.

David offered me his napkin graciously. I snatched it.

# CHAPTER ELEVEN

'How dare you?' I was drunk.

Tom was not. He stopped in front of a red light. We were driving up Pall Mall with its badly lit temples. 'Reggie's obsessed with this referendum. He's taking the chopper to Bristol tomorrow to go join Boris Johnson there.'

'So? What does that have to do with me? With my vote?'

'If you would stop biting my head off for a second and listen—'

'No!' I was about to go on when he turned his head and looked at me. We had reached Regent Street and the glow from all the lights gave his face a bluish hue.

'Fucking hell, woman, it's not about you! It's about my job! The firm expects us to toe the line.'

'Fuck that. What kind of firm tells their employees what or who to vote for?'

'The normal kind. You should get back out there, you'd be surprised.' His voice died. 'It's bad Naomi. It's really bad. I can't believe you're so uninterested in what I'm going through.'

Strings of red, white, and blue lights hung over Regent Street with banners advertising an upcoming American NFL game in London. The road was wet. The windshield wipers were on the low setting. Whoosh and then a spattering of tiny drops of water. Whoosh again. 'Bastard!'

He sighed and went on driving.

We said nothing until we reached Oxford Circus.

'Ok. Tell me then. Who called you?' I waited for him to answer.

He gripped the wheel with both hands. 'Ok. Let's see. The health minister, my friend, the one who invested in Zuidex... he got sacked. His replacement is some communist who wears Crocs with socks to meetings. They've nationalised our company. They've stolen everything: our money, our investment, our time, everything.'

'Is that what made you turn green at the club? I thought you'd found out that the poor woman died because of the sleeping pill.'

'What? No, no. The results of the autopsy were completely clear. The pill, as I predicted, is a winner. So the communist comes out with some bollocks, "*Ze good of ze nation is above ze law*,"' he grossly imitated a Polish accent, 'and he sends me a WhatsApp. Can you believe this? A WhatsApp. And that's it. Case closed.'

He showed me his phone. Next to a little circle with a picture of a cheerful lumberjack type, complete with beard and checked shirt, were the words, ticked twice in blue:

*Thank you but Newspring involvement in national company Zuidex terminated.*

'Yup, that is a WhatsApp,' I admitted.

'It's a disaster.' Tom was on the verge of tears.

Oh God, this was the chance I was hoping for. I didn't think it would happen. Tom in pain, Tom vulnerable, Tom reduced to the human condition. 'Don't you see?' I cried. 'It is because all of this,' I indicated the compressed space of the Porsche, 'can vanish tomorrow that we have to protect who we are. It was you who explained to me that being part of Europe was what made being British acceptable. That it was the part of your nationality that gave you the mental space to aim high, to leave your "place". If you let Newspring pollute who we are, our identity, then yes, Danton will own us body and soul and if or when he pulls the plug, there'll be nothing left.' I leaned over and kissed his cheek. 'Oh, Tom. I fell in love with you when you were poor.'

In my intoxication, I was recognising him, his skin, his smell. We hadn't slept together for a while and I hadn't thought about it but now it was all I wanted. I put my hand on his thigh.

'Do you remember? It was the most beautiful thing I had ever heard. When I asked you what making love was like for you, what it was like being inside of me, you said home. You said it was like coming home.'

'Yes.'

'What happened, Tom? Why can't we—'

'We're no longer twenty-five, Naomi. We can't live on love and water like undergraduates.' He cleared his throat. 'Focus, desires, situations change.'

'I know that.' Sadness overwhelmed me. He obviously didn't have the same need for me. I turned the conversation back before it hurt too much. 'You still had no right to throw me under the bus and decide how I'm going to vote.'

He braked for a red light. 'You're obsessed with this stupid referendum. It doesn't matter. Even my parents are voting Brexit.'

Of course they were. I leaned back on my seat, and it was all I could do not to open my trousers and stick my fingers in between my legs. Oxford Circus was busy, with a constant stream of people emerging from the stairs leading to the underground, while others disappeared down there. Driven by desire. I could tell from here. Why else would you put yourself through this drizzle, through the heat of the over-crowded tube on a Saturday night? Everybody was going to have sex and they didn't need silk sheets and memory foam mattresses to do it.

The light turned green and Tom accelerated hard to speed ahead. He indicated the people we'd left behind, standing on the wet pavement. 'They'd love to be us.'

'They're on their way to make love.'

That shut him up. It was darker now we had left the West End. We were driving along Regent's Park and the frosty empty mansions on its outer circle. We'd be home soon.

Tom spoke up. 'Remember how before Tommy was born and we lived in that one bedroom off Finchley Road, we used to go for long walks on Sundays through Hampstead, St Johns Wood all the way to Kensington? We'd look at all the fabulous homes, the heavy polished front doors with giant brass knobs and stone steps and beautiful cars parked in front, and dream. You don't remember?'

'I remember. But we thought those rich houses were magical because we thought they contained something special. We didn't know.'

'We didn't know what?'

'That they are hollow inside.'

He frowned but said nothing more.

A homeless person wrapped up in a dirty sleeping bag lay on a bench in front of the Everyman cinema on Haverstock Hill. 'I hope this Polish business will be the end of Newspring.'

'Shut the fuck up,' he snapped. The air in the car turned cold. He looked at me as if I had murdered his mother.

I knew it then. No matter what I argued, what I tried, I'd be chucked out like a potato skin if it came down to a choice between his job and me. How about the children? Our family? He flew over a speed bump. I bounced, held back by the seat belt. He kept looking straight ahead.

Who was this man?

We stopped. We had reached our destination. The house looked beautiful. There was an olive tree growing out of a giant smooth stone pot on the landing, casting a delicate shadow against the white wall. An old street lantern that had been refurbished and fitted for electricity was lit above the front door.

'Are you coming?' Tom was standing in the open doorway. I had remained on the pavement.

I didn't want to. But the boys, they were inside. I started towards the door.

Tom waited for me. 'Instead of fighting all the time, why don't you try to show some appreciation for everything I've done for you and for this family?'

I took my time in taking off my jacket and hanging it in the closet. 'And me, what appreciation do you show me?'

'What? You're my wife. You're the mother of my kids.'

No, I'm not your wife, I wanted to say. A wife is someone you touch, you kiss, you fuck, you love. It is not an employee. But I was too tired. I said nothing.

'What happened with that book you were writing with Solange?' His voice had lost its edge.

'Finished about a month ago.'

'Well done! You didn't tell me. Did you send it out?'

'No. We're going to delete it. It's completely outside the point. *Fuera de Tema!*' I declared with my arms up.

'You mean beside the point. But what is the point?'

'We thought when we started it was this!' I waved my arms at our beautiful surroundings. 'But no. We were, like you say, "beside"...' I put my hand over my mouth as I felt the bile rise up. 'No. "Beside" is not strong enough. In Spanish it's better. We were outside the point.'

'You're drunk.'

'*Fuera de Tema!*'

'Goodnight.' Tom walked to the kitchen and poured himself a glass of scotch.

I followed him. 'You'd rather drink than make love to

me?'

'I'm not happy with you. Not happy at all.'

# CHAPTER TWELVE

## June 2016

Tom and I sat with the other waiting parents on the chairs lined in the middle of the school hall. Back to back, two rows, like in that game, *sillas musicales,* and just like in the musical chairs game, as soon as a teacher was free, we all moved up depending on the kind of family. One parent, one chair. Both parents, two chairs. I had nothing to say. Tom looked at the new hall and its sophisticated lights. He looked at the other parents. He looked at the grand piano. 'I'm so happy we can send our boys here. The primary school I went to was nothing like this.'

I nodded.

'You are such a nice couple.' Melanie turned around. Her husband Jon was looking at something on his phone. She leaned in to me. 'Don't look like that. We're all playing our little survival game. Trying to tweak the deals we made without breaking the whole thing.'

Talking about breaking, I couldn't see Solange. I texted her. She didn't reply.

Melanie and Jon were called up next. They went to sit on

the two chairs in front of the English teacher's desk. In spite of Melanie's tales of Slovakian girls in the gym and bank accounts, watching them from behind like this, their shoulders touching, united in their interest and love for Damien, I believed in them, in their family.

I looked at Tom. He was busy on his phone. I opened the file that had been given to us when we walked in. *Tom Barnes 6F* was printed in large bold letters on the front of the blue A4 cardboard folder. The teacher probably expected us to have a look at the boy's work before talking about it. I opened the folder. It was his latest report card. We had received it separately last week and I thought I had already seen it. English was the first subject. He got a D.

Tom was typing something on his phone. 'Darling, we've been invited to Reggie's fiftieth birthday party in the Bahamas. I think we must go.'

The notes from the teacher said Tommy needed more support at home. His homework tended to be sloppy and he should be reading more.

Why had I not read it before? I remembered Tommy giving it to me and I put it on one of the kitchen counters, the one where all the post went.

The English teacher motioned to us. Antheia and Antonio had just stood up from the table beside our own. She didn't notice she was carrying her son's folder upside down and all the contents fell to the floor. Poor Antheia turned bright red and I could see the other parents pretending not to sneak a look at Kostis's grades. She knelt down and started gathering the papers. I was about to go help her when I saw Antonio also on his hands and knees, handing her the notebooks and papers as he picked them up. The gesture was simple but genuine, free of reproach or irritation. Again I believed, in spite of the stories.

'Did you read the notes on the report card?' The English teacher, Ms Day, was bracing herself for an attack.

'Did you?' Tom glanced at me before going back to his phone.

'Yes,' I answered softly. I wanted her to know I wasn't one of those parents who started howling about how much money they paid the school whenever their kids got a bad grade.

'Ah,' she said when she heard my *djes*. 'Now I see. What language do you speak at home?'

'By now mainly English. We're so busy. I still try to speak to Tommy and Sam in Spanish, but it's not regular.' I nudged Tom to pay attention.

The teacher bit her lip. 'Well, it's not a problem to grow up in a bilingual environment. It's just that for Tommy to move from a D average to a B, he needs to spend more time working on his English at home—'

'What? A D? Are you serious? Naomi, what happened?' Tom interrupted the teacher. 'This is bloody unacceptable!'

I could feel the eyes of the parents waiting behind us on our back.

Ms Day cleared her throat. 'As I was saying, things like reading out loud, going over his spellings, making vocabulary lists, all of that will help.'

Tom's phone bleeped and he looked at it and put it down again.

'Which of the books from the reading list has he read?' the teacher asked patiently.

Tom looked at me but then his phone bleeped again. He cursed and stood up. 'I'm sorry, I have to take this call.' He marched off while putting his headset on. 'Hello? Reggie? Of course, of course... Can you hear me?'

I watched Tom disappear through the swing doors. 'Um, he's reading...'

'Mrs Barnes, do you have any secondary schools in mind for Tommy? He's a bright and willing boy. It would be a shame for him to miss out on a good education. After all, isn't that why you both work so hard?'

My eyes fell on my freshly painted nails. Couldn't Ms Day see we were lost? That for all the money and privilege, we were failing? That we didn't know who we were, what we stood for, where we were heading?

I found Tom pacing the pavement outside the school. His coat had been folded over his arm but the hem was brushing the ground, his arms had fallen so low.

'Let's go home.' I took his coat and held it up for him. He buttoned up and we started walking.

The street narrowed and we passed a church to our left and a small cemetery to our right. Night had fallen but a streetlight illuminated those tombstones closest to the railings.

*It is not in the stars to hold our destiny but in ourselves.*

I looked at bit closer. Shakespeare. It was engraved on the tombstone of a certain Benjamin Flynn who lived between the years 1878 and 1960.

*It is not in the stars to hold our destiny but in ourselves.* I looked up in the night sky, something I did often back home but rarely in London. I let my head fall back and opened my eyes. No drizzle fell on my face; the air was crisp and dry. Where were the stars? The sky was complicated with shades of darkness ranging from blue to burgundy and there were strips of thin grey and white clouds, moving slowly. Dots of light broke through. And then I understood why Shakespeare in the sixteenth century figured out something that my people were still struggling with. In the Caribbean, night is black and stars shine bright. But here, like with everything, there is a hesitancy—even in the sky. It must have become tedious to try to read the clouded-over stars.

'If we were no longer together, it wouldn't matter that you have stopped loving me.'

Tom sighed. 'Huh?'

'But because we are still together, it matters. It matters because I am a woman of flesh and blood and I have given my life to you and the boys. You make me feel like I need to earn the right to exist. It is the most terrible thing.'

'You're talking rubbish. It's because you're upset about Tommy. I am too.' He gave me a sideways glance. 'It has been a tough year. And work is getting harder.' He added with gravity, 'I won't make the ten per cent.'

'You can try to make the ten per cent next year but you only get one chance to raise a child. And I know what happens when you blow that chance.' I'd railed for so long against my mother's fatalism and I was doing no better. The little cemetery was now behind us. *It is not in the stars*, nor in the husband, nor in the past *to hold our destiny but in ourselves.*

I found Tommy at his desk, working on a practice English exam. His room already resembled that of a teenager: We had given him a full-size bed and a big desk when we moved in, as well as a small sofa that was now covered with T-shirts, socks, football magazines, and a set of weights. On the walls, he had an old Bart Simpson poster from when he was younger, a framed photograph of him and Tom at the Emirates stadium, complete with matching red Arsenal scarves, and Rudyard Kipling's poem, *If*, that I had printed off the internet two years back and Blu-Tacked above his desk. The paper had turned yellow and curly at the edges.

He raised his head and saw it was me. There was no joy in his greeting. 'Hey Mama.'

'How's it going? I saw your teachers tonight.' I went to sit on the sofa but as there was no space, I sat down on his bed and considered what next to say.

When I was growing up, there were two options: Absolute Groundless Optimism ('Of course you'll make it. Now let's go eat oxtail at Tia's.') or—default option—Fatalism ('You did badly on that test? Oh well, nobody in this family was ever good at maths.') Neither of these was based on reflection. So had been my attitude to the boys. They had everything I had sorely missed. What else could they need? No, I was no longer going to be this way. 'We spoke to your English teacher in particular. What's her name again?'

'Ms Day.'

'Yes, Ms Day. She said you were really bright and motivated. She likes you.'

He swallowed. It occurred to me he was waiting for the 'but'. I must have done that a lot, come into his room right before rushing out in the evening, and like a bird flying with full bowels, drop some advice or what I conveniently considered 'constructive' criticism on his head, before running back to my room to put on my heels and fly out the door.

'You're important to me, Tommy. I love you.'

Tom's love may have made me once but I was going to force myself to matter now. Looking at my boy, I saw we—I had abandoned him, not physically of course, but psychologically. My mind, my heart had been unavailable. 'I'm here to stay.'

He hugged me.

Children forgive. What else can they do? But forgiving is not forgetting and children grow up. Already, his warm, clammy, wriggling body was changing. I put my face against his hair. He was temporary, down to the hands that were holding my waist. One day he'll remember. And then he'll be an adult and God knows they don't forgive.

His father was sitting on the sofa in the lounge with his laptop open on his knees. When he saw me, he pointed at the wire coming down from his ears. 'Conference call,' he mouthed.

I retrieved my own laptop and started researching secondary schools. I found a couple that looked nice and weren't too far away. I downloaded the applications.

'What are you doing?' Tom was done with his call and had come to stand behind me.

'I'm signing up Tommy for secondary schools.'

'Which one is that?' He peeked over my shoulder. 'Christopher something? Never heard of it.'

'It looks really nice. They do a lot of arts and theatre. And they're co-ed.'

'I want Tommy to go to one of the famous schools. That's why we're paying this expensive prep school.'

I clicked on another website, 'Tommy can't get into the Etons of this world. You saw his grades today. Anyway, we missed the deadline to apply.'

Tom began pacing the room like a lion in a cage. '*You* missed the deadline to apply! What have you accomplished exactly in the past four years? And at the expense of your children's education!' He held his finger to my face. 'No son of mine is going to some bloody third-rate school. Not after I've paid so much for his education. You lack rigour, Naomi. I'm not happy with you; I'm not happy with this family.'

This was the second time he said it. And this time we were both sober and it hit home. I remembered Solange telling me that at some point she had stopped listening to Andreas' explanations for leaving. His voice became blurry, muddled and she drifted into a daydream. A nursery rhyme her mother used to sing while she worked. It had to do with a maid walking to the market with a big pot full of honey on top of her head. Her flip-flops make a dry smacking sound against the heels of her feet as she walks down the street, *plap, plap* and with each step, she names something else she is going to buy with the money the honey will bring. Chicks, *plap*, a new pot, *plap*, a comb, *plap*. And so distracted she doesn't see the stone the devil sets on her path. When she trips, ay, the pot with all the honey falls and shatters on the asphalt. '*Misericorde!*' She laments, and her song became Solange's as she sang to herself, *Misericorde, misericorde* over and over again.

'So you are leaving us then?' What else could follow such a statement?

But he went to sit on the couch. 'I'm unhappy here. It's strange: I'm happy at work, I feel alive, even when there are problems, and believe me, there are, but I love being there. And I look forward to coming home at night to see my family, but as soon as I walk in the door... It's a disappointment. I don't understand. I love the boys and I love you too but it never lives up to... work.'

'Work?' I spat out. He flinched.

I couldn't believe this. Abuela Edith must be turning in her grave. A man prefers his job to his woman? What have I done, God, to deserve this? If at least he told me it was another woman, even Reggie, say he had some gay crush on Reggie Danton, but no! This was the coldest thing I'd ever heard.

'I'm competing against a fucking pay cheque.' I tried to laugh, but it came out all strangled.

I had to get away from him. The only room in the house with a lock was our bathroom. I ran in there and shut and bolted the door. The fire started in my throat and burned its way down to my stomach. I sat on the thick square towel on the tiled floor in front of the shower door. It was comfortable, the tiles were heated and I was safe, surrounded by my toiletries and my women things. Fool!

I heard him on the other side of the door. And then a child's whimper. Sam.

Tom shook the door handle. 'Sam woke up. He's asking for you.'

I didn't move.

*By the time I entered my last year of secondary school, I had had so little exposure and read so many books that I had made up my own social position in my head. I had decided I was equal. Once that thought penetrates your brain, it sticks. I decided I was equal to everybody—black, white, rich, poor, male, female—and I expected to be treated as such.*

*I had become friends with a rich white girl. Her name was Alexia Sackler and she invited me to join her and her friends at the cinema one Friday after school, then back to her house afterwards. That night, I went home triumphant and told my mother how all this talk about one's place in this country was bullshit. How everybody confused their own complexes with reality. How if we just chose to behave normally and with self-respect all doors would open for us. Mama, I later realised, didn't have the heart to disagree.*

*Alvaro Sackler was Alexia's older brother by two years. I had been aware of him for years: He was a semi-celebrity in school, a tennis champion who looked like Rob Lowe. And for all my intellectual convictions, I never imagined in my wildest dreams that the son of one of the most famous businessmen of all Colombia would notice me. I thought myself okay but I was too black to be gorgeous; I had a good butt, I knew that from the whistles and lewd comments I got on the street but that came with bad, kinky hair that I spent too long trying to smooth out. Alvaro, on the other hand, was covered in fairy dust. He could have anyone he wanted but that evening, he smiled at me. He came to hang out with his little sister and her friends and it quickly became clear it was because of me. He wanted to sit with me. He touched my fingers. He looked into my face, my eyes.*

*That night, I lay for hours on my back, unable to sleep, flush with virginal fantasies. They started with the cosmos and supernovas. I was everything and everywhere. The sheer immensity of my desires shot out in waves from my bed to shake the entire universe. And he knew. How could he not? His sheets must have billowed with my breath, only two miles away. I heard the neighbourhood around me, the rubber soles smacking dry heels, the clang of pots and pans being washed and put away, the odd radio still playing. The heat. The heat that came from me and made Cartagena hot, even at midnight. I kicked off my top sheet. I pulled down my knickers until they hung off one of my ankles. I spread my legs.*

*With my fingers, I pulled my lips apart and waited for the air shaken by the ceiling fan to tickle me. It was delicious—I was delicious and I never knew one could feel such tender joy for another.*

*The next day, as I left school, I saw Alvaro hanging at the gates with his friends. As I drew close, he left his group to come say hello. He kissed my hand to the whoops and hollers of his friends and told me to ignore them. He asked me in a low voice if I'd be allowed go out with him on Saturday night. I decided there was no way Marina could stand in the way of such a date and said yes, of course.*

*The four days leading up to that Saturday were the best days of my life. That afternoon, Marina saw me getting dressed and asked me where I was going. I was wearing my one pair of branded jeans, the little Guess triangle on my back pocket my proof of belonging, and a sleeveless calico top she had sewn for me. 'To the country club, I'm going with the Sacklers; Alvaro is picking me up. Everybody is going to be there.'*

*My mother didn't say anything.*

*'Can you help me with the hook at the back?'*

*She snapped the tiny clasps at the back of the shirt shut. She already had her hair up in rollers. That's what she did every Saturday night. She went to the salon on Saturday mornings where she would have her hair washed and styled for the entire week. The only way the hair would hold for seven days, in the sun and dust of Cartagena, was to roll it back in curlers that very evening, cover it in hairspray and tie a net over her head before going to bed. 'I don't want you going alone in a car with an eighteen-year-old. I'll drop you at the country club.'*

'No!' I pointed at her rollers. 'You don't want to go out like this. He's Alexia's brother. And the club is so close. And she'll be probably be in the car with him anyway.' I quietly packed my orange lipstick that she thought vulgar in my bag.

'Querida, I don't have a man to send out to rescue you in the middle of the—'

A car horn honked outside the house.

'Don't worry, Mama.' I kissed her on the cheek and ran out. Later, I saw my mistake. I should have let Alvaro park and come ring our doorbell and look my mother with her curlers in the eye, as she entrusted him with her only daughter. As it was, he didn't even have to get out of the car. I let myself into the back seat.

'Naomi, open the door!'

I watched the bathroom door shake with Tom's fists slamming it from the other side.

Alvaro was at the wheel, his friend Miguel next to him, and I was in the back. I loved the smell of the leather seats. Alvaro explained it was a new car and he'd had to beg his father to let him borrow it.

'You're so lucky,' Miguel said. 'My dad insists I only drive my grandma's old Peugeot.'

'No way.' Alvaro laughed. 'With this thing, we can pull!'

I didn't understand what they meant until we entered the downtown harbour area and a woman waved at us from the side of the street. Alvaro pulled over. He lowered his window. She was wearing a red leotard and red plastic heels. Otherwise, she was *naked. She put both hands on the door and leaned into the car, her stretched neckline revealing pendulous breasts. I gasped. She was a prostitute. I stared at the grey flab of her arms, the talcum powder clinging to her unshaven armpits, the heavily painted lips. Alvaro asked her something in a low voice. It didn't occur to me that Alvaro and Miguel would do anything but joke around with this woman.*

*So when Alvaro opened his door and started dropping his trousers, I screamed.*

*They both turned to me. The woman, who until then hadn't noticed my existence, hesitated. 'And she's supposed to watch and learn, I imagine?'*

*'Come on, querida, you know you want to do it.' Miguel smiled across Alvaro to her.*

*She ignored them and knocked on the back window with her knuckles. I lowered the glass, my eyes round like saucers. 'What are you looking at? Stupid girl. You woman just like me. Go home! These boys don't respect you.'*

*My mouth dropped open. But I was in too much awe, the evening so far was too exciting, I was too busy admiring Alvaro's manly grasp of the wheel with his smooth, clean hands. He could have rolled over someone in front of me and it wouldn't have meant a thing. Her words stung, but she was just a* puta *after all.*

*I was thrown back against the back seat. Alvaro must have decided this was no longer fun because he stepped hard on the accelerator. It was only because the prostitute pushed herself off the car that he didn't drive over her foot. As her angry, fist-waving figure shrunk in the distance, he pulled a thousand peso bill from his pocket and threw it out the window. I watched the bill floating in mid-air and I should have closed my eyes then. I could have believed what I wanted to in my heart, that in spite of her poverty, that she wouldn't humiliate herself in running after this scrap, this bone thrown to her as if she were a dog. But poverty doesn't work that way and my eyes remained wide open. My last sight of her before the car turned the corner was of this slow, tired woman on crooked heels, her arms stretched out, running after this money that was hovering dangerously close to the gutter.*

*'Naomi! Wasn't that a riot? That arrogant* puta. *And after all that* preciosa *bullshit, she ran after a thousand pesos like it was worth a thousand dollars.' Alvaro laughed.*

*'Si, si, she was on her knees for thirty US cents.' Miguel rubbed it in.*

*'Meanwhile, she's worth nothing.' Alvaro's eyes sought mine in the rear-view mirror. 'Less than nothing. She deserves what she gets. No one cares.'*

*'She's a human being and a citizen of this country too, you know.' I turned my face away and looked out the window in the night. The boys fell silent. We all knew how cruel our country was. And for the privileged ones, in the air-conditioning and the darkened windows, it was important to mock the poor, to point out their ignorance, greed, backwardness, because this implied that they deserved their lot somehow. But the rich needed those in between, those like me to approve, to endorse their lies. Alvaro and Miguel expected me to laugh with them and cheer them on in their 'boys will boys' behaviour. If I had, maybe they would have pretended, for the evening at least, that I was one of them, and*

*what happened later could have been avoided.*

*Maybe.*


'Naomi?' Tom's voice now was hesitant, solicitous even. 'Will you come to bed?'

He scratched at the door.

I washed my face and dried it with a towel.

'Come on?'

I thought back to that girl, that sixteen year old virgin, who had nothing but a head full of French revolutionary texts and the thin white Bata flats on her feet, a simple calico top and the equivalent of five pounds in her wallet.

'You're not going to spend the night in there! Look,' he coughed. 'How could I know what I said would have such an impact?'

When another rich, powerful guy pretended that he too was just a tourist in this life, that he could do whatever he wanted because he too didn't know it would have an impact, that girl from the nineties with her orange lipstick fought back.

She had already known that Alvaro was talking bullshit, that what he meant was that there'd be no impact for abusing her, Naomi Perez, girl with no father and no power. That fate had created her inferior and ready for abuse. She did not stand for it. Oh, of course, when she finally escaped and got home, she was a mess, she was limping, she was walking with one shoe, her clothes were ruined, she smelled. She cried in the very bed where she'd lain daydreaming about him a few hours earlier. She had loved him and she needed to recover. The next morning, however, the sun, whole and undamaged rose again and with it, so did she.

Fast forward twenty-five years. The world keeps turning. In the morning, in Hampstead just as in Cartagena, the sun would rise again, whole and undamaged (even if clouded over).

'Fuck you!' I shouted across the door.

'Huh?'

'You heard me. Would you like me to say it to you again?' Without waiting for his answer, 'FUCK YOU!'

He kept his mouth shut.

I eventually fell asleep on the floor, on the bathroom rug, with a towel for blanket. It was warm and I slept all night.

I dreamt I was no longer afraid.

# CHAPTER THIRTEEN

The next morning, the sun was bright and the sky was blue. A good omen, I thought, as I lifted the blinds. I unlocked the door and carefully turned the knob. I was worried about the children and wanted to check on them. For some reason I didn't expect to see Tom at all. It was so peaceful now, so quiet, he belonged to the drama of the night before. I looked ahead as the door creaked open and I saw a shape, still dressed with his new grey socks on, sleeping on top of the covers. I crept closer. Tom was fast asleep, his face relaxed and remarkably young again. Who was he? I moved to look at him from a different angle. No, I didn't know him anymore, this husband, and this felt like the greatest failure of all. In spite of knowing all the facts about this man.

Tom Barnes was born on August 10, 1969, the only child of John and Carol Barnes, respectively a car mechanic and an assistant at a local bakery, and residents of a small terraced house on a hilly street with no trees in a town called Ibstock in Leicestershire. One day when Tom was five, he was playing with matchbox cars in the living room of his house while his mother sporadically watched a soap opera while ironing the family's clothes.

'Mum, can I try?' He had grown bored of the metal cars.

'No lad, the iron is hot.' She didn't look at him.

'I don't see it being hot.'

'You ain't gonna see the heat, are ye? I'm telling you, the iron is hot.'

'It's not hot.'

Carol put down the iron on its base, sighed and started folding the shorts she'd just finished.

'Mummy, I'm hungry.'

Carol ignored the boy and put the shorts on top of a neat pile, placing it in the basket on the armchair. She fished a large sheet from the other basket on the kitchen counter, shook it out, and arranged a crumpled edge on the ironing board. She had big wrists and flat hands, Carol, working hands.

'Mummy!' Tom, frustrated, pulled at the section of the sheet that was overflowing the board. The iron crashed down with its hot side on the cream-coloured carpet.

'Tom, bloody hell!' Carol bent down to lift the iron. It had singed a nice patch of the polyester carpet hairs. She put the iron back on its base. 'See what ye done? Do you know how much money it'll cost to fix that? First the boiler, now this…' Her voice rose. 'There goes our holiday.' She picked up the scissors to cut the burnt threads. 'How many times do I have to tell you: The iron is hot!'

'It's not hot.' Tom, blinking away tears, went back on the attack. He'd been that kind of child.

Carol wiped her brow with the back of her hand. The room smelled of Fairy detergent and freshly laundered clothes. 'Aw right, touch it then.' She took the hot iron off its base and set it on top of the ironing board.

Tom hesitated. Somewhere deep down, he knew the iron was hot and that he must not touch it.

'Go on, open your hand. You say the iron's not hot. Come touch it.'

He tried to read his mother but he was only five.

'Come on! What are you waiting for?'

Tom swallowed hard and he opened his right hand and he stuck his palm on the metal plate of the iron.

He screamed for a long time, hot tears blurring his vision. The little boy looked at his mother as if for the first time.

'See? Now ye know. An iron is hot.'

Tom became a quiet boy after that. Which suited Carol just fine. She had dropped out of school when she fell pregnant, but recently she had signed up to finish an equivalent of her GCSEs. She had no intention of remaining poor. And the way out of that did not include a demanding child. She eventually managed to get a diploma in healthcare management and commenced an excellent career at the local NHS trust, rising to the level of manager for a mid-size hospice in Leicester.

Although Tom was not close to his mother, he picked up his ambition and work ethic from her. His father spent most of his time at work, in the union offices, or at the pub, but still Tom got from him his charm and a twentieth century white man's optimism that he'd always land on his feet. Tom became the first of his family to go to university. He chose London. His parents feared and disliked the capital and rarely came to visit him. Tom blossomed at University College. A world beyond the shores of Britain and its class problems was opening up to him and at once he understood the possibilities.

Tom shed his local accent in favour of more neutral vowels. People could never tell when meeting Tom where he came from. Sometimes they weren't even sure he was British; he'd been confused for an Australian or a South African. He only dated foreign girls and explained to them that he was an only child from a small house at the edge of a small town in the heart of England. If pressed, he mentioned what his parents did professionally and stopped again. When he graduated, he joined the analyst pool at one of the New York investment banks setting up shop around St Paul's Cathedral. He worked the slavery hours, seven days a week, with all-nighters every so often. It suited him fine.

Tom had been shipped to New York to help the healthcare team when he saw Naomi waiting in line at the coffee shop. She was a beauty, dark and smooth, but the clincher was when she stayed at the counter, waiting for him. What others called chemistry, Tom called recognition. He recognised Naomi in the way she stood, the way she talked to him. A girl on the make, just like him. Together they would run from poverty, shame, and the parents who didn't protect them. Tom stirred in his sleep. I put my finger to my lips and touched it to his forehead. I knew him but I could only use that verb in the past tense. I didn't know him anymore.

Outside my window was a large London plane tree. Sunlight illuminated its branches and its flat green leaves against the blue sky. I never paid any attention to history because I didn't like the role it had for my ancestors. What my maternal grand-parents called the "unreliable" lineage, the African blood I always felt I needed to atone for, to compensate for, I now knew was the source of my strength. Abuela Edith was smiling down at me from her place of peace. No Tom your love is not what ever made me.

Goodbye.

# CHAPTER FOURTEEN

## 23 June 2016

It was raining when I went to vote by myself. I scratched my X with a vengeance on the Remain box. Reggie Danton had been on TV and in the papers almost every day for the past two weeks. And if it wasn't him, it was one of his cronies. Just last night, there was David Miller on *Newsnight* in his best Harvard voice, extolling the trade advantages Brexit would bring to the nation. Even as I was packing the children's bags last week, Tom had the nerve to ask me to vote the way Reginald Danton wanted.

'And you then? What do you want?' I shouted back at him.

He wanted to keep the house. He never once offered to move out himself.

'Where I come from, men leave. They do it all the time but *they* leave. Not me, not the children.'

'It is your decision to separate, not mine. Why should I be out in the cold? If you want to go, go.' He had that stubborn look he must have had when he opposed his mother. A wound wrapped up in pride. He also calculated it would be too much upheaval for me to leave with the boys.

I said nothing more and continued packing.

'Where are you going to go?'

I stopped. I was waiting for that one. I had two choices: I could play his game and put my arm to my forehead and cry I didn't know, who cared? Which would give him the opening to make me feel guilty about uprooting our poor, innocent children for my own capricious reasons. Or... 'Claridge's,' I said.

'The hotel?'

'Djes.'

'Are you mad? You can't expect me to pay for you and the boys to live in one of the most expensive hotels in London?'

Gotcha. I took my time to fold a jumper neatly and put it in my suitcase. 'I'm finally accepting what you do have to offer as opposed to moaning for what is not on offer.' Prove me wrong, I silently implored him. I searched his face, his eyes.

Half an hour later I put on my sandals and asked the boys to get ready. Tom helped Sam with his socks and trainers. I watched him help his children leave him. Fool. No, there was nothing left to say.

'What about Daddy?' Sam asked. We were on our way to Brook Street. Tommy gazed out the car window, old enough to sense that something was wrong. I didn't know yet what to tell them except that I loved them. Of course, I'd always loved them but from now on, I would love them in a thoughtful way. A love that would be of use to them.

We stood like pawns in the middle of a shiny floor that

looked like a giant chessboard. Business people rushed diagonally across the white and black tiles; porters in uniform carried suitcases in and out. A stately woman in leather trousers, impossible heels and dark sunglasses shoved into Tommy with her stiff shopping bags. He stumbled backwards. She mumbled a 'sorry' to no one in particular and went on. Two elderly ladies, sisters perhaps, emerged from the breakfast room, one holding an open map of London, the other trying to put her reading glasses on while walking. We were out of time and out of place. Two suitcases, a mother, and two boys standing alone in the atrium of a glamorous hotel. If this were a scene in a movie, I'd be wearing a cloche hat. How did I allow myself to fall off the edge of my own century, I thought with shame. I pulled on the boys hands to get out of this place when Tommy resisted.

'Mama, look, it's the midfielder from Chelsea!' he tried to whisper. Sam was grinning from ear to ear. The footballer looked sleek in a shiny linen suit and sculpted hair, and had some eye candy with a perked up butt in skinny jeans at his arm. They left a trail of perfume behind them before disappearing through the revolving doors.

'Let's go check in.' I gave my passport and credit card at the desk and took a look at the prices.

We only stayed at Claridge's for one night. I couldn't do it, not even to spite Tom. Besides, the £500-per-night room was small and it was boring. And it was so meaningless without Tom. We were sitting at breakfast under the dome of the atrium when I became so sad I couldn't swallow anything, not even coffee.

'Yes, it's depressing being self-indulgent. It makes you paranoid,' Solange explained on the phone. She offered for us to stay with her and Baz instead until we sorted ourselves out. I checked out and went straight to her house after the school run. I didn't tell Tom.

That evening, we sat down to a dinner of rice cooked with lentils, lamb chops that she grilled on her BBQ in the garden with a spatula in one hand and an umbrella in the other (it was raining), and a tomato and avocado salad. We played cards with the boys. We stayed up late talking. I felt better than I had in weeks.

'Thank you so much for having us.'

'Can I ask you something? Lily once said to me that there was something wrong with the marriage contract. At the time, I had no idea what she was talking about. But now I wonder… Would you have invited us to stay with you if Andreas was still around?'

'Of course!' Then she frowned. 'But you see where my way of living took us.' She laughed. It was the first time I heard her laugh, her deep, intact laugh, since Andreas left.

It was so good to hear her laugh, I started laughing too.

We sent the kids to bed. I opened another bottle of red wine and we took our glasses to the sofa in the living room. Solange had changed from her work clothes—by then she'd told her boss that her sperm donor decided to procreate elsewhere and that she didn't need the leave of absence anymore—into her pyjamas and sat with her legs folded beneath her. I tried to make myself comfortable.

'Come,' she indicated her thigh.

I hesitated. I laid my head on her lap. She put her hand on my hair. It felt good. She smelled ripe, a woman's smell.

'Hi.'

'Hi.'

'It's a dangerous time.'

'Yes.' I felt the tightening. But Solange was like me, she even kind of smelled like me. I turned my face into her thigh. She kept her hand on my hair. We were both soft and tipsy and wanting.

I thought of something. 'Would you mind if I used pieces of our book for a new one?'

For a moment she just blinked at me. And then she shouted. 'You are crazy!'

I got on my knees on the couch. 'Listen to this: A story that begins with the end of the dream.'

She finished her glass. 'You mean the dream as we understood it?' She looked around herself at all the things that surrounded us. 'Yes…'

'Maybe we didn't have a choice, coming from where we came from. Maybe we had to…'

'Dream like that first and then…' Solange sniffed. 'I should never have introduced your husband to Danton.'

'If it hadn't been you, it would have been someone else.' I remembered what Harriet had said to me earlier that day. 'He was heading there, we both were.'

On a whim I had knocked on my old neighbour's door

after casting my ballot, hankering after happier times.

'Naomi! What a surprise, come in, come in but I must take Ian to his appointment at ten. You should have told me you were coming.' Harriet put the kettle on and took the milk out of the fridge.

I told her I had just voted Remain in the referendum.

'We went at seven this morning, before it got too busy.'

I waited to see if she'd tell me what they voted for. When she said nothing, I told her my big news. 'Tom and I are separated. I'm looking for a place to live with the boys.'

Her hand shook and she spilt some milk next to her cup. 'Oh!'

'Harriet! Can you come here for a moment?' It was Ian. He was calling from the other side of the flat.

She gave me a cup, 'No milk just sugar,' proud that she remembered. I sat on the single stool to wait for her and looked out at their pretty garden. After a moment I went to open the kitchen door to look across into our old garden. The rain had stopped but the sky was still grey. The fence had been rebuilt with wooden slats painted a fresh white that blocked the view and provided a new privacy, but there was still a gap in between some of the slats.

In the two years since we moved out, the wasteland that had been our backyard had been transformed. It looked beautiful. Half the garden had been laid with flat, wide stones and it looked much bigger than when we were there—there was even space now for a large wooden table and eight chairs. The other half had been thoroughly landscaped and looked lush and rich and colourful with bushes of blooming rhododen-drons, red or white, but all of them irresistibly round.

'Naomi?' Harriet was standing at the door.

I went back inside. 'Did you see what they've done in our old yard? It's incredible!'

'I know. A young couple bought the house last year. Can you believe? They did it all themselves. Even the paving. They got the stones delivered and then they carried them to the garden, one by one.'

I could just imagine them, lifting each stone together, at the count of three, running through the house, through the kitchen and out the back door, laying them in the freshly dug earth. She with the shovel, he with the rake. Creating a home with their own bare hands. 'I didn't have the vision.'

'Neither did Tom.' Harriet rinsed my cup in the sink.

'Oh, Harriet.' I wanted to cry. 'We were good when we lived here but I can't say I wish we were here again. That's what's killing me. Because we were good, the family was happy. Why do I not want to go back to more innocent, better times?'

She came close to me. She wasn't shocked or surprised. 'Don't worry love. I wouldn't want to go back either if I were you.' She took my hand, 'Ian always says, you can only go one way in life and that's forward. Be proud. Look how far you've come.'

'Tom made money. I accomplished nothing.'

'You did what a woman does. You turned that money into life. Where do you think he'd be without you? Alone in a hotel room with a bank account.' She raised her eyebrows significantly.

The sound of Solange pouring wine into my glass brought me back to the present.

'The end of the dream is bitter,' she announced. 'It's death. That's what Andreas left me with. It's been a month since he left me and I still don't understand. Why would you destroy your family with your own two hands when God is so ready to do it for you? It's tempting fate, it's like saying, I shit on my good fortune. Look how easily I can throw a family away! *Caca!*' Tears rolled down her cheeks. 'Something really terrible will happen, just to teach us a lesson. You'll see, I'll get cancer or Baz will, or…' She crossed herself and clenched her hands together, 'God have mercy! It's not us. It's him. Andreas the white European man who cannot appreciate that I am Your creature too, who instead thirsts for my tears, who thinks Your grace towards him is endless, who thinks he can make a better family than the one he had.' Her shoulders heaved as she gave in to the sobs.

I ran to get the laptop. It was my intuition, I couldn't explain it, but I felt the solution, not just for me but for Solange, lay in our work together. I opened our book and scrolled to the last chapter. 'Read out loud so I can hear you!'

She was crying too much. I left the laptop on the couch and I hugged her. She collapsed in my arms. We sat back down. She looked unconvinced but she blew her nose and began reading just at the point after she had been sent back to the slum from her uncle's house, having woken the whole household with her screams of terror the night her father's brother decided to climb into her bed. In the morning, her aunt packed her things in a duffel bag and drove Solange herself back to ruelle Nazon.

*Back at my mother's, the struggle to survive was in full force. After my spell in a privileged house, I became even more aware of the scandalous misery we inhabited. Nothing had changed, down to the menu. The whole family still lived in one room with one mattress that we leaned on the wall during the day and threw down on the ground at night. The same latrine was outside in the courtyard. We still had no running water. Every morning at dawn, my mother and I would go with two buckets each and fill them up at a hotel nearby where they allowed poor people to use their hose after they had finished watering their lawn.*

*The day after my return, Maman registered me at the best private school that I could access by foot from our home. By then, I had learned to speak and read French and I had lost the accent of the poor, of the uneducated. I could pass. We had no idea how we would afford the fees. I was sent home every three months or so for non-payment. Maman always sent me back with a message saying that the fees would be paid, but that I couldn't afford to miss any school. After two weeks of such messages, I'd be sent home again. And then Maman would manage to borrow money some-where and I'd be back at school. With her headscarf and factory worker clothes, my mother never went to the school in person. She didn't want to embarrass me in front of my middle-class class-mates. She managed somehow to mend and clean my uniform so*

*I always looked neat and proper, except for the giant holes in the soles of my shoes. So I learned to sit with my feet on the ground, never crossing my legs. Nobody, absolutely no one at school knew how poor I was. It was my great secret.*

*Maman's illness had just taken hold when I graduated. I immediately got a job in a photo lab to take and develop pictures. I moved into a flat with a girlfriend from school who was taking IT lessons. Finally, I was able to help my mother.*

*The owner of the photo lab, a man in his forties who liked to wear polo shirts tucked into his jeans, would hang around with me at the end of the day as I finished sorting and labelling different orders. He was funny and he'd tell me jokes and stories. I was only eighteen but I was attracted to older men who could offer protection, security. I laughed with him. One day, he asked me out after work. We went to a nice restaurant not far from the photo lab, overlooking a roundabout and appropriately called 'Le Rond-Point'. He told me he loved me and asked me to be his 'femme'. Which can mean woman or wife. I asked him to clarify. He admitted that he was already married, with two children, but that he would live with me as often as he could in the flat he was going to rent for us. I said no. I had suffered enough. Maman would be the last mistress in this family. I told him the truth about my background.*

*To my surprise, he did not fire me. Instead he became my friend. His name was Arnold. He helped me pay for my mother's hospital bills. There was nothing to be done: Life had been too hard on her for too long and she passed away. I was overwhelmed with grief. I hated my father, his family, Port-au-Prince, this Haiti that had denied my mother any peace. A poor woman whose crime had been to fall in love with an upper-class man.*

*Oh, how I hated them all. My brother by then was a petty criminal, in and out of jail. My little sister gradually became insane. She sang to herself while picking leaves and twigs and storing them in her pockets. She was arrested one day. She had forgotten to get dressed and wandered outside naked. I sent her to live in Bainet, in the country with one of Maman's relatives. I couldn't bear to go to my mother's church. I hated the priest with his stupid message of endless, toothless love. Turn the other cheek, turn the other cheek.*

Making a face as if she still had those feelings all these years later, Solange stopped reading and turned to me slowly.

'That's when I discovered the Red Sects and Erzulie Red Eyes.'

For a split second, I was sure her eyes turned bloody red too.

She blinked and when she re-opened her lids, it was all back to normal. I had to rub my own eyes. We were all going mad.

There was wine on the floor like a puddle of blood.

# CHAPTER FIFTEEN

## 24 June 2016

The first I heard was in my sleep. A muffled and omni-present voice like that of the tube conductor asking a crowded carriage to mind the closing doors. Sam was snoring lightly next to me, his little body warming the bed. I lifted myself on my elbows. The radio was on in the kitchen down-stairs. The news. The results of the referendum. I jumped out of bed, anxious to hear about the defeat of Brexit. I pulled the duvet over Sam, up to his chin. He didn't need to wake up for another hour.

I found Solange in the kitchen in her bathrobe. Her beloved Italian mocha cafetière with its half-melted plastic handle was on the stove. It was whistling.

'What happened?' I had left my phone somewhere on the kitchen counter.

'Mama, I can't find my boot bag!' Tommy called from Baz's room.

'Shh!' Solange turned up the volume. It was the *Today* programme on Radio 4.

For a second we froze. Solange put her hand on her

mouth. 'Oh!'

'You fucking voted Leave, didn't you?'

'I just wanted them to kick Andreas out. How would I know?'

'I can't believe this.' I'd poured too much coffee in my cup and it overflowed. I went to look for paper towels to wipe my mess. I was a mess; the world was a mess. I thought of Tom. They'd be celebrating today at Newspring. I felt more power-less than ever before. 'I feel like moving out of here.'

'Nonsense! We love having you here, don't we, Baz?' The boys had just entered the kitchen, their eyes widening at our raised voices.

Baz nodded vigorously. Tommy did too.

'I mean, out of England.'

Solange swallowed. 'Are you looking forward to the party, boys?' It was two weeks before they were due to leave St Francis and Solange had offered to host an early farewell party, as much for the parents as for the boys.

'Can't wait,' Tommy said hesitantly, as Sam came in wearing his best dinosaur pyjamas. 'Is Daddy still picking us up afterwards, Mama?'

'That's the arrangement,' I replied through clenched teeth.

'Yay!' said Sam, but Tommy's head dropped. Baz turned away.

'Oh, look at the time! Let's go everybody, otherwise we'll be late for school.'

'I'll catch a ride to the tube with you if that's okay.'

Solange couldn't find her keys. She started shuffling the pot of coffee, the boxes of cereal, the dirty bowls and when she still couldn't find them, she opened a drawer in an old chest I swear I had not noticed before. 'Ouf!' She dangled them. I frowned.

We all piled into the Range Rover and I had just started the engine when Solange pointed at the fading *Vote In* poster on the inside of her front bay window. 'We can't leave the house like that!' she cried. She made me stop, ran out of the car and back into the house. We saw a hand ripping off the poster from the inside. She then came back into the car. The window was bare save for three white streaks from the tape. I started towards St Francis. The streets were quiet.

'The last thing we need is for some hooligan to come break the window.'

'Solange, you make no sense.'

'Why not?'

I just shook my head and focused on the road.

'Mama, are they going to kick you out of the country?'

'Oh, I don't want to be kicked out!' Sam was on the verge of tears.

'No, no, nobody is getting kicked out.' Solange turned to the children sitting in the back. 'Your mum and I both have British passports. I guess that's the advantage of not being European. We couldn't sit on the fence; we had to take the plunge.'

'You didn't need to rip off that poster.'

Solange raised her head to me. 'Naomi, Tom's not here.

You don't have to be more English than the English. People here have been lulled into a false sense of security but you know better than that. When the wind turns the way it just has in this country, you don't know what people will do. We have to be careful.'

I knew she was right, but I resented it all the same. I didn't want to think of myself and the boys as weakened in any way. We stopped at St Francis. The radio was a barrage of shocked commentators and triumphant Brexiteers. Danton would be on air any minute now. I switched it off.

Without the kids and the radio, the car suddenly became very quiet. I turned around to go drop off Solange. A couple was standing at a zebra crossing. I stopped. They moved as one, their arms laced together, their tennis shoes smeared with the same dirt. Young, poor, and happy. I didn't wait for them to reach the other pavement before I accelerated. It broke them apart: they had to jump. The man turned around and gave us a questioning look. He was right. Why would I do that?

'Why did you do that?' Solange was still looking at them.

My phone rang. It automatically switched to the car speaker system. It was my mother. *'Hola, Naomi. Como esta Tom?'*

'Mama, I told you before you have to stop asking after the man before you ask after me. It's bad for my self-esteem.'

Solange pulled a face at me, mouthing, 'Doesn't she know?'

'I want to speak to the boys,' Marina's voice boomed in

the car.

'I'm afraid you missed them, we just dropped them at school. We'll call you this afternoon.'

'I tried your house but no one answered. How is your friend, *la Haitiana abandonada*? Poor thing. I keep thinking about what that husband did to her. How is she going to raise a boy on her—'

'Mama, stop!'

'It's all over for h—'

'Mama, enough. I too am alone! I left Tom and took the boys with me. As a matter of fact, we are staying with Solange until we can find a place of our own.' This was not how I'd imagined telling her but I couldn't let her continue.

She gasped. 'Is this true?'

'Yes. Two weeks now.'

'Naomi! You must go back to him immediately! He'll forgive you if you go back and apologise. Everyone is allowed a moment of insanity, especially in a long marriage, but you must go back now.'

I looked at Solange, my eyebrows raised, but she was lost in her own thoughts. I pulled up across from the Tube station. She stepped out, gave me an absent wave and she was gone.

'Naomi, are you listening to me? Should I come over?'

'Mama, I love you but I have to go now.' I hung up. If I had a daughter I know what I would do. I'd take a machete and clear the jungle of confusing messages and contradictory expectations for her. That way it wouldn't take her over forty years to see clearly. To understand. But I don't have a daughter.

When I felt strong enough, I started the car and I went to buy an enormous cake, some drinks, and the rest of what we needed for the party this afternoon. Back at Solange's, one of the light bulbs in the kitchen had blown. I rummaged through her drawers to see if I could find a replacement. I found a bayonet capped one but I needed a screw top bulb, so the hunt continued. I remembered that old chest at the edge of the kitchen. How did I never notice it before? There it was across from the table. I pulled out one drawer after another. They were all empty except the bottom one. It contained a document. I took it out.

Twenty pages, maybe, stapled together. A pencil drawing decorated the front: A perfect tree with a thick trunk, reminiscent of the oak in front of Reginald Danton's house. And, in a lighter shade, there were horrible things: sharp, pointed triangles and shards and metal hooks and branches flying around with broad strokes to indicate wind and rain. It was a vision of hell and in the middle of it, there was a thin woman hugging the tree. Her arms were too short to encircle the trunk. She had a white scarf tied around her head. Her face was all lines: some horizontal like her eyes and her mouth; others went straight down like her nose, her cheeks, the split in her forehead in between her eyes. Three children with arms too short to encircle her waist were clinging on to her as best as they could.

Hurricane Allen.

I picked up the document and opened the first page.

I was excited to see Solange's writing, to see how close her description of that night would come to what I had put on the page. It was typewritten, in a font I wasn't familiar with.

*There was once a young girl with a name and a family. She'd been sitting on a low chair, peeling beans into a basket with her older sister. They must have been watching her. When the sister moved away, maybe to get something from a neighbour, maybe to go the bathroom, they crossed into the yard and grabbed the girl. They put a jute sack over her head and carried her away quick, over one of their shoulders.*

*The next morning at dawn, the girl was tied to other people like her with a rope. Some were little like her but most of them were older. Some as old as her papa. They were all naked but they put a blindfold on her and she couldn't see anything anymore. They started to walk. They walked like this for two weeks, all the way to the sea. Of course she didn't know it was the sea, she couldn't recognise the bite of the salt in the air, the call of the birds, the wind. She blinked many times when they took her blindfold off, she saw the ocean and they locked her in a fort, a metal ring around her ankle and shackled to a hook in the wall. She was given a bowl of food twice a day and watched new prisoners come in with the sunlight. Every day there were new prisoners and the stench got worse. Many of the prisoners didn't speak her language but one did and he told her that they were being fed because they had been sold to European cannibals who were fattening them up like pigs ahead of their feast.*

*One day they unshackled her and walked her out of the fort, and when she saw the white men waiting outside, she fainted. She was carried onto the ship and shackled again on one of the lower decks. Three hundred people were packed on that deck and the ceiling was too low for even the girl to stand. She had to lie on the floor with her head in-between a man's legs. She was lucky. The man was a priest and tried to keep his urine and faeces as far away from her head as possible. The girl next to her was not so lucky. She kept coughing and choking and one day her body was thrown overboard. The priest explained to the girl that many would die on this passage but not them. His name was Legba and he was from the same country as her. He knew history and told her about the great kingdom of Benin and of the gods that would never abandon them, were in the process of crossing this ocean with them even as he spoke.*

*In Saint-Domingue, she squinted in the brutal sunlight. They threw water at her and brushed her teeth. She was put up for sale at the slave market in Croix-des-Bossales by the harbour of Port-au-Prince. Legba was there too. A Frenchman bought them both. She smiled with relief as she sat next to her friend at the back of the cart.*

*At the plantation, she was taken into the house, given the name of Marinette and dressed like a European. She looked ridiculous. The master had a crippled daughter of the same age and Marinette was to be this girl's slave. Legba, the great priest and healer was sent with the other bossales out to the sugar cane fields. At least he kept his name. They didn't bother naming bossales who worked outside the house.*

*Legba and Marinette met on Sundays after church when the slaves had their weekly break, and sometimes at night when Marinette's mistress fell asleep. Legba started teaching Marinette about the plants and their powers. Marinette was smart and interested. She would make a great mambo, a voodoo priestess. One Sunday afternoon the white girl needed help to get from her bed into her wheelchair and called for Marinette. But Marinette was far away, all the way at the other end of the plantation, studying the plants that grew by the stream. It was her afternoon off after all. But the girl was frustrated and there was no one around and she called and screamed until finally the scullery slave showed up from the kitchen. She was sent to fetch Marinette, who arrived running to her mistress's side. The white girl by then was so blind with rage that she grabbed Marinette by her shirt tail, and slapped her with all she had, ripping her shirt in the process. The commotion brought the white girl's older brother to the room and he froze when he saw Marinette half-naked, her breast exposed.*

*Later that night, when Marinette was walking back to the slave quarters, she heard heavy soles crunching leaves behind her. Her heart stopped. She knew what the sound of boots in the dark meant. She ran. The boots caught up easily with her bare feet. It was the brother. He dragged her by her armpits to the stables and there he raped her. Marinette bit her fist in order not to scream. Just when she thought it was over, he decided to fuck her again. She cracked. She shook and* screamed like a wild animal. The young man got scared and ran away, his pants hanging at his ankles. Marinette was whipped for creating a nuisance and then left for the night tied to a tree, naked.

Marinette was a good student and the next time the brother came for her, she was ready. She first protected her skin with ash. She then put a mixture of crushed ivy and red bonnet peppers over her thighs and breasts. He was drunk and he raped her many times but this time she did not fight or scream. She waited. The itching started. He couldn't stop. It was his turn to howl like an animal. The soft skin on his inner thigh broke. He was bleeding. Marinette started laughing. His penis became infected. They had to fetch the doctor in the middle of the night. Marinette took advantage of the turmoil in the family to run away.

Marinette found refuge in a small cave near a beach, close to Marigot. She calmed down and enjoyed listening to the sea while looking for seaweed and sea urchins to eat. One day she realised she was pregnant. She ripped her clothes to shreds and then she tried to rip the foetus out of her with a twig. She couldn't do it. She had no choice but to wait. So she waited and she grew. Finally she gave birth to a little boy that she wrapped in rags. When the baby was seven days old, she had a dream. In it, Legba her friend and teacher came to her. He had been skinned alive and they poured kerosene on his exposed tissue and set him on fire. No matter, he told her, he never betrayed her hiding place to the white masters. Is that the baby of the white man? he asked, pointing at her *newborn. She said yes. Give me the baby of the white man! She picked up the baby and handed him to Legba. He first chopped off the baby's head and then he cut the baby up like a goat. He cooked his limbs over a fire and they both ate it.*

*Marinette woke up from her dream but the baby had disappeared. She looked everywhere, inside the cave, behind the almond tree, she couldn't find the baby anywhere. An eagle came and rested on top of her head. And then the white men came. They had found her. They tied her to a tree trunk and they doused her in kerosene. They set her on fire. The bird never left her head. Marinette's legs shrivelled and her arms melted in the flames. The ropes were not holding any-thing anymore and fell to the ground. The bird took off with Marinette's head and trunk. As she flew above the heads of her executioners, she cursed them. They all died before dawn the next day.*

*Now she is known as a devil called Marinet Pié Chèch, which means Marinette of the shrivelled feet. She had only known evil in her life and so she only has evil to offer in return. She is very powerful and her followers have superhu-man strength and can drink kerosene.*

I dropped the document back in the drawer and shoved it shut, wiping my hands on my shirt as if the words had burnt them. I tried to tell myself it was just a story, it didn't mean anything, but I packed our things all the same.

It took me a moment to greet Solange when she came back from work.

# CHAPTER SIXTEEN

'Gotcha!' Baz and Tommy bent over in laughter as they soaked their classmates with water pistols. The children on their team cheered. I cheered and clapped my hands too, but I was watching Solange. I wanted to ask her about Marinette's story. I had never taken seriously her brushes with 'red sects' of Haitian Voodoo. I thought it was her bruised ego talking, her frustrations.

The whole time we were writing the book she never even hinted at this... this text. Solange managed not only to leave Haiti, she somehow got a university degree in Chicago, married a Dutchman and ended up on the management team of one of the oldest property developers in England. This is something that normally takes two generations. The first leaves the island and the second maybe gets to realize their potential. Solange does it all before the age of fifty. She must have made a deal somewhere, somehow. How could I have been so naïve to believe that sheer pluck and determination could get a poor black woman with a third-world passport so far?

'Naomi, I'm so embarrassed about the results of this

referendum. I want you to know, this is not the England I believe in.'

I blinked. 'What?'

'No, no. I want to make this clear to all my foreign friends.' Lily's eyes were scanning the room, and came to rest on Antheia. She moved towards her to say the same thing.

Three boys careened past us, splashing each other with water from the bucket reserved for the water pistols and laughing and screaming interchangeably.

'Am I right in thinking you are staying here now?' Ines asked me in Spanish.

'You are,' I looked into her blue eyes. 'It's been good. For all of us.'

'You know that divorce is contagious? It's been proven.' She seemed worried.

'It's not divorce that's contagious.' I liked Ines but I no longer believed in her world. 'It's hope.'

'*Soak me up in a tampon, but keep the lamp on...*' Tommy and Baz were giggling next to the sound system.

'Ines excuse me for a moment.' I ran to the boys. 'Stop it! Give me that!' I seized Tommy's phone. Yes, he had hijacked the Bluetooth and put on this rapper Tyler, The Creator, who to be honest had a lyrical bent, but was so inappropriate for a kids' party. I could already see the rising eyebrows of the mothers around me. I pressed on the phone. Wrong button, it wouldn't stop.

'*Bitch I ate one roach and I made a lot of mon—*'

I slapped Tommy on the back of the head. 'Play

something appropriate. Please.'

'Naomi? There's someone here who wants to see you.'

'Naomi is there any more ice?'

'I envy my parents. I'm sick of London and the selfish, ambitious, user inhuman people who infect this city!' Antheia was shouting at Lily. 'I have tried, I have really tried for years to find meaning, belonging, happiness in this city but look,' she pointed at Solange, 'the people I relate to, they end up screwed.'

'Maybe it's time for you to move back to Greece,' Lily said with concern.

*'The wheels on the bus go round and round…'*

'Funny, Tommy!' I pointed at my eyes with my fingers and then pointed at him. I started towards the hall. Solange was standing in the doorway talking with someone. Tom probably. I braced myself.

But no. Of all people, it was Carol Barnes, my mother-in-law. She was standing at the door, holding a bulky designer handbag in front of her with both hands. I was so surprised, I didn't react right away. Solange invited her in.

'Yes please do come in.' I quickly followed.

Tommy saw her first. 'Granny!' He ran to her. Sam, who'd been holding Baz's pet rabbit, gave it back in order to go hug Carol too. I offered her something to drink but all she wanted was water. She sat on the edge of her seat, with that bag at her feet and held in her puffy hands the smaller, tighter hands of my boys.

*'The horn on the bus goes beep, beep beep…'*

I had not been prepared to meet John and Carol Barnes. It sounds stupid, but nobody had told me that poor English people existed. I had certainly never come across one in Colombia or in America. Even on television or in the books we read, the English were generals or villains or spies or romantic lords and ladies, but they were always top of the ladder. The only poor Brits wore Victorian costumes and so I concluded that's where they lived and definitely not in the twenty-first century.

In any case, I had only been in Britain for maybe two weeks when Tom drove me up to Leicestershire to a small terraced house made of brick and PVC windows. It was a windy Sunday and the low sky had no colour at all. It was raining just enough to mess up my hair. We rang the doorbell. When they opened the door, the hall was too narrow to fit us all in and so we had to queue to walk into the house. And yet Tom's parents looked good. John was tall, fit, still handsome with a good head of blond hair, blue eyes just like Tom and he was well dressed, with a shirt and corduroy slacks and a navy woollen jumper. Carol looked me in the eye, and looked sensible through and through. She would have been on a street in Cartagena and everyone would have thought she was the wife of a foreign dignitary or of an official from Bogota. Why did they live here? In my country, men who lived like this wore wife beaters and the women went out in crotch-moulding leggings and hair curlers. I asked them why had they not emigrated to Brazil or somewhere else in South America when they were young. Had they gone, say, in the sixties, they would have been living like kings now. The fact that they had European training and education, spoke English, knew about order and discipline, were white and had passports that didn't repel immigration officers obviously didn't do much for them here, but over there...

They found my way of thinking insulting and our relationship did not flourish. As the years passed, I came to realise that the very issues of the society I grew up in had made me, if not hostile, at least unsympathetic to the problems of people like Tom's parents.

'How is John?'

'Upset. As you'd expect. He didn't even vote today.' She looked at me. 'Because of you.' She shook her head.

'Did you vote?'

'Of course.' Her outrage said it all.

I sighed. 'How did you know we were here? Tom, I guess.'

'Yes. He's tied up at work now, so I'm here to pick up the boys.'

'Nan, did you bring me a present?' Sam was sitting on her lap.

Carol made him stand up. 'Your present is waiting for you at your home.' She emphasized the word *home*.

'Naomi! Cake time!' Solange called to me from the kitchen.

'Cake!' Sam shouted and they both ran off.

I stood alone with Tom's mother.

'They are good boys.' Carol's eyes followed them to the kitchen.

'Yes.'

'They don't deserve this. They deserve their father.'

'I know. But I couldn't take it anymore, Carol. It was too painful.'

She seemed surprised. 'Was my son cheating on you?'

'I don't know. I... I was dissolving.'

She shook her head. 'You and I, we never got on, did we?'

I said nothing.

She picked up her bag. It was a Mulberry made of thick leather and it had a large statement buckle. She sighed. 'He could have any woman he wants now, my son Tom. Any woman.'

'Excuse me?'

'But he's a loyal man my Tom. And he misses the boys. He told me. He's worked very hard to provide for you and the boys. He doesn't want to lose his family now.'

Again I said nothing.

'I, we would like you to come back too. I never said it before but you're a good mum Naomi. And you're a good wife.'

Through the chaotic fog of the party, a landscape started to take shape. A land already populated with many nice, respectable people. And I had a place with them, in my pretty house with my wholesome, sheltered boys. Tom would follow his destiny and become a rich man and I would do what was expected of me in terms of getting the boys into the right schools, making sure our homes—by then there'd surely be a second home somewhere—were decorated nicely, were running smoothly, that our parents were taken care of and that efforts were made to host lavish family holiday celebrations a few times a year and that I kept myself nice, in character and in appearance.

But where was Tom?

The doorbell rang and there he was. Looking as dapper and in control as ever. He'd even lost that trace of a tyre around his waist. His shirt was tucked neatly into his Italian slimline trousers. The *Evening Standard* was tucked under his arm.

'Daddy!' You'd have thought Tom was Bruno Mars from the way the boys welcomed him. They hadn't seen him in two weeks.

Baz inched close to his mother and stood there, watching. Solange rubbed his hair. Andreas obviously was not coming. As a matter of fact, he hadn't shown up again since Solange threw that hairbrush at his dulcinata's head. She took Baz by the hand away from the hall and towards the cake and called everyone over to the kitchen island. She made a brief speech about the school year about to end. She said she was grateful she had chosen St Francis for Baz. That he had found a home there, a community, and so did she. I clapped. That little prep school had provided an anchor to us all.

Solange then presented the enormous cake I had bought with a flourish. I cut the cake the way abuela Edith did, by tracing an inner circle in the heart of the cake and then cutting slices off that circle. Carol came to help and distributed slices on paper plates. Tom was still standing in the hallway with

Tommy and Sam. Carol went to bring them some cake. Then the guests started to leave. Tom's *Evening Standard* was on the floor. I overheard Inez ask Solange if she had a solicitor.

'I have a *mambo* in Haiti.'

Ines laughed but my heart jumped.

'Naomi, do you have a moment?' Tom was with his mother.

Ines was writing something on a yellow post-it. 'Here. This solicitor can draw blood from a stone…'

Solange took the post-it and looked at it. She tore it into little pieces. 'Ines, what Andreas did, no solicitor can do anything about. I want him to understand that there are mountains behind mountains and that what goes around comes around. The law is for things, not for the heart. What this man has done… No, he cannot get away with just signing some papers, like it's acceptable, like people here do. No! I know what was lost. He must know it too.' Her eyes were red again. Could the others see it too?

'Naomi!'

I shook my head and ran to Tom and his mother.

Carol said she was leaving.

'It was good to see you. Are you staying with Tom?'

'Of course.'

'I don't think the boys are ready to say goodbye to their friends.'

'They want to come home.' She shouted.

'It's ok mum, I'll take care of it.' Tom took his mother by the arm. 'Your cab is here.' He walked Carol out.

'Did you see this?' Solange picked up the paper from the floor. Underneath the obvious headline, *What Happens Next After Britain Backs Brexit*, the paper had started gathering reactions around the city to the vote. And there it was. A small line at the bottom of the front page, *Hedge Fund Cashing In on Brexit: page 3*, and an old picture of Reginald and Lucy Danton at some gala. He was wearing a black tie and she was in a turquoise gown. I turned to the page. It was only a paragraph.

*Newspring Investments, whose founder and CEO Reginald Danton has been one of the market's most prominent backers of Britain's exit from the EU, has had its most profitable day today since the fund's inception ten years ago.*

Tom came back into the house. 'Naomi, please can we talk?'

# CHAPTER SEVENTEEN

'**D**arling, I know what you're doing. It's what we all do. It's what I spend my days at work doing.'

We were sitting in Tom's Porsche outside Solange's house. There was a rectangular green felt jewellery box on the dashboard.

'You're trying to renegotiate a deal you made a long time ago.' He took the green box and handed it to me. 'Here.'

I took the box but I didn't open it. I didn't know what to say.

'Open it.' He smiled. 'What a day. Danton is a fucking genius. The whole time he was pushing for Brexit, he was taking positions against Sterling. He thought the pound would fall against the dollar if the UK voted out and... Anyway, by the end of trading today, Newspring had netted a profit of $400 million.'

'Okay.' I shrugged. To avoid hearing any more and out of some perverse curiosity about my worth to him, I opened the box. A diamond necklace. Spread over a silk cushion. I took it out carefully. I had never seen so many stones together. They sparkled in my hand. It was beautiful, not just to see but to the touch, smooth and amazingly supple. I had never seen anything like it. I wanted to bite them, they were so limpid and soft, like drops tied together and running through my fingers.

'Turn around.' Tom took the necklace and opened the clasp.

I didn't move. 'No.'

'Why?'

'I don't want to be bought with this. I'm not a prostitute.'

Tom cleared his throat. His hands dropped. He was looking hard at the necklace on his lap. 'I see.'

He had tried in the best way he knew and now he was sad, confused and I felt my heart break. I imagined Tommy and Sam when I'd have to confess that it was me, that I refused to come home. I wouldn't be able to explain to them, I...I...'I don't matter. I am trying to convince myself, I don't matter, what matters are the boys, their childhood, you, your happiness... I can't! I can't do it anymore!'

'Ok.' Tom thought for a moment. He took me by the shoulders. 'You're just scared.' He drew me in, he drew my limp body to his and he hugged me. He put a hand on my hair and let my face rest against his chest. He kissed my hair. He pulled the hair away and kissed my ear. He whispered 'I forget where you come from, I'm sorry. It must be terrifying to you, all of this.' He held up the necklace and let it slide through his fingers. The diamonds scintillated with the light. 'You're right. I'm no longer the Ibstock boy from the coffee shop. I've left that boy, that place behind. Forever.' He held my face up with his hand and looked me in the eye, 'Instead of fighting my rise, can you rise with me? Can you leave the little Latina immigrant behind? So we can fulfil our destiny together as a family? Do you have the courage?'

My lip trembled. My mind went blank, I felt completely drained. Tom smiled and hugged me again, 'my dark beauty.'

I collapsed in his arms.

# CHAPTER EIGHTEEN

## July 2016

'Fuck them all!'

The guy was holding his crotch with one hand and a glass of champagne with the other. More and more people were pouring in. What started as an office party was becoming a social event. I recognized the host of a Sunday morning talk show, a couple of Tory MPs' whose pictures were often in the Guardian, there was a blonde woman I suspected was Gwyneth Paltrow. The number of waiters and champagne bottles seemed to rise magically to match the growing crowd.

I made my way to the glass wall. It was still bright daylight. The beauty of England in June. The sun wouldn't set for another two hours. The skyline of London, I could see all the way to the Thames, to Tower Bridge, and all these new glittering high rises with names like the Walkie-Talkie. And still there were so many cranes. I let my forehead rest against the glass. If it splintered or crashed somehow, I would fall. I started writing a story this morning. It was about a bunch of baby girls, born all over the world, some in Madrid, some in Sudan, some in Brazil. What's special about them is that they're all born on the same day and they all share the same fairy godmother. She wants to do good by all her goddaughters but she is a fairy and so wants to be fair. She decides she will bestow the same blessings on each baby, black or white, rich or poor. Will her magic be enough to make a difference? I looked around myself. Asides from an Asian fellow…No, this high up the tower, nothing had changed.

'There you are.' Tom pulled me away from the view.

Someone shouted 'Hear! Hear!'

Reginald Danton was standing on a chair. Behind him, London. His eyes were still as piercing as ever but there was a new ambition to him, a new desire that was making him nervous even as he stood there, literally on top of the world. 'I can't begin to express how special these past few historic days have been for me.' The room had gone completely silent. 'It is such an honour to celebrate our victory against red tape, reckless immigration, and Brussels plutocrats here in this iconic building, a symbol of the glory of London, and our glorious future as a nation.'

Loud clapping. A few of the more roguish traders shouted a couple of 'Reggie, run for parliament!' and 'Danton PM!'

Danton grinned. He liked that. He raised his glass and his voice. 'To you!'

The party erupted. People shouted, we were suddenly surrounded by Pharell Williams' 'Happy'. I looked at all the beaming, excited faces. 'I never knew money could make people so happy.'

'You feeling so rich?'

'No,' I looked at Tom, 'but why turn a business transaction into a political stance? Why not just say, our gamble paid off, we made money, hurray?'

He sighed. 'Do you really care?'

A waitress came by with those little roast beef slices rolled up with horseradish that Danton liked so much. I took one. I chewed while I thought about what he'd said. A better question would be how much did I care. It would be as if Reginald was flying in a helicopter and I was standing on an open field, shouting the truth at him. And he had to bring the chopper lower and lower in order to hear me. And instead of running, I'd foolishly stand there, blinded by my righteousness until whoosh! One of the blades slashes through my neck and chops off my head.

'Barnes! Naomi! Jolly good you are coming to the Bahamas.' Danton hit Tom on the shoulder. 'You make sure she travels in style.' He winked at me. 'He can afford it.'

I laughed, as Danton moved away. 'What is he talking about?'

'Oh, maybe this happened during our, ahem, break. Although, I'm sure I mentioned it. Lucy's been planning this party for a long time. Reginald's fiftieth.'

'I'll make sure I rise to the occasion.'

'Ha ha,' Tom pat me on the bum and walked away.

Carol had been right. The boys needed their father. They also needed their home. To be honest, within hours of coming back to Hampstead everything was back to normal.

As if nothing had ever happened. Except that I was getting with the program. I was learning to accept the choices I had made. Tom's words in the car had not so much convinced as defeated me.

# CHAPTER NINETEEN

I couldn't focus. The stench was unbearable. I couldn't grasp what was on the page I was reading.

The question Tom had asked me so casually at Danton's party, 'Do I really care?' kept coming back to me over and over again. What did I really care about? Once upon a time the answer was clear and it had to do with me and my family's survival. Now I had to 'rise' to a new level of caring, the level of people with money and power. At least that's how I understood it and so I ordered some books on ethics and morality. I started to vaguely see the shape of a new writing project, built upon the ruins of the old one, with a rudder this time that didn't collapse when the story became complex, ambiguous. I was in the process of taking notes, but the smell was driving me mad. Agh, where was it? There had to be a dead mouse hiding somewhere in the room.

I got up and once again moved the furniture around. My desk was against the window in the library, next to the living room. I hadn't moved the books, they were so tightly packed I didn't think there'd be space there for a corpse. Meribel had combed through the room. She lifted the rug. Nothing. I'd have to call a pest control company. Maybe it was underneath the floorboards.

And I noticed it. Behind the leg of my desk. A bottle, half a litre in size, glass, its original label still attached: *Hendon Springs Water* and in a smaller, but no less posh font, *Still* underneath. A dirty rag had been stuffed down its neck. It was about a third full with a liquid that most certainly did not come out of Hendon Springs. It had weird bits floating in it. When I lifted it, the liquid shook and released a stench so violent I dropped the bottle on my desk. I couldn't bear to touch it. I was Caribbean enough to know what this was. A *maldicion*, a curse.

I ran to the kitchen and found the rubber gloves under the sink. Meribel had just made almond milk in the Vitamix and was pouring it through a muslin cloth into a bowl. 'Did you find it? Should I come to take it away?'

'It's nothing a small mouse. Don't worry, I'll do it.' I was breathless but I didn't want her to see or ever even suspect such a thing came into this house. I grabbed a clean dish-cloth and went back upstairs. Holding the cloth to my nose, I picked up the disgusting bottle and, holding it as far away from my body as possible, I ran out of the house, all the way down the street and threw it into a public bin together with the gloves and the cloth. With my heart still pounding, I walked back to the house as calmly as I could. It had to be Solange. That Marinette red sect story came back to me. Crazy bitch. But why?

I locked myself in the guest bathroom and washed my

hands and my arms all the way up to my elbow. I had neither seen nor spoken to Solange since I moved out of her house about ten days before, although I had sent her a text thanking her for her hospitality and proposing to meet up soon. Now that I thought about it, she hadn't replied. With a bottle of bleach and a sponge I scrubbed the floor, the walls, the desk. I damaged the varnish on the wood and the paint came off the walls but I didn't care.

Then I called Solange. She didn't pick up. She'd be home from work by now. I took the car keys, asked Meribel to take an Uber to pick up the boys from football practice, and drove to St John's Wood. I double parked in front of her house. I ran to her front door and started banging on it. I still had a key and I decided I'd use it if she didn't open.

She indeed refused to come to the door although I could see the lights on inside. I took out my key. What the hell, Solange? I was about to insert the key into the lock when I stopped. What was I hoping for? Solange was obviously more dangerous and unhinged than I had ever imagined. Better to give it up, give her up. Go home.

'Naomi?' Baz opened the door. He looked eagerly at me.

I ignored him and continued towards my car.

'Naomi?' He called again. I could it hear in his little voice. The fear. Someone

else who said they loved them was about to turn their back on him and his mum. I bit my lip and turned around.

'Hi Baz.'

'Can I come visit Tommy at your house?'

'Yes of course you can. You can come anytime you want.'
I took him in my arms.

'Solange!' I screamed as soon as I walked into the house,
'Solange!'

'She's in her bathroom.' Baz explained, 'I'll go get her.'
He stopped on the staircase, 'can I come today?'

'We'll talk about it with your mum.' I stayed in the foyer.
It was dark, the only light on was in the kitchen. It was hard
to believe that barely a month ago, I had felt so safe here,
so happy. I heard her coming down before I could see her. I
braced myself: The witch, her face covered in powder, her lips
bloody, her hair electrified, mad, mad woman.

She appeared. She was still wearing her work clothes, a
navy blue shirt dress and brown pumps. her hair was tied up,
her face was plain and calm. I frowned.

'Hi,' she stood on the last step.

'Hi.' I quickly continued, 'I'm sorry to show up like this
but I need to know.'

'What?' She sounded weary.

'This Erzulie "Red Eyes", that slave girl story, is it real?'

'What do you think?'

'Normally I would had said no! Absolutely not.' I looked
at her, 'I don't know.' 'Solange?' I started in a higher pitch than
I intended, 'did you put a bottle of poison in my house?'

'No.' She stepped onto the foyer and motioned to me to
follow her to the kitchen. She put the kettle on. 'In any case,
it's not poison. Trust me, I know the difference. That stuff
wouldn't harm a fly. It was only there to prevent you from

writing.' She took the teapot from the shelf and pulled out a few boxes of tea from the cupboard. 'Do you still drink green tea?'

'So you did put that stinky thing in my house!'

'No.' The kettle began to whistle. She poured the hot water into the tea pot. She took two mugs from the cupboard. 'Here. It was the *Lwa*. She doesn't want you to write about her. About her story. It's a Haitian tale.' She took a sip of her tea and shrugged, 'nothing personal.'

'Of course.' I looked at the green liquid in my cup. It was steaming. I set the cup down on the counter. 'Shit Solange we're friends! How could you do that? Look I don't even feel comfortable drinking your tea!'

'Really? Friends? Naomi I haven't heard from you since you made out with your supposedly ex in his Porsche. I was just material for you and then you used us to lure your man back.'

'Oh!' I was so surprised I didn't know what to say. 'How can you think that?'

'Quite easily. Ah, *bof* we all do what we need to do. Good for you. You've won all your battles. Let me have my Erzulie. My consolation. Have some respect for my privacy. Not all of us have been as lucky as you.'

I flinched as if she had slapped me. 'Solange, you're a director with a listed company. I don't even have a university degree. You're free, you have your career, you can stand proud.'

'You have love.'

I was about to protest, to say something stupid but thank

God I shut up. Rise to the occasion. Maybe I was finally learning. I felt a great tenderness for my friend. I took her in my arms. 'So do you *chica*. So do you.'

Very softly she started to cry. She held on to me.

'It was the hunger you see?' she pleaded in a low voice, 'my brain was formed by hunger. It developed badly like a reptilian brain, like a brain with no cortex. With gorges and ravines.' Solange dried her face with the dishtowel. 'To live here, I had to change my brain. It hurt like hell. But I did it. New maps, new connections but that book, Andreas, you, it was all too much. There was a crack and womp in my head, as if I were changing gears in a car.' She held her head with her hands as if to show me. 'I was back. And Marinette, she didn't like that you found her story. It's not for you.' She squeezed her temples. 'No, not for you.'

'I know. It's ok.' I poured her more tea.

'There's a murder.' Her eyes flashed red.

I took a deep breath. 'No there isn't.'

'Yes! In our book.'

'No, there isn't.' The only death in the book was her mother's.

'It's hidden. Like everything of value in that book, it's hidden inside a lie.'

'What are you talking about?'

Solange started pacing nervously around the kitchen. She walked to the living room and sat on the sofa. I followed her. That's when I noticed that her tights had runs and holes all over them. Even now, she was pulling at the loose threads, ruining them further. 'Arnold tried to keep me from going to the ceremonies. He evoked my mother's spirit, asking what her Catholic soul would think if she saw me mixing with the unwashed, the *san pwel*. He even offered me a promotion. He wanted me to manage the new photo shop he was opening in Pétion-Ville. He came all the way to Seguin, to the pine forest where there is no road. He pulled me away before it was my turn to drink the kerosene. He screamed that he loved me, that the love would be enough, that the love would be the power.'

'But before there can be love, there must be justice.' We both said it at the same time. That line was in the book, and now I knew where it came from.

'Arnold sponsored me to get a visa to leave the country. He paid for my studies. He became a well-known photographer, even outside of Haiti. Especially his portraits. He had these props that clients loved. There was a baby blue Vespa. He got it from a junkyard and scrubbed and polished it for days. The engine was long gone but the young men loved posing on it.

'I had learned from the red sects the secrets of the plants, how to make the different liquids. Arnold wanted to leave his wife to be with me. He loved me. He didn't love her. But she blackmailed him with his children. He was a good man, Arnold, he couldn't live without his children. He had been so good to me. She said if he left her she'd make sure his children would never speak to him again. I wanted to prevent that. Please, Naomi, this is the reptilian brain working, this is not who I am now.' She wiped her tears with the side of her arms. 'What is meant for you, even the deluge cannot take away they say.' She shuddered. 'But that one wasn't meant for him. It had been meant for her. Do you understand?'

# CHAPTER TWENTY

## July 2016

The limousine pulled up in front of a plantation-style mansion. The house, a two-story colonial-style structure with stone pillars, verandas, and balconies was built by a German industrialist in the 1920s as his private estate and he must have been a very rich man, because the location was stunning. We were at the tip of the island, on a plateau that jutted out to the sea. The afternoon was slipping into the evening.

'Look at this. Feel the breeze. Isn't it beautiful?' Tom inhaled deeply.

I nestled my face against his chest. The registration was fast, in reality it had already been arranged, they knew everything about us, when we'd be coming, when we'd be leaving... Two gorgeous young women, barefoot, in beach tunics short enough you could see the elastic of their swimsuits on their butt cheeks, ran giggling past us, holding each other by the arms.

'Pre-dinner drinks poolside at seven. The dress code is festive casual, *les pieds dans l'eau.*' The receptionist smiled suggestively. Obviously, the entire hotel—they called it a club—had been reserved for Reginald's party.

'Are all the guests here?' Tom asked.

'The ones coming from the airport, yes.' Her gaze rose above our heads towards the sea. It was turning dark. Boats. Some guests would be coming by boat.

I held on to Tom. We walked hand in hand to our room.

The room was, noblesse oblige, in that same tropical colonial slow fan blades turning style but with a Danton twist. No peeling walls, no greying mosquito nets. The dark wooden floor was polished to perfection and the glass doors had matching wooden shutters. The silent air-conditioning was at a perfect setting and by—a Danton engineered miracle—there were no mosquitoes, inside or out. The bed was large and impeccable with white calico sheets. I pulled Tom's shirt out of his trousers. I dropped my maxi dress to the floor. 'It's the only reason I boarded that plane', I said, 'to see you…rise.'

Tom smiled, he let himself be undressed by me. I started to unbuckle his belt. We fell on the bed. The sheets were cool. He pulled me up and kissed me. We rolled on the bed until he was on top of me. His shirt open, he put his hands on my hips and I arched my back towards him. His phone started to r

'Hold on,' he lifted his leg and, his boxers and trous hanging at his ankles, he hoped over to the table to che his phone. 'Hello? Yes, so?' I watched him deflate. After moment he hung up and looked at the time. 'We need hurry. Do you want to shower first?'

I rolled over on my stomach and rested my chin in my hands. 'Can I ask you something?'

He stepped out of his clothes.

'Did you see this trip as a chance for us to be together first and as a business obligation second, or vice-versa?'

'Oh darling, I'm tired and dirty and we have to be at this cocktail party in half an hour and we are together so... I'll be quick so you can take over the bathroom after, okay?' He closed the door.

The noise of the high-pressured shower filled the silence. I stood up and opened the plantation-style shutters and the glass doors. It was humid and hot outside, although the sun was gone. Our room was a small bungalow that opened onto the great lawn that stretched all the way to the edge of the land overlooking the sea. I put on one of the robes that had been left folded on the bed and stepped out barefoot. The grass was freshly cut and cool. I stretched my toes in the thick, stiff blades. The pool was at the edge of the lawn, a long, thin line of illuminated water, like light bleeding into the dark sea. Workers were putting the finishing touches on a stage and the lighting nearby. I could have been with my sons now. I could have been writing.

'Naomi! The bathroom is yours!'

I turned around. He had a towel tied around his waist. He was standing on the small deck outside the open doors. He waved at me to come back.

I walked back to the room. He was getting dressed. His fine trousers fit him well. He buttoned up his linen shirt. If this were an advertisement for something aspirational like, say, a man's cologne, it would be perfect.

I went to take my shower. We had made love only once since I came back. The first night. We had gone to Danton's celebratory party at the top of the Shard and then, high from the champagne and our brush with catastrophe, we couldn't keep our hands off each other. As soon as he opened the front door, we tumbled inside, I kicked the door shut. We started on the floor, on the stubble of the doormat. Tom ripped my tights, I helped him. I had to have him inside of me and he had to fuck me. The floor, the clothes, the exposed hallway, nothing else mattered.

When it was over, he lay on top of me, sweaty, lovely, a leg of his trousers still bunched at his ankle. I moved a bit. He lifted himself up. We picked up our things and only then worried that Meribel or one of the boys may have caught us, we ran naked upstairs to our room. We closed the door and started laughing. I fell on our bed. It surprised me, the rush. I recognised it. Love, happiness overflow, and a crazy need to… 'Oh Tom, are you in love with me? I'm so in love with you.'

He smiled, threw his arm over my chest and fell asleep.

The next morning, Tom disappeared back to work and I focused on picking up the family life from where I'd left off.

We met at the airport earlier that day for the direct flight to the Bahamas. I had barely seen him since that first night and he was so happy to have the boys back that he spent every moment he had at home with them. This trip was going to be our little honeymoon. I took my time to pack. Yes, I threw in a couple of dresses for the parties but what I really focused on were the things for us. Lingerie, bathing suits, toiletries. When I arrived at Heathrow, I found Tom at the check-in counter with the rest of the senior team at Newspring.

'Darling! You already know Adam and his wife Laura. And David and Barbara, of course.'

'Of course.' I made myself believe I belonged. That I was standing in the middle of my destiny the same way they felt they were at the heart of their own.

'Where is your son going to secondary school after all? I'm sure he's done very well.' Barbara gazed at me with intensity. She was wearing the uniform of the rich middle-aged wife on her way to the Caribbean: Designer sunglasses on top of her head, white T-shirt, jeans, expensive blazer, Hermès scarf.

'Did you know that Tommy is becoming a really good drummer? And he's the kindest boy in the world. He comes to my room every morning to kiss me hello.' None of your business, I thought with a smile.

Oscar Wilde once said that our first duty in life 'is to be as artificial as possible'. And that people are still trying to decide what the second duty is. I was rising to the level.

'Darling, say hello to Antoine and Vanessa.' Tom hesitated.

'Oh my God, so nice to see you,' I kissed them both on both cheeks. So she lasted after all. I put my arm around Tom's. 'You see?' I whispered to him. My head was throbbing but that's what happens when you're changing and you are aware of it. I wasn't going to be left behind and ruin my life and my family. Besides what is more pathetic than someone who finally makes it and then is too fucked up to own it? Three days in a super exclusive resort in the sun. No children, no responsibilities. Carol had come down from Leicester to babysit. A first. It was all good.

I put my handbag and my shoes in a tray. We got to passport control. They asked me what I did for a living.

I was about to answer 'Writer,' but I couldn't do it. Because ever since the end of Solange's book, I had written nothing. And since that book died, I had nothing to show, not a penny earned since that short story won that magazine competition and they paid me £500. I wrote 'Homemaker.'

That old poisonous fear about vanishing in the shadow of my marriage bubbled down in my gut. It occurred to me that I could have also spent the next three days locked up in some cabin somewhere with a stove, a desk, and a plug for my laptop. That's a minimum of twenty-four hours pure writing time. Probably more. I was wasting myself, my talent, my… no, not my future.

'Naomi!' Tom grabbed me by the hand; our flight had started to board. I followed him. It occurred to me that Tom couldn't care less if I succeeded as a writer or not.

'Wait, I want to buy headphones, I hate the ones they give on board.' He left me with his carry-on and ran into the shop. What did I really care about? I was reading Paul Tillich's book "The Courage to Be". He describes the three inescapable anxieties that torment mankind. We were standing in

Heathrow, a great incubator of the first: Fate and Death. I looked at the digital board with the flight information. How would they show a flight that instead of departing or landing had just disappeared? Fallen out of the sky? Would they leave that entry blank or write something vague and sinister like "Go to Arrivals Desk"? Tom came running to me holding a Dixon's Duty Free bag. Didn't I see the red flashing "Final Call" for our flight on the board? I'd been standing looking at it the whole time he was in the shop.

Back in the hotel room, I put on the dress I had brought for that evening. It was a Roland Mouret style figure hugging white cocktail dress. Tom was outside talking on the phone. I mixed hair mousse and oil in my hands and I put my fingers in the roots of my hair and shook it out. I had decided not to blow dry it and left it to dry naturally in the humid hot air. I put the lipstick in my clutch, put on the white mules I bought for that dress and left the room. Tom waved at me and, still with his headset on, started walking towards the party. The lawn was lit with spotlights along the edge of the pathways. I walked towards one of the lights. I saw or rather heard a man on top of a coconut tree. He was hacking with a machete. I recognised the thump and crack of the blade against the dry stem of the coconut. Another man, in a janitor's uniform, was standing at the foot of the tree, I imagine to prevent anyone from being hit by a falling coconut. The man on top shouted something to the man below. I recognised the sound, the intonation. They sounded like Solange. I walked over to them. 'Are you Haitian?'

The man on the ground looked at me, surprised. 'Yes, Madame. How do you know?'

'My best friend is from there.' Solange my unlucky sister: braver, smarter, more honest than I could ever be, and bearing a load twice as heavy as mine. I got the light version of the Caribbean burdens. She was like these men, invisible in the night.

'Have you known hunger?'

The man climbed back down with his machete. They both looked at me like they weren't sure if they understood my question.

I thought of asking about Erzulie Red Eyes and the sects and the pine forest with no road and the kerosene and shrivelled limbs but instead I just repeated my question: 'Have you known hunger?'

One of them looked me up and down, spat on the ground and walked away. The other man sighed. 'I apologise for my colleague, Madame. He is young. But I can see you have a good soul.' He picked up one of the coconuts on the ground. 'So I will answer your question. Yes, Madame. Every child in Haiti knows hunger at some point in their lives.' With that he turned and went towards the lights of the main building.

I headed in the opposite direction towards the shiny pool and the deck and the laughter and clinking sounds of the rich having a good time with the huge black rolling sea underneath.

'There you are!' Tom called out to me. 'Meet Suzie Fletcher, she's just flown in from London. We were all apparently on the same plane.'

'Hi! Oh my God, don't you love this? Lucy and Reggie are just so incredibly generous.' She couldn't have been older than twenty-five. Porcelain skin, loose auburn waves: Central London beauty. You could hear the fees in her voice, the perfectly rounded vowels, the studied pitch so that her voice sounded rich and sharp at the same time.

'Djes,' I agreed while noticing Tom's over-eager smile. The secret rule in the unwritten Latin Women's Guide to Staying Married is: Don't go there. It's the opposite of what insecure women brag about, the stuff of *telenovelas*. No showdowns, no scenes, no stalking or jumping at the throat of the younger woman. That's entertainment. In real Latin marriages, especially to powerful, desirable men, the wife pretends nor to see or hear any evil and patiently waits for her husband to get bored and to come back home.

I was getting ahead of myself.

'… teach year one in a prep school in Kensington. Anya Danton is one of my pupils. Lucy asked me to come down to give her a hand with Anya and help her get ready for year one.'

Of course.

'We have a four-year-old as well, Sam,' Tom gushed. 'He started this year at St Francis. It's such important work that you're doing.'

'That's a wonderful school. I love teaching Year One. They're so cute and funny!' She giggled.

'Haha!' Tom laughed.

'Hahaha!' I laughed louder.

Tom stopped and frowned at me.

I realised my hands were empty and that I urgently needed a glass in one of them. 'Drink, anyone?' I quickly disappeared towards the bar. The party was getting crowded. There was a pushy urgency to the conversations. It was a Danton party, after all. Vanessa walked by and pretended she didn't know me. The second inescapable anxiety according to Tillich is meaninglessness. The first gong of doubt rang on the inside of my head.

'Oh, Naomi!' Lucy Danton was standing before me. Her skinny shoulders were naked and I noticed she had freckles that went down her arms. 'You've lost so much weight!'

I hadn't but I guessed she was trying to be nice to me. 'You too!'

She gave me one of her condescending smiles. 'I wish. I just can't seem to stop eating these days.' Yes, I understood full well that Lucy Danton didn't 'lose weight'. Because that would imply that there was a possibility in this universe that Lucy Danton could gain weight and pigs would be flying before that would ever happen.

'Reginald must be so happy. What an amazing party you've planned for him.'

She was already looking over my head at the people behind me. She motioned to one of the party planners. I knew they were party planners because they were dressed in white, like me, but had little headphones with ear pieces and microphones. There was a call to go check the seating plan and to move towards the tables. Tom was still talking to Suzie. I started back towards them but Suzie left to go sit at the main family table. Tom waved at me from another table nearby. David and Barbara were at our table too. The stage they were still working on when we first arrived was now ready. It stood in the middle of the lawn so all the tables had a good view. An army of waiters arrived from the main house carrying red and white wine bottles. There was already water on the tables.

'Did you know about the changes in the grading for the A-levels this year? And how they're no longer counting AS results in university applications?' Barbara's lips were shiny. She'd been dipping bread in a puddle of olive oil she had poured onto her bread plate.

If you can't shake the doubt, you must find the courage to accept it without losing your convictions.

The lights changed. A shiver of excitement rippled through the tables. 'Ladies and gentlemen,' a smooth American voice came through the loudspeakers, 'Please welcome...' And then Pasha appeared on the stage.

'Holy shit,' a man exclaimed out loud, 'that's a million dollars right there!'

Pasha was a household name. We are talking the company of Sting, Bono, Jay-Z, or Madonna. His music, from being played for years and years on every pop radio station, is part of our mental furniture. He was smaller than I imagined but his voice was the one, and we all screamed when he took the microphone and invited us to sing 'Happy Birthday'. David stood up first, then Tom, then the rest of us.

Pasha only had eyes for the birthday boy. It must have been a good fee indeed. And then everybody started clapping and cheering, and someone shouted 'Speech! Speech!' They must have agreed the programme before because Danton smiled but shook his head and for a second the party went quiet. And Pasha launched into one of his classics from the nineties. And one hundred arms went up with their phones, flashing, recording, Snapchatting, WhatsApping.

'Naomi! Picture for the boys!' Tom had come to stand next to my chair and was leaning down so his head touched mine. I pushed the lobster salad to the side. Holding the phone up with the camera on us, we turned until we had Pasha clearly in the background. Tom tried to take the selfie but he didn't have that mastery of the angle and of the thumb that all people below thirty seem to have been born with. After three unsuccessful attempts, I suggested he give the phone to David. 'Please make sure Pasha is visible!'

'Yes, yes...' David took a couple of pictures and he gave the phone back to me. I checked the screen. Anxiety number two was right there on my face, I couldn't believe I had become so... transparent. I used to be better at wearing a mask. Tom, on the other hand, was still good at it. Maybe it wasn't a mask. Maybe unlike me, Tom had escaped anxiety. *See the access I have,* his eyes said instead. The expression, I recognised it, it was like Ines's husband in that family shot I had seen on their mantelpiece so long ago. How I had loved that picture. I deleted the photo. I handed the phone back to Tom.

'Where's the picture?' He started scrolling left and right

on the camera app.

A loud cheer drew our attention back to the stage. Pasha backed up as if to welcome a fellow star. Who was coming now? Beyoncé? I wouldn't have been surprised.

But the Dantons had a better idea.

There was a drum roll. There was smoke and blue lights. And out of the mist emerged... Lucy Danton. I glanced at Tom. He, too, was sitting there with big eyes. The party went quiet. Everybody was holding their breath.

She stood ramrod straight before us all with the palms of her hands together in a yogi-like pose and closed her eyes. Her blue dress shimmered in the breeze.

She opened her arms and two teenage boys ran on stage. Handsome lads, they looked about sixteen and fourteen. Their sons, I imagined. And then the music started. All three backed up and came rushing back to the forefront of the stage.

And we all watched as Lucy and the Danton boys put on a dance display. It was extraordinary. It was all driven by her—she was jumping, turning, kicking, all to the beat, and her sons followed her lead. And the whole time the only person she looked at was her husband.

I turned to look at Reginald. He had put his feet up on Lucy's empty chair next to him. Was he impressed? She must have gone through weeks of intensive training to get to this level. The spotlights followed her and settled behind her head like a halo, while she let the beat build in her, tapping her leg, raising her arms. The same man to my right who knew that Pasha's fee was a million bucks volunteered that Lucy had used Rihanna's dance coach to get her and the kids ready for this.

Reginald seemed mildly amused by this public spectacle of his family dancing for him, but if Lucy's aim was to provoke some deeper emotion, if only desire in her husband, she had failed. Before the routine was over, Reginald was no longer watching the stage. At the last glance he was chatting with Suzie, his daughter's school teacher.

The music stopped. Lucy, holding each son by the hand, exhaled and took a bow. Reginald, distracted, took a beat too long to start to clap politely and the crowd followed his lead. I let my eyes fall on the table. Poor Lucy, I didn't want to see her face.

Why did she put herself through this? Maybe just for fun, she always dreamt of being on *Britain's Got Talent* and this was her chance. Maybe she couldn't care less if Reggie or anyone else watched her or not. Maybe she was sweaty happy and proud to have completed a personal challenge. Yeah, right. The reason I didn't want to see Lucy's face was because I hated this way of life. It was still true for so many of us. And when I did catch a glimpse of Lucy, in spite of the flush of the workout, of the adrenalin rush of having performed on stage after one of the greatest pop artists of our generation, of the make-up and shiny hair and perfect body, there was nothing there but sorrow. Why did she put herself through this? For him. To make him desire her again. To show her competition that she was still a force to be reckoned with. To convince herself she was still young, that she still had 'it' after four (okay, three) pregnancies and forty-plus years on this earth? Her sense of self-worth, her value as a human being was attached to him. She was nothing without him. What she did was nothing if not through him. It takes one to know one.

I stood up. I looked around at the seated guests, Reginald first among them with his lame 'proper' applause. 'Go Lucy!' I shouted and I punched the air with my fists and gave her a standing ovation. At first I was alone and I got embarrassed looks. Tom mouthed to me to 'sit back down'. But then a woman I didn't know on another table stood up and joined me in cheering Lucy. And then another, and then a man got up as well. I went on with my arm high above my head, clapping and shouting, 'Go Lucy! Bravo Lucy!'

Reginald stood up. 'What a performance!' he proclaimed. He took control of the party and asked for a new round of applause. Now everybody stood up. My arms were getting tired and I let them down. I expected Lucy to be grateful to her husband for finally acknowledging her efforts. To my surprise she wasn't looking at him. She was smiling at me.

'That was a bit over the top, don't you think?' Tom whispered to me. 'I wouldn't like you and the boys to make a public display of yourselves like that.' Now Lucy had left the stage, a big band was playing Sinatra songs. The tables in front had been cleared away to make room for dancing. Tom had his hand on the small of my back. We were dancing like old people to 'Come Fly with Me'.

'It looked like fun.' I wished they'd play something more Latin. This was too boring. 'Should we go to bed?' I leaned in to him.

'Yes, let's.' He led me off the dance floor and we started towards our room. 'Good night darlings!' someone shouted. It was Lucy. She was standing by the pool. I waved at her.

'Your new best friend.' Tom did not sound happy. 'Why did you stand up for her? It's not like she's ever been that nice or friendly to you.'

'No. But I could relate and she was in an awful situation. She took a big gamble, going out there and Reginald took it completely for granted.'

He didn't say anything. 'Do you have some paracetamol? I drank too much.'

We walked into the room. I went straight to the bathroom and pulled a box of Neurofen from my toiletry bag. 'Here,' I pushed out two pills for myself too.

'Can you believe we've just had a private performance by Pasha?' He filled a glass with water from the tap.

I went to the minibar and took out two bottles of Evian. 'You probably shouldn't drink tap water here.'

'Oh, thanks.' He took one of the bottles and emptied the glass in the sink. 'Do you realise how lucky we are? Newspring is the best thing that ever happened to me. I'm not being penalised for Zuidex. Can you believe that? No other firm out there would pay me a bonus, but Reggie is...' He shook his head with appreciation.

I took off my party dress and hung it carefully in the closet. I changed into a red silk baby doll with a black lace trim I had bought for the occasion. I brushed my teeth while he talked, trying to figure out if there was a connection between us. I loved Tom but I didn't know what to do with it.

'I like this.' He passed his finger along my armpit, around the silken edge of the babydoll. I turned around. His trousers were already down.

In spite of all the alcohol, we managed to make love for a long time. We were both full of all sorts of things and he broke a sweat and I let out a scream and our minds emptied and our hearts filled and so when it was over, he remained on top of me, he remained inside of me and I pulled the sheet over both our bodies and I put my arms over his back, lightly, gently and held him there.

After a moment, he stirred. 'Naomi, we have another big day tomorrow. Let's try to get some sleep.' He rolled off me, folded his pillow in half and turned his back to me.

Ah, yes. Tomorrow was another big party. Supper on a super yacht, some friend of Danton's. I opened my mouth to say something and closed it again. I drifted into a dreamless slumber.

# CHAPTER TWENTY-ONE

I was sitting in the Zodiac, the wind in my hair, the twin engines churning up a trail of white foam, as we sped towards the yacht. There it was, a giant white and black ship with three stories and a giant hold pierced by portholes at regular intervals, a smooth rotating radar, decks at every level lit from top to bottom as if it were a floating commercial for a generator company. There were four of us plus the skipper on the Zodiac. I was on my own. Tom left right after breakfast, his black tie in a dry-cleaning bag on his arm. He had to work with Reginald all day. He called me at some point and said to be at the jetty at six pm for the pick-up. He was already on the ship.

I spoke to the boys back in London. They had just returned from their Saturday football training. Meribel had made them hamburgers and they seemed happy with their grandmother. After the call, I went swimming in the sea. I lay out on a towel on the pebbles and let the sun dry my face, my body. I took a long shower to wash off the salt on my skin. I cupped and weighed my breasts in front of the full length mirror. My mother was right. If I were to remain competitive against the Suzies of this world, I'd need implants. In the meantime, I unpacked the non-intrusive breast enhancers I had bought at Selfridges together with the dress. I opened the pink box and found a pink instruction sheet and two slabs of silicone in the shape and hue of raw, skinned chicken breasts. I towel dried my own breasts carefully. I took each enhancer out of the box and peeled off the paper protecting the adhesive part. After some moderately painful sticking and unsticking and sticking again, I got it right. The slabs of silicone glued under each breast did the job as advertised. My natural breasts were held up in a perky position and their size were double what they normally were. Of course the whole thing looked distasteful in the flesh but the dress would hide all of that.

It worked. The dress, a taffeta gown with a plunging neckline, fit perfectly. I took a selfie, standing against the lawn from the deck. I sent it to Solange. I was so pleased, I thought of sending it to Tom too. My finger hovered over the send button but I didn't do it. Solange replied with a brown thumbs-up emoji. How are you? I texted to her. I put my phone, the room key, and a lipstick in my clutch and I ran in my heels over to the jetty, it was already ten to six and I didn't want to miss the ride. I was sweating by the time I got there. I waved at the skipper, 'Wait! Wait!'

He shouted at me with a strong Australian accent that there was no rush, I could relax. There was a middle-aged couple already there, and a professional-looking young woman with a headpiece who was busy on the phone. The skipper was friendly and offered me a bottle of water. 'We have to wait for this VIP,' he explained. The other guests nodded at me.

I introduced myself and went to lean against one of the poles to wait in the heat.

Now I had the VIP sitting across from me. A famous model, her heels already in her hands. She whispered something to her boyfriend, a floppy-haired prosperous type, maybe a Newspring man. She'd made the cover of both British and American Vogue in the past six months. I could see why, she had that fortunate mix of good bone structure and flawless skin and of course carried as much flesh as a coat hanger come to life. Although she was twenty minutes late, she walked leisurely down the planks. She didn't rest her languorous eyes on any of us, let alone apologise for making us wait, instead she focused seriously enough at the looming ship for me to know—in case I had any doubt—that I was heading straight into a jungle.

I seemed to be the only one who noticed the security men dressed in black holding automatic rifles on the boat. There were two standing on the landing where we boarded and three, if not four, positioned on the top deck overlooking us on the middle deck with their weapons loosely hanging off their straps.

A middle-eastern man welcomed us, holding the little gate open off the boarding steps. 'No shoes, please, come, come.' He was dressed in what could be a black tie if he hadn't put the tie in the pocket of his jacket and opened the shirt. His name was Nassef and although there were no signs of wealth on him—he didn't even wear a watch—I knew he was the owner of this ship. It was in the way he spoke to the skipper and the young woman as they came on board, in the way he welcomed us. The woman with the earpiece whispered in his ear. He greeted me, 'Naomi Barnes, your husband didn't tell me how lovely you are. I would have asked you on board earlier! He's been here since…' his expression changed. 'What's that sticking out of your dress?' He pointed at my chest. It was all he could do not to burst out laughing.

I gasped. My left breast enhancer had slid out of its position and was now hanging out next to my armpit. My sweat must have weakened the glue. The silicone had been coloured with white women in mind and looked like a piece of uncooked chicken fillet against my brown skin. I quickly clasped my left arm down. I had to find a bathroom.

'It's that way.' He could barely contain himself. I said nothing and ran in the direction he pointed. I could hear him roaring with laughter. He laughed and laughed.

Stupid things. I was trying hard not to cry and ruin my mascara. The fucking chicken fillet was continuing its bid for escape towards my armpit. I crossed the party on the deck, avoiding eye contact with anyone and finally I reached the doors and went inside. And yes, there it was, a small guest bathroom.

I locked myself in and took down the straps of the dress. Yes, the right one was still holding on but the left one was gone. And they were both starting to itch with the heat. I ripped them off and wanted to throw them out but there was no waste basket in the bathroom. This perfect boat and they forgot to put a bin in the bathroom. I thought of flushing them. But the enhancers were C-cups and this wasn't even a normal toilet, it was more like an airplane one. I imagined my boob enhancers stuck in there and swelling with the water. No. I tried to fit them into my clutch but it could only fit one. So I put the left one in and closed it and hid the other one behind the toilet bowl. I used the leftover glue to stick it on the back side of the porcelain WC. *Bueno*. I was starting to feel human again. I stepped out into the party, grabbed a glass of champagne from a tray and downed it in one go.

Without my heels, I had to hold up my dress. It looked like I was the only one who didn't know this party would be on a yacht deck with a barefoot policy. I was afraid of tripping against the material and of people stepping on it. The other women looked sexy and confident in their shorter, brightly printed and embroidered tunic-style dresses and their naked, carefully pedicured feet.

'Naomi!' I heard Tom before I saw him. He'd been sitting behind the crowd on one of the banquettes at the edge of the deck. I recognised a Hollywood actor, Ryan something, wearing dark glasses. Tom touched my shoulder, I turned around. 'You made it finally.' He surveyed my outfit. 'Nice dress but a bit too big, no?'

I sighed. He looked gorgeous himself, tanned, relaxed, cool.

I felt like one of my widowed great aunts, all in black. The water was clear and inviting. 'I wish I had a bathing suit.

I'd jump in,' I thought out loud. I looked up at him. 'How was your day?'

'We had a few things to figure out.' He sounded nervous.

I saw two men in black with automatic rifles standing at the balcony of the deck above the party.

Tom followed my gaze. 'They're not goons, they are all ex-officers of the Iraqi army.'

'How does that prevent them from being 'goons'?

A wave passed and there was a slow rocking of the boat. I wondered why the boat was anchored. 'Wouldn't it be more fun to travel around?'

'Naomi.'

I made myself smile. 'I'd love a tour of this super yacht. It's my first time on a boat like this.'

'Tom, come here!' Reginald waved at him. He was standing with his arm now around Suzie the hot school teacher. 'My niece, Suzanna, has an amazing idea. She and a friend of hers want to start a beachwear business.'

'We want to give all our profits to this educational charity in India so we thought our clothes should be inspired by India.' Suzie was positively beaming with beauty and confidence. She looked like a glamorous hippie in an Indian tunic, beads and gold jewellery that sparkled against her fair skin. It all made much better sense now. She was part of the family.

'I told her that you could help her with her business plan, eh Tom? She's got a heart of gold, this girl, but she's useless at numbers.' He squeezed Suzie by the shoulders.

'With pleasure,' Tom said in his most charming voice.

Suzie almost hugged Tom. 'Oh, thank you so much!'

'Suzie, will you give me a tour of your uncle's fabulous boat?' I went to stand between her and Tom.

'Oh, Naomi, we are all just guests here of Nassef's incredible hospitality,' Reginald quickly corrected me. 'I could only dream of owning such a yacht.'

'Yes, of course, I got confused, sorry.'

'I'm sure I can show you around anyway?' Suzie looked at her uncle. 'At least my room and the common areas?'

'Oh yes, Nassef loves showing off his toy.' He blinked at me and for the briefest moment, his eyes flashed crimson.

Suzie pulled me by the hand. 'Come, Naomi, it's the most awesome boat I've ever seen!'

Shaken, I looked back at the party, all these famous, rich people and the others who so obviously drew their oxygen from being around them. And now I was about to go on a tour of a stranger's yacht with a woman I was trying to keep away from my husband. I thought of our night and how lovely it was and forced myself to calm down. I was getting with the programme. Nassef was standing a couple of feet away from us with a woman who looked like his wife by his side.

'Her name's Zara,' Suzie told me. He waved at us, clearly keeping an eye on anyone who left the party and tried to enter the private parts of his boat. Suzie flashed him a wide smile and waved back. I picked up my dress and hung the bottom over my arm, then followed Suzie inside the tinted glass doors.

We walked through room after room of the finest things

a human can buy. The main living room, just off the deck where the party was taking place, was modern with classic Italian designer pieces, a giant flat-screen TV that could rise from a slit in the floor. On a sideboard, framed pictures in silver frames. I went to look. There were pictures of Nassef doing things with movie actors. Golfing with the actor who played Tony Soprano. Eating with Kevin Spacey. Hugging Sofia Vergara. It was immaculate and stylistically perfect. There were no traces of family life anywhere, no Monopoly, no socks, no school letters lying around.

The master bedroom—Suzie decided it was safe to take a peek—was a work of art. The walls were panelled, the lighting gorgeous and subtle and the bed looked huge, with the finest linens, giant pillows, and a throw made of some kind of fur. Assorted night lamps with hand-painted shades framed the bed. There were no books but there were a couple of pictures in silver frames on one of the night stands. I expected in this more intimate setting to see pictures of the children when they were small, perhaps a wedding picture of young Nassef and his wife.

No. Instead there was a picture of Nassef holding a barracuda, Hemingway-style together with Robson Green, a British celebrity with his own fishing show. The other picture was a professional black and white shot, in a photo studio. It was the wife and everything that made her someone. She was sitting in an armchair, in a serious and well-fitted suit with an expensive necklace over her silk top. Her legs were crossed, showing slim ankles and well shod feet. Her children were all around her. The older ones, in suit and tie, were standing behind her and the younger ones were sitting at her feet on the floor. Nobody was touching her; her hands were empty and elegantly folded on her lap. Her eyes were dark, tired, her mouth resigned. She had a large diamond ring on one of her fingers.

'Isn't it just a dream?' Suzie, just like me once, only saw the privilege, the perfection. She loved it, running her hand over the fur on the bed and opening her fingers to better feel the pelt.

'Mmm.' As soon as she moved away, I opened my clutch, took the silicon breast enhancer out, and stuck it under one of the pillows. I hoped it was Nassef's side.

'Naomi? Come see this bath, it's heavenly!' Suzie called from the bathroom.

'Oh, I'm sure!' I joined the beautiful young niece in gushing over the marble and Corian bathroom.

We ended the tour on the top deck where three more armed security men overlooked the pool. Suzie told me she was Reginald's sister Charlotte's daughter. Her mother didn't come because she was in Dorset taking care of Reginald's father, who had cancer. Down on the main deck a man's voice was leading the crowd into a vigorous hip hip hoorah!

'Oh no, we're going to miss everything if we don't hurry.' Suzie rushed down the stairs to join the celebrations.

I started to follow her and then I stopped. The third inescapable anxiety is moral. I sat on the stairs half-way down and watched the crowd below. I saw David Miller leading the guests with his arms while singing with zeal. I saw Lucy carrying a chocolate cake with a multitude of sparkly lights. She stopped before Reginald so he could blow out the candles and waited for the photographer to flash a couple of times and for the party to cheer before handing the cake like a bag of toxic garbage to the waiter waiting behind her. Anya clung on to her mother's skirt. Nassef made a short speech. The Danton boys hung around looking bored but Suzie jumped into her uncle's arms. She wasn't so naïve, after all. She had sniffed the opening Reginald's spoiled and perhaps conflicted children had left in the big man and she was filling it: The daughter the rich uncle wished he had.

And then I saw Tom, my husband of fifteen years, my partner for life, the father of my children. His brown hair picked up different shades of gold from the dying sun. He too was in the front row, completely happy and at home with this crowd. This was his life.

It wasn't mine. I didn't want it to be mine. I leaned my head against the railing and cried. I tried but my life was elsewhere, even though I loved Tom, I'd loved him from the moment I saw him standing in line at that coffee shop on the Bowery. Was this my curse, my *maldición*?

At that moment, at the party below, Suzie Fletcher hugged my husband.

That bitch.

I stood up and raced down the stairs, tripping over my dress in my fury and shoving her away from my husband. I held Tom by the collar, and, indicating the English Rose I had just pushed to the floor, explained to him the facts of life: 'Blue eyes say love me or I die. Black eyes say love me or you die.'

No... that's not what happened. I let the tears run down my cheeks and I stayed on my step and noted how quickly nature will fill a void. Let him go. Suzie was Tom Barnes's kind of girl, just like I used to be. And she may be better suited to the programme than I ever was. Watching her flirt with Tom, she didn't seem to mind the twenty years separating them or the minor fact that he was married with children to the woman she had just shown around.

I wiped my eyes and stood up. It was a beautiful evening. The sea looked oily in the setting sun. I looked once more to Tom. He had his arm around Suzie's waist and stiffened. He had seen me. He looked at me and I recognised our son Tommy in his eyes. It was a questioning look, like when Tommy wanted a playdate or a new pair of tennis shoes. Tom was asking me for permission.

My tears kept flowing but I smiled at him, go. He nodded. He wiped his eyes. After a moment, he turned his back to me.

I cared enough that Danton could actively push his country and millions of people into a dangerous future for the sake of a trade. I cared enough that we had no idea who this Nassef was or why he needed armed goons on his yacht. I cared that most people on this boat were here out of self-interest, to sell themselves, to see who here could be of use to them. My life lay elsewhere. I picked up the end of my dress, stepped from the stairs to the edge of the boat, and jumped

into the sea.
   The water was warm.

# Acknowledgements

I would like to thank Cathryn Summerhayes and Sile Edwards at Curtis Brown for believing. I want to thank Valerie Brandes at Jacaranda for her passion for the book and her invaluable edits and suggestions. She saw what I couldn't see. Jazzmine Breary and Cherise Lopes Baker and the whole team at Jacaranda for their tireless support and enthusiasm in getting this story out. Thank you Julian Friedmann, Wylie O'Sullivan and Bryony Sutherland for your help and support in the early days. Justine Solomons and her superb network 'Byte the Book' for showing me the way. All the staff and friends at the London Library. This book could not have been written anywhere else. I want to thank my London crew, for making this big sprawling crazy city home. Finally I want to thank my family and friends back in Haiti and Miami for never giving up on me although I've been gone for so long.

# About the Author

Isabelle Dupuy grew up in Port-au-Prince, Haiti, studied and lived in the USA and moved to London twenty years ago with a job in the City. She started writing when she became a mother. *Living the Dream* is her first novel.

# THE BOY, THE BIRD & THE COFFIN MAKER

**Matilda Woods**
Illustrated by Anuska Allepuz

■SCHOLASTIC

First published in the UK in 2017 by Scholastic Children's Books
An imprint of Scholastic Ltd
Euston House, 24 Eversholt Street
London, NW1 1DB, UK
Registered office: Westfield Road, Southam, Warwickshire, CV47 0RA
SCHOLASTIC and associated logos are trademarks and/or registered
trademarks of Scholastic Inc.

Text copyright © Matilda Woods, 2017
Illustration copyright © Anuska Allepuz, 2017

The rights of Matilda Woods and Anuska Allepuz to be identified as the
author And illustrator of this work have been asserted by them.

ISBN 978 1407 17869 1

A CIP catalogue record for this book is available from the British Library

Printed and bound by CPI Group (UK) Ltd, Croydon, CR0 4YY
Papers used by Scholastic Children's Books are made from wood grown
in Sustainable forests.

1 3 5 7 9 10 8 6 4 2

www.scholastic.co.uk

*To my family –*
*those with two legs and four*

# THE COFFIN MAKER'S
# FIRST COFFIN

The town of Allora was famous for two things. The first was its flying fish and the second was the beauty of its winding streets. Tourists came from all over the country to watch the fish fly out of the sea while artists came to paint, in pigment, the bright houses that rose like steps up Allora Hill. There were so many colours that the artists did not have enough pigments to paint them, and it was rumoured (at least by the Finestra sisters) that the great artist, Giuseppe Vernice, invented a whole new colour just to paint the roof of their house.

"Splendid Yolk, it was called," Rosa Finestra said to anyone who would listen.

"Derived from the crushed eye of a peacock feather," Clara Finestra added with a wise nod.

Yet though the sisters gushed about their bright home, the one next door was even brighter.

Alberto Cavello's house was the highest house on the hill. If you went any higher you would reach the graveyard at the top. It stood like a bright azure jewel glistening across the sea. And it wasn't just bright. It was loud. It was loud when Alberto and his wife, Violetta, moved in. It grew louder when their first child, a girl named Anna Marie, was born; louder still when their son, Antonio, came into the world; and even louder when a little miracle named Aida wailed for the first time within its bright walls.

Alberto was a carpenter: the best in all of Allora. During the day he would build beds, tables and chairs for his paying clients, and at night he would build toys for his children.

With each new toy Alberto made, a new sound filled the house: squeals of delight as Anna Marie jumped off her spinning chair; screams of anger as Aida cried for Antonio to give back her favourite doll; and cries of "Gallop on! Gallop on!" as this same Antonio raced his wooden horse up and down the stairs.

Their house remained bright, loud and bustling for seven happy years until the sickness came.

The sickness appeared in the coldest month of winter, but it did not reach Allora until spring.

The first to fall ill were the men working on a new railway that linked Allora to the north, then the doctors who tended them and the artists who had come to paint the town. Only one family was wealthy enough to flee. The mayor took himself and his family on a long holiday to a place the sickness had not spread.

"Good luck!" he cried over his fat shoulder as a plush coach drawn by six white stallions carried them far away.

In the beginning, the dead were buried in the graveyard – one, then two, then three to a single plot – but as the sickness spread other measures had to be taken.

A gate was built at the back of the graveyard and a thin staircase carved into the stone with steps leading down to the water. No longer buried, the dead were wrapped in blankets and cast out into the violent, surging sea.

As the number of dead mounted and the number of living fell, the cobbled streets of Allora grew quiet. Houses went unpainted and shutters, once thrown open to greet spring, were pulled tightly closed. Even the Finestra sisters didn't poke their big noses out.

Just like the unfinished paintings that lay abandoned in the streets, the town of Allora itself began to fade.

The sickness rose up the hill – house by house – until it finally reached Alberto's home.

It took the eldest child first. Alberto spotted the purple mark behind Anna Marie's left ear as she read a book in her favourite chair. Then, Antonio fell ill. While he was ailing in his bed, the mark came upon little Aida.

Violetta and Alberto tended to each child as they fell sick. They kissed them when they cried, hugged them when they whimpered and when the time came for each of them to go they answered, "Yes, of course: one day, we will meet again."

Keeping her promise, Violetta joined them two days later. The plague bearers came to collect their bodies that evening, but Alberto wouldn't let them.

"I can't," he had said to the two men waiting at the front door. "I can't let you throw them away. Not into that cruel sea." Even from where he stood outside the highest house on Allora Hill, Alberto could see foam shooting up from where the waves crashed against the grey stones below. He could not bear to think of his family thrown in there.

"You must get rid of them somehow," the men had replied. "You can't let them stay inside. It will spread the sickness quicker."

"I'll bury them."

"All the coffin makers are dead. We collected the last one this morning."

"Then I'll make their coffins myself."

And that is what Alberto did. He went into his workshop and for the first time built something for the dead instead of the living. He carved a coffin for his wife, a coffin for his eldest daughter, a coffin for his only son, and a coffin for little Aida. Each was smaller than the one before and, like Babushka dolls, could fit inside the other.

When the coffins were finished and his family buried, Alberto returned to his workshop and began to make his own. But by the time he finished, the plague had left the town. The mayor returned from his holiday, the Finestra sisters reopened their shutters and people passed gaily up and down the streets of Allora once more.

But instead of joining them, Alberto sat beside his coffin every day, waiting for the purple mark to come back and claim him too.

# THE MAYOR'S EARLY ORDER

*Thirty Years Later*

"I want it made of golden oak," said the mayor grandly. "Nothing beats golden oak. Strong as an ox and light as a feather. They say—" He tried to lean across the table, but his vast stomach got in the way. "You can throw a whole tree in the ocean, roots and all, and it would float all the way to the wilds of Africa."

"Are you planning a sea burial?" Alberto asked. He wasn't used to asking questions. His clients were usually dead by the time they arrived.

"Of course not," the mayor spat. "I'm not a sailor."

"No one in Allora is," Alberto agreed. No man, sane or insane, would set sail across that tumultuous sea.

Almost like it had heard, the sea chose this moment to send a colossal wave crashing into the rocks below. Water sprayed so high it battered the kitchen window. A second later, a giant sea bass battered it too. Luckily, it didn't break the glass.

"So," Alberto said as the fish flapped about on the cobbles outside, "why do you want it to float?"

"I don't." The mayor took a sip of his tea and then, tasting it, spat it back out. He only drank tea steeped from the finest leaves and Alberto's were clearly the cheapest.

"But you just sai—"

"Oh, I don't care about all that floating nonsense." The mayor flapped his hand about like the fish in the lane outside. "I just care that it's..." He searched for the right word. "Rare!"

"And expensive," Alberto added. You couldn't buy a more expensive wood, not unless you shipped it in from Africa itself. "Are you sure you don't want to use something else, like elderwood or ash?"

The mayor gave him a scathing look. "I'm not poor either, Coffin Maker."

Alberto eyed the mayor's golden lace and velvet cloak. "No one could ever accuse you of being that. Golden oak it is." He dipped his pen into a jar of ink and wrote *Golden Oak* beneath the mayor's name. "Now." He looked up from his notebook. "Measurements."

"Measurements?" The mayor lost some of his vigour. "What measurements?"

"*Your* measurements, Mister Mayor. Height and girth will do. After all, I'm no shoemaker."

In truth, there were no shoemakers in Allora. Not any more. The last one had died two weeks before. Alberto had made his coffin:

*Master Luigi Scarpa*
*Elderwood*
*75 × 23 inches*

"Er, right. Well. . ."

"I have a tape measure," Alberto offered. "I could get it if you would like."

"No. No. It's quite all right." The mayor waved him back into his seat. "We can leave the measurements for now."

"I'm afraid I can't do much without measurements. They're a vital part of the coffin-making process. Normally, I'd measure the body myself. Most people don't come to me when they're still alive."

"Well, I'm not like most people, am I? I'm the mayor: the mayor of all Allora." He stuck his chest out importantly, and the fat of his stomach broke over the edge of the table. "And as the mayor it's my right, nay, my responsibility, to have the largest and grandest coffin this town has ever seen."

*He'll certainly have the largest,* Alberto thought to himself. He had never met anyone, alive or dead, who was as fat as the mayor.

"What was that?" the mayor snapped.

Alberto's eyes widened. Had he voiced that thought out loud?

"On second thoughts, I think it was my stomach." The mayor hauled it back under the table. "She always gets temperamental in the evenings. You don't happen to have any cakes or sweets in the cupboard? Just to quell the gentle beast." He gave his stomach a fond rub and glanced hopefully around the kitchen.

"There's some stale bread on the bench," Alberto offered. "And some cheese on that plate. Though, it's looking a bit green, even from here."

"Never mind," the mayor said, though he looked like he minded a lot.

"So?" Alberto asked.

"So, what?"

"What are your measurements? Just an estimate will do, so I can order the wood. If you want the grandest coffin, I'll have to start work on it soon."

"Right, well, seventy inches by – er..." The mayor's fat cheeks turned a deep shade of red. "Seventy inches, I suppose."

"Seventy by seventy?" Alberto said, unable to hide his surprise.

"What's wrong with that?"

"There's nothing wrong with it. It's just curious."

"What's curious?"

"I usually make rectangular coffins, not square ones."

"If it's too much of a challenge," the mayor said, trying unsuccessfully to stand up, "I'm sure I can find someone else to build it."

"It's no problem at all, Mister Mayor." Alberto dipped his pen into the ink and wrote the measurements down. "Now..." His voice wavered. He had a feeling the mayor would not appreciate the next question. "When would you like it by?"

The mayor's face turned from red to purple. "How would I know?" he blustered. "One doesn't exactly *know* these things. Death can be very unexpected."

"It always is," the coffin maker agreed. "One moment you're breathing and the next you're not."

"Still," the mayor said with a nervous laugh, "you shouldn't work too fast. I'm not planning on popping off anytime soon."

Outside, the clock tower rising from the graveyard chimed twelve. To block the tolls, the mayor began to yell.

"Good genes, I have. Mother lived to eighty-three, and even then she was killed by a runaway cart. Clean bill of health except for the broken skull and punctured lu—"

The mayor was cut off by three loud knocks on the front door. He frowned and looked across the table to Alberto.

"Do you usually have visitors this late?"

"Not living ones," the coffin maker said, and leaving the mayor alone in the kitchen, he went to answer the door.

"Put her down there." Alberto pointed to a table near the back of his workshop. He had carried a candle from the kitchen and now used it to light five more around the room. One by one, little pools of yellow-grey light spluttered into life. When they formed one constant glow, he joined the two men who had carried the body in.

Alberto recognized the woman. It was Miss Bonito. She had moved to Allora just over a year ago. In the four seasons she had called the town home, Alberto had only spoken to her once. He had helped her to read a sign in the market square: *Two pears for the price of one!*

"What happened?" Alberto asked. He knew both men, one far better than the other. The older man was Enzo the baker and the younger was his apprentice, Santos.

"She died," Santos said.

"I can see that. How did she die?"

"Um. . ." Santos looked to his master.

"A growth, Alberto." Enzo coughed to clear his throat. "Right there. Just above her heart." He pointed towards her chest where, above the cut of her faded dress, a lump the size of a small apple could be seen.

"Ah," Alberto said sadly. "I have seen this type of thing before. Many a time, in fact." He pulled back from the body and looked at his old friend, Enzo. "Who found her?"

"My wife. She used to give her our stale loaves for free. Poor thing couldn't afford them fresh. Hadn't seen her for two weeks, so went out to the cottage to check if she was OK. Found her like this, alone in her bed, the sheets still warm."

"Warm?" Alberto frowned. "Are you sure?" By the state and smell of her, he was certain Miss Bonito had been dead for at least a week. If it had been high summer, she would not have even looked like Miss Bonito any more.

"Si. Si, Alberto," Enzo said with a sad nod and even sadder eyes. "My wife was most sure about that."

Ah, Alberto thought. That explained it. Enzo's wife was prone to exaggeration, almost as much as the Finestra sisters who lived next door.

"She could not afford food, Alberto, let alone a coffin." Enzo's voice took on the tone of a proud man about to ask a favour. "But I remember – how could I forget – that you helped my father when we couldn't afford..."

"Of course. Of course," Alberto said. "You do not even have to ask, Enzo. Don't worry. I'll look after her now."

"Thank you, Alberto." Enzo shook his hand. "I knew she'd find a friend in you."

"Alberto's had a busy night," said Clara Finestra. She pulled her head inside the window and turned to face her sister.

"Really?" Rosa asked. She was sitting in an armchair decorated with roses to match her name.

"Oh, yes. The mayor and Miss Bonito."

"The mayor's dead?" Shock rendered Rosa speechless, but only for a moment. "Well, I can't hardly be surprised. When one's of a certain size, death does come rather early."

"No." Clara's sharp face lit with delight. She loved knowing things before her younger sister. "The mayor isn't dead. Miss Bonito is. Enzo and his apprentice just carried her up now."

"Let me see." Rosa clawed herself out of the chair and raced towards the window. Pushing Clara aside, she poked her head out into the lane. But she was too late. All of Alberto's living guests had left, and the front of his house was dark.

One by one, Alberto blew out the candles in his workshop.

"There you go," he said, placing the final flame beside the body of Miss Bonito. "That's better. Don't you worry yourself now. I'll look after you. You'll have a proper burial, just like everyone deserves. You can have my coffin." Though she could not see, he pointed to a short, dusty box resting in the corner. "And I'll buy you a plot in the graveyard too. You can have a stone and everything."

To keep the flying fish away, Alberto closed the back window. He turned to leave but something made him stay. Miss Bonito may have died alone and lain alone for a whole week, but she did not have to lie alone any longer. So, instead of going upstairs, Alberto sat down beside her.

"Good night, Miss Bonito," he said, and in the final pool of light, he laid down his head, closed his eyes and eventually fell asleep.

# THE CURIOUS BIRD

That night, while Alberto lay sleeping beside the body of Miss Bonito, a bright little bird flew high overhead. Each beat of its wings made a patch of the stars flicker out, and another made them flicker back on.

The bird was heading out to sea, but it wasn't getting very far. The wind was strong and the bird's wings were weak. So, instead of flying forward, it kept circling round and round.

"*Twrp!*" the bird cried. "*Twrp!*" it cried again. Its calls echoed across the water, but no calls echoed back.

The bird flapped and wailed for almost an hour before a small light caught its eye. Turning its back on the sea, it soared towards the town of Allora. Houses as bright as its feathers flashed past as it spiralled downwards. It flew over cobbled lanes, shingled roofs and glass that glistened white in the night. Then, with a gentle sigh, it landed on a stone windowsill.

The bird shuffled towards two wooden shutters that covered a window. Through a thin gap where both shutters met, it peered into a dim room that flickered with golden light.

A woman's body lay stretched out on a cold table and an old man, his hair grey, lay sleeping beside her. The bird looked at the woman and tilted its head. A sad cry, formed deep in its chest, echoed across the room. Then it looked at the man. Its inky eyes studied him for several minutes. Finally, as if seeing something it liked, the bird's eyes flickered gold.

"*Twrp!*" the bird chirped. "*Twrp!*" it chirped again.

With a flap of its glistening wings, the bird returned once more to the sky. This time, instead of flying south, towards the sea, it turned north and headed towards the hills that surrounded Allora.

\*

"Would you look at that?" said a toothless man sitting in the gutter of Allora's main square. He was talking to a bucket of fish squirming near his feet. "No brighter bird I ever did see."

The man craned back his head and watched the rainbow bird circling by. He'd never seen one like it. Not in the south or in the lands to the north he used to call home.

The man's name was Alessandro Diporto, and as a child he'd heard stories of Allora: stories of how the fish flew out of the sea and fell down, like rain, on to the cobbles below. Then, as a man, he'd had a great idea. An idea as bright as the bird flying high above. An idea that would make him rich.

He left the calm rivers of the north and headed south to make his fortune as the one and only fisherman in all of Allora.

But there had been a fault in his plan. A fault so big, in fact, that it had ruined his plan completely. For what need did a town have for a fisherman when the fish basically caught themselves?

So despite catching three thousand and eighty-nine fish, Alessandro Diporto had failed to sell a single one. This fact had led the townsfolk of Allora to give him a new name. A name that had become so well known everyone had forgotten his old one.

"There he is," people would say as they passed him sitting in the streets with a basket full of flapping fish and a faded sign that read *Ten for a Single Copper.*

"Keep away from that one," mothers would warn their children as they raced up and down Allora's thin lanes.

"Who's that?" the tourists would ask of the man lying in rags by the gutter.

"Ah," the townsfolk would reply, "he is the foolish fisherman. The one and only in all of Allora."

The foolish fisherman sighed and stared up at the bird in the sky. Yes, he had been foolish to come to this town in search of his fortune. But he knew it would be even more foolish to leave. For what other place in the world could be as magical as this? Where else would he get to spend his nights watching silver fish rain down from the sky and bright birds that were so rare they had never been sighted by a grown man before?

That is why Alessandro Diporto had chosen to stay in the town where everyone called him a fool. He had chosen to stay because when you came to Allora you just had to tilt your head towards the sky to see magic every day and deep into every night.

# WHO WERE YOU, MISS BONITO?

A lberto woke with a start. During the night, cold air had crept through the shutters and now a piercing chill filled his workshop. He sat up and rubbed his frozen hands together. Slowly, blood and life returned to them. He relit the candle beside him, and a small pool of yellow light warmed the air.

"Good morning, Miss Bonito," he said when her body came into view. "I trust you slept well. We've got a busy day ahead of us." After shaking his legs awake, he opened the shutters and clean, salty air flew into the room. The hour was early and a few stars still shone in the sky. His garden smelled of salty dew and two silver fish lay, as if sleeping, in a flower pot below.

"Right," Alberto said when he had taken the fish into the kitchen and returned to Miss Bonito. Behind him, the bushes jumped like they had awoken too. "Time to get to work."

Though Alberto had finished his coffin thirty years before, it was not ready for Miss Bonito. He had to clean it, sand it, add handles to both sides and engrave her name on top.

"It won't be the best fit," he admitted to Miss Bonito as he began to wipe away the dust. "It will be too wide and far too long. But at least you will fit inside, and I will try to make it comfortable."

While Alberto worked, he spoke to Miss Bonito as if she was still there. In the morning, he told her about his work.

"The trick is in the measurements," he said as a bird tweeted outside the window. "Not too big and definitely not too small. I've never, not in my whole life, made a coffin that was too small."

In the afternoon, he spoke about the weather.

"The sea is wicked today. Wickedly windy too." As if confirming this, the bushes outside rustled loudly and a giant mackerel flew through the window. It landed with a thud inside the empty coffin.

"I don't think I'll be burying you," Alberto said. He pulled the squirming fish out and hurried towards the kitchen with it. "I might have you for dinner."

And in the evening, he talked about the woman herself.

"Who were you, Miss Bonito," he asked, "and why did you come here?"

He could guess where she had come from – she had spoken with a northern accent in life – but he had no idea why she had come to Allora. It was not exactly in the centre of things. In fact, it was right on the edge: the final place you went before you could go no further: the last stop on the railway line before you reached a sea too wild to cross. Had she hoped to start a new life, or did she know her first would soon end?

The sun was setting when it came time for Alberto to place Miss Bonito inside.

"There you go, Miss Bonito." He placed a pillow beneath her head. "Nice and comfortable, see?" The setting sun caught the side of her face and the same golden glow that had lured artists to Allora made her dark hair shine a deep mahogany and her pale skin glow like honeyed milk. If Alberto had not just spent the day building her coffin, he would have mistaken her for being alive.

"Oh, Miss Bonito," he said, as he rearranged her hair over the cushion. "You were far too young to die. It should have been I who went instead."

# A FUNERAL AND A
# THIEF

Miss Bonito's funeral was one of the smallest funerals Alberto had ever seen. The only funeral smaller was the one he had held for his own family. Even the priest hadn't shown up to that one. He had died of the sickness three weeks before.

In total, five people braved the windswept graveyard at the top of Allora Hill: Enzo the baker, the Finestra sisters, the town's current priest and Alberto himself. The clock tower chimed eleven when they arrived but fell silent when the service began. Unfortunately, two people standing at the back didn't show the same respect.

The Finestra sisters had dressed for the funeral as if it was a wedding. They wore wide straw hats and hideous floral dresses that floated around them in the salty sea air, giving the unfortunate, and unintended, impression that they were as fat as the mayor.

At first, Alberto thought they were making up nasty rumours about Miss Bonito, but when the wind carried their words his way he heard the mayor's name instead. Apparently, his late night visit two days before had not gone unnoticed.

"What do you think it means?" Rosa whispered.

"You only visit the coffin maker for one thing," Clara said wisely.

Rosa nodded just as wisely, before asking, "What's that?"

"A coffin, Rosa."

Clara spoke so loudly that the priest paused in the middle of a prayer to see what was wrong. Upon seeing the Finestra sisters, he gave a little sigh, said a silent prayer – *Lord, save me from their wicked tongues* – and carried on.

"He must be dying," Rosa said. "And quickly too. He looked in a rush the other night."

"But of what?"

"Tuberculosis? Our cousin had that."

"Or nephritis," Clara mused. "Our other cousin had that. It was awful, wasn't it? Her whole body swelled up—"

"—that fits with the mayor," Rosa was quick to observe. "He's been swelling up for forty years."

"And then all that blood," Clara continued. "Remember the mess it made of the carpet?"

"Remember?" Rosa exclaimed. "I was the one who cleaned it up, and it wasn't just blood..."

Thankfully, Alberto didn't hear the rest. The wind changed direction and blew their words across the sea. He hated gossip, but at least they were not gossiping about Miss Bonito. Their words were wicked when it came to men, but their tongues were like acid when they spoke of women, particularly the younger ones.

When the service was over and Miss Bonito buried, Alberto headed for home. He had work to do. For the first time in thirty years, he didn't have a coffin of his own and he felt almost naked without one.

Though Miss Bonito's life had ended, the other lives in Allora carried on. Enzo continued to bake bread every morning, the mayor continued to make laws every day and the Finestra sisters continued to gossip every evening.

As life continued, deaths did too. Alberto spent the daylight hours working on coffins for those who had just passed away and when night fell he worked on his own. Despite the vast number of coffins he made, Alberto never forgot the names of the people he placed inside. Miss Bonito joined this list, unique because he did not know her first name. He tried to think of her often, for he feared no one else would, but as the weeks passed his mind drifted to other things.

With each coffin Alberto made, he went to another funeral. He had not missed a single one in thirty years. It was when he returned from one of these funerals – *Adamo Totti, maple, 85 × 25 inches* – that he first noticed something was missing.

The first thing that went missing was Alberto's lunch: a sandwich layered with salted ham and cheese. Then, a few nights later, his dinner disappeared: a bowl of stew and two slices of buttered bread. Soon, every time he left the house he returned to find another item gone.

In the beginning, the thief took what Alberto left on the kitchen table. But soon he or she took things from the cupboards as well: jars of chutney, pickled eggs and two whitefish he had caught floundering on his doorstep.

But while the food in the house was disappearing, something new took its place. Alberto started to feel a change – a *presence* – in the house. He had never been a superstitious man (as a coffin maker he couldn't afford that), but now as he worked he could not shake the feeling that eyes were watching him. Not the eyes of the dead, looking up, unseeing. But the eyes of the living, looking everywhere and seeing everything.

Alberto put up with the sneaky eyes and the missing food for three weeks, but when a whole loaf of fresh bread went missing and half a wheel of his favourite cheese, he could stand it no longer. So he came up with a plan to catch the thief.

Alberto set out early for a funeral that did not exist. His plan was simple. He would walk up to the graveyard and then turn straight back. He would be gone for all of ten minutes: long enough to lure the thief out of hiding, but not long enough for them to finish the bowl of steaming porridge in the kitchen.

But as soon as Alberto closed the front door, his plan went awry.

"Coffin Maker! Coffin Maker!" a breathless voice called from further down the cobbled lane.

Alberto turned to see the sweaty face of the mayor wheezing up the hill.

"Glad – I – caught – you." He came to a stop outside Alberto's front door.

"What can I do for you, Mister Mayor?" Alberto said, trying to hide his annoyance.

"Could we, er, go inside?" the mayor asked, still struggling to catch his breath.

"I'm actually on my way out."

"Oh." The mayor's face fell. "I just brought those measurements you asked for." With one eye on the Finestra sisters' house, he pulled a piece of folded paper from his pocket and handed it to the coffin maker.

"Oh, good," Alberto said. "I'll be able to order the wood. It might take a while. Golden oak is ve—"

"Shh," the mayor hissed. "I don't want the whole town to hear." Again he glanced towards the sisters' home.

"Of course. Forgive me, please." Alberto slipped the note into his pocket without another word. He said goodbye to the mayor and walked on a little further. Then he turned back and hurried down the hill. When he reached his front door, he silently pressed the key into the lock and pushed it open.

Alberto stepped into the hall and listened. Sounds came from the kitchen: cutlery clinked, a bottle opened and liquid sloshed into a cup. His eyes lit with triumph and he edged down the hall. But before he could open the door, a person spoke on the other side.

"That was some nice milk, Fia. Real nice."

Alberto paused, one hand on the handle. He did not recognize the speaker, but he could tell they were a child.

"And this porridge," the boy in the kitchen said, delight clear in his voice. "It's still warm. Would you look at all the steam?"

Alberto wondered what to do. He had assumed the thief was an adult. Not for a moment had he thought it might be a child. Should he confront the boy or sneak back outside and leave him be?

Before Alberto could make up his mind, a little bird made the decision for him.

"*Twrp!*" came a chirp from inside the kitchen.

All sounds of slurping, chewing and clinking stopped.

"What is it, Fia?" the boy whispered. He spoke with a faint northern accent. "Is someone there?"

Alberto pulled back from the door so suddenly that the floor beneath him creaked. Not wanting to frighten the young thief, he edged back down the hall. But he was too late. The kitchen door flew open and a boy darted past. A bird – the brightest bird he had ever seen: a bird that swam with shades of gold, turquoise and lapis lazuli – flew in panicked circles around his head.

"Wait," Alberto called. "Come back. I won't hurt you." But the boy and the bird were out the back door before he could catch them.

Alberto stepped into his garden and peered over the fence. The hill was so steep he could see the white froth of the ocean crashing below. He feared the boy would trip and topple down into the raging sea. But thankfully his legs remained steady as he bounded through the shrubs with the little bird flapping around his head. Alberto was about to call out again, when someone called to him instead.

"Alberto, is that you?" a woman yelled from the garden next door.

"Yes, Clara," he said with a sigh. Further up the hill, the boy jumped over the gate of the graveyard and landed safely on the other side.

"It isn't Clara," the same voice replied. "It's me, Rosa. Why do you always think I'm Clara?"

Alberto didn't bother replying. He was too busy thinking about the thief. Though he had only seen the boy's face for a moment, it had looked very familiar. That hair. That nose. Those eyes. The likeness of that face he had seen before. He could not be mistaken. It looked like the face of a woman he had buried five weeks before.

# A MOTHER'S BROKEN PROMISE

The boy did not stay in the graveyard for long. As quick as he fled the house at the top of Allora Hill, he fled the town of Allora itself. Keeping to the shadows he slipped through the town gate and headed north, towards Vita Valley. His legs did not stop until he reached the small cottage that stood in its centre.

The boy raced inside and closed the door. Fia – his little bird and only friend – fluttered down the chimney to join him.

"That was close, Fia," the boy said in between gasps for air. "Real close."

41

"*Twrp!*" chirped the bird fluttering beside him. Her wings shone green and then blue and then gold in the dark.

"But at least we got some porridge. And hot porridge at that!"

Fia settled on to the boy's shoulder and he walked into the next room. In the cold darkness, he picked a faded blanket off the floor and went to sit beside the unlit fire. He wrapped the blanket around himself and Fia and stared at the three pieces of grey wood lying in the fireplace. He had no matches to light the wood but sometimes, if he closed his eyes extra tight, he could feel heat crackling off imaginary flames.

After the boy's breath returned and his racing heart slowed, a different feeling fell upon him and he sighed.

"I'm still hungry, Fia," he said. "Almost like I haven't eaten anything at all."

The rainbow bird peered out from under the grey blanket and stared into his face.

"*Twrp*," she said and pointed her beak towards the door.

"But we can't!" the boy replied. "We can't go to Allora. What if we get caught? What if they find out the truth? What if they make me go back?"

Fia gave a stern, "*Twrp*," and gently pecked his cheek. *Well, you've got to find food somehow,* she seemed to say.

The boy looked around the small room. His eyes fell upon an old suitcase and an empty jar that once held strawberry jam. His stomach started to rumble. There was no food here, not even a single crumb on the floor. And even if a fish somehow managed to fly this far inland, he had no fire to cook it. The only food was in the town of Allora.

"This is not how it was meant to be," the boy whispered to the bird beside him. "She said we would be safe. She said we would be OK. She promised that once we got to Allora we would never go hungry again."

# A LITTLE THIEF
# GETS A NAME

"Miss Bonito had a child," Alberto said to the man lying before him. The man's name was Mr Adessi, and even in death he smelled of tobacco. "But how?"

One day had passed since he spotted the boy and his bird stealing porridge from his kitchen and he was still trying to figure it all out. He had never seen Miss Bonito with a child nor heard mention of one from someone else, not even the Finestra sisters and they mentioned everything, far more than they should. True, Miss Bonito rarely came into town, but surely after a whole year someone should have seen something. Unless... ?

"She was hiding him." Alberto began the sentence as a question but ended with certainty. "But why?"

Alberto looked down at the silent form that used to move with the life of Mr Adessi, but was now still.

"You never were much of a talker, were you, Carlo? Never mind. I don't think two minds together could solve this mystery. Yet there is a more important mystery to solve and that is this: who is looking after the boy now?"

By the look of him, Alberto didn't think anyone was. There was no mistaking the thinness of his bones and the sallowness of his skin: a sallowness only a shrinking stomach could bring. Twice he had seen death by starvation and if this boy did not get more food he would become the third.

So many questions filled Alberto's mind, but amongst them shone one certainty. The boy was here, he was real, and he needed help.

"So," Alberto said to the stony and silent Mr Adessi, "that is what I will do. I will help Miss Bonito's son as best I can."

The next day Alberto made breakfast for two instead of one. He ate a bowl of porridge himself and placed another outside in the garden. While he worked on Mr Adessi's coffin, he snuck glances outside. But the boy and his bird did not return.

Alberto ate the porridge for dinner and the following day left out a fresh one. Yet it too went uneaten.

For four days the food remained untouched and Alberto feared he had frightened the boy away for ever. But then, on the fifth day, the lure became too much, and the boy and his bird returned. Alberto didn't see them come, but he found the empty bowl in the evening.

He wanted to speak to the boy – check that he was OK – but he did not want to frighten him away. After the first sighting, it had taken five days for him to come back. What if he never returned after the second? So, for now, he would leave the food out in the morning, collect the empty bowl in the evening and leave his garden alone in the hours between.

One morning Alberto was getting a plate of food ready to take outside when he heard a knock on the front door. He wondered who needed burying this time. Miss Donati had been looking off colour, and Mr Grimaldi's cough had gained a worrying tone. But when he opened the door, he found neither.

"Ah, Master Alberto," said the mayor with a jolly rumble. The day was cold, so he wore a thick coat of grey wolf skin. "Glad I caught you. Not too busy, I hope?"

"No, no. I was just making breakfast."

"Breakfast?" The mayor's face grew even brighter. "Why, I might join you." He squeezed his humungous body inside. "What are we having?"

"Sour milk and mouldy bread," Alberto lied. In truth he was going to have smoked cod on three slices of Enzo's freshest bread. But he didn't want to share *that* with the mayor.

"Er, right, well. As it would happen, I've already had my breakfast today. Maybe we could go straight to your workshop?"

"Of course."

When the door to Alberto's workshop was closed and they were inside, safe from prying eyes, the mayor pulled a thick envelope from his pocket and handed it to Alberto.

"What's this?" Alberto asked. He took the envelope and opened it.

"Money. For the coffin."

"But it is too much. Even for golden oak it is too much."

"I put in a little extra, for some additions."

"Additions?" Alberto asked.

"Yes. Just a few things." The mayor pulled a scroll from his pocket. It was so long that when unravelled it reached all the way to the floor. "Jewels and cherubs and the like. You know, all that sort of thing."

"Cherubs?" Alberto repeated, making sure he had heard right.

"Yes. Those little things with wings. My mother used to call me her little cherub. I'm going to be buried beside her. Got the plot all sorted. The priest gave me two. It's true. I said, 'No, no. Just the one will do.' But he insisted. Said it would befit one of my position."

The mayor cleared his throat and looked down at his list. "Now," he said importantly, like he was introducing a new law. "Addition one..."

The talk with the mayor took longer than expected: three hours longer, in fact. A few additions ended up being one hundred and ten. The coffin would still be square and made of golden oak, but the measurements had increased by three inches all around and new fittings had been ordered for the inside and out.

By the time Alberto saw the mayor out, he was

exhausted. Listening to him speak was more tiring than building a coffin. Remembering the food he had left in the kitchen, he hurried down the hall. When he arrived, he discovered someone else was already there.

The little thief Alberto had been feeding for two weeks was now feeding himself a honey sandwich. He must have grown hungry and snuck inside to help himself.

"You eat faster than me, Fia," the boy said in a break between mouthfuls. He took a slurp of milk and tore off another piece of crust. "Here you go." He handed the bread to the bird perched on the bench below. "Don't eat it all at once. It'll get stuck in your throat, and you'll look like a snake that's swallowed an egg."

Though the bird had taken the bread gently, it swallowed it in one gulp and tweeted for more. The boy had just pulled off another bit when he noticed they had company. His eyes darted around the room, searching for a path of escape. The coffin maker blocked the door, but there was a window near the sink.

"Please," Alberto said as the boy raced towards the grimy glass and tried to pull it open. Behind him the little bird flew in panicked circles around the room.

"Please," he pleaded again. "I won't hurt you. Just stay and finish your food. Then you can go out the back way, so no one sees."

The boy gave a final tug before giving up. With his eyes locked on Alberto, he edged back to the sandwich. Forgetting his own warning, he shovelled the food into his mouth even faster and started to choke.

"Be careful!" Alberto raced over to help. "Here." He picked up the glass of milk. "This will wash it down."

The boy took the cup and began to drink. When all the milk was gone, he handed it back to Alberto. With his throat clear, he picked up his sandwich. This time when he took a bite he chewed it carefully.

"She's a lovely bird," Alberto said of the feathered creature hopping about on the counter, gobbling crumbs as fast as she could. "I've never seen one like her."

The bird was as bright as a peacock but five times smaller. Her right wing was crooked, but her eyes were bright and her beak sharp.

"That's because Fia's special," the boy said.

"I don't doubt it," Alberto agreed with a kind smile. "Fia? Is that her name?"

The boy nodded. He swallowed a piece of

sandwich and said, "She fell out of the sky when she was a baby. She broke her wing. That's why she flies in circles. Her brothers and sisters flew away, even her mother left, but she stayed here with me. I didn't even make her; she wanted to. I think," he said with a shy smile, "she loves me." To stop himself saying more, he took a big bite of his sandwich.

"Well, it's a lovely name for a lovely bird. Do you. . ." Alberto paused for a moment, unsure if he should go on. "Do you have a name too?"

When the boy did not reply, Alberto said, "What a silly question. Of course you do. Are you going to tell me or will I have to guess?"

The boy remained silent, so Alberto made his first guess.

"You look like a Jacob to me. Yes." He nodded. "Very much like a Jacob."

In reply, the boy took another bite of his sandwich.

"Or how about Pablo?"

Again, silence.

"Bruno?" Alberto asked. He was getting nervous. As soon as the sandwich was finished, he was sure the boy would leave. "Or are you called Antonio?"

At the sudden brightness in Alberto's voice, the boy looked up.

"Antonio?" he said.

"Yes." Hope made Alberto breathless. Had a new Antonio, just like his only son, come back to him?

But the boy looked at him with confusion. That was not his name.

"No," Alberto said sadly. "I did not think so. The silly dreams of an old man. You are a new boy, all himself."

The kitchen fell silent, and Alberto debated his next guess. He decided to take a new approach. "I know! I've got it. I'm sure. Absolutely certain."

Intrigued, the boy stopped eating.

"Emilia," Alberto said. "You are called Emilia."

The beginnings of a smile touched the boy's face.

"Ah, a smile," Alberto said. "Though, I fear, not a name." He frowned for a long moment. The boy watched his face. "I know. How about Teresa?"

The boy's smile grew.

"That must be it," Alberto said triumphantly. "You are called Teresa. I should have known. Would you like some more milk, Teresa?" He reached for the bottle on the bench.

The boy's smile widened and then broke into

a laugh. Startled, like she hadn't expected to hear such a sound coming from the boy, Fia flew off his shoulder and flapped twice around the room.

"I'm not Teresa," the boy said as Fia returned to his shoulder and began to preen her feathers. "That's a girl's name."

"So? Some girls are called Peta and some boys are called Jess."

"But Teresas are *always* girls."

"Then what should I call you?"

Alberto feared another silence but instead the boy opened his mouth and said, "Tito. Tito Bonito."

"Tito?" Alberto repeated. "Why, what a fine name." He liked it so much, his chest swelled as if it were his own.

"Do you really mean it?" Tito asked shyly.

"Absolutely. The finest name I've ever heard. Tito Bonito. Tito Bonito," Alberto said again and again. "It rolls right off the tongue. Even an old, tired tongue like mine."

At this compliment, Tito held his head a little higher and a glint of pride shone in his eyes.

"Well, it's very nice to meet you, Tito Bonito. And if you're ever hungry, you may come back here again."

# THE COFFIN MAKER'S
# APPRENTICE

Tito Bonito came back every day. At first he took his food into the garden and ate with Fia. But as the days grew colder they began to eat inside with Alberto. The moment they were finished they would leave – like they feared something bad would happen if they remained in one place for too long – until one day it started to rain and they decided to stay.

Alberto had work to do, so he left Tito and Fia in the kitchen toasting crusts of bread over the fire. A few minutes later, he heard footsteps near his workshop. He looked up to the sight of

Tito standing in the doorway and Fia fluttering in the hall.

"Don't be frightened," Alberto said. "The dead cannot hurt us; only the living can do that."

Finding truth in Alberto's words, Tito stepped down into the workshop.

"Who's that?" Tito asked, nodding towards the body that lay on a table beside Alberto.

"Miss Alletori. She was a lovely lady. Always took great care in her appearance. She wore the most delicate clothes and bred the ugliest dogs. Awful things, with big, squashed-up faces."

Tito looked down at Miss Alletori. He looked at the brown leather shoes that covered her feet, the light cotton dress that covered her body and the thin necklace that adorned her neck. Then he looked up at the coffin maker and said, "Did . . . did my mum come in here too?"

Alberto wanted to lie. He did not want Tito to think of his mother lying in here. But something in the boy's face made Alberto certain he already knew the truth.

"Yes," he said.

The fear that had made Tito's body tense for weeks disappeared. His shoulders drooped and a deep sadness formed in his eyes. Fia fluttered on to his shoulder and rubbed her head against his cheek. He was so lost in sadness, Tito didn't even notice.

"I know it's hard to lose someone you love," Alberto said, "but try not to think of her in here. Instead, think of her before she came. Think of her when she smiled and laughed and helped you fall asleep at night. It won't take all the sadness away, but it will help you think of happier things."

Tito slowly nodded his head, but the sadness remained in his eyes. Alberto wanted so much to make him happy, but he knew of no words that could do that. It would take time for the boy to heal, just as it had taken time for him.

To help take Tito's mind off his sadness, Alberto picked up a plank of wood and said, "Look here, Tito. Come and have a look at this. This is called spider wood. Can you guess why?"

Tito studied the piece of wood in Alberto's hand. At first he didn't seem to notice anything, but then he focused carefully and spotted something strange. "It looks like its covered in spiderwebs."

"That's right!" Alberto said. "Now..." He put the piece of spider wood down and picked up another. "Can you guess what this is called?"

*

On that first day in Alberto's workshop, Tito learned the names of five different woods. Then he sat by the window and watched the coffin maker work. Alberto took Miss Alletori's measurements, gathered the wood, cut it to size and began to piece it together. A few times the coffin maker went to speak to her, but then Tito would ask a question, so he'd answer the living boy instead.

With each passing day, Tito's chair crept further across the room until it was right beside Alberto's workbench. Before Alberto knew it, their conversations turned from the dead to how they would be buried.

"Most are buried in poplar wood," Alberto explained. "It's nothing fancy, but it's easy to work with and doesn't rot."

"Is that what this is?" Tito picked up a scrap of wood lying beneath his feet.

"That's right," Alberto said. "People die without warning, so I have to work quickly. If I work from dawn to dusk, I can make two in one day. The frame is the simplest part – six bits of wood measured, cut and hammered together – but then comes everything else: smoothing the wood, carving it and adding wooden handles."

"Who's this one for?" Tito nodded to the

coffin lying before them. Miss Alletori had been buried a week ago, and there was no body in the workshop today.

"For me," Alberto said.

"You?" Tito's face filled with worry. "Are you dying too?"

"I don't think so."

"Then why are you making a coffin?"

"I – I'm not sure. It's just what I do."

"Can I help?"

From that day on, Tito helped Alberto in his workshop every day. Sometimes he was in such a hurry he forgot all about the food waiting for him in the kitchen and went straight there.

Under Alberto's gentle guidance, Tito learned many things: how to smooth the wood, how to cut it, how to join it and how to shape it. He did not work on any of the real coffins. Instead, Alberto gave him scrap wood and a workbench of his own. While they worked they talked, and for the first time in thirty years the room echoed with two voices instead of one.

"You know, Tito," Alberto said as the end of another day neared. "I never thought I'd find an apprentice."

"Apprentice?" Tito asked. "What's that?"

"Why, it's someone who is training to do what I can do."

"You mean, I can be a coffin maker too?"

"Tito, you can be all sorts of things. Anything you want."

When he heard this, Tito's eyes grew as bright as the candle burning beside him. Alberto imagined he was dreaming of being a doctor, a sailor or a great explorer. But when Tito opened his mouth he said: "I want to be a coffin maker, just like you."

# A PARADE OF
# GOLDEN OAK

The wood for the mayor's coffin arrived early one Monday morning. It was brought by train from the north. It took five days and four nights to chug through the wild mountains that split the country in two. There was so much oak that two extra carriages were added to fit it all in. Alberto was at the station when it arrived, along with ten donkeys who were normally used to pull carts laden with fruit to market.

The donkeys were loaded with wood and led up Allora Hill. The sound of their hooves clobbering against the stony lane and workmen yelling, "Keep

it steady! Keep it steady!" ensured hundreds awoke to the parade. And if anyone slept too deeply, they soon heard about it from the Finestra sisters.

At the first sound of hooves, the sisters threw open the shutters of their house and cast their whole upper selves outside. Though they had been spying over his back fence for forty years, Alberto had never seen their necks so long. They looked like those grand, speckled creatures in books – giraffes – that lived far across the sea.

The wood came on and on. But for a forest, no one had ever seen so much in one place, not even Alberto who worked with it every day.

"Just take it through to the workshop," he said at least forty times.

When all the wood had been delivered and the train had left the station, Alberto could barely fit inside his workshop. The room was crammed so tightly with wood he had to send Tito in to fetch a tool, darting between the tiny spaces.

For all the crowds that had gathered, one person was not there. The mayor had stayed away while his order was carried into town. Even so, the Finestra sisters pieced it all together. After all, so much wood could only be needed for someone of a certain size. So by midday the whole township of Allora spoke of the mayor and his secret coffin.

The mayor came to check on the wood late in the afternoon. He tapped quietly on the front door and waited for Alberto to answer.

"Well, where is it?" he asked when Alberto led him into his workshop.

"Pardon?" Alberto tried to close the door, but there was so much wood spilling out that it wouldn't shut.

"I said, where is it?"

"Where's what?" Alberto was certain he had heard incorrectly. Surely he was not asking about the wood.

"Where's my wood?"

"It's right here." Alberto pointed to the wood covering the floor. "And there." He pointed to the five piles weighing down his workbench. "And out there." He pointed to the wood stacked in the hallway.

"But. . ." The mayor's face drooped as much as his sagging stomach. "It's not gold."

"Well, of course it isn't. No tree is made of gold."

"But it's called *golden* oak."

"It's just a name. It doesn't actually mean anything, not the gold bit anyway."

"But . . ." The mayor looked on the verge of tears. "If it isn't made of gold, why's it so expensive?"

"Because it's as strong as an ox, light as a feather and can float all the way to the wilds of Africa."

"But. . . But. . . It isn't gold," the mayor said weakly.

"Would you like me to order something else?" Alberto asked. "It might not arrive until spring, and you would still have to pay for all of this, bu—"

"No. No." Sense found the mayor and he shook his little head. "Money doesn't grow on trees."

"It would if they were gold."

The mayor did not appreciate Alberto's joke, but a boy chuckled in the hall.

"What's that?" The mayor's head snapped around, but by the time he looked towards the door Tito was gone. "Never mind. Must have been my stomach. You don't happen to have any food about, do you?"

"Afraid not," Alberto said. "Though there might be some mouldy cheese I use to catch the mice."

"Mice?" The mayor's face paled. They had spread the purple sickness that had killed so many people thirty years earlier. "You have mice?"

"Only in the kitchen," Alberto lied.

And on that note, the mayor decided it was time to leave.

Alberto saw the mayor off and returned to his workshop. He found Tito waiting.

"Did you hear that?" Tito asked. Like a tightrope artist, he was walking along one of the planks of wood. "He thought golden oak was gold. Even I know it isn't gold."

"Well, the mayor isn't like most people," Alberto pointed out.

"Yes," Tito agreed. He jumped off the plank and landed lightly on the dirt floor. "Most people aren't that stupid."

"You rascal of a boy!" Alberto said with a fond shake of his head. "Come now." He waved Tito closer. "Come here and look at this wood."

Quick as a greyhound, Tito was by his side.

"Golden oak is a special wood that must be shaped in a special way." Alberto ran his fingers along the largest section of oak. It would form the base of the mayor's coffin. "Would you like to learn?"

"You mean. . ." Tito's eyes grew wide. "I can help make the mayor's coffin?"

Alberto nodded and they got straight to work.

# A FAINT FLUTTER

Winter came early to Allora and what a terrible winter it was. Storms built over the sea, and the instant they reached land the rain turned to snow. The grey cobbles that wound up Allora Hill turned white and the fish jumped even higher to escape the icy sea. The snow fell so steadily that the tombstones at the top of the hill had a white lining, like a dusting of sugar on one of Enzo's baked sweets.

Though the days grew shorter, Tito spent longer and longer at the coffin maker's house. He said he was enjoying the work. Though judging by how close he stood to the candles and the fireplace in the kitchen, Alberto had a feeling he was enjoying the warmth even more.

With the mayor's wood ready to be shaped and the yearly influx of winter deaths, Alberto needed all the help he could get. Even Fia was given a task: to fetch tools in her sharp beak. She'd grown so big and strong she could carry whole hammers by herself and soon, Alberto hoped, she would be able to fetch planks of wood as well.

They were so busy that large blisters appeared on Tito's hands that cracked and hardened over. Yet despite the thickening of his skin, Tito himself grew softer, calmer and more at home in Alberto's house. Soon he spent more time there than out. But leave he always did, every day one hour before dark. Alberto would watch him race towards the graveyard and vanish, like a shadow, into the approaching night.

Alberto wanted to know where Tito went, but he was too afraid to ask. Though Tito spoke freely about work and Fia, he froze every time Alberto questioned him about anything else. The coffin maker could tell the boy was frightened – he was hiding something – but he had no idea what. And he feared that if he tried to find out, the boy and his bird would disappear from his life all together.

All was going well until one night a giant storm settled over the town.

"I was down at Enzo's this morning," Alberto said one evening while he and Tito worked on the mayor's coffin. "And he thinks it's going to snow."

"It's been snowing for two weeks," Tito pointed out.

"Ah, but this isn't a little snow. This is a huge storm. Enzo can tell by the fish. Their scales turn grey and they jump so high they look like tiny pebbles in the sky. There's a saying, here in Allora, that when it snows the roofs sing. They beat like a thousand drums with the sound of fish pummeling down."

"I thought I saw one fly by the window at lunch," Tito said.

"Ah yes, it was a tuna if I'm not mistaken. You know..." Alberto stopped working on the mayor's coffin and looked at Tito. "You can stay here tonight if you'd like."

Straight away Alberto knew the offer was a mistake. Tito's whole body tensed and Fia, feathers ruffled, swooped to his side.

"Down here in the workshop," Alberto clarified quickly. "Or in the kitchen by the fire."

"I – I think I better go." Tito put down his hammer and chisel and hurried towards the door. "It's getting dark."

"Of course." Alberto tried to hide his disappointment. It would have been nice to have another life in the house at night. "But can I get you a blanket first? I'm sure there's a spare one upstairs."

Alberto hurried to his room and opened his cupboard. A bright red blanket lay folded at the bottom. It had belonged to little Aida.

"And you haven't had dinner," he said when he handed the blanket over. "Don't worry, I'll fetch you some stew. You can take it with you."

Alberto went into the kitchen and ladled thick fish stew into an empty bowl. When it was filled to the brim, he carefully carried it back to his workshop.

"Here you go, Tito," he said as he stepped into the room. "I've given you a bit extra just in ca—"

Alberto looked around his workshop. Tito and Fia were gone. With a sigh, he walked over to the back window and poked his head outside. A light sleet had begun to fall and wind swirled his grey hair. In the failing blue light, he caught a glimpse of red near the graveyard on the hill and then Tito and Fia were gone.

"Goodnight, Tito," Alberto said softly. He closed the window against the chill and went to eat his dinner.

The world was white when Alberto awoke. A fierce storm had swept across Allora during the night depositing a thick, snowy silence. He made his way downstairs in his nightcap. After refueling the dying fire, he placed a pot of tea and another of stew over the flames. While they heated up, he set the table for three.

The tea boiled and the stew bubbled, but Tito and Fia did not appear. Fearing he had locked the back door, Alberto hurried to check. But it opened without need for a key.

Alberto peered outside. Snow covered the world like a blanket. He had to squint against its brightness to see. Everything – the garden, the graveyard, even the sky – was white. Only the sea remained its usual churning blue.

Alberto scanned the snow for Tito, but there was no Tito to see. He feared something was wrong – had he fallen down in the snow, or perhaps he was sick? – but then convinced himself there wasn't.

Tito was probably running late. It took a lot longer to walk through snow than grass.

When a full hour had passed, Alberto could wait no longer. A body had been brought in the previous afternoon, and he had yet to get started on the coffin. So, for the rest of the freezing day he worked alone in his workshop. Every few minutes he glanced towards the door to see if Tito was there, but he never appeared.

"I hope he is okay," he confided to Mr Vetrotti.

But, being dead, the old man did not answer.

Fia squawked and soared through the darkening sky. Snow flew into her eyes. She scanned the land below, looking for the town of Allora, but everywhere looked the same. In panicked circles, she flew round and round, searching for a sign of the bright town. Finally, she saw two thin, metal lines: the train track that led into Allora.

Fia swooped towards the ground and flew along the tracks. She moved in large circles, as her injured wing dragged her down. She flapped and flapped until the tall stone walls of Allora rose before her.

Too weak to rise above the stone, Fia soared through the town gates. Two Carabineers turned to watch the wondrous bird flying through the main square. But Fia did not turn to watch them. She circled past bakeries, taverns, blacksmiths and sweet shops as she searched for the last house on the hill. A few times she fell headfirst into the snow, her wings too weak to carry on. But she always flew back up before the snow had time to settle. And then, as the sky above Allora grew dark and stars began to twinkle above the icy, swirling sea, she saw the house she was searching for.

Alberto was just sitting down to dinner when he heard three loud knocks on the kitchen window. Leaving his stew uneaten, he opened the shutters to find a bird fluttering on the other side.

"Fia?" Alberto said. Snow covered her bright blue head like a hat. "Where's Tito?" He poked his head into the lane, but the boy was not there. "Has something happened?"

"*Twrp*," Fia chirped. To rest her wings, she flopped on to the windowsill.

"What is it? Where is he?"

In answer, Fia rose back into the air and tugged on Alberto's sleeve. *This way*, she seemed to say.

Alberto grabbed the bowl of stew, an unlit lantern and raced towards the door.

Alberto followed Fia down the winding lanes of Allora. The cobbles were as icy as the wind that nipped his cheeks and he wished he had brought his coat. Lines of light crept out from behind closed shutters, but no one else in Upper Allora was out.

When Alberto reached the market square, he saw two Carabineers standing guard outside the prison. The foolish fisherman lay asleep nearby, huddled under some rags beside a basket full of fish. Keeping close to the shadows, Alberto crept past all three unseen. The last thing he needed was to get caught sneaking out of the town so late in the night. How would he explain himself to the Carabineers? He had a feeling Tito wouldn't be happy if he told them the truth.

Upon reaching the walls of the town, Alberto lit his lantern and a warm orange light spluttered into life. Above him, little Fia turned right. She flew away from the sea, heading along the train tracks.

Only two trains came to Allora each week: one on Monday morning, the other on Friday evening. Tonight was a Wednesday, so the line was still. As Alberto followed the tracks, clouds scudded across the sky. Each time the moon appeared, a patch of

the world brightened and the wolves in the hills howled. Alberto hoped that none were howling near Tito.

The railmen had kept the train tracks clear, so their progress was swift. But then, a mile out of Allora, Fia left the tracks and flew towards the right. Alberto recognized the direction they headed: they were going to Vita Valley.

Away from the tracks, the snow was thick and fresh. Each time Alberto took a step forward snow swallowed his legs, and it took all his strength to haul them back out. As the minutes passed he grew weaker and feared he would have to turn back. Then, despite the thickness of the snow, he felt the ground slope downwards.

Vita Valley stood to the north of Allora. A little cottage rose in its centre. Built by a farmer one hundred years before, it had lain empty for seven decades before Miss Bonito moved in.

The cottage was small and made of stone. It had a little chimney, a door at the front and four windows spaced evenly around. A thin pile of firewood was stacked against one side. The wood was frozen solid and laced with icicles that shone blue in the fleeting moonlight.

When they reached the cottage, Fia left Alberto's

side and flew on to the roof. She hopped along the tiles before disappearing down the cold chimney. Alberto was too old to climb up there and too large to fit down the flume, so he used the front door instead.

At first the door appeared locked, but with one strong budge it swung open. Snow rolled inside, taking Alberto with it.

Alberto got to his feet and cast his lantern around. The cottage looked more suited to animals than people. Hay covered the dirt floor and a broken trough rested in the corner. He followed the wall of the room until it met with another door.

The door creaked when Alberto pushed it open and air as cold as outside washed over him. He stepped into the room and almost tripped over an iron bed. The bed was empty and he began to fear Tito wasn't there. But then Fia chirped, and he saw a mound of blankets beside the unlit fire.

"Tito?" Alberto hurried forward and dropped to his knees.

Tito's head lay upon a stained pillow. His body was curled up tight beneath Aida's red blanket. Even in the warm light of his lantern, Alberto could see that his skin was blue.

"Oh no, Tito," Alberto said. He put the bowl of

stew on the ground and placed the lantern beside it. Then he raised his hand to Tito's neck. He searched for a pulse, but could not find one.

"I'm too late," Alberto said, sitting back on his legs. Tito must have fallen asleep during the snow storm and been too cold to awaken. "I should have come this morning. I knew something was wrong. Now the next coffin I make will be for you. I'm so sorry, Tito."

Alberto began to weep, but Fia refused to let him weep for long. She flew down beside him and poked him sharply on the cheek with her beak.

*Try again*, she seemed to say.

And so, in hope, Alberto raised his old fingers to Tito's thin neck. He searched for a pulse and searched again until finally he felt a faint flutter of life.

"Tito!" he cried. "You're alive!"

# THE FLIGHT OF THE LANTERN

Alberto could not carry Tito and his lantern together, but luckily he had help. Using the trick Tito had taught her – the trick of fetching tools from the workshop – Fia carried the lantern in her beak while Alberto carried Tito beside her.

The trip back to Allora took a lot longer than the trip to Vita Valley. By the time they reached the main square, the Carabineers had fallen asleep and Fia was so tired she had taken to sitting on Alberto's shoulder.

Silently, Alberto crossed the square and headed up the hill. The house next to his own was dark, and he breathed a sigh of relief. If the Finestra sisters had seen them arrive back, by first thing tomorrow the whole town would have spoken about the little boy Alberto had carried home in the snow and the bird that had held a bright lantern to guide the way.

Still holding Tito in his arms, Alberto slid the key into the lock and pushed the front door open. He stepped into the hall and headed towards his workshop. He only stopped when he saw his coffin lying inside. Realizing his mistake, he turned around and headed upstairs.

Dust greeted Alberto when he opened the door to his children's room. Three beds lined one wall and a boarded fireplace stood in the other. He placed Tito in the bed closest to the door and took the lantern from Fia's beak. She gave a grateful chirp before flopping on to the pillow beside Tito.

Alberto pulled a dusty blanket over Tito's cold body. Then he prised open the old fireplace. A pile of dead leaves and twigs lay inside. Using his lantern, he set the kindling alight and went downstairs to fetch some wood. He built up the fire until it crackled and flared. To keep the warmth in, he closed the door and sat down in a chair beside Tito.

\*

Alberto watched over Tito all night. He kept getting more blankets whenever the boy shivered and putting more wood on the fire whenever the flames grew low. It burned so brightly and so fully that by midnight it felt like high summer inside the old room.

Alberto heard the hours pass as the graveyard clock tolled one o'clock – two o'clock – three o'clock – on and on until morning. But the clock on the wall inside never moved, nor did the boy lying beneath it.

That first day, Alberto barely left Tito's side. The blueness faded from his cheeks at midday, but in the afternoon they turned red and his forehead burned with a high fever.

Alberto hurried up and down the stairs fetching pails of cold water and placing wet cloths atop Tito's burning head. In his workshop, he would have been terrified if one of the people lying before him had spoken. Yet now with Tito, he wished, hoped, even prayed, that he would speak again.

"I just don't know," Alberto said as day turned to night and he pulled a scorching cloth away from Tito's head. "I just don't think I can do it. I've never saved anyone before. I've only buried them."

And out of everyone still living in the world today, Alberto wanted to bury Tito Bonito least of all.

The next day Alberto awoke to the sound of two women calling to him from the street.

"Yoo-hoo!" Clara Finestra called as she rapped her knuckles on the front door.

"Only us!" Rosa hollered from beside her.

Alberto moaned and opened his eyes. The last people he wanted to speak to at any time of the day, let alone right after waking, were the Finestra sisters. But he knew he had to answer the door. Otherwise, they'd fetch someone to open it for them.

"Can you look after Tito while I'm gone?" he asked Fia. Though he had spent thirty years talking to the dead, he felt silly speaking to a bird. Yet Fia seemed to understand. She chirped in reply, and he went downstairs to answer the door.

"Rosa! Clara!" Alberto said with forced cheer. "What are you doing here?" Neither was dead, so they weren't after a coffin. Unless they too were hoping to place an early order.

"We've come to check on you," Clara said.

"We were very worried," Rosa agreed.

"Worried?" Alberto laughed. "Why were you

worried about me?"

"Because you missed the funeral."

"What fu— Oh, *that* funeral." Alberto lost his cheerfulness. He had forgotten all about Mr Vetrotti and his burial yesterday at noon. "Oh, right. I'm just coming down with a . . . a cold." As proof, he offered a little sniffle.

"Ah, we noticed the fire." Clara nodded to the line of smoke trailing out of the bedroom upstairs. "You must be very sick."

"Positively terminal," Rosa agreed. "You haven't lit that fire for thirty years. Would you like us to make you some soup?"

"No. I'm fi—"

"We'll make you some soup," Clara decided. "What neighbours would we be if we didn't make you soup?"

"All right then," Alberto said with a resigned sigh. It was common knowledge that the Finestra sisters could not cook. They doubled some ingredients, left out others completely and added their own "secret" ingredients that technically weren't even food.

"We'll be back before lunch," the sisters said, and they bustled off to make Alberto some of their infamous fennel soup.

# CAKES AND SWEETS
# AND STRAWBERRY JAM

Despite taking several sips of Rosa and Clara's soup, Fia got better first. Within days she had recovered from the flight with the lantern and begun to fly in circles around the room. Her beak was a little bent from when she had carried the light, but at least now it matched her wing.

Alberto continued to burn wood at a furious pace, and a constant plume of smoke billowed from the chimney. Every day that passed the temperature dropped another degree until it was too cold even to snow. Alberto realized that if he had not brought Tito in, he would have died in the same room as his mother.

When he was not forced to work on a coffin, Alberto spent every moment caring for Tito. Despite his doubts, he did not give up on his quest to save the boy. He kept the fire burning constant and bright, kept the blankets warm and sat beside him all through each night. But no matter what Alberto did, Tito Bonito would not wake up. The old coffin maker would have to try something else.

Leaving Fia on guard, and one window open so she could fly for help if need be, Alberto went down into town to buy Tito Bonito a treat so sweet it would surely wake him up.

On the first day, Tito went to Enzo's bakery.

"Good morning, Enzo," he called as he stepped into the warm shop. Steam filled the glass cabinets rising before him. Through the milky mist he could see cream buns, doughnuts bursting with blackberry jam and raisin cakes as big as his fist. In the corner, he spotted the foolish fisherman. Enzo must have let him in during the night so he could escape the cold.

"Morning, Alberto," the baker replied with a smile as warm as his shop. He stepped past the sleeping fisherman and approached his friend. "Haven't seen you for a few days."

"Been a bit under the weather."

"Ah, so has my wife. I'll just go and fetch you a fresh loaf."

"Actually," Alberto said as the baker turned around, "I'm not after bread today. I was hoping to buy something sweet."

"So you've finally found your sweet tooth?" Enzo had a little chuckle. "I knew you'd find it one day. How about a little orange cake?"

Alberto looked at the small, round cake Enzo was pointing to and shook his head. He didn't think Tito would like that.

"Do you have anything sweeter?"

"Of course. How about a lemon cream pie?"

Again, Alberto shook his head.

"Sweeter still?" Enzo said.

"The sweetest thing you've got."

Enzo walked behind his glass cabinets, studying each treat in turn. A few times he nodded to himself, but then shook his head. Eventually, he said, "Ah, this is the one. No doubt. You can't get anything sweeter than this," and pulled a treat off the highest shelf. He placed it on a piece of parchment paper and presented it to Alberto.

"What is it?" Alberto asked.

"A triple cream gateaux with extra layers of custard and butterscotch jam. There's almost half a bag of sugar in that."

"Good," Alberto said. "I'll take it."

On the second day, when Tito had failed to stir for the triple cream gateaux, Alberto returned to Allora's main square and studied the shops rising around him. His eyes soon settled on a pink one in the corner. He walked across the square and entered Madame Claudine's sweet shop.

"Alberto?" old Madame Claudine said when she saw who had just walked through the door. "Why, I haven't seen you in here for thirty years. What was it you bought?" She paused for a moment and stared at the ceiling. "Ah. I remember. A chocolate wolf for Anna Marie, a speckled frog for Antonio and a raspberry fish for little Aida." Her smile turned into a frown. "May those sweet children rest in peace with their dear mother." After making the sign of the Gods, she bustled closer. "Now, Alberto, what can I do for you today?"

Alberto took off his frost-laced cap and said, "I'm hoping to buy something sweet."

"Then you've come to the right place. No sweeter shop in all of Allora. Here, let me show you my wares."

Madame Claudine, in her bright, twirling skirts,

led Alberto around her shop. She pointed out every sweet that lined the store and told Alberto a little about each one.

"These are the chocolate wolves that Anna Marie loved so much. They're our highest seller, especially in summer when all the tourists come from the north. They don't have wolves up there, you see. The Great Mountains are far too high for them to cross.

"And these ones here –" She pointed to a barrel full of rainbow, jelly birds "– are called the Birds of Summer. The colour in them will stain your tongue and teeth for two weeks straight.

"And these," she said, stopping before a barrel full of green and brown pinwheels, "are peppermint creams. Nothing wakes you up as swift as one of Madame Claudine's famous peppermint creams."

Alberto was sure the peppermint creams would do the trick. But, alas, they did not. And so, for a third day, Alberto made his way down to Allora's main square. This time he entered the town's only jammery and asked for the owner's finest jar of strawberry jam. He'd heard Tito talk several times about how much he loved strawberry jam.

"Coming right up, Alberto," jam-maker Cirillo

said. He pulled a large jar off the shelf behind him and wrapped it in red ribbon. As he went to hand it over, Alberto held out three copper coins.

"No, no," the jam-maker said. "This jar is for free."

"But I insist." Alberto placed the coins on the counter.

"And I insist even more so," the jam-maker said. He picked up the coins and stacked them on the lid of jam. Then he held both out towards the coffin maker.

"But why?" Alberto said. He could not understand.

"We could only afford spider wood for my mother," the jam-maker explained. "But you, Alberto, buried her in poplar. I'd give you every jar of jam in my store for free in thanks for that."

Alberto had been certain that the strawberry jam would wake Tito up. But, alas, just like the triple cream gateaux and the peppermint creams, it failed to make the boy stir.

Alberto began to fear he could do nothing to halt Tito's impending death. He even thought about measuring him for a coffin, but when he had the tape in his hands he couldn't bring himself to do it. But luckily, twelve days after he carried the boy's frail body home through the snow, Tito Bonito woke up.

"Tito!" Alberto cried. He pulled a steaming bowl away from his pale face. "You're awake!" He could not believe it. He had done it. He had saved Tito Bonito.

Tito looked up at Alberto and then turned to the bowl. He took a deep breath and spoke his first words in twelve days.

"Is that chocolate?" he croaked.

Alberto laughed. "Yes, it is. Chocolate pudding. I made it myself. It was my wife's recipe. It's still warm, and there's cream with it. Would you like some?"

Alberto helped Tito to sit up. When he was propped against the pillows, he spooned some pudding into his mouth. Tito swallowed. Coughed. Spluttered. And swallowed again.

"It's brilliant," he said with a big, chocolately grin.

When all the pudding was gone, Fia began to peck the bowl clean. In the twelve days Tito had lain still, she had grown bigger and bigger. No longer the size of a sparrow or a magpie, she was now larger than a hawk.

Tito looked around the room. "Where am I?" he asked.

"In my house."

"I've never seen this room before."

"That's because it's upstairs. This was my children's room. But, if you would like, it can be your room now. For as long as you want."

# TITO'S FIRST STORY

Tito couldn't believe it. He'd never had his own room before and though his first was filled with things that belonged to other people – dusty books, hand-made dolls and wooden horses – he still thought it was the best room in the whole world.

While the winter days grew colder and darker, his new home grew warmer and brighter. After eating lots of chocolate pudding, fish stew and a whole bag of peppermint creams, he grew strong enough to walk and within days was exploring every room in the house. He looked under every bed, opened every cupboard and examined every tool in Alberto's workshop. He only steered clear of one thing: the windows.

Aware that Tito did not want to be seen (though why, he could not be sure), Alberto warned him of two dangers living next door.

"You must be careful," he said one day while Tito was eating breakfast in the kitchen. "Next door live two old sisters called Clara and Rosa who love to gossip. They tell everyone everything, and if they were to learn that you are here the whole town would know by lunchtime."

Tito took the warning very seriously. He left his half-eaten porridge on the table and went upstairs to fetch an old sheet. Then he spent the rest of the day tearing it into pieces and placing the cloth over every window.

As Alberto watched each room in the house grow dark, a bad feeling formed in the pit of his stomach. Tito wasn't just worried about being seen. He was absolutely terrified. But why?

Though it only took one extra fireplace to make the whole house warm, Alberto lit them all anyway. Soon, despite all the cloth covering the windows, every room grew bright, and the four chimneys jutting from the roof sent cheerful puffs of smoke into the air, like a signal to another land.

While Tito refused to let Alberto take him down into the town, he did occasionally sneak out into the garden during the day when Rosa and Clara were out shopping or at night when the gossiping sisters were snoring like two freight trains in their beds. Afterwards, he would sit beside the fire in his room and Alberto would read him a story.

Before he came to the coffin maker's house, Tito Bonito had never been read a story. So when it came to choosing his first one, he picked it very carefully. He pulled out every book from his bedroom shelf and studied each one in turn. He examined the drawings on the front, the drawings inside and the strange words that covered both. Then, finally, he made a decision.

"Can you read me this?" he asked Alberto. He held up a large cloth-bound book with a drawing of a giant mountain on the front.

"Ah," Alberto said. "*The Story of Isola*. That was Anna Marie's favourite. It's very long," he warned Tito. "It will take many nights to read."

"That's OK." Tito held the book out towards

Alberto. "That's why I chose it."

The coffin maker took the book and cleared his throat. "Right," he said. He put on his reading glasses and, for the first time in thirty years, opened the dusty pages.

*There once lived a famous explorer who was born Giovanni Moretti, but went by the name of Gio. When Gio was a child he would look upon trees no one had ever climbed and climb them. When Gio was a young man he would look upon raging rivers no one had ever crossed and cross them. And when Gio was no longer young but not yet old he would look upon mountains no one had ever scaled and scale them. Gio was the greatest explorer the world had ever seen and his greatest discovery was made at the age of thirty-three.*

*The mountain Gio decided to climb on the morning of his thirty-third birthday did not look like much from the ground. But once he reached the peak, its true wonders were revealed.*

*Like fog rising on a winter morning, he saw the mountain for what it truly was. On this mountain the trees weren't made of wood, but silver; the flowers weren't made of petals, but rubies; and the grass, every blade, was made of emeralds. And in amongst*

these wonders roamed even more: fish that walked on land, horses that cantered through the air and birds that couldn't simply fly, but swim.

Gio looked down upon all of these wonders and tried to think of a name to call the mountain he had just scaled. But before he could, he heard a whisper on the wind and the whisper said this:

*Isola.*

"Isola?" Gio said. "Yes. That is a name. That is the name. That is the name I shall call my mountain."

Plucking a ruby flower for proof, Gio returned to the dull world below and began to tell everyone – everywhere – about the wondrous mountain he had found. But even with the proof of a ruby flower, no one believed a word he said.

"It could not be possible," men would say when they heard about Gio's latest adventure.

"It could not be real," women would agree when their husbands told them the tale.

"But it is possible!" Gio would cry when he heard them call him a liar. "But it is real!" he would scream to the crowds that gathered to listen. "I swear it is the truth. Here. See. This map." He would throw down a piece of parchment and point to a cross in the middle. "That is it. That is the magical mountain: the magical mountain of Isola."

*Most did not believe a single word Gio said.*

*"The ravings of a mad man," they all agreed with a nod of their heads.*

*But some, just a few, looked upon this map and began to wonder if maybe the magic Gio spoke of was not false but real. And so, within a moon of Gio finding Isola Mountain, a small group of men, armed with a map, set out to find it for themselves.*

Having reached the end of the story's first chapter, Alberto closed the book and took off his glasses.

"Can you read some more?" Tito asked. He hadn't moved an inch during the story and Fia hadn't either. She'd listened so closely her tail feathers had singed on the fire.

"Not tonight, Tito. I'm feeling quite tired."

"Then tomorrow?"

"All right. I'll read you the next chapter then."

"And the next day?" Tito asked as he helped Alberto return the book to its shelf. "Can you read us another chapter then?"

"I'll read you one every night. On and on until we've read the whole story. Now, Tito Bonito, it's time for all of us to get to bed."

\*

"Alberto's house is looking warm," Clara said as she peered out the window. The sound of a giant mackerel throwing tiles off the roof had pulled her wide awake. Unable to fall back asleep, she'd taken to staring down Allora Lane, searching for the scent of gossip. "Look at all that smoke." Four trails rose out of the coffin maker's house.

Rosa, who had woken to the sight of that same mackerel crashing into her fireplace, hurried over to see. "Why do you think they're all burning?" she whispered.

"Maybe he's cold or—" Clara gasped and her eyes widened with horror. "Oh no," she said.

"What is it?" Rosa asked.

"You don't think. . ."

"Think what?" As usual, Rosa was one thought behind her older sister.

"You don't think he's started to *burn* the bodies, do you?"

Rosa gasped even louder than Clara. Then she poked her head outside and spent the rest of the night trying to catch a glimpse of what the coffin maker was up to.

# THE MAN WHO STOLE
# THREE APPLES

Tito had been living at Alberto's house for two weeks when they finished the frame for the mayor's coffin and began work on the first cluster of cherubs that would adorn the lid.

"That's very good, Tito," Alberto remarked as he watched the boy carve feathers into a wooden wing. Tito's small hands made the work easy. But it wasn't just that. Tito had a way with the wood that some people were just born with. It was like his heart knew how to shape it and his hands did all the work. Even Alberto's own son, Antonio, had not been able to work wood like that. "I bet you'd make a wonderful blacksmith too. Maybe you could have some lessons with old master Luca down in the forge?"

At the suggestion Tito's hand slipped and he scraped a deep mark right across the cherub's right cheek.

"Don't worry," Alberto said when he saw Tito's shaking hands. "It was only an idea. You don't have to go anywhere you don't want to."

Tito's hands began to still. He looked up from the coffin and said, "I'd rather just stay here."

"Are you sure?" Alberto asked. "There are many wonderful things out there." He motioned towards the window and the wide world that existed beyond.

Tito shook his head and turned his attention back to the mayor's coffin. He adjusted his grip on the chisel and began to carve another feather into the cherub's scarred wing.

Alberto returned to the cherub he had been carving, but his eyes did not leave Tito. Though he had been looking after the boy for weeks he still knew hardly anything about him. Tito was like a puzzle he desperately wanted to solve. But how can you solve a puzzle when so many pieces are missing? Hoping to discover one today, Alberto cautiously asked the boy another question.

"Tito," he said. "Why don't you want to leave the house? Are you frightened of something? Please," Alberto said when Tito didn't reply. "Please tell me the truth. Maybe I can help."

Tito looked up from the coffin and studied Alberto. Seeing something he liked, he said, "I don't want to leave because then I might be seen."

"By who?" Alberto asked.

"Everyone."

"What's so bad about that?"

Tito paused for a moment, like he wasn't going to answer. But then he did. "People talk about what they see, and if they talk about me he might hear. Then he'll come to get me."

"*He*?" Alberto asked. "Who's he?"

"My father."

Alberto gasped. "You never told me you had a father, Tito. I should contact him. Tell him you're safe."

"But you can't!" Tito's eyes widened with a fear so great they doubled in size. "He can never know I'm here."

"But why not? What's so bad about your father?"

Tito's eyes flickered around the room. He looked at the dusty roof. He looked at the empty coffin.

He looked at the saws, in five different sizes, hanging from the wall. Then, finally, his eyes returned to Alberto.

"Everything," he said softly. "That's why we ran away."

"From the north?" Alberto asked.

Tito nodded. "We came from the other side of the mountains: just me and my mum. We travelled by train. We would get off at each station and try to live there. But wherever we stopped he found us. He found us hiding in the town of Trento. He found us sleeping in the stables outside Verona. He even found us hiding in the northern woods, ten miles from the nearest town. Then he'd drag us back home."

"Did he hurt you?" Alberto asked. Worry made the wrinkles on his face grow deeper.

Tito shook his head. "My mum wouldn't let him. She was my protector." When he spoke of his mum, Tito's face lit up like the sun shone upon it, but then a cloud rolled over. "He wouldn't let us leave the house after that. But then one night, while he was on patrol, we escaped. This time when we got on the train we didn't get off until we reached the end of the line. My mum used to call this place magical. She said that whenever anyone got hungry in Allora they just held out their hand and plucked a fish from the sky."

"Tito," Alberto said. "You have been living here for over a year. Perhaps, just maybe, your father has stopped searching."

Tito shook his head. "He'll never stop searching for me."

"How can you be sure?"

For the first time since he came into the coffin maker's house, Tito decided to tell Alberto a story of his own.

*One day a man broke into our house and stole three apples. My father is the lead Carabineer in all of Bolzano, so he knew the thief had to be punished. He offered a reward of one gold coin to whoever handed him in first.*

*It did not take long. The next day a woman came to our house and said the man who had stolen the apples lived on a farm just outside of town.*

*My father gathered his three best Carabineers and marched out to the farm. He found an old man standing in a small paddock that held one cow, one sheep and one chicken.*

*The animals were the only three things that the old man owned. He would drink the cow's milk for breakfast, eat the chicken's egg for lunch and, in winter, knit himself a warm jumper made from the sheep's wool.*

My father looked down at the old man and said, "Are you the thief who stole three apples?"

Hunger had made the man into a thief, but he was not a liar. So he told my father the truth.

"Yes," he said. "It was me. I am the man who stole three apples from you."

"Every thief must be punished," my father said. "You stole three apples so now you owe me three things."

Winter had only just passed and it was late in the day so the old man had already drunk the cow's milk, had already eaten the chicken's egg and had already made a jumper from the sheep's wool. But then he had an idea.

"Tomorrow you can have my pail of milk. The next day you can have my chicken's egg. And, when winter next comes, I will knit you a jumper made from wool."

My father thought over the offer and then shook his head. That was not enough. He turned to the first Carabineer and said, "Take his cow."

Then he turned to the second Carabineer and ordered, "Take his sheep."

Then he turned to the third Carabineer and screamed, "Take his chicken!"

"Please," the old man begged as the Carabineers started to drag his animals away. "They're all I have.

*Please, just take one. Just take the sheep. Or take two – the sheep and the chicken. Just leave me the cow. Please, you must leave me something."*

But my father said, "You stole three apples. Not one."

And then he and the three Carabineers took the animals away.

"You see," Tito said, "that's what my father's like. When something is taken from him he doesn't stop until he gets it back or he's hurt the person who took it."

"But . . . but surely all that about the man and three apples is just a story," Alberto said.

Tito shook his head. "No it isn't. It's the truth."

The workshop grew so silent that they could hear a lone fish flapping about on the Finestra sisters' roof. Alberto did not know what to say, but Tito did. He had a request. All this talk of his father had made him desperate to see someone else.

"Alberto?" he said. "Could you take me to my mum?"

Now that he knew who Tito was hiding from, Alberto wanted to keep the boy inside for ever. But then he looked at Tito's hopeful face and knew he couldn't say no.

"Of course," he said. "I will take you there tonight."

Alberto checked to make sure the lane was clear. Behind him, Tito peered out into the night. It was so late all the lights in lower Allora were out and two rounds of snores filtered through the shutters next door.

"Come on," Alberto whispered to Tito.

Wrapped in a set of Antonio's winter clothes Tito, for the first time, stepped into Allora Lane. Fia flew beside him, enjoying the late-night air flowing through her wings.

The sound of giant whitecaps crashing into the black water below drowned out the clap of Alberto and Tito's shoes as they climbed Allora Hill. When they reached the graveyard at the top, Alberto opened the gate. It creaked at the familiar touch of his hand.

"She's over here," Alberto whispered. He led Tito to a small grave near the front gate. "I didn't know her first name or her age, but I did the best I could."

Tito stared at the grey stone for several minutes, his eyes scanning the words engraved on top. "What does it say?" he finally asked Alberto.

HERE LIES
# MISS BONITO
WHO DIED ALONE
BUT SHALL LAY ALONE NO LONGER.

"But she didn't die alone," Tito said. "I was there with her, all the time."

Alberto's mind travelled back to the night Enzo carried Miss Bonito into his workshop. Enzo's wife had said the sheets of the bed had been warm. Alberto had dismissed her words, but now he realized she spoke the truth. The sheets were warm because of Tito. He must have been lying beside his mother. When Enzo and Santos carried her away, he had followed. That was how he had found himself at Alberto's home.

"Her name was Anita," Tito said. "But her mum called her Ani."

"Her mum?" Alberto's eyes widened. "Do you have other family, Tito? Do you have grandparents?"

Tito shook his head. "They're all dead. My father's the only one left."

To give Tito some privacy, Alberto visited four special graves of his own. His family lay far deeper in to the graveyard. Though he attended at least two funerals a week, it had been a long time since he had visited them.

When Alberto reached their plots, he knelt down and spoke to each one in turn.

"Ah, little Aida," he said to the grave that marked the smallest coffin. "I have been giving my scraps to the stray cats every day, just like you asked. And my little Antonio." He turned to the next grave along. "Tito is taking very good care of your things. And Anna Marie, I have been brushing my teeth every night. Well, most nights, and you were right. They have started to look less green."

Alberto cast his eyes upon the final grave. When he read the words on top, his eyes began to water. "Ah, Violetta, my dear Violetta, what can I say to you? We always hoped for another child and now I have found one. Tito is his name. He's a giant of a little thing. You would have had your hands full with him."

Alberto stayed with his family until the clock tower chimed in a new hour. Then he kissed each stone goodbye and went to fetch Tito.

# ALBERTO HEARS A RUMOUR

The rumour started two days after Tito and Alberto returned from the graveyard. Clara was the one Alberto heard it from first. He was cleaning the tools in his workshop one evening when he heard the sisters gossiping over the fence. Usually he ignored them, but when he heard two words in amongst so many – "Bonito" and "child" – he began to listen closely.

"It's true," Clara was saying. Alberto could not see her, though he imagined she was nodding her head with an eagerness only good gossip could bring. "Miss Bonito had a child."

*Oh no,* Alberto thought. Someone must have seen him and Tito go to the graveyard.

"What type of child?" Rosa asked.

"A little one, like a small person."

"But what *type* of child, Clara?"

"Rather small, I believe."

"No. You misunderstand. Is the child a boy or a girl?"

"Oh. A boy, I believe, called Nito or Beto or Sito or – Tito. That's it!" she exclaimed so loudly Alberto feared Tito would hear. "Tito Bonito."

Both sisters laughed.

"What a silly name," Rosa said.

From where he stood inside his workshop, Alberto's face darkened.

"So where is he?" Rosa enquired when they had stopped laughing. "Where is this Tito Bonito? He didn't die too, did he? Maybe we should ask Alberto."

At the mention of his name, Alberto pulled his head inside. When neither sister called out, he leant back out into the night.

"No. No. He didn't die. That's the thing. The *mystery* of it all." Clara paused for effect. She paused for so long, in fact, that it lost all effect and Rosa got annoyed.

"Well?" she said impatiently. "What's the mystery?"

"The mystery is that ... no one knows where he is."

"Then how do you know he even *is*?"

"Because, I believe," Clara said delightedly, "his father has come looking for him. He has come to Allora for the child. *His* child. He has come to take Tito Bonito home."

Alberto Cavello had never been one for gossip, but now he listened closely and learned all sorts of things. Though which things were true and which were false, he could not be sure.

Apparently, or so Clara believed:

"Mr Bonito has been searching for two years. His wife left with the child one night while he was working an—"

"Working?" Rosa interrupted. "Working as what?"

"The lead Carabineer of all Bolzano."

"Ooh," Rosa said. "That's almost as powerful as the mayor."

"He's been following the train-line south ever since," Clara said, continuing with her story, "stopping at every station and searching for the son who was stolen from him."

"She must have been crazy to leave a man like that," Rosa added.

"That's what he said. She wasn't right in the head. Kept on making up stories. Saying people were trying to hurt her."

The next night Alberto pressed his ear to the fence even harder than the sisters usually had theirs pressed to his, and he learned of what happened on the night Mr Bonito arrived in Allora.

"He came asking for a Mrs Bonito and her son. He went all the way to the mayor who told him about our Miss Bonito. Said he was right there when they brought her body in. But he assured the man that she didn't have a son."

"Then how did he find out our Miss Bonito was his Mrs Bonito?" Rosa asked.

"Well, at first he didn't think she was. But then he asked the mayor to describe her and said that was the one."

"But what about his son?"

"Thought he was dead too, but then he went to the cottage and found a pile of blankets and a bowl of stew. He's been living there in secret without her for all these mon—"

"*Twrp!*"

Alberto jumped and spun around. The back door had just opened. Tito poked his head outside.

He was holding a large red book under his arm.

Before Tito could speak, Alberto hurried inside and closed the door.

"What were you doing?" Tito asked.

"Oh, nothing," Alberto said lightly. He checked to make sure the door was locked. "Just pruning the flowers."

"Come on." Tito pulled on Alberto's hand. "It's time to read the story."

After all the rumours he'd just heard, Alberto didn't feel like reading a story. But the look on Tito's face made it impossible to say no. So when he had tucked Tito safely into bed and all the shutters were firmly closed, Alberto opened the big red book and continued to tell him and Fia the story of Isola.

*When the men armed with Gio's map reached the Mountain of Isola their faces hardened with anger.*

*"It was a lie!" they screamed.*

*"I knew it was impossible!" they yelled.*

*For the mountain rising before them did not look magical. Not at all. In fact, it looked just like every other mountain: plain and green and positively ordinary.*

*They were ready to turn back then and there, when one amongst them recalled something Gio the*

Explorer had said.

"Like a key that must be turned in a lock, we must climb the mountain to see its wonders."

And so, instead of turning back, they continued on. They climbed up the mountain, past trees made of wood, flowers made of petals and grass that was just grass, until finally they reached the peak.

"Would you look at that," the men said, as the true wonders of Isola were revealed.

"He was telling the truth," they all cried at once.

Within seconds of their eyes falling upon the wonders, the men began to grab them for themselves. They filled their pockets with rocks of chocolate; stashed snowflakes made of pearl in jars meant for jam and put droplets of never-ending fire into their dark lanterns. Then they threw ropes into the sky and hauled flying horses to the ground, crammed dancing fish into their hats and pulled swimming birds from the ponds. When they could carry no more, they took the bright wonders of Isola down into the dull world below.

The group of men had intended to keep quiet about the wonders they had discovered. But then one got drunk and told his wife who told another. And soon word got out. Isola Mountain was real and, for a small price, you could buy one of its wonders for yourself:

A flower of rubies for five gold coins.

A ball of chocolate for three.

And, for ten gold and three silver, you could purchase a lantern full of light that never went out.

But there was one item that was not sold in the streets. Instead, it was auctioned to the highest bidder for the price of three thousand gold coins.

The map that led to Isola was won by a mayor from the north. But, strangely, the mayor had no intention of trekking to Isola Mountain himself. Instead he ordered an army of scribes to make ten thousand copies of the one map he had bought. Then he sent these copies out into the world and sold every single one. Without even setting foot on Isola Mountain he became the richest man in the world.

But the number of maps did not stop there. For the men and women who had bought maps from the mayor made copies of their own. And soon, within five moons of Gio's thirty-third birthday, every family in the land had seen a map that led to Isola.

# TITO LEARNS HIS
# A-B-CS

After the rumours began, Alberto made sure Tito remained inside even more. He did not want the boy to worry, so he kept the sisters' words to himself. For all he knew, Mr Bonito would leave – give up the search in Allora – before Tito even learned he was there.

But luckily Alberto did not have to worry about keeping Tito occupied. As soon as the rumours started, he began to teach him how to read. Alberto had never seen anyone so excited to learn something new. Tito was like a sea sponge that had lain on land for ten years and now, finally, had been thrown into the sea and could soak all the churning knowledge up.

Alberto gave Tito an old A-B-C book he had used to teach himself how to read fifty years before. On the first day, Tito learned the alphabet all the way to F. He was so excited by his progress he did not fall asleep until three o'clock in the morning and was up again at six to learn the letter G.

Tito was so busy learning letters he did not have time to listen to any stories, not even the one about Isola. Instead, he spent every night sitting in bed with Fia who proudly listened as he recited his ABCs.

While Tito practised his letters, Alberto would go downstairs and work on his coffin. But one night, as he shaped a piece of poplar into a handle, he paused.

Alberto turned the wood over in his hands. He spun it. He touched it. And when his old fingers finally stopped he didn't see the handle of a coffin any more but what could, with a little work, be something very different.

A loud squeal woke Alberto at quarter past seven in the morning.

"Look, Fia," Tito exclaimed in the room across the hall. "It's a boat. A real wooden boat. Too little for me, but just the right size for you."

Alberto heard footsteps crossing the hall. A moment later, a shy hand knocked on his bedroom door.

"Alberto?" Tito whispered. "May I come in?"

"Of course." Alberto sat upright to the sight of Tito and Fia charging into his room.

"Look," Tito said, running over to the coffin maker. "Look what I found right at the end of my bed." He held out a little wooden boat that smelt of fresh sawdust. "Did you make it?" he asked.

Alberto nodded sleepily. He had been up all night carving the wood and fitting a piece of cloth to its mast for a sail.

"Is it for me?" Tito sounded afraid like it would, in a moment, be taken away.

"Of course it is for you."

"I've never had my own toy before." Tito looked down at the boat and then up at Alberto. "What do I do with it?"

"Why, you play with it."

"And where do I keep it when I'm not playing with it?"

"Anywhere you like."

"And – and—" Tito bounced with another question. "And can it float?" he finally said.

"Why, I don't know. Should we go and see?"

\*

That night when Alberto returned to his workshop he pushed his own coffin aside and made a wooden train with five carriages. The following night, he made a set of miniature birds that fitted one inside the other. Soon he had made so many toys for Tito he had to build a large chest to store them.

While Alberto made toys for Tito at night, during the day he played with him. They played marbles in the kitchen, blindman's buff in the workshop and hide and seek all over the house. Hardly a sound left their lips for fear the sisters next door would hear, but despite the silence their days became full of fun and, for the first time in thirty years, the house at the top of Allora Hill became a bright and happy home once more.

# ALBERTO'S PROMISE

Though Alberto could keep Tito inside most of the time, he could not deny him visits to his mother. So late at night, when the moon was the only other thing up, they would sneak out to the graveyard at the top of the hill.

Tito would go to his mother's grave while Alberto went to his family's four. Sometimes Tito was there for hours, whispering whole days of conversation in one night. Alberto did not know what he spoke about and though, of course curious, never asked. Those words were meant for Tito's mother alone.

One night Tito spoke for so long that the clock tower chimed in a new morning. Alberto, for the first time, had to go over and interrupt. But before they could leave, someone else entered the graveyard.

"Quick, Tito. Hide," Alberto whispered. But he need not have spoken. After one glance at the approaching man, Tito had jumped behind a gravestone and was now hidden from sight.

Alberto watched the man approach. In the dark of night, he couldn't see much. He was tall and dark and, instead of walking, marched.

"Hello," Alberto said when the man drew so near he could ignore him no longer.

The stranger jumped and reached into his pocket. The handle of a pistol appeared. It glistened white in the moonlight.

"Strange time to visit a graveyard," the armed man said.

"And yet," Alberto replied, unable to stop his voice quivering, "both of us are here."

The dark stranger stepped nearer. When Alberto's form grew clear, he loosened his grip on the gun. "Good point. Are you the caretaker?"

"In a way. I'm the coffin maker."

The man's eyes flashed with interest. "Then you

might be able to help. I'm looking for someone. My wife. She's in here somewhere. Bonito's the name."

"Why, you're right here." Alberto pointed to the grave before them. He had suspected the man was Tito's father – they shared a likeness in the shape of their faces – and now he knew for sure.

"So I am," Mr Bonito said. His eyes skimmed the gravestone and settled on something small and white that stuck out of the winter grass below. "What's that?"

"It's a flower," Alberto said.

Mr Bonito picked the flower up and snapped the thin stalk in two. Droplets of juice, like morning dew, seeped out. "A fresh flower that has just been placed."

"Yes." To block the gravestone Tito hid behind, Alberto shifted his body to the left. "I just put it there."

"You?" Mr Bonito's eyes jumped with surprise and then suspicion. "Why would you—" He took a step forward. His large shadow fell across the old coffin maker. "Leave a flower on *my* wife's grave?"

"Because I knew her," Alberto said with only a slight gulp.

Mr Bonito's eyebrows rose. "Oh, did you? And in what *way* did you know my wife?"

"I made her coffin. I already told you that. I'm the coffin maker."

"Oh." A little of Mr Bonito's suspicion fell away, but some remained. "Do you place flowers above every coffin you make?"

"Well, of course not. There aren't enough flowers in my garden to do that."

"So why place a flower on my wife's grave?"

"Because no one else does."

"And why would they?" Up until that moment Mr Bonito had been quite civil, but now his voice cracked through the air like a whip. "She thought she could take him away from me. But she couldn't. You see, a boy should be with his father. He is mine, and I will have him. That's why she was punished. Death was her curse and so shall it be the curse of anyone who has helped her." Anger made his mouth froth like the sea after a storm.

"Mr Bonito," Alberto said calmly, "death will be the curse of everyone. Even you."

"Well—" Mr Bonito's voice grew as icy as the late winter air. "I wouldn't bother leaving any more." He kicked at the flower lying broken on the ground. "She didn't deserve flowers. Besides, I'm sure there's a little hand that's eager to leave another."

"If you're talking about your son, I wouldn't be too sure about that. Miss Bonito lived in this town for over a year and no one saw this so-called son, not once."

"But I know he was here," Mr Bonito said. "I found his things, and she never went anywhere without him."

"But perhaps he is here no longer. You have missed a nasty snap in the weather. A chill so deep it almost froze the very sea. I doubt any child living by himself could have survived that."

"Ah, but who said he was living by himself?"

Alberto frowned. "Whatever do you mean? If no one has seen the boy, no one could be helping him."

"No one has *said* they have seen him. They're two very different things."

"Yes, well, it is a possibility," Alberto admitted. It would have been suspicious to deny that.

"A very real one," Mr Bonito said. He looked across the sea for a moment, as if thinking, and then turned back to Alberto. "You're right," he said. "Someone must be helping him."

"Well, you can't be sure of tha—"

"Yes I can," Mr Bonito snarled. "There was that bowl of stew. No other bowls in the house had looked like that." His eyes lit with triumph. "Here I was waiting for the boy to come back to the cottage. But if he has help, I'll have to do far more than that."

Without another word to Alberto, Mr Bonito spun on his heel and marched towards the graveyard gate, trampling over graves as he went.

Alberto watched Mr Bonito leave. When he was long lost to sight, he leant over the tombstone behind him and whispered, "Tito, are you still there?"

The young boy slowly stood up. The tombstone was so large, he remained in its shadow.

"Did he see me?" Tito whispered.

"I don't think so."

Tito's body relaxed, but when he spoke his voice was filled with worry. "What I said isn't false. It's the truth. He really did hurt my mum and do those bad things. I swear it."

Hearing the despair in Tito's voice, Fia poked her head out of his jacket (she was now far too large for his pocket) and nuzzled him gently on the chin.

"I know, Tito," Alberto said. "I believe you."

"Please don't let him take me."

"I'll try, Tito."

"But trying isn't enough. My mum tried every time, and he caught us every time. You have to promise."

Alberto was not the type of man to make promises he could not keep, but more than that he was not the type of man who wanted Tito to worry. So, though he feared a day might come when he couldn't keep it, he opened his mouth and said:

"I promise, Tito. Now, come around here. There'll be no more hiding behind gravestones for you."

# THE SAILING COFFIN
# MAKER

Now that Tito knew his father was back, he had no desire to leave Alberto's house. Even the garden became too dangerous in Tito's eyes. And so, as winter turned to spring, he remained inside, trapped not by a key and lock but by fear: the fear that his father would find him and take him far away.

As the seasons changed, Mr Bonito remained in Allora. After his conversation with Alberto, he had stopped waiting for Tito to return to his mother's home and now waited for someone to return the boy to him. He had offered a reward of twenty, then fifty, then one hundred golden coins to whoever returned him first. Alberto had never seen so much money – not even the mayor's coffin had cost that much – but he wasn't tempted in the slightest.

Alberto tried his best to keep Tito busy. Their reading lessons continued, and soon Tito could read whole words by himself. Alberto's old ABC book was cast aside in favour of books with proper stories, and it wasn't long before Tito knew all sorts of long, tricky words like gingerbread, bumblebee and pomegranate.

The more Tito read the more curious he became. No subject was dull to him. Alberto could not enroll him in school, so he tried to bring school to him instead. He taught him all that he knew, not just about wood and coffins, but about history, geography and arithmetic. He even tried to teach him how to cook. Yet no matter how much Alberto told Tito, the boy always had more questions than he could answer.

While Tito could not leave the house, Alberto left every day. In the morning he would walk down the cobbled lanes of Allora, buy a fresh loaf of bread from Enzo and a small bag of sweets from Madame Claudine and then he would sit in the main square and wait.

Alberto wasn't waiting to meet someone. Rather, he was waiting to hear someone – anyone – who spoke of the Bonito name. By now the reward had climbed to one hundred and fifty golden coins and false sightings of Tito Bonito had risen to at least three each day.

"I saw him climbing the town wall," said a man outside the tavern. "Almost tripped over his own feet. But by the time Mr Bonito arrived he had disappeared like a ghost into the air."

"I heard a child crying down by the rocks," said a woman about to enter Madame Claudine's sweet shop. "Weeping for his long lost father and cursing his evil, crazed mother. But by the time I reached the water the child was gone, swept clean out to sea."

"It's true. The sea has claimed him," said the foolish fisherman as he awakened from a deep slumber. "I saw it just now, in my dreams. The waves came and took him away, so very far, far away."

Alberto always breathed a sigh of relief when he heard these lies and imaginings. There was no way Tito could climb the walls of the town, they were far too high; and he was not stupid enough to go and sit by the rocks near the sea. But there was one rumour whispered amongst the people of Allora that was actually a truth. And it made Alberto very worried.

"He's started to search the houses," Enzo said one morning as he fetched Alberto a fresh loaf of bread. "Not all of them. But he has searched three already at the bottom of Allora Hill. Apparently someone saw a child's face looking out the window of the first, a child's shoe lying suspiciously outside the door of the second and a whole child – legs, arms, head and all – running in the garden of the third. The mayor says Mr Bonito can search any home he wants, as long as there has been a sighting. He's even talking about making it a new law."

To keep Tito's mind off his father, Alberto continued to read him stories every night. Or rather, just the one. Tito's favourite: the big red book about Isola.

By now they had heard all about the robbers who had raided Isola Mountain, the crazed queen who had claimed it as her own and the kind farmer who toiled upon its land and bred a whole flock full of diamond sheep. And now, finally, after months of reading they had reached the final chapter.

*Over the space of three and fifty years, men and women, queens and kings, farmers and robbers, all made their mark upon the mountain called Isola. But it was not a good mark. For as the pockets used to smuggle chocolates and pearls turned into buckets and then carriages and carts, the mountain itself began to die. Rubies turned to dust, never-ending fires faded to ash and snowflakes fell to the ground as ice not pearl.*

*But the bad marks did not stop there. For, you see, Isola Mountain was far more special than anyone could know. It possessed a wonder that could not be seen or stolen and that wonder was this: Isola Mountain was alive. Just like you and me, she could think, she could feel and she could dream. And as she felt person after person trampling over her body and tearing wonders from her skin, she began to cry.*

*A mountain is a big thing, far bigger than us, so her tears did not form puddles on the ground, but a whole sea across the land. Waves surged up around the mountain as she sobbed, and the people on Isola fled before they drowned. In a single day Isola Mountain became Isola Island.*

*Isola's tears were as magical as the island itself. She could tame them, control them and move the whole sea at her will. In her anger, she made the water rage without rest for days, weeks, months, even years. As her land remained untrodden all of its stolen wonders grew back.*

*But just like every living thing, Isola grows tired and must sleep. While she sleeps her tears still and if you are fast enough and brave enough you can sail all the way to her island and tread upon the magical land yourself. And if you are good and true and kind, Isola will let you stay. She will treat you like a mother and fiercely keep everyone else away.*

"Wow," Tito said as Alberto closed the final page of the book. "Do you think all that stuff's real?"

"It could be," Alberto replied.

"I'm going to go there one day," Tito said with a stubborn nod of his head. "I'm going to become a sailor and sail all the way to Isola."

"A sailor?" Alberto said. "I thought you wanted to be a coffin maker like me."

"Can't I be both?"

Alberto laughed. "Why, of course you can. You can be the first ever sailing coffin maker. The one and only, sailing from town to town helping to bury the dead."

"And I'll go to Isola first. You can come too," Tito offered.

"That is a kind offer," Alberto said. "But I think I might stay here. I'm far too old for an adventure like that. But I'm sure Fia would be very pleased to join you. The way she stares across that wild sea, I think she'd feel right at home out there."

"*Twrp!*" sang Fia, in her most cheerful tone yet.

"Maybe the two of you could bring me back a present. How about a flying horse? Or perhaps a diamond sheep? Or, I know, a flower made of rubies?"

"All right," said Tito. "I'll bring you back two."

# THE MAYOR TAKES A TUMBLE

Tito and Alberto were eating breakfast one morning when they heard a knock on the front door. By now Tito was used to running when death knocked, so he ran upstairs to his room with Fia. Alberto waited for the door above to click closed before opening the one below.

"Ah, Master Alberto," said the man standing on the other side.

"Good morning, Mister Mayor. What can I do for you?" It had been a long time since his last visit.

"I just came to check on my coffin." He didn't

bother keeping his voice down. His coffin was no longer a secret. The Finestra sisters had made sure of that. "Can I come in?"

"Of course." Alberto stepped aside so the mayor could enter. It was a tight fit, and he feared that if the man got any larger he would need a new coffin. "We're making good progress."

"We?" the mayor asked.

"Yes. You and me." Alberto was quick to correct his mistake. "I think we make a very good team."

"Right you are," the mayor said with a chuckle. "Now, lead the way, Master Alberto. Take me to my glorious coffin."

For once the mayor was pleased with Alberto's progress and, despite the wooden frame, couldn't help admiring his speed and workmanship.

"Particularly those cherubs," he said, pointing to a little cluster near the coffin's base. "What skill you have, Master Alberto."

"Thank you," Alberto said, making a mental note to commend Tito on his work.

"Now, I best be getting on. Wouldn't want to keep you from your work. Though, like I said before, there's no need to rush." The mayor stepped into the hall. "No need at a—"

A loud crash filled the hall, and the whole house shook as if a ship had ploughed through the front door.

"Mayor, are you all right?" Alberto called, racing to his side.

"Yes. Yes. I'm fine." The mayor rocked back and forth like a tortoise stuck on its shell. "Just need a little help getting up."

"Of course. Here, let me." Alberto offered his hand and hauled the great man up.

"Thank you, Master Alberto," he said with an embarrassed chuckle. "Must have tripped over my own fee— hang on. What's that?"

The mayor hadn't tripped over his feet after all. He had tripped over a little wooden sail boat lying in the hall.

They didn't come until later that night. Tito and Alberto were fast asleep. When they heard the knocks, their eyes flew open and they hurried into the hall. They met in the centre, both wearing their nightcaps.

"Who is it?" Tito whispered. Fear robbed his face of all signs of sleep. He had lived with Alberto long enough to know the knock of death. That knock was sad, resigned and, at night, apologetic. This knock was different. It was fast, insistent and angry. Even the mayor did not knock like that.

"I'm not sure." Alberto crept into his room and over to the window. Silently, he opened one of the shutters and peered outside. The sky was dark but the lane was bright.

"Oh no," Alberto said. Four men were gathered below. The mayor stood at the back and Mr Bonito at the front. He could not see the two who stood in between.

"What is it?" Tito rose on to the tip of his toes and tried to peer outside. Alberto closed the shutter before he could see.

"They have come for you," Alberto said.

"What do we do?"

"We must hide you, Tito."

"Just like in our game?"

"Exactly like our game."

"But where?" Tito asked.

Alberto pictured every corner of his house: every fireplace, every cupboard and every bed. But they wouldn't do. Mr Bonito was sure to check there. He needed some place else. Some place no one would even think to check. His eyes lit with an idea.

"Come, Tito. Quickly."

In silence, Alberto, Tito and Fia crept downstairs and into the workshop. Two unfinished coffins lay inside. Alberto couldn't hide Tito inside the mayor's coffin – he would get suspicious if his own was closed – so he led Tito to another.

"Quick, Tito. Get inside, and take Fia with you. Make sure she doesn't chirp. Can you do that?"

With a nod as short and sharp as he was, Tito crawled on to the bench and into the coffin maker's coffin.

"Don't worry," Alberto said as he pulled the lid over the top. A long shadow fell, like a setting sun, over Tito's small body. "I'll come back. I promise."

Alberto closed the lid and nailed his coffin shut.

"Sorry about the wait," Alberto said when he finally opened the door. "I was working on a coffin."

"In your pyjamas?" Mr Bonito asked.

"Yes, well, I couldn't sleep."

"We heard hammering," one of the men said.

Alberto recognized the voice. He searched the shadowed faces before him. To his surprise, he saw his childhood friend, Enzo. Beside him stood his apprentice, Santos.

"Just closing one up," he said sadly. "So..." He

turned back to Mr Bonito. "What can I do for you? Has someone died?"

"Of course not," Mr Bonito said. "We're here about the toy."

"Oh," Alberto said. "That was nothing. Just a misunderstanding."

"I think you misunderstand *me*, Coffin Maker," Mr Bonito said. "I have not come here to listen to you speak. I have come here to search your house for my stolen son. Now, step aside or these two men can hold you down while I search."

"Of course." Alberto stepped back so all four men could enter.

"Sorry about this," Enzo whispered as he walked past. "The mayor roped me and Santos in while we were closing the store. Ordered us to come or he'd lock down the shop for ever."

They searched the kitchen first. Everything looked in order, but as they turned to leave Mr Bonito spotted two bowls drying beside the basin.

"Hang on," he said, coming to a stop. "I recognize the pattern on those bowls." He picked one up and held it closer. "It is the same as the bowl I found in the cottage."

A triumphant gleam shone in Mr Bonito's eyes.

Alberto feared it was all over, but then his oldest friend spoke.

"Why, I recognize them too," Enzo lied. "I have the same set. Do you, Mister Mayor?"

"Of course not! They're far too common for me. I get mine ordered in from France."

"Si, si. Common indeed," Enzo said. "Why, I wouldn't be surprised if half the town owned bowls like those."

Mr Bonito growled in frustration. He dropped the bowl into the basin where it smashed into twenty pieces. Then he turned towards the stairs and climbed up to Alberto's room.

Alberto did not think they would find any sign of Tito in his own room, but then he saw Tito's nightcap lying on the floor. It must have fallen off when he tried to peer out the window. With horror, he realized he was still wearing his own.

"Ah," Enzo said. "I, too, keep a spare nightcap in my room." He picked up the material and placed it in Alberto's hand before the others could notice its small size.

"I think all is in order here," the mayor said with a smart nod. "Shall we move on to the next room?"

Dread slowed Alberto's feet as he followed the four men into Tito's room. Though he had time to hide Tito, he hadn't had time to hide any of his things.

Tito's room smelled of milk and chocolate. The sheets on his bed were ruffled, toys littered the floor and ashes filled the fireplace.

"It was cold this last winter past," Enzo said, nodding to the cinders. "We lit every fireplace in the house, even the rooms we kept closed."

"And what about all of these toys and that lantern?" Mr Bonito snapped. He was starting to suspect the man who had come to help him search was not helping at all. "What excuse is there for a floor full of toys and a bright lantern beside the bed?"

Enzo searched for a lie. When he failed to find one, Mr Bonito turned to Alberto.

"How do you explain all of this? Is there a special guest staying in this home? A friendly little ghost living in this room?"

"I, er..." Alberto fumbled for a lie. In desperation words tumbled from his mouth. They came so quickly he did not know what they were until he spoke them. "I used to have a son, Mr Bonito. Just like you. Only I do not have to search for him. For my son died many years ago. I know, for I made his coffin myself."

Mr Bonito stifled a yawn. He had not come to listen to this old man's story.

"Lately," Alberto continued, before Mr Bonito could interrupt, "your presence in the town and all this talk of your son has opened old wounds: wounds that I have kept bandaged for thirty years. Three decades have I kept this door closed, but lately my thoughts and memories have led me to open it back up. Now, some nights, to my shame, I imagine they are still here with me. Antonio, playing with his toys." Alberto nodded to the wooden train set covering the floor. "Aida, playing with her dolls." He nodded to the dolls in the cupboard that Tito had barely touched. "And Anna Marie reading her books." He nodded to the open book resting by Tito's bed. It was the one about Isola.

"I blush to admit that I also leave their things lying about the house. So then, when I am tired and walk into a room, I suddenly light up because in my tiredness I forget the past and believe they are still here. My devilish Antonio, my wise Anna Marie and my sweet Aida have just left the room, and if I go upstairs I will find them lying asleep in their beds."

The room fell silent. Three of the men stood

with their heads down, but one, Mr Bonito, kept his up. He kept scanning the room hoping for a sign, proof, that it was his son living in this room and not the ghost of someone else's. But he could not find one.

"Come on," Mr Bonito snapped. "We have yet to search the workshop."

Alberto's legs felt like lead as he followed Mr Bonito, Enzo, Santos and the mayor down the stairs. When they reached the workshop, Mr Bonito began to search through Alberto's things. He threw aside all of Alberto's tools, kicked away stacks of wood and peered into the mayor's coffin. Then his eyes fell upon the one that had just been nailed shut.

"Master Umberto Romano," Alberto said, nodding to his own coffin. "Poplar wood. Seventy-one by twenty-five inches."

Even though Enzo and Santos had watched Master Romano's coffin – *Maple, 76 × 18* – be lowered into the ground two weeks before, neither said a thing. Luckily, the mayor had not bothered to attend that funeral so he was oblivious to the lie.

"Well, go on." Mr Bonito nodded towards the coffin. "Open it."

"But..." Alberto searched for another lie. He had told more lies tonight than all other nights of his life put together. "But I can't," he finally said.

Mr Bonito stepped closer to Alberto and reached towards the pocket that held his gun. "Can't or won't?" he said softly.

Alberto gulped and looked to Enzo for help. But the baker looked as lost as he did.

"You see..." Alberto said. "I can't open it because – because..."

Mr Bonito was losing what little patience he possessed. He took a step away from Alberto and reached for a hammer so he could open the coffin himself. But just as he was about to prise the first nail free, Alberto thought of something that just might work.

"We can't open it because I'm not entirely sure what killed Master Romano. However just before I closed the coffin, I noticed a mark. A purple one, behind his ear."

On the other side of the workshop, the mayor's face paled.

"Out," he said, already heading towards the door. "Out!" he screamed as he tripped over a saw that Mr Bonito had thrown on the floor. "Everyone out!"

"Pull yourself together, Mayor," Mr Bonito yelled, "and order this man to open this coffin!"

"Are you crazy?" the mayor blustered. He hauled himself to his feet and took another step towards the door. "We can't open that. We'll catch what he caught. We'll be dead within days."

Mr Bonito looked ready to object. But then the mayor threatened him with an order – "I order you to leave this house immediately or I'll lock you away for three and twenty years" – and he decided it would be best to go. He glanced around the room one final time, his eyes lingering on Alberto and the closed coffin beside him. Then, he reluctantly followed the mayor into the hall.

Alberto saw them off from his front door. He waited for all four men to disappear down the lane before returning to his workshop.

"Tito?" he whispered. "It is safe."

He picked up a hammer and began to prise his coffin open.

# THE COFFIN THAT COST MORE THAN A HOUSE

It may have been safe inside Alberto's house, but outside was more dangerous than ever. When it came to potential gossip the Finestra sisters were like hawks to mice. They had not missed the bright lights outside Alberto's house, and by the next morning they had formed a story that soon spread throughout the town.

"They thought the coffin maker had the missing child. It's true," Clara said to Enzo as they bought their daily loaf of bread. "But he didn't. He was just pretending he still had his own."

"Or so he says," Rosa added with a knowing nod.

"Now I'm sure there's no truth in that," Enzo said as he handed Rosa the oldest, crustiest loaf he could find. "After all, they didn't find him, did they?"

"Just because they didn't find him doesn't mean he isn't there."

"Well, *I* was there," Enzo said, "and every inch of that house was searched and not a single sign of a boy was found."

Enzo had hoped his words would put an end to all the gossip, but it made the sisters gossip even louder. Not only that, they gossiped about him as well. Apparently, or so Rosa and Clara believed, Enzo was helping Alberto hide the missing boy until Mr Bonito increased the reward to two hundred golden coins. Then they could hand him over and claim one hundred each.

News of Mr Bonito's reward had spread and now tourists didn't only come to see the flying fish but to spot the stolen boy. Rumours swirled, gossip grew and every day a stream of people walked to the top of Allora Hill. There hadn't been a procession that long since the mayor's golden oak was carried up.

With so many people clamouring outside, Tito did not dare leave the house. Even his late-night trips to the graveyard stopped. He could not go into the garden either. So enthralled with this gift of gossip living next door and the promise of a bucket full of gold if their rumour proved true, the Finestra sisters no longer pressed their ears to the fence but climbed up and looked over the top. One day Rosa even fell in. Alberto heard the crash all the way from his workshop. Tito did too. He jumped like a startled hare and dived behind the mayor's monstrous coffin.

Now locked off from the outside world completely, Tito threw himself into another world: the magical world of Isola where horses raced through the air and the pebbled shores were made of chocolate. He had reread the story so many times that the pages were fading and some had even fallen out.

While Tito read each chapter over and over again, Fia would sit on his shoulder watching. For weeks she had refused to leave his side, like she too could hear the rumours whispered in the town and understood the danger that Tito was now in.

Tito spent so much time reading that he barely found time to help Alberto work on the mayor's coffin. By now most of the cherubs were carved, but they still had to embed jewels into the wood.

So while Tito escaped into the imaginary world of Isola, Alberto pressed ruby after ruby into the wings of butterflies, sapphire after sapphire into the eyes of angels and diamond after diamond into the hair of cherubs. He had only encrusted eight out of eighty motifs when he realized the mayor's coffin was now worth more than his own house.

Tito never complained about being inside, but sometimes Alberto caught him peering through the cloth on the kitchen window as children ran past, playing in the lane. Tito was missing the real world, and Fia, perched restlessly on his shoulder, was missing it too.

# TITO LOSES A FRIEND

**D**eath came to Alberto's house not with a knock this time but a wail, and what a horrible wail it was.

"Master Alberto!" cried a woman in the earliest hour of the morning. "Master Alberto!" she cried again.

With eyes full of sleep, Alberto made his way downstairs and opened the door to Clara Finestra. She was wailing so loudly her breath made a wind that swirled her dressing gown round and round. The moment she saw the coffin maker, she threw herself upon him and said:

"Please, Master Alberto. Please. You must come and help. It's my sister. I think Rosa's dead."

And dead Rosa Finestra most definitely was. Alberto could find no signs of life as she lay alone in her cold bed.

By the time Alberto carried her into his workshop, half the lights in the town were on and little inky heads peered up towards the top of the hill. It was too dark for them to see what was happening, but Clara ensured they all heard.

"My sister," she cried as she followed Alberto into his house. "My sister," she wailed like a banshee. "Oh, my sister," she sobbed. "Dead!" she screamed. "Dead in her bed!"

After sixty-three years of spreading nasty gossip, Miss Rosa Finestra became the subject of gossip herself.

"It was enteritis," a woman told Enzo one morning while she ordered a cake. "It's true. Clara Finestra told me herself. Been sick for weeks, rolling about in her bed. Couldn't even get up to go to the toilet."

"It was a growth deep inside her head," said another. "Had been growing bigger for years and years. That's why she said such silly things. Finally grew so big her brain stopped thinking altogether and she just dropped dead in the street."

But one rumour was spoken far more than any else.

"It was her sister," the townsfolk whispered as her coffin – *rosewood, 65 × 29 inches* – was lowered into the ground. "Clara poisoned her just to get inside the coffin maker's house. She wanted to search for the stolen boy herself and claim the full reward. She always hated sharing things with her little sister."

But despite all the gossip, nobody heard a word from Clara. After Rosa's death, she grew strangely quiet. She hardly ever left the house and on the rare occasions when she hobbled down into the town alone, she refused to say a thing.

After Rosa's death, Clara Finestra was not the only thing in Allora to fall silent.

"The sea is calming," said Enzo one day when Alberto went to fetch his daily loaf of bread.

"The beast sleeps," Madame Claudine intoned when Alberto bought a bag of chocolate wolves for Tito. "The water's so still even the fish aren't jumping."

This last bit of news sent the townsfolk of Allora into a panic. No one could remember a time when the waters off Allora had stilled, nor a time when the fish had chosen to swim instead of fly.

"It's not natural," murmured men in the tavern.

"What will we feed our children?" wailed women in the streets.

Only one man in all of Allora seemed happy with this change in the weather.

"A tuna for a silver!" yelled the foolish fisherman as he raced up from the rocky shore. For the first time in eighteen years he had caught a fish using a line instead of a bucket. And, also for the first time in eighteen years, there were people willing to pay for it.

With no waves crashing below, an eerie silence fell over Allora, pierced only by the foolish fisherman screaming that he had reeled in another fish. Tito was forced to keep quieter than ever, but Fia started to grow loud.

Two days after the water stilled, she sat by the window in Tito's room and screeched – *"Twrp! Twrp! Twrp!"* – over and over again. Tito tried to hush her with food and pats, but she kept on crying out. The next morning when he opened the shutters she let out a great cry and flew outside. She soared and dived across the sea for hours, and when she returned she brought them a gift.

"Look, Alberto," Tito whispered as he raced into his workshop. A giant tuna squirmed in his arms.

"Why, you've caught a tunny!" Alberto cried. "I haven't caught one of them in forty years."

"No," Tito said. "I didn't catch it. Fia did."

After that, Fia flew out of Tito's window every morning and returned late in the evening with a new fish squirming in her mouth. She would fly down the stairs, land in a salty puddle on the kitchen table and present Tito and Alberto with their dinner.

With each flight Fia took, her wings grew straighter and stronger. She did not fly in circles so tight, and sometimes Tito swore he saw her flying in a straight line. She flew further and further out to sea until one day she went so far that Tito lost sight of her. In the evening, she did not come back.

# TITO'S TELESCOPE

Tito sat beside his window and looked out across the calm sea. He had been sitting there for two weeks, waiting for Fia to return. He'd even made a telescope out of paper to help him search. He'd learned about them in one of the books Alberto had used to teach him how to read. But it was no use. Fia wasn't there.

A quiet knock on the door interrupted the silence. Tito turned around, but only for a moment. He knew who it would be: Alberto bringing some type of treat to tempt him downstairs to eat. But it wouldn't work. No matter what it was. He wasn't going to eat a thing until Fia returned.

"Tito?" Alberto called softly from the hall. "May I come in? I've brought you some pudding. It's chocolate. Your favourite."

At the word "chocolate" Tito's empty stomach rumbled and his mouth began to water. But he wouldn't give in.

"No thanks," he said.

"Please, Tito," Alberto pleaded. "You must eat something."

"No," Tito said. "I'm not ever eating again."

Tito heard the clink of a bowl being placed outside his door and then fading footsteps as the kind and gentle coffin maker walked away. He turned back to the sea and stared at the silent water. No waves crashed against the rocks below. No fish jumped on to the roof above. And no rainbow bird soared and dived and sung as it flew back to him.

Tito wanted to call out to Fia: call out across the sea and beg for her to come back. He knew that if she heard his voice she would. But he couldn't call out. Not ever. If he did, someone would hear and tell his father. Then he would be dragged all the way back to the north and he would never see Alberto or Fia again.

\*

Alberto climbed the stairs that led to Tito Bonito's room. A bowl of untouched chocolate pudding lay outside the door. He picked it up and replaced it with a new plate.

"Tito?" Alberto tapped on the wooden door. "Tito?" he said again. "I've bought you a slice of Enzo's apple pie."

When Tito didn't respond – he always said something – Alberto grew worried. He opened the door and let himself in. The chair beside the window was empty. All three beds were too.

"Tito?" he said. "Where are you?"

Just like their games of hide and seek, Alberto began to search the house. When he had checked every inch of every room, every bush in the garden and every coffin in his workshop, he realized the truth. Tito wasn't hiding. He had run away.

All the lights in Allora were out when Alberto stepped outside. The water below was so calm that even the stars were reflected, like pinpricks of diamond lace. In all his life, Alberto had never seen the sea so still.

Alberto could think of no reason for Tito to go down into the town but he could think of a reason for him to go up.

Despite the dark houses below, Allora graveyard was bright. In the moonlight, Alberto opened the gate and stepped inside. He made his way to Miss Bonito's grave – certain that Tito would be there – but he wasn't.

Panicking, Alberto began to search the graveyard. It wasn't until he looked on the other side of the clock tower that he spotted a small figure standing alone at the peak of Allora Hill.

Alberto weaved through the graves until he reached Tito's side. The boy stood with his telescope pressed to one eye. He didn't even lower it when Alberto began to speak.

"Tito?" he hissed. "What are you doing?"

"Looking."

"For what?"

"For Fia."

"She is too small to see from up here. And it is far too dark. You need the light of a sun, not a moon. Come now, Tito. We must go home before you are seen."

"But what about Fia?" Tito lowered the telescope and looked up at Alberto. A round, red mark covered one eye. "Where is she? She wouldn't leave me. Not ever. She loves me. Just like my mum."

"Oh, Tito. The sea is a dangerous place.

Perhaps – Perhaps..." Though they stood in a graveyard, Alberto could not bring himself to speak of death. "Perhaps she is injured and someone is looking after her until she gets better."

"Do you really think so?" For the first time in weeks, Tito's eyes lit with hope instead of despair.

"How about we go home and make her a bowl of porridge? If we place it on the window she might see it and fly back. Come now, Tito. We must go. It is so late even the wolves are sleeping."

But while the wolves may have gone to bed, someone else remained up. An old woman missing her sister and thinking of her as she looked out to sea, saw something else: an old man and a little boy standing on the peak of Allora Hill.

For the first time since the death of her sister, Clara Finestra thought of something to say.

# A FRIENDLY WARNING

The afternoon felt fresh and bright as Alberto made his way down into town. The air was hot with high summer and the warmth of the cobbles passed through his shoes and warmed his feet. Today had been a good day, because today was the day he and Tito had finally, after twelve months work, finished the mayor's coffin.

Despite the events of last night, he and Tito had woken early to complete the piece. Together they had created the greatest coffin Alberto had ever made. Soon he would present it to the mayor, but for now he had something more important to do. He had to go into town and buy his little apprentice a treat.

The bell of the bakery tinkled as Alberto stepped inside.

"Good afternoon, Enzo," he said as he walked towards the counter. He had been into the bakery countless times since the search of his house, but neither had mentioned that night or the lies Enzo had said to help his friend. "Do you have any of those little buns with cream inside?"

Alberto scanned the glass counter. This late in the day most of the shelves were empty, but there were still a few small treats and a very large pie.

When Enzo didn't reply, Alberto looked up at the baker. His heart skipped a beat. The man looked unwell.

"Are you all right?" he asked.

"Si, si. I am fine, Master Alberto. But I fear you are not."

"Whatever do you mean?" Was he the one who looked sick? He did not feel sick on the inside but perhaps he looked it from the out?

Before he replied, Enzo walked out from behind the counter and flipped the sign on the door from *Open* to *Closed*.

"Clara has seen you and the boy," he said. "She swears on the freshly made grave of her sister.

She did not spread it around the town this time. She went straight to the mayor and he to Mr Bonito."

"But how? When? Wh—?" Fear jumbled every question Alberto had, but finally he got one out. "How do you know?"

"Mr Bonito came in here only just the hour passed. He's looking for men to help him search. He said he is going to your house tonight when the bell tolls twelve and you and the boy are sure to be asleep."

Alberto's face whitened with terror, but things only got worse.

"The mayor said he doesn't have to knock this time. He can go straight in. The Carabineers are coming too. Six of them. Before it was just a toy, but now it is a child that has been sighted. There is proof."

"But it's Clara's words," Alberto said. "When did they become proof of anything? I doubt she's spoken a truth in all her life."

"I would have believed you in winter, but this spring just gone has changed her. Since her sister died, she hasn't spread a single rumour. So why now and why this?"

"But – But. . ." Alberto struggled to understand.

"Why are you telling me?"

"Because I have known Mr Bonito for less than a year, and I am certain he is bad. But you, Alberto, I have known a lifetime, and I am certain you are good. If what Clara says is true then I believe, I am *sure,* there must be a reason you have hidden this boy. You are trying to protect him, from something or someone, though I'm not sure which."

"What should I do?" Alberto said.

"I don't know. This time Mr Bonito said he will not stop searching until he finds him. He will tear down your whole house and break apart every coffin. In his anger, I don't dare to disbelieve it."

Alberto searched his crowded mind for a plan. "Can I hide him here?"

"I wish I could help, but you know my wife. She is almost as bad as the Finestra sisters. She knows everything that passes into our house, even a fleck of dirt on my shoe, and makes sure the rest of the town knows it too."

"I understand," Alberto said. "I will think of something. Thank you, Enzo. For all you have done." He turned towards the door, but Enzo called him back.

"It would look suspicious if you left without

buying something. Here." He ducked behind the counter and pulled out a large strawberry pie. It was big enough to feed twenty and dusted with large granules of golden sugar. "Good luck to you, Alberto," he said as he handed the pie over. "You have been a good friend to me."

"And you to me."

"I will try to delay them as long as possible."

When Alberto stepped outside, Enzo closed the door and flipped the sign back to *Open*.

Alberto returned to a silent house, but it did not remain silent for long.

"Is that strawberry?" Tito asked as he followed Alberto into the kitchen. The smell of freshly baked pie had lured him from the window upstairs.

"It is," Alberto said. He put the pie on the kitchen table and sat in the chair beside it.

Tito stared longingly at the pie, but made no move to eat it. He still hadn't eaten anything, not a crumb, since Fia flew away. To keep his mind off it, he turned to the coffin maker.

"What's wrong?" he asked. Alberto looked sad.

Alberto looked down at Tito's bright face – his cheeks were as rosy as Enzo's strawberry pie –

and then around the kitchen. For the first time in decades it was bright and clean. He looked at all the life that had returned to his house and to the boy before him, and then he started to cry.

"What's wrong?" Tito said. "Why are you crying?"

"Because they know, Tito. Clara saw us last night. I'm so sorry." His eyes filled with tears and Tito became a blur.

"Don't worry," Tito said. "I'll hide. Just like last time." And without Alberto's asking, he turned and raced from the room.

Alberto found Tito hiding in the mayor's coffin.

"Out you come, Tito."

"No," the boy replied. He sat up and began to pull the lid over the box. "You have to cover me up. Nail me in, like last time."

"You can't hide in there," Alberto said. "The mayor would grow suspicious if his own coffin was closed."

"Then we'll make another one. If we both work together it wouldn't take long."

"But it would be too long. They're coming for you tonight."

"Then I'll hide somewhere else. In one of the fireplaces or in a cupboard, just like our game.

I can hide in there all day and night if I have to."

Alberto looked down at the frightened face peering out of the coffin, and his heart broke. "Hiding won't be enough. Not this time, Tito."

"What do you mean?"

"He knows you are here. You have been seen. Now he is sure and he won't stop until he finds you. Like he searched every town for your mother, he will search every corner, every fireplace and every coffin in this town and this house for you."

"But why won't he leave me alone?" Tito wailed from inside the coffin.

"Because he thinks that you are his."

"But I'm not. I'm my own person. Just like you said. All myself. And I don't belong to him. I don't want to go with him. I want to stay here with you."

"Even I can't stay here with me, not any more."

"What do you mean?"

"They know I have hidden a child that is not my own, and I have lied to the mayor. Very few people would look favourably upon that."

"But you didn't do anything wrong. It isn't fair. What will they do to you?"

"Lock me away."

"In prison?"

Alberto nodded. At the prospect he sank, tired and hopeless, into a chair. Tito climbed out of the mayor's coffin and sat beside him.

"Don't worry," he said. "I know what to do. I'll go back to him. I'll say I was hiding here in secret, all the time, and you didn't know. I was stealing food whenever you went out. They won't be able to get you in trouble then."

"Oh, Tito. How kind. How very generous. But seeing you go back to him would be worse than spending my life in prison."

"It's better than both."

"No, Tito," Alberto said firmly. "You can't go back to him. I promised."

"Then what will we do?"

Alberto thought for so long that the sun fell below the sea, and a dark shadow spread over his old house.

"We will run," he finally said.

"Again?" Tito's face fell. "I'm tired of running."

"I'm sorry, Tito," Alberto began. "But it's all I can thi—"

At that moment, a loud crash came from upstairs.

"What's that?" Tito asked.

More thuds sounded in the room above their heads.

"I think it is your father," Alberto whispered. "We have been tricked. He has lied to Enzo to keep us off the scent. He isn't coming tonight. He is coming now. He is already here."

# FIA'S GIFT

Though he had just said it wouldn't work, Alberto helped Tito back into the mayor's coffin and closed the lid. He grabbed a plank of wood and headed towards the kitchen.

All was silent as Alberto climbed the stairs, but when he reached the landing he heard a scraping sound in Tito's room. He tightened his grip, mustered his courage and threw open the door.

Alberto raised his arms in the air, ready to swing, but he didn't. Instead of finding Mr Bonito on the other side of the door, he saw a very bright and very large bird standing in the centre of the room.

Upon hearing the door open, the bird turned to face Alberto. Lumpy, cold porridge dripped from the tip of its bent beak.

"Fia?" Alberto stepped into the room and checked behind the door. No one else was there. Relief made him laugh. The crash they had heard wasn't the mayor breaking in. It was Fia landing on the windowsill. She had knocked the bowl of porridge over before greedily gobbling it up.

Remembering Tito still hiding downstairs, Alberto raced back to his workshop.

"Tito?" He pulled off the coffin lid and a little head poked out. "Do not worry. It is not your father. Come and see. Come and see who has flown back to us."

At the mention of flight, Tito jumped out of the mayor's coffin and raced out the door.

"Fia!" he cried when his eyes fell upon the bird standing in his room. "I knew you'd come back. I knew you'd never leave me."

Abandoning the porridge, Fia flew into Tito's arms. She was now so large her wings spanned half the room and she knocked a bowl of flowers off the mantel.

As Alberto watched Tito hugging Fia, he forgot all about the danger they were in. But then the clock tower tolled seven times and he remembered who else was coming.

Alberto walked over to the window and looked outside. He knew they would have to run, but run where? No trains left Allora tonight and the Carabineers would surely be guarding the town gate. In despair his eyes dropped from the tower on the hill to the porridge splattered around his feet. It took several moments for him to notice something red lying beneath the largest clump of oats.

Kneeling down, Alberto picked up the porridge and wiped it on his sleeve. When the oats fell away, a little rock of red glistened in the palm of his hand. It was a flower: a flower made from rubies.

Alberto gasped. "It can't be," he said, his voice barely a whisper. Across the room, Tito and Fia rejoiced too loudly to hear. "It's just a story. It's impossible."

But then Alberto thought of all the impossibilities around him – the flying fish that called Allora home; little Tito, the frightened boy who felt so safe in his house; and the biggest impossibility of all: he, the sad, lonely coffin maker who had found a new reason to live – and he began to think that maybe it was possible after all.

"Tito?" he said. "I know where we can go."

Tito stopped playing with Fia and turned to Alberto. "Where?"

"To Isola."

"But that's just a story."

"No it's not." Alberto held up the ruby flower. "That's where Fia must have gone. She flew all the way to Isola Island and brought us back this flower as proof, so we could go there too."

"But we can't. The sea's too dangerous."

"It has been calm for many weeks, and no trains lead to Isola. Your father would never find us there."

"But how would we get there?"

"The water is calm, so we will take a boat."

"But we don't have a boat. Unless. . ." Tito's own eyes flashed with an idea. "Should we steal one?"

"There isn't a single boat in Allora for us to steal. No one's sailed out into the sea for years." Alberto felt his dream slipping away, but then he had another idea. "Come, Tito. I think we can use something downstairs."

"A coffin?" Tito looked at Alberto like he was going crazy.

"Not just any coffin, Tito. The mayor's coffin. It's

180

huge. We can both fit in there. Even Fia could too."

Across the room, Fia let out a happy trill.

"But a coffin isn't a boat," Tito pointed out.

"Yes it is," Alberto enthused. "After all, a boat is just a wooden thing that floats."

"But what if Isola Island isn't there?"

"Then we will keep sailing, on and on, until we reach the wilds of Africa. And look." He pointed to the jewels encrusting the mayor's coffin. "We can sell all of these when we get there. We'll have enough money to buy a new house. We can start a new life where you won't have to hide."

"Can I go to school?"

"Not just school, Tito. You can go to university."

Tito gasped. "What's that?"

"A place where you learn how to build ships, save lives and draw maps of the world."

Tito liked the sound of university very much, but he still had one concern.

"What will we eat?"

"Why, we'll take Enzo's strawberry pie. That will keep us full for weeks."

Tito and Alberto had to hurry, but they couldn't leave the house yet. The lights of the town were on and they would surely be sighted. But if Mr Bonito stuck to his plan, they had until midnight to get ready.

The first thing they did was pack their belongings. Then they packed all of the food in the house: yesterday's bread, half a wheel of cheese and today's strawberry pie. When they were ready, they waited in the kitchen for the lights of Allora to go out. The clock tower chimed twice and the fire behind them dimmed but finally, well past ten, they slipped outside.

Keeping to the shadows, for Clara would be on the lookout tonight, they made their way up to the graveyard. They hid their things beneath the clock tower and returned for the mayor's coffin.

For all the jewels encrusting it, the mayor's coffin had grown heavy. Yet Alberto and Tito could still lift it and they hoped it would still float.

Alberto and Tito hauled the mayor's coffin up the hill. The clock tower chimed eleven as they placed it beside their things. Alberto was ready to go right then, but Tito insisted on doing one final thing.

"Please," he said as he pulled on Alberto's hand. "It's important."

So they hurried back to their house and gathered every flower in the garden. Then they sped back up the lane and laid whole bushes of flowers across five graves.

"Enough flowers for a year," Tito said as he arranged the last cluster above his mother's.

"Don't forget this one," Alberto said. He reached into his pocket and pulled out the ruby flower Fia had dropped in the porridge. "This one will last a whole lifetime."

Tito took the flower and gently placed it on his mother's grave. In the moonlight, it twinkled like a lonely ember star.

It was halfway to midnight when Alberto opened the back gate. It let out a pained, piercing creak as its hinges moved for the first time in thirty years. Then, with their belongings stored inside, they carried the mayor's coffin down to the rocky sea.

Warm water lapped at their feet as they moved amongst the rocks. Carefully they lowered the mayor's coffin into the water. Despite all the additions, it floated with ease. It barely moved when Tito climbed in and only lowered an inch when Alberto joined him.

Alberto looked up at Allora – at the town that had been his home for fifty-five years – for one final time and then pushed off.

The surface of the sea was calm, but the water carried them out quickly. The moon lit their way, and Fia swam through the air as if to guide them. Soon they were so far out that if they turned their heads back to shore, they could see all of Allora branching before them.

Alberto and Tito had been on the water for ten minutes when the clock tower chimed twelve. It echoed on and on across the water, making twelve chimes sound like sixty. The last echo fell silent and a light appeared at the bottom of the hill. It left the prison gates and marched up Allora Lane. Many more joined it until a whole chain of flames snaked their way towards Alberto's home.

When the men reached the front door, Alberto's breath caught inside of him. He imagined them smashing the windows and charging inside: their yells and flames and searching eyes. Horror filled him as he realized how close Tito had come to being taken. Before he could imagine any more, Tito spoke.

"Can you see it?" he asked.

"Yes," Alberto replied gravely. "They are at the front door."

"No. Not back there. Out here. Look."

Alberto turned around. Tito held the telescope towards him. The paper was worn and wrinkled, but when he raised it to his eye he could still see through to the other side. He searched the distant horizon, but could not see a thing. A flicker of doubt formed in the pit of his stomach. Was this all a mistake? Was he taking Tito to a place that didn't exist? But then Fia flew down and pecked the paper a little to the left.

"Yes, Tito," Alberto said, his voice flooded with wonder. "I can see it." Tears glistened in his old eyes. "Truly, I can." Lights – thousands of them, each one as bright as Fia's feathers – clustered together on an island far out to sea. They were invisible from Allora, but the moment you left land they came into sight, as if you had to be on the sea to see them.

"Here." Alberto put down the telescope and handed Tito a piece of wood. "Take it, Tito, and row. Row as hard as you can."

And so, in the mayor's coffin, the boy, the bird and the coffin maker sailed towards those distant lights and the promise of a new life on the magical island of Isola.

# ACKNOWLEDGEMENTS:

For Polly, who believed in this story before anyone else did.

For Lucy and Lauren, who took this story and turned it into a book.

And for Anuska who made this book come to life with her wonderful drawings.

Thank you.

# ABOUT THE AUTHOR

Matilda Woods lives in the Southern Tablelands
of Australia, where there are no flying fish but
there is the world's largest cement sheep!
*The Boy, the Bird and the Coffin maker* is
her debut novel.